THE SWALLOW'S NEST

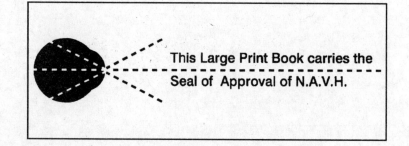

This Large Print Book carries the
Seal of Approval of N.A.V.H.

THE SWALLOW'S NEST

EMILIE RICHARDS

WHEELER PUBLISHING
A part of Gale, Cengage Learning

GALE
CENGAGE Learning·

Farmington Hills, Mich • San Francisco • New York • Waterville, Maine
Meriden, Conn • Mason, Ohio • Chicago

GALE
CENGAGE Learning°

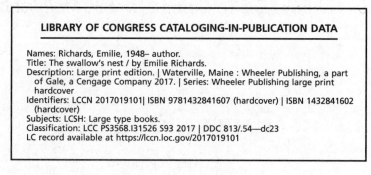

LIBRARY OF CONGRESS CATALOGING-IN-PUBLICATION DATA

Names: Richards, Emilie, 1948– author.
Title: The swallow's nest / by Emilie Richards.
Description: Large print edition. | Waterville, Maine : Wheeler Publishing, a part
    of Gale, a Cengage Company 2017. | Series: Wheeler Publishing large print
    hardcover
Identifiers: LCCN 2017019101| ISBN 9781432841607 (hardcover) | ISBN 1432841602
    (hardcover)
Subjects: LCSH: Large type books.
Classification: LCC PS3568.I31526 S93 2017 | DDC 813/.54—dc23
LC record available at https://lccn.loc.gov/2017019101

Published in 2017 by arrangement with Harlequin Books, S. A.

Printed in the United States of America
1 2 3 4 5 6 7 21 20 19 18 17

To Jessie, my daughter, who has been and always will be a great joy in my life. Thanks for insisting I watch *Maleficent.*

■ ■ ■ ■

PART I

■ ■ ■ ■

Choosing the right colony is the first of many tasks for Petrochelidon pyrrhonota, the cliff Swallow. As primary homemaker the female investigates existing colonies before she decides where she and her mate should reside.

Male and female build a nest and raise their young together, but sometimes both mate with others, too.

"Our Songbirds, Ourselves:
A Tale of Two Species,"
from the editors of *Ornithology Today.*

1

THE SWALLOW'S NEST

FEATHERING YOUR NEST WITH IMAGINATION AND LOVE

March 3rd:

All of you know how I've longed for this day. One year ago, my husband, Graham, was diagnosed with Burkitt's lymphoma. You've been with me as he progressed through treatment, as our spirits soared and plummeted, even with me during my absences here. I can't count the encouraging emails I've received, the suggestions, the promises of prayers. Now, today, we will celebrate the best possible news. Graham's cancer is in remission, and he is really, at last, on the road to recovery.

Before this I never considered how I would adjust to news as horrifying as a cancer diagnosis, but now, one year later, I know. Life moves on and so do we. Graham and I came through this year stronger and closer, and my gratitude for your support knows no bounds. *Mahalo,* the Hawaiian word for thank you, doesn't begin to cover what I'm feeling today.

I wish you could be right here to share

every moment of today's celebration party with us, but watch for photos and recipes. In the meantime, here are the instructions for welcoming a loved one with a flip-flop sign — or "slippahs" as we call them in my home state.

Aloha! Lilia

Lilia Swallow was on speaking terms with reality, but only just. For the past year she had questioned everything she believed in, while trying to make sense of the disasters raining down from above, the way Haimi, the yellow Lab of her childhood, had pawed and rattled coconuts when they fell from palm trees in her family's yard on Kauai. In the end, unlike Haimi, she had concluded that while life often hides something delicious, too often the best parts remain out of sight and unattainable.

"And Haimi never once cracked a coconut."

Regan Donnelly was looking on as Lilia painstakingly shot photos of a moisture-beaded glass pitcher nearly overflowing with pineapple chunks, citrus slices and a haze of red wine floating on top of white. At Lilia's words her friend cocked her head. "What on earth are you talking about?"

Lilia hadn't realized she'd spoken — or more accurately, mumbled. She had begun talking to herself during the long stretches when her husband was in the hospital. She had been so lonely, she had needed the sound of her own voice.

"Nothing. I was just thinking about happy endings and failures."

Regan sing-songed in a high-pitched voice. "Lily-ah, Lily-ah, you are being Silly-ah!" She grinned. "Today *is* your happy ending."

"I wish I'd never told you my brothers used to say that."

"But you did."

Lilia straightened and stretched before she moved the pitcher to the back of the counter where sun from a large window over the sink wouldn't strike it quite so directly. She turned the handle to one side and took another shot.

"Well, if nothing else, my pineapple sangria *is* a happy ending. I worked on and off for a week on this recipe. I think you'll like it. My readers will, too."

Regan would not be deterred. "Graham's in remission. His last two CT scans were clear. You're afraid to be happy, aren't you? You're afraid the gods will descend and whack you all over again."

Lilia sent her just the faintest smile, because as different as they were, Regan knew her inside and out. Although they were the same five foot five and both twenty-eight, Regan was fair-skinned with a collar-length bob the color of butterscotch. Her pale green eyes had been Lilia's inspiration the last time she had painted this kitchen. In contrast Lilia's

11

hair was nearly black and waved down her back, and her skin turned a distinctive brown in the sun. She had what novelists liked to describe as "almond eyes," in her case the *color* of almonds, although the crease of her eyelids also hinted at whatever Asian ancestor had bequeathed them to her.

She decided the pitcher had finished its moment in the spotlight and stepped away. "I come from superstitious people. This morning I blogged about how happy I am. I don't want to jinx Graham's recovery."

"We Irish can match you Hawaiians, superstition for superstition. But I think you're allowed to be happy. His doctor told you relapses occur quickly, right? It's been a year since the initial cancer diagnosis, but he's here today, having a great time."

It *had* been a year marked by nearly insurmountable hills and valleys. Lilia was still too exhausted not to question fate.

"My tutu trotted out an old Hawaiian proverb whenever things went wrong. *'He ihona, he pi'ina, he kaolo.'* It means we go down, we go up, we walk on a level road. A level road is all I'm asking for. Graham, too."

"He's looking so much better. Hair's appealing on a man, don't you think?"

Lilia allowed herself to laugh. "We weren't sure what color it would be after chemo, but I think it looks the way it did before he lost it, only shorter."

Graham, dark blond hair a couple of inches now, was standing outside their sunroom door with newly arrived partygoers, receiving good wishes. Employees and clients from Encompass Construction, the design-build firm he had created from the ground up, were shoulder to shoulder with neighbors, college friends and some of Lilia's clients, too. But in the middle of a conversation with another young man, he stopped and turned, looking straight at her, as if he knew she was talking about him. Then he smiled.

For a moment she fell back in time to the first day Graham Randolph had smiled at her. She'd been ten; he'd been eleven. She'd been barefoot, and he'd worn stiff leather loafers with heavy dark socks. Until that moment she'd written him off as sullen and self-absorbed. Then she fell in his swimming pool trying to make an impossible Frisbee catch.

Remembering that now she winked at him, and his smile widened before he turned away.

Graham, even after months of chemotherapy, after losing all his hair and almost twenty pounds, was still easy on the eye. He was handsome in a prep school way, even though he was still puffy from steroids and sported nearly invisible chemo ports in his chest and scalp. Once again his blue-gray eyes were rimmed with dark lashes shaded by darker brows. Despite his illness he was still broad-shouldered and narrow-hipped, and today, as usual, he was clad in scruffy jeans and a T-shirt — the more or less official dress of the Silicon Valley.

Best of all he was alive and hers.

"Do you ever get tired of this?" Regan swept a manicured hand at the pitcher and at a platter of hot and sour wings that Lilia had photographed first. The wings weren't quite finished, but sometimes food photographed best when it was still slick with sauce that later would darken in the oven.

Lilia set down her camera so she could slide the wings back to a foil-lined baking sheet. "As much as I'd like to forget my website this once, I don't have the luxury. These days my online presence is the largest portion of our income."

"Didn't readership grow during Graham's illness?"

The larger audience had surprised Lilia, but so many people had hung on every word she'd carefully crafted about Graham's illness. Prayers had been said all over the world. Uplifting emails had flooded her in-box.

"It did grow, but now my readers want a celebration after a year of gloom."

Regan was still piling up the happy endings. "*The Swallow's Nest* will be even busier and more productive now that you won't be at the hospital so much."

The Swallow's Nest had been named after the Tudor Revival cottage in San Jose, California, where they stood. Lilia's aunt Alea Swallow had always called the house "my nest" and, on her death, had bequeathed it to her niece, who had taken care of her at the end of her life. Now Lilia's website and blog were devoted to nesting, to creating a snug, beautiful home in a small space like this one, to feeding loved ones and launching fledglings.

That last, of course, was something she wouldn't be doing, at least not for some time.

She closed the oven door, setting a timer with her voice. At that moment Carrick Donnelly, who'd circled the house to the patio, abandoned his date and came inside through the sunroom, bending over when he reached Lilia to kiss her cheek.

Carrick and Graham had been friends since childhood, and Lilia had known him almost as long as she'd known her husband. He might be Regan's older brother, but in the sunshine there was only a faint tinge of red in his brown curls, and his eyes were a much deeper and muddier green. He was also as different from Lilia's husband as the ocean from the shore, lankier and less patrician, but equally as pleasurable to look at.

For just a moment he rested his hands on her shoulders. "Anything you need help with?"

"No, you ought to get back to Julie." Lilia hoped she had his date's name right. She'd met the woman once, another associate at

15

Carrick's Palo Alto law firm, but keeping up with the names of his ever-changing girlfriends wasn't easy.

"She's already engrossed in a bitcoin discussion with somebody from Google. She'll never realize I'm not standing beside her."

She held out the sangria. "Would you take this outside and put it with the other pitchers and check to see if there's enough beer and soft drinks in the ice chest? I have plenty in the fridge if there's not."

He reached for a dish towel and wrapped it around the bottom of the pitcher where moisture was beading. Unlike the man she'd married, who had grown up with housekeepers and maids, Carrick and Regan had grown up in a family where everybody pitched in.

He inclined his head toward the patio. "Graham looks happy."

"I invited everybody he loves."

His expression changed to something less pleasant. "His mother?"

"I did ask Ellen. She sent her regrets."

"She's capable of regret?"

This was so unlike him, a man who always struggled to be impartial, that Lilia didn't know what to say.

He shrugged. "I'll see about the drinks."

Regan waited until her brother had gone. "He won't tell you, but he called Ellen when Graham was first diagnosed. He told her she needed to make peace with her son because

16

if she didn't, and Graham died, she would regret it forever."

Carrick hadn't told Lilia, but he wouldn't have. She'd had enough on her plate. "Carrick was a guest in their house for a lot of years. He knows Graham's parents better than I do. I guess he was in a better position to plead with them."

Of course Carrick hadn't bothered to speak to Graham's father. Like any lawyer he understood lost causes.

"Plead probably isn't the right word," Regan said. "I think he told her straight out."

"Maybe the phone call worked. Ellen did visit the hospital at least once. I was there."

"How did that go?"

Lilia could still see the scene in her mind. Illness hadn't rested well on Graham's shoulders. Depression was part of cancer, for reasons nobody had to explain, and too often he had shut out the people who loved him when they tried to help. That morning she had prayed his mother's visit might turn the tide.

She tried to describe it. "When she walked in and asked Graham how he was feeling, she wrapped her fingers through a long strand of pearls and twisted them back and forth, until I was sure they were going to explode all over the floor. Maybe she wanted me to scoop up a few to help with the hospital bills."

"Casting pearls before swine?"

Lilia hoped not. "She stayed about five minutes. Then she told me Graham needed his rest and offered to walk me to my car."

"Did she have something she wanted to tell you?"

"I'll never know. He needed support more than he needed rest, and she knows our phone number."

"Well, look at all the people who *are* here to celebrate."

Lilia could see the backyard, and in the other direction, all the way through their dining area to the living room. More guests had just let themselves in through the front door. From the looks of things, everybody she had invited might be coming.

"You go and mingle. When they're ready I'll take the wings out of the oven and put them on a platter," Regan said.

Lilia nodded to two sheets of quinoa-stuffed mushrooms she'd made for their vegan friends and already photographed. "Great. And would you put the mushrooms in once the wings are out? I'll get them when I come back through."

"Done. Go say hi."

Outside, the welcome sign she had crafted from spray-painted flip-flops hung from a tree, and three surf board tables Graham had created from replicas that had once hung outside a surf shop were already groaning with food.

For the past year, instead of enjoying leisurely nutritious meals, Lilia had eaten vaguely edible items packaged in cellophane. Convenience store sandwiches with sketchy expiration dates, salt and vinegar potato chips and cartons of yogurt had been staples. Today she had been too happy to stop cooking. But even if the wings flew away and the mushrooms formed a fairy circle behind the garage, the party would still be a knockout. Relief and joy scented the air.

Guests she hadn't yet spoken to came to say hello. She greeted them with "Aloha," and a hug, the way she always did, an expected ritual for those who had been here before. She warned first-time guests they might see her taking photos for her website, and if they didn't want to be in a shot, to let her know. The Hawaiian sangria and the wings would probably be featured this week.

Carrick, who shared Graham's taste in music, had put together a playlist of songs about fresh starts and homecomings. By the time Lilia got back to the kitchen to arrange the stuffed mushrooms on a platter, the music was so loud that Graham was able to sneak up behind her. He wrapped his arms around her waist without warning.

"Another awesome party," he shouted.

"An awesome reason to have one." She set the tray on a nearby counter and turned in

19

his arms to kiss him. "You need to eat, *Pili-kua.*"

He brushed a strand of hair over her shoulder, and his fingertips lingered against her neck. She was wearing a turquoise sundress he loved, but it was the neckline he loved most, just low enough to hint at everything it hid. He liked the way the fabric cupped her breasts, or had before she'd lost so much weight. She hoped the dress would fit perfectly again very soon.

"You okay? Not too tired?" she asked.

He kissed her again. "Flying high."

He looked happy enough, but pale. The scans might be clear, but there had been so many side effects from the disease and the treatment that he was far from recovered. He had spent two mornings of the past week on his latest job site, and both afternoons he'd fallen into bed, so exhausted he hadn't even taken off his shoes.

Over the hubbub she heard more music, this time guitar chords from the front of the house. Last year Graham had replaced their old doorbell with a programmable one. When Carrick had dropped by yesterday with his playlist, he had uploaded the opening riffs of Steely Dan's "Home at Last."

She would probably blog Carrick's playlist *next* week.

"I'll get the door." She was surprised whoever was standing on the porch hadn't walked right in. Clearly the party was underway. "You get something to eat, okay? I'll send the stragglers along to greet you."

As she went to answer the door, she glanced back and smiled as, outside, he draped his arm over the shoulders of his master plumber, who was politely examining the sangria. Graham pointed the heavily tattooed man toward an ice chest filled with beer.

The front of the house had a slight entry alcove framed in by a narrow bookshelf. Over the past three years as Graham renovated the cottage, she had refused to let him incorporate that space, with its coat closet, boot tray and umbrella stand, into the rest of the living room. She liked the idea of a transition from the porch, a chance for guests to catch a breath, like actors waiting and preparing in the wings for their next big scene.

Stepping into the alcove she opened the door, preparing to prop it open for the rest of the afternoon.

A moment passed before she recognized the woman clad in tight jeans, showy metallic platforms and a formfitting black tank top. Marina Tate, a leggy and unashamedly voluptuous blonde, was an outside sales rep for a supply company Graham worked with. He had introduced them at some company function, and now she remembered that Marina had been to a party here. She tried to think

21

when. Sometime before the world had caved in.

Lilia hadn't invited her today, but she guessed Graham must have.

She was glad that with everything else going on she remembered the other woman's name. "Marina, right?" She smiled. "Aloha. It's nice to see you."

Something stirred in Marina's arms. Lilia glanced down, noting several canvas bags at her feet before her gaze lifted to the bundle resting against the woman's chest. For a moment she fumbled for something to say, coming up with the blatantly obvious. "A baby." She leaned over, searching her memory for a husband, boyfriend or even a lover. "He's adorable. How old is he? She?" She looked up in question.

"*Toby* is three months." Marina didn't sound happy, and certainly not like a doting mother. Most of Lilia's friends with children answered the same question in weeks and days.

She tried a second time for a better look so she could say something complimentary. "I'm so sorry. I didn't even know you were pregnant. I would have —"

Marina cut her off. "I doubt you would have. And whether you found out about the pregnancy wasn't up to me."

The baby seemed to be asleep, and Lilia couldn't get a good look because, despite

22

moderate temperatures, he was swathed in blankets. She stepped back and met the other woman's eyes. Marina's expression was as hostile as her tone.

She searched for the cause. "I hope you know he's welcome at the party. There aren't any other children, but he's really too young to need a playmate, isn't he?"

"I don't think he'll be welcome, Lilia. But here he is." Marina held out her arms. "Let's just see."

Lilia felt her smile disappear. She had no idea what she was expected to do. "I'd love to hold him, but I'm still taking food out of the oven —"

"You'll get used to that. Wanting to do other things and not being able to."

Now she was completely at sea. This time she said nothing. The conversation obviously belonged to Marina.

"Take him." Marina lifted the bundled baby higher. He whimpered, beginning to wake, but Lilia shifted her weight back and away.

"Take him!"

Lilia knew better than to let this continue. "Let me get Graham, or maybe I can call somebody else for you?"

"You know, I'm glad it worked out this way. I'm glad *you* were the one to answer the door."

Lilia stepped back, preparing to slip inside, but Marina tucked the baby against her own chest and grabbed Lilia's arm with her other hand to stop her. "Take him."

The baby's name finally registered. "Toby?"

"Toby. Right. Toby *Randolph.* After his father. Don't you think a boy should carry on the family name? Tobias is Graham's middle name, right?"

Lilia managed another step back, trying to shake off the other woman's hand, but with no success. "You need to leave right now."

"Oh, I'm leaving. But I'm leaving Toby here when I go. With you. With his father. I've finished my part of this bargain. Now it's up to Graham to take care of the rest."

She thrust the blanketed bundle forward so forcefully that Lilia grabbed at it. She had no choice, panicked that Marina would let go and blame the resulting disaster on her.

Satisfied, Marina stepped back and dropped Lilia's arm. "You'll have lots of time to think about this moment and what a horrible person I am. But while you're at it, don't forget, I gave this baby life. Think about that, Lilia, when you're feeling superior. I did something you couldn't be *bothered* to do. And think about what it was like for me to manage everything on my own up to this point, when I was promised so much more."

She didn't glance down at her son for a final goodbye. She turned and walked along the flowered brick pathway to the street. She was out of sight almost before Lilia could form another thought.

In her arms the baby stirred. Stunned, Lilia looked down, and the tiny infant opened eyes the china blue of her husband's. With shaking fingers she pulled back the blanket. What hair the baby had was blond, like Graham's. But Marina was blond, and surely her eyes were blue, as well.

This was a scam, a horrible, ill-advised prank.

She lifted him slowly for a better view, and then, without a legal document, without confirmation from anyone except a crazy woman, with no proof whatsoever except a vague resemblance that might not even exist, she was 100 percent certain this was no scam.

This child belonged to her husband.

She wanted to drop the bundle and run. She wanted to race after the near-stranger who had just handed off her beautiful baby like a football in play.

But most of all? She wanted to scream right along with Graham's son, who was now wailing inconsolably in her arms.

2

Marina Tate pulled into her private space in the parking lot of the three-story apartment building that had once symbolized how fast she was rising in the world. Her one-bedroom was on the top floor, not exactly a penthouse, but still superior to anything she'd grown up with. The view from her narrow balcony was a freeway, but sometimes at night she sat in a folding chair and watched headlights blooming through banks of fog. She'd sat there many times after Toby was born. She hadn't been able to get away from his screaming, but closing the door and listening to the roar of traffic had been an improvement.

As she had during the trip home, she wondered again if the baby was okay.

Clearly Graham hadn't gotten around to telling Lilia about his son. Maybe announcing a love child between one dose of chemo and the next just hadn't seemed sensible. Maybe in his shoes she would have kept silent, too. After all, if he'd made the announcement, who would take care of him? No man could drop a bombshell like that one and expect even the most supportive wife to spoon-feed him chicken soup, much less clean up his vomit and wash his sheets.

But no excuse was really good enough, was it?

She was still behind the steering wheel, and she drooped forward to rest her forehead against it. She was so tired she wasn't sure she was going to make it up the stairs to her apartment. She was so tired she considered taking a nap before she tried. In the end, after two cars screeched into the lot with radios throbbing, she pushed away, opened the door and swung her feet to the asphalt.

In the midst of flipping her seat forward she remembered she had no baby to retrieve from the back. For a moment she stood staring at the infant seat. She had considered carrying the baby to Graham's door nestled inside, but the seat was used and worn, and at the last minute — not blind to the irony — she'd rejected the idea. She had been embarrassed to give Graham and Lilia the car seat, but not the infant.

Tomorrow she would chuck it into the Dumpster.

So many months had passed since she'd had an entire night's sleep. She couldn't remember when she hadn't been sleep-deprived. Even in the weeks before the birth

27

she'd slept fitfully because she was so huge, getting comfortable was a joke. And no man had been around to rub her aching back or get her a glass of water.

One of those nights Graham had called. She couldn't remember which, but *why* was stamped on her heart. He wanted her to know he had made the arrangements for a paternity test. She listened to him recite the clinical details, as if he were reading them from a list. At the birth someone would collect blood from the umbilical cord, and a lab would process the results. He confirmed he would not sign the Declaration of Paternity document agreeing he was the father until the test results were official. Without that, she would not be allowed to list him on the birth certificate. When paternity was finally confirmed, she would then have to fill out another form to have the birth certificate amended.

Finally, as if this were a small thing, he said that at that point everything would be official, and she would get the rest of the lump sum he had promised when she agreed to have the baby.

At the time she'd wondered, and still did, if delaying the test and refusing to sign the document were stalling mechanisms. A more expensive but equally reliable test could have been conducted during the pregnancy. Had he hoped these small rebellions would deter her from announcing the identity of the man who had carelessly planted the baby inside her?

Had he thought about it at all? Or had he been so immersed in the present, ensnared in a mass of twisted and unshared emotion, that he hadn't given the future any real thought?

At the beginning Graham had been so anxious for her to carry the pregnancy to term, but all those months later, had he come to regret it? As his health improved, and the possibility of survival improved with it, had he wished that the baby and the baby's mother would disappear and leave him to the good life he'd had before his diagnosis?

Whatever his reasons, she'd been given no choice in the matter. After Toby's birth the hospital had filled out the health department form without Graham's name. Weeks went by before he was officially the father of record. Then once he was, the money he had promised to give her, the second half of a trust fund he had cashed in to help her through the pregnancy and early months of Toby's life, had never materialized. Nor had a satisfactory explanation. He'd said she and the baby would be taken care of, and he had promised to find a way to be part of Toby's life. By now she knew what his promises were worth.

Today there was no more room for lies. Everybody would know Graham was officially

Toby's father. A copy of the baby's amended birth certificate was among the items she had left in one of the bags at Lilia's feet.

She started toward her apartment and trudged up the three flights of an open stairwell. For a moment after she unlocked the door she stood on the threshold and drank in the silence. She'd grown up in a noisy home, but the months since she'd brought Toby here from the hospital had been filled with screaming that only tapered off when the baby grew too exhausted for more. At one point the noise had been so overwhelming her neighbors had threatened to report her to the landlord. She had been forced to move his bed to the center of the living room, away from common walls.

By that point she had lowered herself to begging for help. Toby's pediatrician had insisted the problem was colic. Along the way the woman, fresh out of medical school, suggested different formulas, modeled a baby carrier to keep Toby snug against Marina's chest, prescribed white noise, swaddling, massage, letting him cry. Finally, at this morning's visit, after pointed questions about her state of mind and how vigilantly Marina had followed her useless suggestions, the clueless young doctor had decreed that Marina was a first-time mom, and Toby probably sensed her insecurities.

That had been the final straw. Marina had

no insecurities when it came to babies. She had raised her younger brothers while her mother worked two jobs or "socialized." She had a niece named Brittany whom she'd been unable to avoid in infancy, and a short-lived romance with an otherwise perfect man who had just divorced the mother of his newborn. She'd chucked him quickly, but not before managing weeks of diapers and bottles.

Toby was born a nightmare. Or maybe Toby was punishment for trying to steal another woman's husband, although a year of misery seemed like a pretty stiff sentence.

She flicked on her lights and stepped inside. Her apartment was furnished in leather with chrome accents and neon table lamps. She was a fan of sleek surfaces with no hint of clutter. The walls were mostly blank, and she liked them that way, clean white paint and no memorabilia from a past she wanted to forget. The tile floors were unmarred by rugs. Toddler Toby probably would have cracked his head a hundred times.

No longer her problem.

She wasn't hungry, but she crossed the living room to the tiny kitchen and searched the refrigerator for beer. She found a tall bottle hiding behind half a gallon of milk, but only one, because that's how she bought them, one at a time, just enough to split or enjoy alone without temptation to drink another. Her mother, Deedee, was a bartender who had lost at least one job for over-sampling the wares. Her youngest brother, Pete, had lost his driver's license for two years after his second underage DUI and, judging by his continued drinking, showed no signs the lesson had any impact. She had no intention of following the family tradition.

She tossed the milk carton in the garbage because she couldn't remember when she'd bought it. Then, using the hem of her tank top, she unscrewed the beer cap and drank half the bottle slouched against the granite counter.

Many people were not going to understand what she had done this afternoon. But Toby Randolph was alive today because she had, against her better judgment, given birth to him. Even after she learned that Graham was likely to die before their baby was born, and if he did, his mega-wealthy parents probably wouldn't want anything to do with her or the baby. Even after she realized that, whether he lived or not, Graham was never going to make the three of them a real family.

She was too tired to think about Graham.

She left the half-empty bottle on the counter. In the bedroom she kicked off her shoes and jeans and fell facedown on the unmade bed.

Hours might have passed or just minutes when the doorbell buzzed, then buzzed again. She was so foggy-headed she was clueless about time or place. As the buzzing continued she rolled over and sat up, and the world came into focus again.

If Graham or Lilia or, worse, their lawyer friend, Carrick, was standing on the other side, she didn't want to answer the door. But whoever was waiting was insistent, and she could hardly pretend she wasn't home. Anyone who knew her would spot her yellow Mustang Fastback in the lot. She pulled on her jeans, walked barefoot to the door and squinted through the peephole.

Silently cursing she unlocked it and stood back to let her mother inside.

"I hated to ring the doorbell, in case I woke up little Toby . . ." As she spoke Deedee Tate's voice gathered enough volume to wake every corpse at the Odd Fellows Cemetery miles away.

Marina had dreaded this moment, but now that it was here, she mostly felt annoyed. "If Toby had slept through the doorbell, your shouting would finish the job."

"Where is he?"

"Safe and happy. Why are you here?"

Deedee looked puzzled, but she never meditated on a problem when she could talk instead. She held out a wrinkled paper bag. "I found some cute baby clothes at a neighbor's garage sale. You don't owe me much. They were cheap."

Marina squinted through sleep-fogged eyes.

33

From photos, she knew she resembled Deedee when she, too, had been thirty. It was a sobering thought. Now her mother was fifty-one. By the time Marina was that age would she resemble the woman standing before her? Deedee made no effort to eat well or exercise. She was overweight, with sagging breasts and a roll of fat that bulged over the elastic waistband of a broomstick skirt. Her shaggy hair was haphazardly dyed an improbable shade of gold, and her graying roots were inches long.

"I didn't ask you to buy a thing," Marina said. "I wish you would stop buying things I don't need and then asking me to pay for them."

"I'm trying to help. I can't afford to do much on my own. I'm barely getting the hours at Frankie's that I need to make ends meet. And your brothers —"

Marina made a chopping motion with her hand. "I don't want to hear about my brothers." Both Jerry and Pete, twenty-five and nineteen respectively, still lived at home and never helped Deedee with rent or food.

Her mother lifted her chin proudly. "Well, aren't you snippy today."

"Yeah, well, try not getting any sleep for months."

"I had babies, too, you know."

"Yeah, you did, and I raised two of them for you." Marina didn't sigh as much as force air from her lungs. "Look, I have half a beer I just opened. It's yours."

"One of those bombers you like so much?"

"There's plenty left."

Deedee followed Marina into the kitchen and watched as she took a go-cup from a cupboard. "So who's got Toby?"

"His father." Marina poured the beer and handed it to her mother. Most likely by now it was almost flat, but Deedee wouldn't balk.

"What? His father's in the picture all of a sudden? Like that?" Deedee flicked a glittery fake nail against the plastic cup for emphasis.

Marina watched her mother take two long swallows. "Isn't it about time?"

"What about that wife of his?"

"We can definitely say she's in the picture, too." Marina had a sudden flash of Lilia's expression as she handed the baby to her. She had expected to feel victory followed by the sweet aftermath of revenge. But she had felt neither. Lilia Swallow had never done anything to her except marry the man Marina had wanted for her own, and married him long before Marina even met him. At the one party Marina had been invited to at Graham's house, Lilia had been a thoughtful hostess. She'd even made a point of introducing Marina to Graham's best friend, Carrick Donnelly, then backing away, as if she hoped sparks might ignite.

"They'll give him back, won't they?"

Deedee didn't wait for an answer before she finished what was left in the cup.

"Deedee, I don't want him back." Marina pushed away from the counter. "I never wanted to be a mother. Don't you think I had enough mothering with Jerry and Pete? You remember who took care of them when you were working and in the wee morning hours when you were off having fun? I gave Petey more bottles than you ever did, and I rode herd on Jerry until he got bigger than me. You think any of that made me want to be a mother again?"

"You were their big sister. *I* was their mother. You were helping out. Helping is good for kids."

"It was *not* good for me. I didn't have a childhood. I had children. Your children."

Deedee was angry now. She banged the go-cup on the counter. "Family is important!"

"Yeah, right. You mean like the father you told me was mine, only it turned out he wasn't? Is that your idea of family?"

"He wasn't much of a father. You hardly noticed when he disappeared."

"Right. Maybe I hardly ever saw him, but at least I had a name and a face when I needed them. Until the state went after him for child support and he demanded a paternity test."

"I told you then, I'll tell you now. I *thought* he was your father. I never lied. I thought he

36

was the one."

"Uh-huh. And by the time you found out you were wrong, you couldn't remember who else might have been in the running."

Deedee ignored that. "I was mother *and* father to you. To all of you."

"You were gone most of the time. I had no mother, and the boys had me, which was probably worse."

"You can't really mean you don't want your own baby."

"I do mean it. I left Toby —" she couldn't admit she'd left the baby with Graham's bewildered wife "— with Graham, and I walked away. I couldn't do this another minute. This morning I —" She stopped.

"You what, Rina Ray?"

Marina hated to remember that moment. "I came so close to shaking him. I just wanted him to stop screaming. I was this close." Her thumb and forefinger were nearly touching. "I took him to the doctor instead. *Again.* I begged her to help me figure out what was wrong, and she said I just had to tough it out, that things would get better soon. Only she's been saying that and saying that. It didn't get better and it won't."

"You just have that post-pardon depression thing, like Brooke Shields. I've read about it. It'll go away, you watch."

"Don't you get it? I don't care what it's called. Post*partum* depression or just good

37

sense. I just know now it's Graham's turn to listen to him cry and not know what to do. And if by some miracle he does know, or that wife of his knows, more power to them."

"I can't believe it. You gave him away? Just like that?"

Marina pushed her short blond hair off her face, raking her fingers through it until undoubtedly it stood on end. "I did. And before you showed up I was finally getting some sleep."

"Where's your heart?"

"Protected. Right here." Marina put a fist to her chest.

"You've always been a cold fish."

Marina knew if she was a fish at all, she was just a fish afraid of getting hooked. She certainly hadn't been cold the night Toby was conceived. She had acted on impulse when Graham came to this apartment, supposedly for a drink, and they ended up in bed, instead. For once in her adult life she had allowed her imagination to take control. Graham had confessed that he and his wife were deadlocked over having children. He wanted one right away, and Lilia didn't.

Of course he hadn't explained that any woman would be hesitant to conceive a baby with a man who might not be alive for its birth. He hadn't explained there was a cancer diagnosis and lethal chemotherapy he would have to undergo very soon. He'd presented her with a different picture: Lilia, as a selfish career-driven woman who was the wrong wife for a man who wanted a family and a supportive helpmate.

Blinded by hope and a foolish infatuation that she had nurtured since the day she'd introduced herself to Graham Randolph, Marina had imagined *she* was the right woman. As if in silent agreement that night he hadn't used a condom, and God help her, she hadn't asked him to.

She pulled herself back to the conversation. "I'm not cold. I'm just determined. I don't want your life, Deedee. And that's where I was headed."

"You think you need to insult me to make yourself feel better?"

"Not really. I think you got what you wanted. And I plan to do the same."

"What am I going to tell your brothers? They love that baby."

"Oh, please! Neither of them loves anybody. Try telling them the truth, that I'm not going to settle for a small slice of life. I want the whole pie. They won't understand, but tell them anyway."

"I'm ashamed of you. My own little girl."

"Look, keep the clothes, and don't buy anything else. I'll give you some money."

"Keep your money. The way you *didn't* keep your own flesh and blood." Deedee turned and stomped out the door. Marina wasn't

39

impressed. Her mother never stayed angry for long. Without Toby to care for, Marina would be more available whenever Deedee needed her. Everything else would fade. Before long she would tell her friends her daughter had acted heroically to give her son the best possible life.

And who knew? Maybe it was true.

Just as she was pulling off her jeans again to get more sleep the bedside telephone rang. She studied the caller ID and saw that this caller was welcome.

She licked her lips and cleared her throat before she answered.

"Hey, stranger." She swung her legs to the mattress and propped pillows against her padded headboard.

"Rina, how's it going?"

Blake Wendell probably thought using a nickname signaled they were closer than they were, like promising an expensive piece of jewelry without making the cash outlay. She was Marina Ray Tate, but only Deedee called her Rina, and then added the Ray for good measure. Even her brothers knew better. Unfortunately she'd made the mistake of confiding the nickname in a long phone conversation. She'd been six months pregnant, and conversations with Blake had been one of her few distractions. At least he'd forgotten the Ray.

"It's going fine." She examined her chipped

nails. Professional manicures had been impossible with a screaming baby, so she'd taken to doing her own.

He cleared his throat. "You're okay? It's been a while since we talked."

In reality they had talked earlier that week. She envied him for enjoying the kind of life where one day flowed gently into the next. Or maybe, there was an even more positive spin? Maybe he really *had* missed her.

"We should get together," she said.

"Would you like me to come over? I haven't seen your place."

She realized then how badly she wanted to get away from the apartment where Toby's presence still hung in the air. "Why don't I meet you at your place instead? Just give me an hour."

She hung up after jotting down his address, glad that Blake wanted to see her, although she wished he had waited until she had gotten some rest.

She got up and stretched, hoping a shower would revive her. She would wash and style her hair, do her nails, and choose something sexy to wear.

Halfway to the bathroom she felt something soft under her toes. Glancing down she saw she was standing on a small fleece blanket, the white one she'd always used to swaddle her son. She had wrapped his tiny flailing arms against his body to calm him, and

41

walked in circles around the apartment, crooning the closest thing to a lullaby that she knew. Toby had seemed to prefer this blanket to others, and sometimes swaddling him had even helped a little. But this morning he had rejected swaddling the way he had rejected her and everything she tried to comfort him.

She should have left the blanket on the porch with Toby's other things.

Should she send it to Graham now with a note explaining it was special? Would anybody understand or care?

She lifted the blanket off the floor and held it to her nose. The fabric still held the scent of baby shampoo and baby powder, along with the indefinable essence of a brand-new human being. Her hand dropped to her side, but she stood in the same spot, holding the blanket for a very long time.

Finally she changed direction and moved to the far corner of her room. She carefully folded it into a square and laid it under a pile of her shirts in the bottom drawer of her dresser.

3

The baby was screaming now, a shrieking siren that seemed incompatible with the featherweight human being in Lilia's arms.

After one examination she didn't want to look at him. Early in their marriage she and Graham had put off having children, certain they had all the time in the world to start a family. Later when she'd been ready, he had still wanted to wait. Then Burkitt's had entered their lives. He'd frozen sperm before chemo so that someday, when he recovered so completely they no longer had to worry about his future, they might be able to conceive through artificial insemination. But no baby birds would be hatching in this nest anytime soon, something she had tried hard not to think about.

Now she had no choice.

Instinct told her to set the child down and never pick him up again. Before she hurt him. Before the betrayal washing through her washed over him, too, and caused irreparable harm. But there was no place to lay him, no carrier or car seat. He had arrived in his mother's arms, and now he was in hers, the only place on the porch even halfway acceptable for an infant.

She'd been raised with other people's babies. Cousins, nieces and nephews, neighbors. As a teenager, she'd been in demand as a babysitter because she always seemed to know what to do. Yet she had no inclination to rock this one in her arms, to snuggle him against her shoulder or pat his tiny back. She was so angry that every ounce of goodness inside her had already been summoned. She was struggling just to remember that no matter the circumstances of little Toby's birth, he had not asked for this moment any more than she.

But quite likely his father had.

She knew then what she had to do. Suddenly it seemed simple. She held the infant against her shoulder so she could open the door with her other hand and walk inside, walk through the house she and Graham had so lovingly renovated together, walk through the kitchen where Regan was piling her carefully marinated chicken wings on a platter.

Her friend looked up and smiled. "Hey, who's that?"

"Where's Graham, do you know?"

They'd been friends so long that Lilia's tone wilted Regan's smile. "Still out back, I think. Mingling. But —"

"He may be calling on you tonight for help. Say no."

"Lilia, what —"

She stalked into the sunroom and threw open the door to the patio. The music was so loud that even the baby's screams were muffled. She was aware enough of her own feelings to be sorry that was true. Everybody should get the full benefit of Toby's misery.

At first she didn't see her husband, but somehow a path cleared. Friends who had smiled at the sight of her with the baby quickly sensed all was not well and stepped away. She wasn't surprised. She had learned to cover her despair in the past year, but fury was a different matter. Since she'd never been this angry, not in her entire life, she made no attempt to hide it.

Graham was in the far corner of their yard. He'd set up a dartboard against their tiny garage, and he, Carrick and several others, including Carrick's date, were playing. She should have gloried in the sight, one that at times, she had worried she would never see again. At the moment her husband was up, darts in hand, and carefully, one after the other, he was aiming at the board. She watched as he scored a bull's-eye.

Carrick moved to join her, but she waved him away. He paused. "Whose baby is that?" He looked completely baffled, and she wondered if Graham had kept Toby's presence in the world a secret, not just from her, but from his best friend and attorney, too. Carrick usually saved his acting skills for the courtroom, but until now, she'd never had reason to doubt her husband, either.

She watched as Carrick floundered toward the truth. At that moment Graham finished his turn and turned away from the board. His smile of satisfaction died. His gaze flicked to the baby screaming against her chest, and suddenly, he looked as unwell and frightened as he had during the worst moments of his illness.

If she'd had lingering doubts that Marina had been telling the truth, they fled forever. She expelled a long, harsh breath, and then she lowered Toby until he rested in the crook of her arm, moved closer and held him out to Graham.

"All your best friends are here. I'm sure they want to meet your son, and they'll want all the juicy details. I suggest you practice telling the truth for once and explain how this happened. They'll be dying to know."

When he didn't step forward, she did, until there was nothing between them except one wailing infant.

"Lilia —"

"Don't even try to explain. Take your son."

He was frozen in place, as if the horror of the moment had stripped him of the ability to move.

She spoke through gritted teeth, and only for his ears. "I have managed to carry this baby all the way through the house, but if you don't take him right this minute, I can't say that either of you are going to survive unscathed."

He reached out and grabbed Toby, holding him awkwardly.

"Just confirm Marina's story," she said. "This is your son? And all the months I was taking care of you, working to support us and doing everything I could to make sure you survived, another woman was pregnant with your child? Were you just waiting to tell me until you didn't need my help anymore?"

"It wasn't like that."

"He's yours?"

Graham looked down. If possible Toby was screaming louder, his tiny face screwed up in misery. "Yes."

"Then I suggest you get used to taking care of him. His mother left and didn't look back. She doesn't want him, and as you probably figured out a year ago, neither do I."

Then she turned and walked back through a parting Red Sea of guests who looked as if they would rather be slaves in Pharaoh's Egypt than at this party to celebrate Graham's good fortune.

4

From the master bedroom addition over the sunroom Lilia listened as the last of the guests fled. At first she had simply trembled with her back to the door and stared out the windows. But by the time someone called her name from the hallway she had positioned a carry-on suitcase on the Hawaiian appliqué quilt her mother had given her on her wedding day and begun to pack. She didn't answer, but the door opened, and Carrick appeared in the doorway.

He was the first to speak. "Regan has an extra bed at her place. And you know I have a spare bedroom."

She glanced over her shoulder. "You should be with your date."

"We drove separately. Julie's gone."

"Thanks for the offer, but I'm going home." She was torn between continuing to pack so she could leave faster, or asking him the question she hadn't outside. The question won. She faced him.

"Did you know, Carrick? About Toby? I hope to God you weren't keeping Graham's secret, too."

"I had no idea."

She studied his expression. Carrick looked both furious and wounded, but she knew her question wasn't the cause of either. "Okay."

"He *knew* what I would say if he'd told me. Maybe he was trying to use every bit of strength just to stay alive."

"Don't make excuses for him!"

"I'm not."

"He was your best friend before I even met you. I'm not going to ask you to choose. I'll make it easy. I won't be here."

When she turned away he joined her at the bedside where she had begun packing again. He perched on the edge, long denim-clad legs stretched out in front of him, but his posture wasn't relaxed. Carrick was holding himself like a man walking a tightrope.

"Lilia, these past awful months I've been right there with you. I know what you've gone through. Days, even nights at the hospital, then home to change clothes and go out to design appointments, or work on the website, or head out to your storage unit to be sure *The Swallow's Nest* orders were being processed correctly. Dealing with your employees and doing whatever you could with Graham's. You hardly ate or slept. Nobody could have done more to keep everything going until Graham recovered. *If* he did."

She remembered an evening when Carrick had asked if she was experiencing sympathy lymphoma. He'd offered to shave her head if she wanted to enhance the effect. Then he'd marched her out of Graham's hospital room for fish tacos and a chopped salad and sat with her to make sure she ate every bite.

Her hands hovered over the suitcase, but she couldn't force herself to fold the T-shirt she was holding. "How could he have done this to me? To us?"

He touched her shoulder, his fingers warm against her skin, but he removed his hand quickly. He didn't move closer, aware, she supposed, that she would either fall completely apart if he held her or, worse, she would shove him away. "I don't know. I really don't, but you need an answer. I don't think you can leave without knowing."

"Do you know what she said to me? What *Marina* said? She said I might hate her, or something to that effect, but at least she'd given that baby life —" her voice broke "— when I couldn't even be bothered to have Graham's baby."

"Lilia . . ."

She cleared her throat. "I wanted children. Before he got sick I thought we were ready. Graham was the one who held back. We had that possibility of a television show, and he kept saying the time should be exactly right.

50

Then when it wasn't, when it was the worst possible time to have a baby, when we had absolutely no idea whether he would live or die, he begged me to get pregnant. Just like that. After the diagnosis and before chemo. Out of nowhere. He wanted me to do everything to keep us going and have a baby, too. And we had no idea if he would even live to see it born!"

She took a deep breath and closed her eyes. "Although I guess that question was answered. He did live to see his son, didn't he?"

"You have to talk to him."

"No, I'm going home. I stayed in San Jose the whole time he was sick. I missed a wedding, a christening. I need my family."

"Plan to come back."

"Are you speaking as my lawyer? Can Graham divorce me for desertion if I leave?"

"Not in California. I'm talking about *The Swallow's Nest,* Lilia. You've built your whole business on making a home and a happy marriage, and you need to figure out how you're going to explain this to your readers. If you leave Graham and leave this house, everything crumbles to dust. And we both know your financial situation is beyond precarious. You can't afford to walk away."

He was right. The house was her one real asset, but she couldn't sell it to fund a new life because it was heavily mortgaged, first to pay for renovations and the audition tape she

51

and Graham had made for a potential television series, then refinanced yet again to help with medical bills and the loss of his income. If she sold it now she would be homeless and *still* in debt.

Then there was her life's work, her reputation as a designer whom local and internet clients could count on. And what about the readers who loved her website because she shared her own stories to help them gain the confidence to share theirs?

She was too confused to think it through. She spaced her words for emphasis. "I am too angry to talk to him now."

"Then just listen. Regan has the baby. Your guests are gone —"

"No surprise."

"Graham's a mess."

She hoped it was true. "Apparently I've used up my store of sympathy."

"You don't have to sympathize. You need facts. After you hear what he has to say you can take time to think this over."

"What is Graham going to do with that baby? I've never seen him hold one. Does he know he'll have to support his head? Put him on his back to sleep? When he's with my nieces and nephews he watches them like he's at the zoo."

"I guess he's about to learn fast."

"Right, or maybe he'll go back to his baby-mama and ask her to take them both in. A happy little family."

"I don't know what Graham was thinking when he slept with Marina Tate, but I do know she's not the one he wants."

"Well, I don't want him. I don't want a husband who sleeps with somebody else, finds out she's pregnant and forgets to tell me."

"He's been suffering. The depression? The way he pushed us both away at times? He was ashamed and probably torn up about what to do."

"You're defending him!"

"No, I'm just struggling to figure it out. And it *is* a struggle, but then nobody's ever told me I might only have months to live."

Still clutching the T-shirt, she met his eyes. Part of Carrick's nature was to see both sides of every situation, which made him an excellent lawyer. But while he was fair, he was also human, and she heard anger resonating in his voice. Now she saw it shining in his green eyes. And he wasn't angry at her.

"Will you drive me to the airport? If you feel that's taking sides, I'll ask Regan."

"Of course I will, but do you have a reservation?"

She gave a shake of her head. "I just want to get out of here."

"I'll see what's available and when."

"I would appreciate that."

He got up, but he didn't move away.

"Please, take your time making big decisions."

"It's too bad you didn't give Graham that
advice, what . . . a year ago?"

"He didn't make a decision. He made a
mistake."

"That poor little baby." Despite everything,
Lilia felt a stab of sympathy for Toby, whose
entrance into this difficult world had been
doomed from the start. A mother who didn't
want him, a father who hadn't acknowledged
him, and a stepmother who until today
hadn't even known he existed.

She was a *stepmother.* For as long as she
stayed married to Graham, her relationship
to the little boy who had been dumped into
her arms as unceremoniously as a bag of
garbage actually had a name. It seemed
inconceivable, like everything else that had
happened in the past half hour.

Carrick started toward the door. "I'm going to send him up."

She wasn't going to stay in the house a moment longer than she needed to, so it was
now or not at all. She finally folded the shirt.
"You do that. But tell him he only has as long
as it takes me to finish packing."

She was returning from the bathroom with
a bag of travel-sized toiletries when she saw
Graham had come into their bedroom and
closed the door behind him.

He looked as pale as she had ever seen him,

paler than the terrible day in the hospital when his heart had stopped, and she had been evicted from his room as hospital staff revived him. His blue eyes were almost startling against his white skin, and his forehead was dotted with sweat. He leaned against the door, as if he was afraid his knees might buckle without support.

For the first time since his diagnosis, she felt no trace of sympathy and no surge of love. She only felt anger, cold and deadly.

He didn't quite meet her eyes. "I don't even know where to start."

She was shaking with emotion, but she managed to hold her head high. "How about this? You slept with Marina and she got pregnant. And you decided to keep that little tidbit to yourself."

She went to the closet, took down her largest purse and slipped the bag of toiletries inside it. When he didn't answer she took a deep breath to steady herself before she turned.

"How many times did you sleep with her, Graham, or have you become such a practiced liar you'll lie about that, too?"

"Once, Lilia. Just once, I swear. The night you and I fought about having a baby."

"As a kid you probably got everything you asked for. I guess having somebody say no to you didn't compute."

"There are no excuses or explanations good

enough."

"Just tell the truth then. All of it. And quickly, because I'm leaving in a few minutes."

His speech was halting, as if he were dragging the words from a deep well. "I was an emotional disaster. I guess I can't say 'was.' I still am. I saw a black hole instead of a future, and all I could think about that night was that I was going to die and leave nothing important behind. I was going to die and no part of me was going to live on. I latched on to the idea of having a baby as proof I'd been on this earth. Of course you knew better than to go along with me, but that night I couldn't see how right you were. I went to a bar near a house I was renovating, and Marina was there. We'd gone there together a few times with others from the project. It was a place she liked."

"What exactly was going on between you?"

"Nothing." He paused, and then he shrugged. "I liked her. She liked me, but she knew I was married. She even came to a party here and met you. I guess there were a few harmless sparks. It never bothered me and maybe it was kind of nice to flirt a little. I knew nothing was going to happen."

"And then it did."

"If I say I wasn't myself that night it'll sound like I'm using cancer as an excuse to behave badly. But I wasn't myself. I wasn't thinking rationally. She invited me back to her place for a drink. I didn't want to come home. I was too upset you were refusing to give me the one thing I thought I needed. I went."

She was shaking; her voice was shaking. "Let me guess. Out of nowhere Marina seduced you. None of this was your fault. You went along for the ride because you were too sick to resist."

"No. I didn't try to stop what happened. I guess I knew right from the moment I followed her home how the night might end, but I also knew what was waiting for me in the months ahead. For that night I just wanted to be a man, not a man with cancer."

"And birth control?"

"She had condoms. At the last minute I didn't use one, and she didn't insist."

"You hoped she would get pregnant?"

"The chances seemed so small. I left it up to the universe."

She was glad he was standing too far away to slap. "What a strange place to get religious. In bed. You think God wanted a baby to be born into those circumstances? First cancer made you do it, then God?"

"There are no words that even begin to cover how sorry I am or how stupid I was. I know how screwed up the whole thing is."

"Did you think that she and that baby were just going to disappear? That a woman like

Marina was just going to let this catastrophe go on and on and never tell anybody? Were you hoping you could have two happy families and one of them would never know? How stupid could you be?"

"I haven't thought about anything else. Not since Marina told me she was pregnant. I knew I had to tell you. I knew I had to fix this somehow so I could keep you and Toby in my life, but I couldn't find a way."

"You've had almost a year to come up with one, haven't you?" She waited a moment until she had swallowed angry tears. "And in none of that time could you think of any way to tell me what you had done?"

"How could I? I was terrified you would leave. And not because I needed your help. Because I need *you*. I love you."

"But the moment I refused to give you what you wanted, you found another woman who would."

"Please, don't leave, Lilia. I know it's asking too much, but please, don't leave me. From the moment I walked out of Marina's apartment I've wanted to beg you to forgive me. I just couldn't find a way to say it. Because I was afraid of this, afraid you'd go."

"Here's a tip. You can find a nanny in the yellow pages. Or a day care center."

"I don't want a nanny. I want you."

She met his eyes. "I'm going home, Graham. That's another thing I gave up for you

58

this year. My family. Now I'm going to see them."

"Please come back."

"You've said what you came to say. I've listened, which is all I said I would do. Is there anything else you haven't told me?"

He didn't answer.

She hadn't really believed things might get worse, but now she realized that something else was coming. "What about Toby? You don't know anything about babies. Are you going to ask Marina to take him back? Maybe she just wanted you to acknowledge him."

He put his hand to his forehead, as if to brush away hair that still wasn't long enough to be a nuisance. "There is something else. You need to know one more thing."

For a moment she wasn't sure she could listen. "Make it fast."

"Marina didn't want to have the baby. Especially after she found out I was sick and might not be around to support them both."

She knew better than to respond. She clenched her teeth and waited.

"I . . . convinced her to finish out the pregnancy by promising to pay her. A lot."

He stopped, but he didn't have to go on, because suddenly she knew. "Your trust fund? The one that tanked the last time the stock market dipped? The one we really needed for medical expenses so I didn't have to mortgage this house?"

"I lied to you. That money was well invested. But I couldn't live with myself if Marina hadn't gone through with the pregnancy. The whole thing was my fault, and an abortion would have been, too."

"You gave her all of it? At one time the fund was worth, what, almost a hundred thousand dollars?"

"I gave her half and promised to give her the rest when Toby was born. But at the last minute I had to use it for my final round of chemo. Our insurance refused to cover the drug the doctors wanted to try, and they rejected the claim. They called the drug experimental, but my team said it was vital."

"I know that, but you told me the insurance paid it after you appealed."

"Because I couldn't tell you I'd paid the bill myself with money from a trust fund I'd already told you was worthless."

"What an accomplished liar you are!"

"Marina was furious, as she had the right to be, and that's probably why she brought Toby here today. But that's the end of the lies, Lilia. The absolute truth. All of it. One terrible mistake that just kept growing."

"And now you have a baby to take care of when you can hardly take care of yourself. And nothing to live on."

"I'll figure it out."

She was rarely sarcastic, but nothing stopped her now. "Maybe Marina will take you back. You can tell her how awful I am, like you did the night you used her like a broodmare."

He winced. "Lilia, Marina won't be in the picture. She hasn't wanted Toby from the beginning, and now she's abandoned him to me."

A stab of sympathy for the other woman surprised her. "As strange as it seems, maybe I can see her point. She told me on the porch that you had promised her so much more. You lied to both of us."

"I never promised her anything except money. We never talked about a future together, I swear. She was reading what she wanted into a one-night stand."

"A one-night stand with a man intent on proving his manhood and his fertility. It's no wonder she was a bit confused. *If* she was."

"I've screwed up so many lives. I'm so sorry."

"As exit lines go, that works. I'll be out of here in a few minutes, and then you'll have lots of time to wallow in all the damage you've done."

She thought she was finished, but she realized she couldn't be. Not yet. Because even though her flash of sympathy for Marina had come and gone, she was still worried about the other person in this drama.

She turned her back to him. "That baby is the biggest loser here, isn't he? He never asked to be born. And he sure never asked to be born to the two of you. Whatever else you do, make sure he's taken care of. Toby's more than your selfish bid for immortality. He's flesh and blood, and no matter how he came into this world, he deserves better than you wallowing in self-pity and wringing your hands for the next weeks. His mother doesn't want him, and his self-absorbed father has no clue how to give him what he needs. Find somebody to help you who can act like an adult, and find somebody fast."

"Please, come back when you're ready."

"I'll have to come back to settle things. Other than that?" She shrugged. "In the meantime if you have any suggestions on how I explain this little upheaval in our perfect marriage to my readers, let me know."

"Is there anything I can do except tell you again how much I love you and how sorry I am?"

"You can leave. Now."

A moment later the door closed behind him. She was alone.

She dropped to the side of the bed where Carrick had been and closed her eyes, trying to calm her roiling stomach. Through all the turmoil and terror of his illness, she and Graham had stood together and faced whatever came their way. Now she was alone. When it seemed his chances of survival were slim, she had learned to face a future without him. But she had never expected to face a future without him because he had betrayed her.

No part of her wanted to call him back to forgive him. But a part of her wished it were yesterday, when whether her husband lived or died was her worst problem. Yesterday she wouldn't have believed how insignificant life and death could seem today.

5

No one knew exactly which ancestors had passed their genes to Lilia or her four brothers. From their mother's side they were Hawaiian, Filipino and Samoan. From their father's they were Chinese, along with a large dose of the UK. International bloodlines weren't unusual on the island of Kauai, where she'd been raised. Neither were they atypical in the South Bay area of California where she had moved at age eighteen to care for her aunt.

Now looking at her oldest brother, Eli, who had picked her up from the airport in a four-seater beach buggy, she remembered a game they had played as children. Each sibling had imagined that ancestors long departed had personally chosen him or her as a favorite. Their personal guardian angels.

Eli had always claimed their Samoan great-grandfather had chosen him. He was big-boned and substantial, with the darkest coloring of any of the Swallow siblings, although that was never easy to document because of the hours each child spent in the sun. As a teen he had come home sporting an intricate Samoan shoulder tattoo, and since then he had added to it until now most of one muscular arm was covered.

Eli owned a shop that gave tours and rented buggies, like the one he was driving today, and he swore the more Polynesian he looked, the more business he attracted. Some of his steadiest customers were female. When he'd threatened to knot a lavalava around his waist and show up for work bare-chested, his wife, Amber, had put her foot down. Business was fine just the way it was.

Eli was a man of few words, so Lilia knew he was waiting for her to tell him why she had come home with such short notice. He would never ask outright.

"Do you remember what we used to pretend about our ancestors?" she asked.

"You thought you were descended from some English princess or maybe a Chinese courtesan. I don't think you knew what that meant."

"It was all about the palaces. There was a book in the school library with amazing photos. I wanted to live in one."

"California doesn't have a lot of palaces."

"Kai decided he was all Hawaiian, remember? That was the year he borrowed his first ukulele from Uncle Ike." Kai, who sang and played beautifully, was the second oldest Swallow, followed by Micah and then after Lilia, Jordan. Lilia was the only girl, and for the first five years of her life she had been treated almost exactly like her brothers, including short haircuts, hand-me-down clothes and freedom.

"We had a great childhood." As she spoke she envisioned baby Toby, whose childhood so far was anything but, and unexpectedly her voice caught.

Eli glanced away from the two-lane road to search her face. "You didn't say what's what with Graham."

She had debated this question since she boarded the plane to Honolulu, and then during the hours she had waited for the final flight to Kauai. She had managed to get home, but not on the best schedule. She was exhausted and still too emotional to trust herself.

"Graham's last two CT scans were clear."

"Yeah, I knew that."

"Our relationship took a bad turn, Eli. I'm guessing it won't take a good one again."

He didn't say anything for miles of tropical foliage and red dirt fields that had once grown sugarcane and pineapples and now nurtured a variety of crops. She tried to focus on distant mountains instead of her pain.

"Marriage, it's hard." Eli gave one definitive nod, as if that said it all.

66

"Yours still good?"

"Oh yeah, she puts up with me, with everything, Amber does. But three kids under ten? Not much time to think about anything else."

"Would you want something different?"

"Nobody's life is perfect. Good is a lot to hope for, and we have more than that. We work together, raise our kids, put food on our table. We're thankful."

She remembered the teenage Eli, who for a school project had memorized a Samoan grace and made everyone in the family sing it for months before meals. He was the Swallow who attended church most regularly, who faithfully tithed and volunteered whenever he was needed. He was a good man, and Lilia wasn't surprised he was the one who had volunteered to drive her home.

"Good would be good enough for me. That's really all I wanted." She stared out the window. "I never asked for more."

He continued the conversation, which was a sign he was worried. "Illness takes a lot out of a family. Amber's brother nearly died in that accident, remember? For a while her mom and dad split up over it." Amber's brother had wrapped his car around a kukui tree after too many beers at a graduation party. He still walked with a cane.

"Does illness make a man forget his marriage vows?"

He whistled softly, and that was all she got

until they passed through the quaintly scenic town of Kapa'a, ten square miles that were large enough for a few stoplights, a variety of shops and hotels, and stretches of palm tree–lined beaches. In English *Kapa'a* meant solid, and the solid little town had been built on rice, pineapples and now, tourism.

Out of town Eli followed a winding two-lane road past one-story houses screened by extravagant clusters of oleander and banana trees, along with chain-link or concrete block fences. In the past decades the area had built up steadily, but homes, by mainland standards, were still modest, even though in the islands the most substandard housing was expensive.

Roosters crowed, a familiar sound, and Eli waited patiently at a one-lane bridge until traffic coming from the other direction had crossed. She could see the Sleeping Giant, a mountain that had shadowed her childhood. Her family had owned the land and house they lived on for generations and watched the landscape change to suit new residents. This still felt like home.

"Graham is hard to know," Eli said at last. "But one thing I always figured? He loves my sister."

"Words mean so little."

"You're taking time to think?"

"I don't expect anything to change. But that's why I'm here."

68

"Will you move back? If you decide to leave him?"

She had asked herself the same question on the plane. Family surrounding her would be wonderful, and she loved her childhood home. But everything else she loved was in California. Her house, her friends, Swallow's Nest Design, her small but thriving interior design business. While she could run her website from Kauai, she would be forced to scale down. Her online store and design consultation would be impossible because the cost of travel and shipping would be prohibitive. Opportunities here would be different, but they wouldn't suit her needs or talents nearly as well.

She put the other reason into words. "I think I was born with island fever. I love the mainland, but I would come home more often. I missed coming home so much this past year. I didn't think I could leave Graham."

"Be sure you have all the facts straight, Lilia."

"I heard the facts directly from him. And saw the proof." She gave up pretending she could keep what had happened a secret. "He has a son, Eli. He claims it was a one-night stand, but he used the trust fund we needed to pay his medical bills to support the baby's mother. Then Graham let me nurse him back to health for a year without telling me."

He whistled again. Then he surprised her. "He was afraid to lose you."

Anger was white-hot and immediate. "Why would you say that? It's just as likely he didn't tell me because he needed me when he was sick!"

"I say it because I've seen the way he watches you."

She couldn't let that pass, and she told him something she hadn't told anyone else, because she had always been able to share her secrets with Eli. "Do you remember the last time we came here? Before we found out about the cancer? Graham and I had talked about having a baby of our own very soon. Then he came here and saw little Jonah."

Jonah was Kai's youngest son, a particularly beautiful child, who at birth had resembled his Georgia peach mother, rosy-skinned and blue-eyed.

She spoke faster. "Jonah had grown so much and suddenly he looked like an island baby. And Graham was shocked. He didn't know babies' skin color deepens, or that their eyes can change colors. Suddenly Jonah looked like our Polynesian ancestors, not his *haole* mother, and will probably look more like them as he grows up. Graham never said so, but I think he took a look at our beautiful nieces and nephews, with their rainbow diversity, and realized his baby might look like them because, hey, I'm Hawaiian, too.

Like the rest of you. Same gene pool, right? So to spare himself that possible calamity, his baby's mother is blonder than he is!"

Eli slowed because they had almost reached their destination. "I'm not surprised you're angry."

"I don't think you believe me."

"I believe everything you've said, but this man married you when his parents disapproved. He showed every sign of wishing he was Hawaiian, too, not wishing you were more like him."

"Well, now he has a son who looks like him. And the baby has come to stay."

He turned into the long unpaved driveway leading to their parents' house. "The baby's mama?"

"She dropped that little boy in my arms and announced he was Graham's, then walked away and left me holding him on my own front porch."

He surprised her and stopped, turning in his seat to look at her. "I know you hurt. I wish I could make that better."

"Please, don't be condescending."

"It's just that I understand better than you think."

"How could you?"

He grimaced. "Amber kept a secret from me, too. Aleki is not my biological son, but nobody else knows it, although I think Mama suspects. Amber was pregnant when I mar-

71

ried her. I knew she had been in a bad relationship before we met, but for months before we married she didn't tell me she was pregnant. Then when hiding it was impossible, I wrestled with the pregnancy, the deception, the responsibility. Everything."

She was stunned that in a family as close as theirs, this had been kept a secret. "But you married her anyway and never told us?"

"I married her, maybe *because* of the baby. By then I loved her and didn't want her to go through that alone. And when he was born I loved Aleki as much as I love our other children. And after a while I didn't hold Amber responsible for the hard choice I had to make. The whole thing? It made me think about what really mattered."

Then he surprised her, because Eli was rarely demonstrative. He touched her braid, hanging limply over one shoulder, then he gave it a slight tug. "Maybe that's what you'll need to think about, too."

6

Ellen Randolph had been wealthy all her life, so she knew for certain that having money did not automatically make anybody happy or widen their world. Protecting one's assets was a cheerless, thankless task, and the narrower one's world, the easier it was to stay at the top of it.

Having lived with Douglas Randolph for thirty-six years, she knew the view from the top was limited, too. Every single day as chairman of the Randolph Group, Douglas acted on his conviction that a wider view was an unnecessary distraction, and every single day he got wealthier and more rigid.

This morning Douglas stood in their designer kitchen, with its custom rosewood cabinetry and enameled lava countertops and pinched his features together in disapproval.

"I don't quite know what you expect me to do about this, Ellen."

She had caught her husband right before he headed for his corporate offices in Oakland, and from long experience she knew that this was exactly the wrong time to bring up anything personal. But truthfully there were no good times. Douglas was 99 percent business and only 1 percent father-husband-lover, and mentioning their son's name at any time of day wasn't just a distraction, it was an act of treason.

For Douglas, removing Graham from his life had been a business decision, and his business decisions were evenly divided between pragmatic and spiteful. He was not a man to cross, and Graham had crossed him one time too many. The spiteful Douglas would never forgive his son, and Ellen knew better than to ask him to.

But he still had to know the latest news.

Her tone was solicitous, more personal assistant than wife, which was the way he liked it. "I don't expect you to do anything. I just thought you had to know that apparently we have a grandson." She played her ace. "In case someone mentions it. I know how you hate to be taken by surprise."

He made the same noise low in his throat that he made whenever he was skeptical or didn't want to admit anybody else had a point. "And the person who told you the story is reliable?"

"Jenny Lurfield's daughter is a friend of Graham's, and she was at the party to celebrate his better health. She told Jenny about the baby."

"Well, you have a little spy network everywhere, don't you? You should have gone into the CIA instead of marrying me."

"I needed the bigger challenge." She moved on before he processed that. "I'm going to see Graham this morning. I just thought you should know."

"Don't expect anything from me. I don't want to hear about this again, you understand? This has nothing to do with me. Nothing Graham does has anything to do with me. I thought that was clear."

"You are the master of clarity. And now that I've let you know, I'll keep the rest to myself."

"What rest? I would like you to ignore this scandal and hold up your head if it's mentioned. Can't you do that?"

"Do you mean am I capable of doing that? Of course I am."

"Don't play games!"

She didn't back away, not even when he stepped forward. At sixty Douglas remained a force to be reckoned with, in full possession of all his hair and a trim waistline, still erect and broad-shouldered, but Ellen had learned long ago that he would never raise a hand to her no matter how loud his voice. He intimidated by attitude and gesture.

She was nearly his height, and now she met his eyes, which were blazing with anger. "I'm just going to visit Graham today and see what

I should do next. My head's always up, but I'm not nearly as adept at ignoring our only child as you are."

"You coddled him. If you had ignored that boy a little more when he was growing up, then maybe I wouldn't be so ashamed of him now."

The problem was just the opposite. She'd spent Graham's childhood ignoring him. Between her own lack of experience, her inability to dredge up what she thought were appropriate maternal feelings, and her desire to please and placate her husband, hadn't she ignored her son's all-too-fragile development until he had finally developed without her and gone in his own direction?

She chose her words carefully. "Your son almost died this year. He's still not out of the woods, and now he has a child and, as I understand it, his wife has fled. If I could ignore that, then *I* would be less than human."

"Watch what you say to me."

She wondered why. Years of watching every word and placating Douglas had gotten her right to the place where she was standing.

She turned away. "I won't bother you with whatever I find. I just told you what you need to know."

"More than I need to know."

"Douglas, if I were you, I would prepare a response in case anybody else brings it up."

Then despite a lifetime of training she added: "Something between passing out cigars and what you've said here."

The sound of angry footsteps disappeared slowly down the hallway until the door to the garage slammed. Today he was driving himself to work. At the last minute his driver had taken a personal day, and Douglas was fuming about that, as well. She was afraid that between the son in trouble and the absent driver, the driver bothered him more.

When she looked back on her fifty-eight years, after she peeled away the superficial layers that first jumped to mind, deleted all the social events she had helped with for charity, deducted all the money that Douglas had donated to causes that propped up his financial interests? When she did all that, hoping for some sign that deep inside she was a good woman? She found next to nothing.

But today, no matter what Douglas said, she was going to see Graham and the baby.

Upstairs in the master bedroom she stared out the window and considered what to wear. The Randolphs' house on Belvedere Island had priceless views of Sausalito and the Golden Gate Bridge, but she was too preoccupied to notice. Casual was probably in order, but casual in her closet meant expensive resort wear, nothing particularly baby proof. She remembered how, as a newborn, Graham had spit up on everything until she had asked the nanny to feed and burp him before she picked him up herself.

Had she really been that concerned about appearance and so little concerned about bonding with her son?

She chose gray pants and a matching knit top that she planned to donate to the Tiburon Thrift Shop. These days she needed brighter colors anyway. Her hair was carefully blond, like Graham's, her face as young as the best plastic surgeon in San Francisco could make it. She still saw inevitable signs of aging.

She wondered if Douglas ever looked at her long enough to see them, too.

The drive to San Jose would probably take at least two hours, unless she waited until well after rush hour. She decided not to wait, and not to call Graham. If he wasn't home she would settle somewhere and wait. She didn't want to risk having her son tell her that he didn't want to see her. She wasn't sure what she would say to him, but her Tesla practically drove itself, and even in heavy traffic she would have time to plan. She told herself she would be ready.

Two and a half hours later, the drive hadn't worked any magic. By the time she drove into the Willow Glen neighborhood in the south part of San Jose, she still didn't have a speech prepared, and worse, she was lost. So much time had passed since she had visited her son and daughter-in-law that she had to pull over and set her GPS to find their house. Two turns and a few minutes later she parked on the right street, but she didn't get out of the car. She gazed up and down the block.

Willow Glen was charming in a way that the fabulously beautiful Belvedere was not. The houses were small, cozy and individual. She had never studied architecture, but she didn't need a college course to see that a number of styles and eras were represented here.

Yards were small, most carpeted in flowers or shrubs instead of grass. Graham and Lilia's house was one of them, asymmetrical beds of roses and perennials, a bench and a birdbath. While she didn't really like her daughter-in-law, she had to give Lilia credit for making the most of the tiny Tudor cottage she had inherited from an aunt. A brick walkway wound its way up to a brick porch. A vine, probably wisteria, ran from one side to the other along the front. These days the house was painted a subtle pine green. The door was ivory and the trim a bright seashore blue. Everything was too quaint, too picturesque, to suit Ellen. But she could see the appeal.

She blamed herself for Lilia. In a way she had been the one to introduce the girl to her son. Lilia's mother, Nalani, had been the house manager for the Randolphs' estate on

Kauai's North Shore. Douglas had bought the seven-acre property as an investment, but he had been in no hurry to sell, hoping for a zoning change that would let him subdivide and make a significant profit. So the family had visited there several times a year, and Nalani had both cared for the property while they were away and acted as housekeeper and occasional cook when they were in residence. She managed other properties, too, and when the house had to be opened in a hurry, her five children often pitched in, a family business of sorts.

On one of those occasions, ten-year-old Lilia was introduced to eleven-year-old Graham. And from that point on, until the year that Douglas forcibly broke up the friendship that had formed between Lilia, Graham and later Carrick — who had often visited the estate with the Randolphs — Lilia and Graham had taken far too enthusiastic an interest in each other.

To this day Ellen wondered if the grown-up Lilia had stalked Graham to renew their "friendship." Both claimed their meeting years later, at a party in Berkeley where he'd been a student in the architecture department, was accidental. But the heir to the Randolph Group was an extraordinary catch. For all the laid-back, not-the-way-we-do-things-in-Hawaii attitudes that Lilia laid claim to, Ellen still wondered if the girl had known

Graham would be at that party and traveled all the way from San Jose to reacquaint herself with the man who could make her life so much easier.

Of course it certainly hadn't turned out that way.

Ellen had delayed long enough. She tucked her handbag under her arm, got out and locked the car before she started up the street, then the walkway. She'd considered bringing gifts, but that had seemed hopelessly positive. She wasn't sure if she was here to celebrate or commiserate. Graham had survived cancer and now had an illegitimate son to deal with. Celebration would have to wait for more details.

At the front door she rang the doorbell and heard music. Not chimes, but snatches of a song. She shook her head and waited, trying again when nobody answered the door. She was just beginning to plan where she would wait when it opened.

Graham was so pale, so clearly exhausted, that for a moment she wasn't sure this was her son.

"Graham?" She stretched out a hand and touched his arm. "Are you all right?"

He raked fingers through hair too short to need grooming. "What are you doing here?"

"Word gets out. I heard about . . ." She shrugged. "I heard you have a son. I heard Lilia left you."

"And you swooped right in. Here to gloat?"

"Of course not."

"Then why?"

"To see if I can help, I guess."

He faked a laugh. "Cancer didn't spur you on, but the baby did. I'll have to think that one over."

Early in his life Graham had learned to be cool and polite, to combat his father's sarcasm and criticism with aloof good manners. She had never heard him be so dismissive.

"Nobody knows better than you do why I had to stay away," she said.

"Actually I don't know. I figure you're an adult, and unless I missed something, my father doesn't chain you to a chair when he's not around."

"I didn't come here to fight or defend myself."

"So tell me again why you did come?"

"I'd like to see my grandson. If it's true that I have one."

"Oh, it's true. But he's actually sleeping. For once."

"You look like you're going to fall over. Let's go inside."

"Please, keep your voice down. He's upstairs, but God knows what wakes him up and sets him off."

"You were a monster for your first few months."

"How nice he inherited that particular

trait." He stepped aside and swept his hand behind him to usher her in.

The house was anything but tidy. Signs of a party were still in evidence. Crumbs on the floor, dishes on the dining room table, a congratulations sign hanging askew. Clearly Lilia wasn't here. Ellen's daughter-in-law loved order. Whether Ellen liked Lilia's design ideas or not, the house was always picture perfect. Never fussy, but comfortable and welcoming. Anything that looked out of place was meant to be.

She followed Graham through the house, through a kitchen piled with dirty dishes, and into the sunroom. She thought the room must have been an addition because she didn't remember it from her last visit. It was small but flooded with light, and the tropical-style furniture, old-fashioned rattan with a glass table on a coral stand, probably made Lilia feel right at home. She picked up a floral cushion from the floor and placed it on the love seat before she sat.

Graham dropped down to a chair in the corner and closed his eyes. He looked so beaten. She searched for something to say.

"You cried for the first three months of your life. Even a professional baby nurse wasn't sure what to do with you. And me? I felt so completely inept. It seemed like I should know the magic key, that you should have emerged with instructions. Everybody told me not to worry, that crying was normal, but I was sure it was my own fault. Something I'd eaten in pregnancy, a glass of wine I had before I realized you were on the way. Bad genes."

At that he opened his eyes. "Really? Bad genes? I thought the Randolphs and the Grahams were perfect in every way, that you and my father thought I was some sort of genetic mutation."

"Not even close to being perfect."

"There's nothing you can do here to help. I have to deal with it. I brought this on myself."

"Do you want to tell me what's going on?"

"Why?"

"Maybe there's something I can do."

"Unless you can zoom back in time and keep me from acting on the worst impulse I've ever had, then no."

"You had an affair?"

He gave a bitter laugh. "Nothing that interesting. A one-night stand. Right between what sounded like a death sentence and chemo."

"Oh, Graham . . ." She didn't know what else to say.

"Toby is the result. As you can imagine, Lilia is not happy about it."

"She's gone?"

"In Kapa'a with her family. I don't know if she'll be back for more than packing and shipping."

She wanted to be angry at Graham's wife. He was still recovering, and Lilia had abandoned him to handle everything on his own. But how could Ellen fault her? For the past year her daughter-in-law had shouldered every possible burden, with no help from anyone except the long-distance support of her own family.

"Did you really think you could keep the baby a secret from Lilia? Or were you waiting until you felt you could cope with the fallout?"

"I don't know, Mother. I was trying to stay alive. Half the time I was so sick I couldn't remember where the bathroom was."

"And you were ashamed. You're a good man. You would be."

"You have no idea what this kind of shame feels like."

She did, but it wasn't helpful to admit that now. She was saved from trying, because a wail began somewhere in the distance. She put out her hand when Graham started to rise. "He's upstairs?"

"A friend gave me some kind of contraption for him to sleep in. He's in our room."

"I'll get him."

"Do you know what to do?"

"Has it changed that much in thirty years?"

"Did you know what to do *then*?"

The question should have hurt, but both of them knew that Graham's childhood had been managed by competent professionals, and she had looked on from the sidelines. "I do know how to change a diaper."

"I think he looks like me."

"Then he's a beautiful baby."

"He should have dark hair and brown eyes like the mother I didn't give him."

"I'll bring him down. Will he need a bottle?"

"I'll get one ready."

The upstairs must have been expanded in her years away because the wail was coming from a room she didn't remember. She followed the sound, opened the door and saw a small mesh-sided crib beside a queen-size bed. She picked up a beautiful hand-stitched quilt from the floor and folded it carefully, setting it on a chair before she dared go to the baby.

And then it was like looking at the infant Graham again.

She reached down and scooped him up, holding him against her breasts. Time stood still, although the baby didn't. He arched his tiny back and screamed, just the way his father had.

"Well," she said when she could speak, "Hello, Toby. I'm your grandmother."

The baby was not impressed. She laughed. "I know. I know!" She looked around and saw a box of diapers on the floor. She set him carefully in the center of the queen bed, grabbed a baby blanket from the floor and tucked it under him before she stripped off his little footie pajamas, then took out a diaper. He screamed as she changed him, but she hummed loudly, and she thought that the screaming paused from time to time as he listened.

His clothes were dry, so she pulled them back on and folded the blanket snugly around him until he looked like a burrito. She smiled and kissed his forehead. "Let's get you something to eat."

Downstairs she found her son with a bottle ready. "When was the last one?" she asked.

"When he was hungry."

"They always seem hungry when they're screaming, but overfeeding can cause problems, too."

"So I'm told."

"Good. You have help?"

"I have a few friends who are still speaking to me, if that's what you're asking."

"The baby's mother?"

"Is not among them."

"You haven't spoken to her?"

"She won't take calls or texts from me. She probably feels like she's on vacation."

He stretched out his arms, but she shook her head. "Let me." She held out a hand for the bottle. He shrugged and gave it to her.

She settled Toby into her arms, propping him carefully because she remembered being told that keeping the head high might help.

Toby sucked at the bottle's nipple like he hadn't been fed in weeks.

"He's beautiful, and yes, he looks remarkably like his father. I never quite knew what to do with you, but I did appreciate what a gorgeous little boy you were."

"Why did you have me?"

"It's complicated."

"I'm not going anywhere."

It took her a while to answer. Toby had taken enough formula that she decided to burp him, despite his protests. Frequent burping was something else she remembered. "I wanted to feel connected to somebody. I saw women with their husbands and children and knew they had something I didn't. Your father was always busy —"

"Not to mention rigid and controlling."

"Let's not talk about that."

"Why start now?" He closed his eyes again.

"I believed having you would make us a real family."

"Sorry it didn't work."

"Graham, I was never sorry you were my son. And that's the truth. But I'm also not sorry I didn't give you a brother or sister." She didn't go on. She knew she didn't have to.

After a loud burp Toby settled back to his bottle and opened his eyes to stare at her. She smiled at him. He smiled back, and the nipple fell out of his mouth. He wrinkled his little face to cry, but she slid it back in.

"He smiled at me!"

"Aren't you the lucky one." Graham didn't sound quite as cynical as he had.

"I *feel* lucky. A baby's smile is magic." She looked at her son, although pulling her gaze from her grandson was hard. "This is going to get better. His nervous system is going to mature. Pretty soon he's going to seem like a real person to you."

He surprised her. "How can I blame you for having *me* after what I've done?"

She didn't know how to answer, but Graham's question almost sounded like absolution, like he might actually forgive her for being such a distant figure in his life. In the end she shook her head. "I wish I could do more."

"I don't want help. I'll manage."

"And Lilia? Is there any way you can make this up to her?"

"Can you think of a way?"

He didn't expect an answer; she knew that. But she gave him one anyway. "You know I never really approved of your marriage."

"Yes, for some reason you didn't think Lilia was good enough for me. When the opposite was clearly true."

She knew better than to address that since whatever she said would make her sound racist and undemocratic, although she was sure she was neither. Instead she moved the discussion sideways. "I can't help you with that. I've never felt close to her, and I probably never will. I felt I lost you for good once you found her."

"What exactly did you lose?"

"And I've always felt she prodded you into confronting your father the way you did. He gave you a job, a future at Randolph Group, and instead of listening to him and following his lead, you went out on your own and brought a stain on all of us."

"I took the truth to the places where something could be done about it."

"Your father doesn't forgive easily."

"I knew that when I did what I had to."

She wondered, with Lilia out of the picture, if a miracle might happen. "This could be a time, Graham, when Douglas might soften a little. If you tell him you made a mistake and you're sorry, he might be willing to let bygones be bygones. Toby is his grandson, perhaps the only grandchild he'll ever have, and even your father has a sentimental streak."

"I'm *not* sorry, and I didn't make a mistake. Not that time, at least."

"Is it beyond you to say so, even if it's not precisely true? Is it beyond you to say it to assure this baby's future?"

Graham was silent so long she thought he might be mulling over the idea. But when he spoke she realized how wrong she had been.

"I hope my son has a long, happy future

with me guiding his steps. And if she can ever forgive me, I hope he'll have a future with Lilia as his mother." His voice hardened. "But I would apply for food stamps, Mother, I would stand in bread lines before I would allow my father to sink his talons into anybody in my family, especially Toby. I will never humble myself in front of a man without an ounce of humility or goodwill in his soul."

As if his own words had spurred him to action, he got up and held out his arms for the baby. "Feel free to tell him I said so."

7

Blake's "villa" overlooked a golf course, which didn't surprise Marina. The day they'd met waiting in line at a popular restaurant downtown, he had been dressed in a bright blue polo shirt with the Pebble Beach logo. Three months into a pregnancy she regretted, she had started an idle conversation with the attractive older man who had lost none of his graying dark hair and held himself like a soldier. They'd cut their mutual wait time by taking a table together, and she'd learned that Blake was adjusting to being a widower. He had seemed lonely, in spite of admitting to a new romantic interest. Before parting, they'd exchanged phone numbers. "Just to chat."

In the following months they *had* chatted occasionally, talking about everything, except her pregnancy. She hadn't told him about the baby, preferring to pretend to herself, as well as to him, that she was carefree and single. After all, who did it hurt? But a month after

Toby's birth, he had invited her to dinner. The new girlfriend was out of his life, and by then, Graham was definitely out of hers.

The community where he lived was divided into villages sprawling over land where a vineyard and winery once stood, and his village was near tennis courts and the clubhouse restaurant. The villa, while small, was still three times larger than Marina's apartment, with every possible amenity.

Blake fell into the amenity category.

This morning Marina woke slowly and saw the sun was high in the sky. She could hardly remember days when she had slept until she was ready to wake up, but she was rapidly getting used to it. Even before the baby she'd needed to be at her job early, and weekends had been filled with shopping and cleaning or helping Deedee with some project she couldn't complete on her own. But this morning no alarm had awakened her, and now Blake stood beside the bed they'd shared for a week with a cup of steaming coffee in his hands.

"Sleeping Beauty," he said fondly.

She slid up to a sitting position and pulled the top sheet over her breasts before taking the cup. On the evening she had volunteered to meet him here, Blake had invited her to stay the night, and she had never gone home. Although he had taken her on a surprise shopping trip during her second day in residence, she hadn't bothered with a nightgown.

She took her first sip and realized he'd added cream, exactly the way she liked it. She tried to remember when a man had remembered even the important details about her, much less what she put in her coffee.

"This is such a lovely treat. Thank you." She lifted the cup to her lips. "How long have you been up?"

He smiled, teeth white against tanned skin. "I had a little work to do, so I got up at seven."

Blake was semiretired from a company that had something to do with network processors. He'd started the business himself, and his two sons — one of whom was a year older than Marina — were now in charge. Blake still went to his headquarters occasionally and worked each morning on a laptop in the kitchen dining nook. If he thought about work when they were together, he never let on.

Cream in her coffee was just one example of the attention he had lavished on her.

She patted the place beside her, and he sat. He was wearing khaki slacks and one of his endless supply of polo shirts. His cheeks were ruddy from shaving, and his brown eyes sparkled. He smelled like soap and aftershave, and she wasn't at all sorry to wake in his bed.

"I have to go back to work on Monday,"

she said, "so I'll need to go home this afternoon and get all my things ready. But haven't we had a good time?"

"You're sure you have to go?"

She pursed her lips seductively. "I'm a working girl."

"How well do you like your job?"

From the beginning he'd seemed interested, so she'd already told him a little about her position with a building materials supplier, about the way she facilitated sales and analyzed data, about the endless trips to construction sites with promotional items and a ready smile.

She answered truthfully. "I like putting together sales presentations. I like traveling to job sites but not the waiting around."

"Are you looking for something else?"

She wondered if Blake was going to offer her a job at his company, and then she wondered how his sons would like *that*. "Right after college I got a great job in public relations in LA, and I loved it."

She didn't add that even more, she had liked the fact that single executives had been plentiful, and she'd dated her share. She'd been in no hurry, looking at net worth, future prospects and work habits before she went on to appearance, intelligence and humor. She hadn't viewed her assessments as particularly calculating. She had simply done for herself what parents in other cultures did for their daughters.

Blake still seemed interested. "Why did you quit?"

She'd quit because Deedee had suffered a heart attack, and of course, Marina's brothers hadn't lifted a finger to help. She'd left behind a new lover who owned a chain of blue chip financial planning firms and called a congressman from northern California "Cousin."

She bent the truth. "I missed my family. And it's no sacrifice to live in San Jose, is it?" She smiled. "Just think, I never would have met you."

"My lucky break."

"What do you have planned for the day?"

"Bridge at noon."

"Are you going to teach me to play?"

"You're too smart. As it is I'm going to have to watch myself on the golf course."

He had escorted her to the Par 3 course yesterday and given basic instructions. She'd realized the real meaning of senior living when he'd introduced her to his golfing buddies who had looked her over the way a starving man looks at a steak dinner. Blake was just old enough to be her father, but his friends were straying into grandfather territory.

"I probably like being outside or in bed better than I'd like being at a card table anyway." She winked at him.

96

His eyes lit approvingly. "Do you like it here?"

"Why wouldn't I? The place is gorgeous."

"Sometimes I miss my house. Four bedrooms and a view of the mountains. My wife's garden was her life. After Franny died I couldn't stand to see it going to seed."

"Is that why you moved here?"

"I wanted something smaller. Everything I could possibly want is here." He had long, slender fingers, like a musician or an artist. He touched her hair and pushed a strand off her cheek, his fingertips lingering. "Especially now that you're here, too."

"I'll come back if you want me. Maybe on weekends?"

"You could move in, Rina. There's room."

She took a moment to imagine life here. She would still have to keep her apartment, in case Blake got tired of her. She'd have the usual bills, although he always paid when they went out. After Toby's birth he'd taken her to the symphony, expensive restaurants, a play. Deedee had been persuaded to take Toby for those hours, and Marina had wanted to forget everything about her real life and pretend she was the woman she'd been before the pregnancy.

Somehow, because she hadn't wanted to scare him away, even then she hadn't gotten around to telling Blake she was a new mother.

For a week now she'd carefully schooled

herself not to think about the baby. Graham's frantic texts — unanswered — had assured her that Toby was still alive and screaming. She wondered where Lilia fit into that scenario, or if she even did. Since Marina didn't want to think about any of it, after one text too many she had blocked Graham's number.

Did she feel guilty? If she did, guilt was buried under layers of disappointment and anger. She had fulfilled her part of their bargain, but Graham had not. Now the baby she had never wanted was his to fix. And okay, that made her a bad person, or at least a bad mother. But sadly she had never felt like a mother, just an overworked babysitter.

The whole situation had finally come to a head one night on one of her marathon phone calls with Blake. Realizing she couldn't continue to keep such a big secret, she had finally broached the subject of children. He'd confessed he was glad child rearing was behind him. His sons were adults, and he wasn't sorry they were.

She'd hung up once more without telling him about Toby, but in that final week before Graham's party, when her thoughts about the baby had frightened her, she'd realized that, like Blake, she needed to put child rearing behind her, too.

"You could, you know," he prompted, "move in with me."

She smiled in answer. Did she love him? Of

course not, and besides, what did love have to do with it? But money and security? Those were different matters. She liked him. Wasn't that a good enough start?

"I would like to live here with you," she said, feeling her way. "But I really can't afford to, Blake. I'd still have all my expenses and a longer commute. And with my hectic work schedule, we wouldn't see that much of each other, anyway. But when I'm free, I hope we'll get together."

"I like having you right here."

"And I like being here." She set down her coffee and held out her arms, letting the sheet drift to her waist. He might be dressed already, but they could fix that. Blake was past fifty, but his libido hadn't suffered. He was an enthusiastic lover and surprisingly intent on making sure she found as much pleasure as he did.

And every time, he seemed to get his way.

"One for the road?" She winked at him.

"You could be the death of me."

She pulled him closer. "Oh, I don't think so, but what a way to go."

8

THE SWALLOW'S NEST

FEATHERING YOUR NEST WITH IMAGINATION AND LOVE

March 10th:
  I'm home in Kauai after an unexpected challenge in my life. Your patience during my
  absence means everything to me.

                              Aloha, Lilia

In the days since she'd left California, Lilia
hadn't answered any communication from
Graham, or Carrick, either. Carrick probably
had been as much in the dark about Toby as
she had. She believed he was furious at Graham. But the two men had been friends since
they began rooming together as young teens
at a New England boarding school. Since
then Carrick had proven his loyalty over and
over.

Of course so had she, and look where that
had gotten her.

Today she planned to think of other things.
Her parents were having a party in her honor,
and now her mother, Nalani, came out to the
yard behind the Swallows' plantation-style
house carrying platters of food to the picnic

100

tables. The family had given Lilia a week to recover, but everyone knew the time to publicly welcome her home had come, whether she felt up to it or not. She couldn't hurt the people who loved and wanted the best for her.

Unlike the man who had hurt her.

When family came for a meal, people sat on the lanai, in the kitchen or in the yard, wherever they could squeeze in. Here the outdoor tables were shaded by a spectacular Poinciana tree which in summer would set the yard ablaze with brilliant red flowers.

"You feeling more rested after your nap?" Nalani asked.

"A little." Lilia hadn't napped as much as collapsed in a lounge chair after breakfast. She was fairly certain she hadn't slept more than an hour at a time since her arrival. She was still too angry, too torn, and despite herself, in the deepest part of her heart, too worried about her husband and his son. Some habits were hard to break, and she'd spent a year thinking of little other than Graham's survival.

Nalani read between the lines. "If you disappear after you've greeted everybody, no one will ask where you are."

Nodding her gratitude, Lilia took two of the platters of her mother's shoyu chicken and set one on each end of two wooden tables placed end to end. Cabbage salad topped with crunchy ramen noodles, macaroni and cheese dotted with Spam — a local favorite — and a platter of fresh fruit had preceded them. Steaming bowls of rice would be set out when the family began to arrive in a few minutes. Identical bowls adorned two tables inside, and her brothers' families would bring their own additions, as would the relatives and neighbors who came and went through the evening. Kai had agreed to sing and play, probably with friends from his band, and music magically turned the welcome home party into a luau. Children would chase each other, too excited to sit and eat. Grown-ups would "talk story," which was local pidgin for chatting.

"Talk stink" was trash talking, and considering that by now everyone already knew why Lilia had come home, there would be plenty of that, too.

The usual family gathering.

The preparations reminded her of the party she had thrown for Graham. She had learned to entertain from her mother, who loved having guests as much as she did. Nalani was short and plump with a round face and shining salt-and-pepper hair that just cleared her earlobes. While Lilia most resembled her father, the two women were much alike in every other way.

She took a step backwards and nearly squashed a chicken parade, a hen and three chicks who were cleaning up crumbs behind her. Ellen had come to the island for Lilia and Graham's wedding and shrieked when a rooster pecked at her sandaled toe. That memory brought the first smile of the day.

"You know we'll have chaos, like usual," Nalani said from the other side of the table. "You're ready?"

"I've missed everybody. I'll never stay away this long again."

"Sounds like you're planning to go back home then."

"I'll be back and forth." There was no point in pretending. She hadn't decided much, but she had decided that. "My life's in California now."

"Even without Graham?"

"I guess our friends will choose sides. But enough will choose me. I won't be alone."

"Then you've decided to leave him?"

Lilia had expected these questions soon after her arrival, but she wasn't surprised Nalani had waited until now. She and her mother always had their most serious talks while they set out food. Until now she had asked very little, letting Lilia begin the healing process first.

"I make a decision. Then I change my mind. I'm a mess."

"You love him."

Lilia was no longer sure present tense worked. "I did love him. I don't know what I feel now."

"You think he was unfaithful more often than he said?"

"I don't know." She straightened the bowls of food until they were in a perfect line, although nobody would notice. "Wouldn't somebody have found a way to tell me? Our marriage was out there where people could watch it. My website, the how-to videos we did together, the renovations Graham did on our house. Our relationship was almost public property. Wouldn't somebody have told me if things weren't the way they seemed?"

"People don't always like to give bad news. But before this happened? Most people would have said Graham was honest no matter what it cost him. When he stood up to his father and went public with the problems at the Randolph Group, he lost his parents. But he did it anyway."

"Some might. But he never *had* his parents, so what was there to lose?"

"And after having you, would he take a chance on losing you?"

"He clearly did."

"So you're still not sure he's telling the truth?"

In the past week Lilia had asked herself that question over and over. On long walks at the beach and hikes on a mountain trail. "What he told me may be true. But what about now,

Mama? He has a son. Not my son. *His.*"

She thought about Eli's confession on the way home from the airport and wondered how her brother had found the inner strength, the goodness, to raise Amber's firstborn as his own. At the moment she couldn't find hers.

"You need more time. And a friend to talk to."

"I have you. That's enough."

"There's a difference in generations, and a difference between mainland and here."

As her mother went into the house for more food, Lilia thought about that. The difference wasn't imaginary. In the islands, family or *ohana* was primary, but it was far more than blood ties. Boundaries were fluid, and family included those who might be related or even wanted to be. Lilia shouldn't have been surprised Eli had chosen to raise Amber's son as his own. The individualism that was held up as an American value was not as valued here.

The Swallows heritage was mixed, but in this way, they were most like their native Hawaiian ancestors. When her Auntie Alea could no longer care for herself without help, various family members had taken turns staying with her in California until Lilia took on the job full-time. Nobody had considered engaging professionals. Help came from within.

Lilia sometimes felt she was walking a high wire strung between cultures, but when her mother returned, one thing was easy to put into words. "There might be a difference between generations, Mama, but nobody's advice is as good as yours."

"I have no advice. You have to walk your own path. I could tell you to forgive, and if you couldn't, then you would carry the burden of my advice, as well as your own sadness."

"I want somebody to fix this."

Her mother was close enough to reach out and stroke her daughter's cheek. "There is no one but you, Lilia Alea."

The next half hour was filled with greetings, serving, sharing stories and catching up on family and local gossip. For the most part Graham's absence was ignored, although a petite cousin pulled her to one side and told her she would personally go to San Jose on her next business trip to the mainland and slap him around if Lilia just gave her the go-ahead.

The air was filled with the scents of plumeria, pork roasting in an outdoor oven her brothers had built for her mother, fragrant pikake and ginger leis. For the most part the women were clad in flowered sundresses or muumuus, although some of the younger ones wore jeans, and the men wore aloha shirts patterned with flowers and local scenery. Her youngest brother, Jordan, a professional surfer, arrived in the striped board shorts he'd worn in his last successful competition and announced he planned to wear them until the next one.

Lilia noted that her father kept track of her, and when he sensed she was trapped in conversations for too long, he came to the rescue. Joe Swallow, former cop and now the owner of his own security firm, wasn't a man who was comfortable talking about feelings, his or anybody else's, but nobody ever doubted his devotion.

Several hours into the commotion, as Kai's little band turned up the volume, new supplies of food arrived, and more neighbors arrived to listen, her father sought her out.

"A friend of yours is here."

Lilia thought everybody she'd met in her years on Kauai was already at the party. Her head was beginning to ache, and she wasn't sure she would be able to talk to one more person. An hour ago she had reached her saturation point, and now the evening was becoming a complicated jumble of thoughts and emotions.

Her father motioned. She followed him to the front of the house in time to glimpse a woman with strawberry blonde hair getting out of a cousin's old Toyota. A moment passed before Lilia recognized her.

"Regan?" She moved forward, past her

father, and the other woman ran straight into her arms. "I can't believe you're here!"

"Tell me I really am, okay? I feel like I'm still on an airplane."

They held each other until Lilia thanked her cousin and finally backed away. Now Nalani's comment about a friend made perfect sense.

"My mother knew you were coming?"

"She thought you would enjoy the surprise. And the company."

"She didn't think I had enough company?" Lilia nodded toward the house and the roar from the back.

"Not exactly like me."

Lilia linked arms with her friend. "I'll introduce you to everybody. That will take hours. Don't worry about how any of us are related because we never do. Call all the older women Auntie and you'll be fine. And then when we can, we'll sneak away. If you're not too tired?"

"I can only stay till Tuesday. I don't plan to sleep."

"I've subscribed to that plan lately. It's not a good one." She stopped walking and turned to face her friend. "Just tell me Graham didn't put you up to coming."

"Lilia . . ." Regan frowned and shook her head.

"Your brother?"

"Is sick with worry. But coming was my

idea. In fact I didn't tell either of them, not that I've talked to Graham."

"You're not in charge of the baby?"

"You told me to stay away, remember? I listened. In his favor, he never asked."

Lilia realized how much she wanted to know about the situation back in Willow Glen, and at the same time, how little. She was glad that right now, she had other priorities. "Are you hungry?"

"Starving. I smell food."

"You'll never go hungry here."

"I'll eat if you will."

Lilia was surprised that eating actually sounded good now. In fact what she'd thought of as a permanent knot in her stomach was beginning to unravel. "Let's load our plates. Then we'll make the rounds."

"So, I'm a good surprise?"

Lilia squeezed her friend's arm. "Of all the surprises I've had lately, you are the very best."

9

Plantation architecture arrived in the Hawaiian islands in the early twentieth century. The houses, for workers in the pineapple and sugarcane fields, suited the climate. They were often framed in wood, with wide-hipped roofs, vertical plank siding, and lanais for ventilation and extra living space.

The Swallows' cottage had been built by Lilia's great-grandparents and added on to, as was common, but the lanai that wrapped around three sides of the house was the crowning jewel.

On the morning after the family luau Lilia found Regan sprawled in a chair in the front with her eyes closed. She was wearing fresh clothing topped with a sadly wilted ginger lei she'd been given at the party. Last night she'd slept on the bed in the loft, where island breezes swept across the narrow expanse from opposing windows. For the Swallow children, sleeping there had been a reward for good behavior.

Invariably Lilia and Graham had slept in the loft on their visits. This time, for obvious reasons, she was sleeping on the daybed in what was now her mother's sewing room.

With a cup in one hand she plopped down in a neighboring chair to sip her mother's excellent coffee. She closed her eyes, too. "How'd you sleep?"

Regan didn't open her eyes. "Am I awake?"

"You'd better be. This is our only full day together. I wish you could have gotten more time off."

"You have any idea what a miracle it is that I got any time off at all? Hello? Remember tax season?"

Lilia knew March and April were crunch months for Regan, an accountant at a prestigious firm. "I appreciate that, and you."

"I'm sorry we never got to talk yesterday."

"If I'd dragged you away from my brother, he would have pulled out every embarrassing story he remembered and shared it."

"I'd forgotten how cute he is."

"And how *young* he is . . ."

"Three years, Lilia. Just three years younger than I am. That's nothing."

"Jordan's married to his surf board."

"He's coming to Huntington Beach in September to compete."

"You're so funny. You won't even remember his name by September."

Regan didn't deny it. Like her own brother,

she never seemed to settle down. "I think I kind of disappeared last night. The party was still going on when I went upstairs and tested the bed, just to see how it was, and that's what I remember. I'm sorry. What are we doing today?"

"There's not enough time in the world to do everything you'll want to."

"Whatever was in that punch Jordan gave me was lethal. I need advice, preferably delivered in short sentences."

"We can swim, snorkel, hike, shop." Lilia opened her eyes. The sun was creeping steadily across the lanai. In a few minutes they would need to move. "Whatever works best with your rum-addled brain."

"Where would we hike?"

"We could walk up the Sleeping Giant." Regan had forced her eyes open, too, and Lilia gestured to the mountain beyond them. "Can you see his profile?"

Regan squinted. "Maybe. The view's priceless even without the fantasy. But now I remember what I'd really like to see. The Na Pali coast. Carrick told me all about his visits to the Randolphs' house there. He said the house overlooked a fantastic beach."

The long hikes Carrick and Graham had taken along the coast to get away from the Randolphs had later bloomed into Carrick's passion for exploring. These days he spent whatever time he could eke out of his law practice backpacking through the West, an antidote, Lilia supposed, to too much time in offices and courtrooms.

"I know they sold the property a long time ago," Regan said, "but can we still get down to the beach from there?"

Lilia certainly knew which beach Regan was referring to. She wondered if her friend knew the story of her last day there with Graham and Carrick, when they were still teenagers. Or had Carrick told his sister about his trips to Kauai and left out that account?

She hadn't been to Kauapea Beach in years. There were plenty of other beaches that didn't come with memories, but since her future might well be spent putting memories behind her, she supposed she could start today.

"The path down is steep, and this time of year the currents are probably too strong to swim. But we might be able to splash around in tidal pools."

"Just lying in the sun for a while sounds great."

"Done deal then." Lilia got to her feet. "I'm going to change. Did you bring sturdy shoes?"

"Running shoes. Nothing fancy."

"Perfect. The trail down is red clay. You'll get dirty. Wear your suit and a cover-up you don't care about."

"I'll get up in just one minute. If I can remember how."

Lilia held up her mug. "This is my mother's Kona coffee, and there's a cup in the kitchen with your name on it."

Regan stood and stretched. "I just remembered."

On her first trip to the mainland, Lilia had found traveling in straight lines as amazing as the number of cars in California. The trip to Kauapea Beach, known as "Secrets," meandered along the coastline past Kealia Beach, Anahola and inland before it took a sharp turn north. Since they were on Hawaiian time, they meandered, pulling over for better views. Once they were on the North Shore they took a detour and visited the Kilauea lighthouse and wildlife refuge to stretch their legs and look for nesting seabirds. Back on the road they stopped at a farm stand, and Lilia bought Regan a lei from a woman who had made them herself that morning.

She had asked her father for directions to the parking lot, accessible but not advertised, so it wouldn't attract crowds. He had warned that a number of new homes had gone up along this familiar stretch of coast, and now she witnessed the reality.

After parking she gathered herself to relive the past. "We can walk along the road, and I'll show you where Graham's family stayed."

"Carrick used to talk about that house until

I wanted to scream. I was so jealous. I was too young to realize traveling with the Randolphs came at a price."

"Carrick got along. He figures out what people need, then he gives it to them."

"Within reason."

"But that's how he managed the Randolphs. Ellen needed polite conversation, and Douglas needed strict adherence to rules and no interruptions."

"Is that how *you* got along with them?"

"Me? I was a shadow. My mother was the estate manager, and my father's company provided security, but our whole family pitched in whenever a job had to be done quickly. Douglas never even realized I was alive until . . . Well, until."

"That's not a bad thing. It's when he *does* notice that things get uncomfortable."

They got out and chatted about nothing for a few minutes, stepping to the side of the road when cars approached. Lilia tried to get her bearings. Finally she stopped. "I think this is where their property was." She pointed ahead where five magnificent homes were set back from the cliff overlooking the water. "It looks like they took down the original houses and built those in their place. Douglas was just holding the property until he could get permission to subdivide and build, but it took years. I can't even imagine how much money he made when permission was finally granted."

"A drop in the Randolph bucket."

The new homes were lovely and lavish, but Lilia could still remember what the land had looked like years ago. "The old house was graceful, plainer than these and dated, but it had four bedrooms, views from every window. There was a guest cottage with a lap pool built to look like a natural lagoon, an orchard with avocados, mangoes, lychee, a gatehouse. The Randolphs only came a few times a year, but sometimes guests arrived and stayed a week or two without them. From the beginning, this was an investment. I doubt either of them had a sentimental thought about it."

"How old were you when you met them?"

"Ten. Graham was eleven." She turned away from the memories. "Let's find the path down to the beach. It's behind us and not always easy to spot."

The trip down was steep and in places rugged, although more cultivated now than Lilia remembered. They moved through a hala and ironwood forest. She had a backpack with their lunch and towels, and they took their time to negotiate the narrow root-choked path. While the locals hadn't managed to keep the beach a secret, getting to it still took experience or careful instructions. By the time they emerged onto pale golden sand, Regan was panting.

"Wow!" Regan moved forward and spun

around. "Lilia, this is heaven."

"It is pretty amazing." In front of them was the turquoise ocean, behind them the rugged cliffs. Outcroppings of black lava dotted the waterline, and waves crashed against rock, sending silver sea spray high into the air.

"I've never been anywhere this beautiful." Regan started forward but Lilia took her arm.

"Just remember to stay back, okay? Surf's high today, and people get carried out more often than you think. We'll head east and see if we can find a tidal pool where we can cool off. There's a waterfall, too."

An hour later, after splashing in the pool under the waterfall and immersing themselves in a larger one close to the shore, they walked far enough that they were well away from the dozen or so people who had gotten to the beach before them. To the east the lighthouse stood guard high above, and behind them, red cliffs anchored with evergreens and ferns towered like castle walls.

They spread towels and reapplied sunscreen. Then they lay down where the cliff provided a little shade.

Despite sunglasses Regan shaded her eyes with her hand. "Shade? Sunscreen? I'm still a redhead. I'd better not stay here too long."

Lilia was staring at the water. "This is one of the longest beaches on the island."

"I'm surprised you haven't been here lately."

"Carrick never told you about our last afternoon together on this beach?"

"Not in so many words. But I have the feeling it didn't end happily."

"We were teenagers. It might bore you."

"Tell you what, I have a story to tell, too. We can trade."

Intrigued, Lilia settled back and closed her eyes. "Graham and I were friends first, but you know that. The day we met? Ellen called my mother early that morning to say they were coming sooner than planned and asked her to have a meal ready. They had a chef for the rest of the week but would need her help that day."

"That's how I always travel. With a chef, butler, lady's maid. You, too?"

Lilia laughed. "I was trying to stay out of my mother's way while she finished setting out the meal she'd prepared. They'd brought guests, and Douglas was at his most charming, but Mama knew how quickly that could change. So before he could complain about me, she chased me outside. She'd roped my brothers into coming with us, to get everything ready outdoors while she cooked. They drove separately, and I expected to leave with them when she stayed on, but they took off without me."

"Brothers." Regan knew.

"Graham was tossed out, too, or left on his own. I thought he was from another planet."

118

She paused. "Too bad I didn't roll my eyes and walk away, huh?"

"Things might be simpler now."

Lilia pushed on. "I thought he didn't know how to smile. We played Frisbee until I fell backwards into the pool with the Frisbee clutched to my chest. He did smile then, even laughed. And he kept smiling and laughing afterwards, every time I saw him. We became friends, although his parents didn't realize it. I was just the little brown-skinned babysitter. Eventually they brought your brother along to take him off their hands even more."

"Carrick always knew that."

"Since he loves Graham like a brother, he was willing to go along. And hey, this is Hawaii. Why wouldn't he come?"

"Did you ever wonder why the Randolphs chose *him*?"

"I assumed because they were roommates at school."

"Did you wonder how *that* happened, too? My father's a college professor, an immigrant from Ireland, no less, so we're not exactly in their social or economic class."

"They take what they need, right? They tolerated little ol' foreigner me."

"Um, Hawaii is a *state*."

"Too recently to count. Carrick used to say he and I were founding members of the Wretched Refuse Society. Anyway the two of us were acceptable enough to make sure Graham left them alone."

Regan rested her hand on Lilia's arm. "Here's the real reason Carrick was acceptable. Douglas wanted my father to come to work for him."

Regan's father taught economics at a small Pennsylvania college. He was known in academic circles for having eccentric ideas about the world economy and publishing papers nobody wanted to read. He was as charming as his son.

"Douglas wanted your *father*? At Randolph Group?"

"Douglas may be cow poop on the heel of your favorite sandal, but he's brilliant, and he knows Da is, too. Douglas was probably instrumental in getting Carrick a full scholarship to prep school and maneuvering them into letting Graham and Carrick room together."

"Why is this news to me?"

"Why would either Carrick or Graham talk about it? If it's true, they were manipulated into becoming friends. But whether or not it is, Da was happy teaching and working on a book nobody will ever read, so he refused all offers. But he does give Douglas financial advice from time to time. Which means if any of this is true, his plan paid off. At least a little."

"I remember the first time I met Carrick. I think he was fourteen. I liked him right away."

"Did you have a crush on either of them?"

Lilia crossed her arms under her head and tried to remember how all this had started. "I was surrounded by boys at home, so they held no mystery. Graham and Carrick were nicer than my brothers, and I just liked being with them. They came from a different world, too. Of course as the years passed, things changed a little."

"How so?"

She wasn't sure how to phrase the difference. "We all became more aware of each other. They began to compete for my attention, and I liked it. The two were so different, but they were both attractive and fun to be with. Carrick is open and easy. Graham is more closed off. I'm sure every time he tried to open up, a door was slammed in his face by one parent or the other." She realized she sounded sympathetic, and that annoyed her.

"What happened on the beach?"

All these years later the scene was absolutely clear, because all of them had been so humiliated. "I was fifteen, and it was summer. I think both Ellen and Douglas finally realized I might be more than unpaid help, because my invitations to visit dropped off."

"You were probably a knockout. How could they not notice?"

"One afternoon Graham called to say he and Carrick were at the house for a week and asked if I wanted to go swimming. My mother

121

was going to a neighboring estate to oversee the installation of outdoor lights, so she gave me a ride. When I got there I found out that Graham's parents were in town having lunch with business associates."

"Maybe that's why they called you."

"I'm sure. Graham wanted to hike down here to swim. In those days the path was even more challenging, and two years before he'd tried it after a heavy rain and broken his wrist. Ellen had strictly forbidden him from coming here, but that day he said it was ridiculous to live so close to a beach he couldn't use. He was determined to come down again with or without us."

"Sixteen and finally ready to challenge authority, huh?"

"I suppose. I didn't want him going alone, but it was clear he planned to, unless we went along. Once Graham makes up his mind, there's no stopping him. Witness the fact that he decided to have a baby without his wife."

"Is it hard to talk about him? You could just leave me hanging."

Lilia grunted. "I showed them the best way down. The water was a lot calmer that day than it is now. We bodysurfed and watched for dolphins and whales. Then we walked this way to see the falls before going back. Graham wanted to make sure he was home before his parents got there."

Regan sat up and slapped more sunscreen

on her legs. "It's strange to be right here while you tell this story."

"When he asked what we would see farther east I told him the truth."

"Which is?"

"Farther that way," she pointed, "people like to take off their clothes to sunbathe. The far edges on both ends are known as nude beaches."

"Whoa. Sixteen-year-old boys. Nude beach."

"Uh-huh. I might as well have tossed a lighted match into a gallon of kerosene. I was embarrassed, but I was persuaded to walk with them because they were going to go anyway, and I wanted to be sure they knew how to get back up the path. I told them we would look from a distance, and that's as much as we would do because it was getting too late to go farther. Some couples were sunbathing, but without binoculars that was all we could see. Even so the possibilities made me uneasy."

"I can see why."

"I was with two guys whose place in my life had quietly reconfigured. I was confused about my feelings, and thrilled when they agreed to turn around and start back. That's when we saw a man stalking toward us. Of course it was Douglas. I hung back with Carrick, and Graham went ahead to meet his father."

Regan lay down on her side and propped her head to look at Lilia. "I can imagine this."

"Douglas has a way of diminishing anybody who disagrees with him, but you know that. Graham took the abuse, but when his father accused me of putting him up to this, Graham told him he was wrong. Douglas didn't listen and called me a number of names I have managed to forget."

"I'm sorry he put you through that."

"When I arrived back at their house my mother was already there. Ellen was furious, most likely because Douglas was. She told Mama I would no longer be welcome, and my mother told her to find someone else to manage the estate. By then Graham had taken off in one of the family cars, and Carrick had gone along, probably to calm him down. Not only was I totally humiliated, I lost two friends I thought I would never see again."

"They didn't find a way to see you before they left?"

"No, that was the last time for years. They left the next day. Carrick emailed to say he was sorry things had gone the way they had. Graham never did, and he didn't answer my email. But I wasn't surprised. I knew that, of all of us, he was the most embarrassed by everything that had happened."

"Did you and Carrick stay in touch?"

Lilia considered her answer. "I think Carrick knew that Graham had a thing for me, even then. His first loyalty was to him."

"I don't think that's true anymore."

Telling the story to Regan had taken some of the sting out of it. Still she didn't want to talk about herself anymore. She turned on her side to view her friend. "Now it's your turn."

Regan bit her lip and didn't speak for a moment. When she did her voice was low. "This is harder than I expected. Even after you just gave such a great lead-in about how painful it is to lose people you care about."

"Are you about to lecture me?"

Regan waved her to silence. "Oh, please, not even vaguely. It's just I'm something of an emotional coward."

"You're somebody who will fly all the way to Kauai during tax season just to support a friend."

"I came for more than that."

"Why don't you tell me then?"

Instead Regan crossed her arms over her chest and stared at the sky. "I love my family, but we never really talk about feelings, so I never learned how. Actually we never talk about *ourselves.* It's that Irish Catholic thing. Don't get a swelled head. Put yourself down, so nobody else has to."

Lilia knew Carrick better than she knew his sister. Regan had grown up on the East Coast and gone to college and graduate school there. They hadn't become good friends until she had come West to take a position in a Silicon Valley accounting firm. Now she realized that Regan was right. Because whatever Carrick was feeling, he rarely shared it, and Regan was much the same.

"Are you saying you have something you want to say, and you don't know how?" She paused but Regan didn't answer. "Don't tell me you were having an affair with Graham, too?"

Regan whacked her on the arm. "You'd better be kidding."

The mood had changed, which is what Lilia had intended. "So spill."

"I've never told you about Devin."

Regan had discussed some of the men in her life, but only with humor. Lilia remembered that one blind date had suggested they should have sex immediately to see if they were compatible, and when Regan had wondered out loud if anybody in the restaurant would notice, he'd taken a good look around while he considered.

"I've always counted on you to remind me how little I enjoyed being single." Lilia realized she might be in that category again and soon.

"Devin was different. I met him in my senior year of college. We both headed for the same graduate program, and after a year together, it was clear we were also headed for

126

a life together. Things seemed perfect. You're sure Carrick never told you this?"

"I have a bad feeling this is the kind of story Carrick wouldn't share."

"Because I'm not going to look good after I tell it?"

"No. Because it's personal to you and not a happy ending. I'm right?"

Regan didn't answer directly. "That Christmas he gave me a ring. A really beautiful diamond. We decided we'd be married the next summer, something small and informal so we could spend whatever money we had on a backpacking trip through Europe. I wanted to see family in Ireland. His roots were in France. It seemed perfect.

"He was a top student. Lightning quick. A creative thinker. But in January he started not showing up for classes. A professor sought me out and asked what was going on. I was living with a family as a part-time nanny, and Devin and I had decided I should stay there the rest of that year to save for our wedding. Anyway, we weren't living together, so I didn't know he had been missing classes or why. When I asked him, he told me he was fine. He was using that time to catch up on another class. He said it was temporary, and he was getting good notes from another student."

Lilia knew even if that had been true, it would have been a problem. "Did he take too many hours?"

"He'd moved out of accounting into corporate finance. I figured the work might be a lot harder, but Devin knew what he was doing. He'd found a way to handle things." Regan faced Lilia. "I should have pushed him instead of just choosing to believe him. You can start counting the 'I should haves' now. After Devin died I spent an entire year starting every sentence that way. I'm better now. I know his death wasn't my fault. But still . . ."

Lilia tried to read Regan's expression. "You left out a lot."

"Drugs."

"Oh . . ."

"He was pushing himself really hard, so he started with the easy stuff, to give himself a way to unwind. Pretty soon that didn't work, and he moved on. Prescription drugs, then cocaine. He was smart. He was sure he could beat it. He was even sure he could beat heroin."

Lilia had seen too much addiction among family members and college friends not to understand. "How did you find out?"

"I should have seen it sooner, but remember what I said about myself? When he didn't tell me what was bothering him, that just seemed natural."

"Because that's how things were for you."

Regan nodded. "Of course there were more signs, but I wrote off his lack of appetite, his restlessness and everything else as exhaustion and stress over the future. I told him we could postpone the wedding, but he said no. And here's the zinger. He told me he wanted to take my ring back to the jeweler to have it cleaned and the prongs repointed. He said a friend had lost the diamond right out of one that was newer than mine. So I gave it to him, and for weeks I didn't even worry when he didn't return it. When I finally asked, he said the jeweler was busy. He'd had to send it away because there was a problem . . ."

"He sold it."

"Oh yeah. But not for enough to feed his habit, because about a week later he was caught in his academic adviser's apartment stuffing anything that glittered into a pillowcase. He'd been given the key so he could study there. By then Devin didn't care about anything except where his next fix was coming from."

"You must have been devastated."

"I was furious! I can't begin to express how angry I was, except that I don't have to, because you know what that kind of betrayal feels like."

The analogy made Lilia flinch. "What happened?"

"Since it was a first offense the judge gave him a choice between jail time and a drug treatment center. You can guess which he chose, and he was lucky. His parents mortgaged their house to give him that chance. They loved him enough." Regan lifted her hand in emphasis. "Me? I didn't."

"He hurt you badly."

"Another thing about the Irish? We hold grudges. Just look at our history. Anyway, I can't blame this on ancestry. The day Devin left for the treatment center I told him we were through, that I didn't want anything to do with him ever again. And I meant it."

Lilia was pretty sure what was coming next. "Whatever you said didn't kill him, Regan. Wasn't Devin in charge of his own life?"

"The statistics were pretty clear — 40 to 60 percent of addicts relapse. He had ruined everything, and that was that. I didn't write him. I didn't take phone calls from his family. I finished my course work and took the job in Mountain View to be near Carrick. I told myself I didn't love Devin anymore. I dated jerks. I was pretty sure I deserved jerks, considering how stupid I'd been not to see what was happening."

Jerks or guys like Lilia's brother Jordan, with whom Regan had absolutely no possibility of a future. But Lilia knew that revelation was out of place and waited for her to go on.

Regan turned to her back again. "He found me and called one night after I'd been in California for a couple of months. He was back in school in a different state but doing well. He knew addiction would be a lifelong

130

battle, but he had tools to fight it. He wanted my forgiveness. That's all he was asking for. And I couldn't give it to him. I kept thinking he'd chosen heroin over me, that he'd ruined both our lives. I told him I didn't want to hear from him again." Her voice was suddenly thick with tears. "And I never did."

Lilia moved closer to put her hand on her friend's shoulder. "Did he die of an overdose?"

"No. He decided to spend his spring break in Haiti with some other guys from his program. They were helping build a new wing on a treatment center there. His program is big on community service as a way to return self-confidence and give back to the world. His second night there one of the residents got high, found a knife, and when he went after another resident, Devin stepped between them."

"I'm so sorry."

They lay that way for a few minutes until Lilia finally moved away. She was sure of one thing. Regan hadn't traveled this far just to acknowledge her own past. "You're trying to tell me I should forgive Graham and go home. That people really can change."

"I don't have any idea if you should go back to Graham. I really don't." Regan wiped tears off her cheeks. "Only *you* can know that."

"Then what?"

"We never know whether change will stick

or what the future's going to hold. And we're never under an obligation to play somebody else's games. But I'll be haunted forever because I didn't tell Devin I was glad he'd made progress and wished him well. Even if I'd opened the door for another chance at a life together, he probably still would have gone to Haiti and died trying to help other addicts. But if I had just said those words? Both of us would have had closure. And who knows? Maybe we would have had that second chance."

"Don't marriages have to be built on trust?"

"We like to say that, but isn't marriage just a merger between two flawed, fragile human beings who make mistakes, sometimes really terrible mistakes, and somehow come through them together? Trust is a shaky foundation because it can be so easily destroyed. The question is whether a relationship is worth rebuilding. Maybe more than once."

Lilia cleared her throat, which was suddenly clogged with tears. "You're afraid Graham's going to die, aren't you? And you're afraid I'll have the same regrets you do."

"All of us are going to die. But I wish I had asked myself what really mattered for whatever time I had left on this earth, or Devin did. And I guess that's what I came to say. Maybe that's what you need to be asking now. What do you have to say to Graham that you haven't said? What, if anything, do you need to forgive? Because nobody knows the future. You can trust me on that."

10

Marina hadn't yet cooked for Blake, but on Friday night he had a cold and didn't feel like going out. Even though her work week had seemed a hundred hours long, she had volunteered to feed him.

She wasn't a gourmet. Her talents ran to macaroni and cheese, spaghetti, tuna fish sandwiches, anything her brothers would deign to eat when she had been in charge. She still specialized in food that arrived at her local Safeway in a box, jar or can. Tonight, for a change, she was going to prepare something more appealing. Even she could bake a potato and broil a steak, and these days salad came in a plastic bag with dressing. At the grocery store she added frozen garlic bread to her cart and half a gallon of Neapolitan ice cream. Blake's fancy wine cooler was already well stocked.

As she unpacked and started dinner she took stock of the kitchen. The space was expansive, only separated from the living room by an island. Drawers were crowded with every possible utensil and gadget. Since Blake relied on pre-prepared meals from the supermarket freezer, she suspected his wife had been the one to revel in complex recipes. She also noted that the black granite countertops were spotless, which meant the kitchen probably hadn't been used since his cleaning service had come on Monday. She wondered how much he missed being married.

She wondered if he wanted to be married again.

As the garlic bread warmed in the needlessly complicated oven, and the potatoes baked in a microwave with enough settings to fly a space shuttle, she poured orange juice and took it into the living room.

After work she had changed into her shortest micro-miniskirt without tights, even though she hadn't enjoyed the modesty challenge as she slid in and out of her car. But when he'd opened the door to find her standing on the porch with groceries, Blake had enjoyed the sight of her bare legs enough for both of them.

He was enjoying them again, this time as she held out the glass. "Pretend it's a screwdriver. You're not taking care of yourself, are you?"

He took it and began to sip. "If you were living here, I bet you'd make sure I did."

She smiled, although the thought of being in charge of somebody else sounded woefully familiar. "And if I was taking care of you, I would never make it to work, would I? You're usually a pretty hands-on guy. You must be sick."

Reluctantly he wrapped both hands around his glass. "*Somebody* ought to take care of you."

"I'm a big girl." She paused just long enough. "But I won't be around much next week. Sales meetings, and in-service training in San Francisco. I'll be driving back and forth since my company's too cheap to spring for a hotel, so I'll be getting back too late to see you."

"You'll be missed."

"I'll call and check on you. And you'll go to the doctor if your cold gets worse, right?"

He sent her a warm smile, which must have taken some effort. "Do you like being back at work?"

Blake thought she'd been on leave to recover after minor surgery, so she couldn't tell him the truth. No, she didn't like being back. She didn't like the way the other employees looked at her, the way they didn't ask about her baby son because they knew he was no longer with her. None of her sales colleagues had been at Graham's "celebration" party, but word traveled fast in the construction community. While she'd spawned a little sympathy as a pregnant woman alone in the world, now it had vanished. She'd had an affair with a man they had previously respected, and now she had given him their child to raise. Publicly, too. For a mother there was no greater crime.

And maybe they were right.

When she didn't answer, he continued. "You shouldn't have to work so hard. You need more fun."

If that was true, clearly somebody had forgotten to tell Deedee, Graham and God. Her brief sojourn in Los Angeles had been as close to "fun" as Marina had ever experienced, too little and over too fast.

She lowered her lashes. "I imagine I'll have fun at the sales meeting. They pull in executives from all over the world. I've met some great . . ." She paused, as if to reconsider word choice. "*People.* There's always a little social time built in."

He hadn't missed the hesitation. "Do you work with many women?"

"Mostly men. I do try to keep work and play separate, though."

"Do you go out of town a lot?"

"Depends on what's in the pipeline. The job pays my bills. I can't refuse."

"I might be able to find you something closer to home."

She pictured a deadly dull office job. Creating a marketing plan for the latest innovation

137

in denture cream. Putting out a company newsletter with feel-good stories about the new water dispenser and the tenth anniversary of the underpaid cleaning service.

She chose her words carefully. "I like being out in the field. I was born to travel. I love seeing new things. So the job suits me well enough. We'll find time to be together."

"Have you traveled much? Real travel, I mean?"

"Not nearly enough." In truth, not at all.

"My wife didn't like it. I always wanted to go, and she always wanted to stay. Mostly we stayed."

"You didn't go anywhere?"

"Europe once. We came home two weeks early because she missed her garden and our dog. Somebody was supposed to come in, weed and water, but they didn't do it the way she wanted, so she never went anywhere for more than a weekend again. And even then, we had to take Doolittle."

"I guess each person is different. I haven't been able to travel and always wanted to. She could and didn't." Her sigh was real. "And what about you? Now that you can, do you plan to?"

"It's not the same without somebody you love."

Marina thought traveling alone would be great. Nobody to answer to; nobody to take care of. Just her, doing whatever she wanted.

"Maybe we could travel together," he said.

She squeezed his shoulder. "I would like that. So many places to see and all of them interesting. But I won't have any time off, Blake. Not for most of the year. I had to use most of my personal days for the surgery."

He sneezed and ended the conversation by blowing his nose.

She took that opportunity to head into the kitchen to broil the steaks and finish their dinner. When she took out the garlic bread to replace it with the steaks she saw she hadn't, as hoped, mastered the complicated oven settings. The bread was charred. She wrapped it tight before she tossed it in the garbage, but the burned smell lingered. She was glad Blake had a cold.

When they finally sat down to eat he complimented her on the meal, but she could see he was only going through the motions. He wasn't running a temperature — she had checked — but the first stages of a cold were often the worst. When he set down his fork, she did the same, even though she was only half finished.

"I think you need a shower and bed, my boy." She got up and removed his plate. "I'll tuck you in, but I think you've got a long night of sneezing and coughing ahead of you."

He was as docile as a lamb, getting up as ordered to head into the master bedroom. In a few minutes she heard the shower running.

As she cleaned the kitchen she ate the rest of her own dinner standing up. Then she tucked both plates and the serving dishes into the dishwasher and got it going, did one final swipe of the counters and prepared to leave.

As she gathered her purse and the jacket that dangled lower than the hemline of her skirt, the doorbell rang. The shower wasn't running, but Blake was still in the bedroom. Shrugging, she set down her things and went to peer through the peephole. This was a gated community, and two men about her own age in jeans and sport shirts had made it through security and now stood on the porch. She opened the door a crack.

"Can I help you?"

The taller of the two, a man with perfectly normal features that were one size too large for his face, wrinkled his oversized nose. "Who are *you*?"

"Since I'm on this side of the door, I think I'm supposed to ask that question."

He glared at her. "I'm Wayne Wendell, and my father lives here."

She saw the resemblance now, although Blake, at his son's age, would have been much better-looking.

She opened the door all the way and held out her hand. For the first time that day she was sorry she'd chosen her shortest skirt. "Marina Tate. I'm a friend of your father's."

Wayne hesitated a moment before he took

her hand, then he inclined his head toward the man beside him. "My brother, Paul."

Paul Wendell looked nothing like Blake. He was at least four inches shorter than Wayne, with a belly that hung over his belt and close-set eyes that were even closer now because he was scowling. Marina shook his hand, too, then gestured for both to come inside.

"Your dad's not feeling well. I'm almost sure it's just the start of a cold, but I came over to make him dinner. He's on his way to bed now. He needs to sleep."

"How well do you know my father?" Paul asked.

She pretended not to understand. "I'm sorry?"

"I said, how well do you know my father? I don't think he's mentioned you."

"I've known him a while."

"In what capacity?" Wayne's eyes traveled down her legs.

For a moment she didn't understand. When she did she stepped back and stared at him. "You think he pays me for something?"

He sniffed the air, where the smell of burned bread still lingered. "Not for your cooking."

She could feel heat rising in her cheeks. Blake took that moment to come out of the bedroom wearing a robe and slippers. His hair was damp, and clearly he had been in the shower.

The moment he saw his sons, he frowned. "Is everything all right?"

"You said you weren't feeling well. We were checking on you." Wayne gestured to Marina. "And look who we found."

Blake didn't respond immediately. Instead he lifted one eyebrow before he went to Marina and put his arm around her. "Marina made me dinner. Not that I need to explain."

"I think I'd better go." Marina kissed Blake's cheek, then pulled away. "You need your rest. I'll call tomorrow from San Francisco if I get a break. But drink plenty of juice. I bought extra, and there are cold meds on the counter. Please, call the doctor if you start feeling worse."

"We can take care of our father." Paul stepped aside, leaving a clear path to the door.

"I'm so glad you can." She smiled at him. Then, just because she could, she winked. "But not in all the ways that *I* can."

Blake laughed.

If the gloves had still been on, now they were off. Wayne stepped forward. "Dad, what are you doing? This woman is probably younger than I am."

"But with much better manners." Marina cocked her head. "I, for instance, would never jump to conclusions."

Wayne acted as if he hadn't heard. "I would appreciate it if you would leave so we can talk to our father."

142

"You're the one who's leaving," Blake told him. "You and your brother. Right now. This is my house, and you're not welcome if you can't treat Marina with respect."

Marina stepped between them and touched Blake's cheek. "Look, you're not feeling well, and you don't need a fight. We'll all part friends and leave you alone to recover. Okay?"

Paul's voice rattled with anger. "We don't need your help. And my father doesn't need your *attentions.*"

"That's it!" Blake walked to the door and held it open. "Out!"

The two younger men stalked to the open door. More words were exchanged, but Marina, too angry to trust herself, stayed out of the fight. When it was over, and the door had closed behind them, she shook her head.

"Just what you didn't need, huh? I'm sorry, Blake. If being your friend upsets your family, maybe I ought to stay away."

"It's my own fault. I had to be away a lot when they were growing up, and they still resent me. I let them take over the business when their mother was sick and I needed to be with her. And after that I got tired of working so much and let them take over even more. Now they want to take over my life."

She was still furious, but fury had never worked in her favor. She didn't let it show. "I'm sorry."

He ran his hand over his wet hair, leaving

tracks where his fingers plowed through it. "You're the first good thing that's happened to me in a long time."

"I like being your good thing."

"Don't you dare stay away."

She thought about how *not* staying away would make his overbearing sons feel, and she had to work hard not to smile. "Then I won't. I definitely won't."

"I was thinking in the shower. Can you take at least one day off so we can go somewhere for a long weekend? We could get a flight to Las Vegas, see a show, have some great meals?"

She had been to Las Vegas — hadn't everybody? But she'd gone for one night on a budget, eaten at cheap buffets and played the penny slots.

She didn't have to think. This was her chance to do everything differently. "I'll see what I can do. I might be able to take a day without pay."

"That job of yours is going to be a hurdle."

"Maybe I'll quit someday." She hugged him hard, but her mind was on other things. Like how she could use his sons' anger against them. Like how her life could change for the better and quickly.

Then she thought of Toby. If she had kept him, she wouldn't have this chance. She had traded her son at least partly for Blake, but maybe it was going to work out best for everybody.

"Stranger things have happened," she said. "Someday I just might quit. Who knows?"

11

At age ten Lilia had fallen in love with her aunt's "nest." She'd stepped out of the taxi on her first visit to her grandparents and aunt in San Jose, and the tiny house had beckoned to her and whispered "home." In those days the stucco exterior had been pale gray and the trim charcoal. Unkempt evergreens had flanked the house and hidden the lower panes of windows. As she and her mother walked up a crumbling concrete sidewalk, Nalani told her that while Auntie Alea could still walk, keeping up with the house was difficult now that she had Parkinson's, and hard, too, for Lilia's grandparents, who had moved from Kauai to help.

"It doesn't matter what shape the house is in, because Auntie Alea will never leave," her mother added. "Leaving would kill her faster than any disease. She loves her nest the way I love my children. And while we're here, we'll do everything we can to make it a happy place for her."

Now, as Lilia stood at the curb after saying goodbye to the driver who had picked her up at the airport, she remembered how she had felt that day. While her brothers were completely content living where they had been born, she had known immediately that when she grew up, she would live on the mainland. And while the boys and her cousins had taken their turns helping an increasingly fragile Auntie Alea when their grandparents went home to Kauai, Lilia had come most often, until the day she'd moved in permanently to attend San Jose State.

Even if she had hated San Jose she would have come to help her aunt, who by then was wheelchair bound. That's what family did. But from the beginning she had known just how lucky she was to be here. The city, and particularly Willow Glen, felt like home.

It still did.

Twilight deepened as she gazed up at the house, in no hurry for what lay ahead. Her aunt had left her cozy little nest to Lilia just months before Lilia married. Her brothers and cousins had received money and stock, but nobody questioned the reason Lilia was given the house. Everyone knew Auntie Alea had left it to the one person who loved it as much as she did, and would keep it in the family.

She came from strong, solid people, people who, when decisions were made, thought about what was best for everyone. They trusted each other and the future they would share, even when things went wrong.

Her trip home had been a reminder of that strength, and her own strength was beginning to return. But still, the decision to come back today had been the hardest of her life.

The moon was coming up over the house, bathing it in silvery light. After their marriage Lilia and Graham had lovingly restored and renovated, and finally built the addition to ensure they could live here forever. Despite living in much more extravagant houses all his life, Graham loved it as much as she did. When property values increased, when he found a better investment or a more prestigious location, Douglas Randolph had moved his family. Unlike any house Graham had lived in with his parents, this one had love and family woven through every room.

Together they had added their share.

She wasn't sure what she was going to say to him tonight. Two weeks had passed since the moment Marina thrust Toby into her arms and disappeared. Regan had been short on particulars, but she *had* said that Toby was still living with his father. Whether Marina was back in the picture was a mystery, as were details about how Graham was managing.

As a child, when a night was hot or something particularly bothered her, Lilia had gone out to her family's lanai, sometimes to find a brother in one of the lounge chairs, too. She had slept better there, as if she'd nestled into the loving arms of Papahanau-moku, the earth mother, who with her sky husband, Wakea, was the ancestor of all people.

Here in Willow Glen, when she and Graham had added the master bedroom suite upstairs, she'd done her best to replicate that feeling, insisting on skylights so she could see the stars, and cross-ventilation so she could feel the breeze.

But last night back on her family's lanai, she had made a decision.

Before going inside she allowed herself one more look at the house. How many times had she changed the color of the door, the trim, even the stucco? The wisteria vine running along the eaves was finally coming into its own after years of training and nurturing. The walkway no longer led straight to the door, and perennials bloomed in the curves. Except for the beds of old roses rimming the back patio, everything she planted was drought resistant and colorful. And during the driest season, she'd been known to catch buckets of "greywater," the water that normally ran down the drain as her morning shower warmed, to soak the roses.

The house belonged to her, and most likely since it was hers before marriage, even with

California's community property laws, it would remain hers in a divorce.

Not for the first time she wondered how much worse Graham's death would have felt than his betrayal.

Lights were beginning to flick on in houses, but not in hers. The porch light was off, and none of the windows were lit. If Graham was home, he was doing a good job of hiding it. She had no idea what she would walk into, but she was about to find out.

On the porch she unlocked the door, then gathered herself and went inside, pulling her carry-on behind her. The downstairs wasn't completely dark; the light on the microwave glowed softly from the kitchen, and light shone through windows where shades hadn't been drawn. She left her suitcase and shoes by the door and walked through the familiar rooms to the staircase.

Graham hadn't wasted their time apart cleaning. Dishes lay on the dining room table, still dotted with food. In the kitchen more were piled in the sink, and unopened mail, magazines and keys littered a counter. She wondered if he had given up hope she would be returning soon, or if he just expected her to clean up after him when she did. More likely he just hadn't given her reaction any thought. And that seemed like a bad sign.

She was halfway up the stairs when she heard a wail. Not a loud one, more the sound of an infant just waking, or one who had worn himself out with louder cries. At the top of the stairs she listened and realized the sound was coming from the small bedroom they used for guests. Someday they had hoped to use it for a nursery.

The door was open, but the light was off. She didn't need light, though, to know the room was now occupied. Toby was in the nursery they had planned for their own child. She hadn't considered the possibility, but it stabbed her now. Toby was not *their* child. He belonged solely to Graham and the woman he had impregnated. And now his baby was firmly implanted in the room, in the dream she had shared with him. A dream of a baby they had created together.

She didn't go inside despite continued wailing. Toby was Graham's to care for. She walked slowly down the short hall to the master bedroom. The door was open, and here, at last, was light shining from two lamps and spilling brightly from the connecting bathroom. Graham, fully dressed, was face-down on the bed, as if he had collapsed there because he didn't have the strength or energy to strip off his jeans and slide between the sheets.

For a moment she wondered if he was breathing. She held her own and watched until she could make out the steady rise and fall of his back. She wondered how long he had lain that way, clearly so exhausted he couldn't do anything but sleep. Even quiet, cheerful babies took enormous energy. Constant feeding and diapering and toting from one place to another. After an evening of babysitting she had always been relieved to give infants back to their parents. She'd loved the cuddling, the nurturing, the singing of lullabies, but she had also felt drained.

How much more drained was a man who had just endured a year of cancer and chemo? Considering the state of the downstairs, no one else was helping. From all the signs, Graham had been on his own.

One part of her felt sympathy, another thought he deserved exhaustion. Graham hadn't asked for cancer, but he *had* asked for his son.

The wailing was louder now. So the baby wasn't giving up; he was just getting started. And Graham? Graham was sleeping too soundly to hear him.

Lilia knew she should wake him. A part of her was ready and willing. She could tell him she would be downstairs in the sunroom when and if he got Toby back to sleep. She almost did both.

Instead she found herself in the hallway again, and this time she entered the room where the cries were growing louder and louder and stood in the doorway. The shades weren't drawn. A street lamp was all she needed to see a crib had been installed in a corner, along with a changing table and a dresser. Everything looked brand-new and possibly expensive. She wondered which credit card Graham had used.

She nearly turned away, nearly went downstairs to let the baby cry and Graham sleep on until the cries woke him. But none of this was Toby's fault. As angry as she was, as hurt, she couldn't let a baby who had asked for none of this suffer. She padded slowly to the side of the crib and stood looking down at him.

Toby was so impossibly small. She always forgot how tiny babies were, how fragile. They had no defenses except their cries. And how sad, how forlorn he sounded, as if he believed that nobody cared about his distress, nobody even recognized it.

She scooped him into her arms before the desire to do so registered. He was so light. For a moment she wondered if she dropped him if he'd simply fly away, if his bones, like a bird's, were hollow, and he would gracefully soar to the heavens.

Miraculously the cries stopped. In the lamplight she examined his face, and oddly, he seemed to examine hers. On that awful day she'd seen Graham in his features. Now she saw her husband again. Since the beginning of human reproduction fathers had seen themselves in babies that weren't their own.

But this was no mistake. She certainly didn't see herself when she looked at Toby, but she did see the man she had married.

He whimpered, and without thinking she rested him against her shoulder. He squirmed, but he didn't cry. She adjusted him so his face was turned toward hers, and he seemed to relax.

She wondered when he'd last eaten. Had he been hers she would have offered him a breast, sat in the corner rocking chair — and yes, she saw now that there was one in the corner away from the window — and sung to him as he nursed. But he wasn't hers. She had no idea what Toby ate and when. She did know, though, that he was wet. The dampness was seeping through the little footie pajamas he wore.

As she changed him she murmured. Of course the wailing began again. Few babies enjoyed being changed. But she turned on a lamp so he could see her better and told him who she was as she stripped the pajamas off his impossibly tiny body and warded off the chill with a flannel blanket over his chest as she removed his diaper.

"I'm Lilia, Toby. And this is my house. I hope you never remember the day you arrived, because it wasn't a good one for you or for anybody else."

She wondered how true that was. Had it been a good day for Marina? Had she been

154

so relieved that after she drove away she'd gone somewhere to celebrate?

She found wipes and cleaned him thoroughly, noting the beginning of diaper rash. Would Graham know it if he saw it? Wasn't anybody helping who could point out the need to change Toby more frequently? Clearly the baby had sensitive skin, and despite a quick search through the changing table drawer, she saw nothing to relieve it.

Tomorrow she would shop.

That thought surprised and annoyed her. "Except that you're not mine to worry about, are you?" Still pinning him to the table, she pulled dry pajamas from a drawer in the dresser. *Somebody* had folded and placed baby clothes in drawers. *Somebody* had made certain the dresser was an easy reach from the table.

She pulled the pajamas over the baby's flailing arms, then scooped him up again and took him to the rocker, grabbing a blanket from the foot of the crib as she passed.

Seated, she tucked the blanket around him. "I guess we'll find out if you were just wet or hungry." A pacifier sat on the closest window ledge, and she tucked it into his mouth. Then she began to rock. He squirmed; he protested. But in a minute he began to settle.

"So I was saying . . ." She was surprised that her voice quieted him even more. "I'm Lilia. And you're Toby. If I'm not mistaken

155

you are now my stepson. What you are for sure is a surprise. What a way to start your little life, huh?"

One arm shot up, and he batted at her chest, surprising her. He was no longer crying. Now he was squinting at her, as if he was trying to figure out who she was. She remembered that babies saw faces, that faces intrigued them.

"I have four brothers. All but one of them have children. They're a rowdy group, Toby. They would eat you alive. Then they would spit you out and teach you to surf and fish and hike up mountains."

She wondered why she was telling him this, and she thought of Eli's oldest son, the child who wasn't his by birth, but was as much a part of their extended family as any other child.

"Lilia?"

She looked up and saw Graham in the doorway. She didn't speak.

"You're home," he said.

"It appears so. When did this baby last eat?"

"He's probably due for another bottle, but —"

"Just get it, okay? You can do that, right?"

"Of course, but —"

"Not a good time for a conversation."

He disappeared and she continued to rock. Toby was still staring at her, his little eyes narrow slits as he tried harder to focus.

156

"I'm not your mother." She put out a finger for him to grasp, and he locked his own fingers around it. "I'm sorry."

She realized how much she meant it, and the tears came. She thought she had cried them all.

By the time Graham came back Toby was crying, too. He was more than ready to be fed. Graham collapsed on the floor beside the rocker, tucking his legs campfire style beneath him. "Do you want me to take him?"

She reached for the bottle. The pacifier had long since been rejected. She put the nipple in Toby's mouth, and he began to suck.

Graham didn't touch her, but he leaned forward. "There aren't enough words in the English language to say how sorry I am."

"You're right. There aren't."

"I was out of my mind."

"I've been thinking about that. I don't believe it. Your childhood wasn't good, but you got everything you ever wanted except love. I'm not sure you ever got over that."

He was silent.

She looked up from the baby. "And how did all this work out for you, Graham? You have the son you were sure you needed. Was it worth any price? Including losing me?"

"Did I? Lose you?"

"I don't know. I know I have to be here for a while. We have to straighten out our finances and our futures. I have to do some work. I haven't done any since I left. I can't do it from Kauai. So I'm back. And this house belongs to me. So I won't be leaving again. If anybody goes, next time it'll be you."

He nodded.

"Is Marina in the picture?"

"No! I haven't heard a word from her. She wouldn't even answer questions about Toby. I had to figure out everything."

"Do you have help?"

"Mike and Judy came over a few times to help me put the pieces together."

Mike was Graham's foreman, and both he and Judy, his wife, had been at the party.

She looked back at the baby who was still watching her as he sucked. "You've set up quite a nursery here." The crib slats were gracefully curved, and the headboard had a ship's wheel on the side nearest the door that looked like it might actually turn when a toddler needed something to play with.

"The furniture was delivered on Monday, and they came in and set the whole thing up." He hesitated before he added, "An anonymous gift."

That surprised her. "Anonymous? You have no idea?"

"I know the set is cherry. The crib converts to a bed. Judging by the quality and the white glove service that came with it?" He let that hang in the air.

She was stunned. "Your parents?"

"Of course not, but maybe my mother. She was here. She wanted to see Toby."

"She was probably deliriously happy to find I was gone."

"She probably was, but she wasn't foolish enough to say so." He paused. "She did ask me to reconcile with my father so we could be a family again."

"Well, that would be one way to take care of your future."

"You know better."

She looked up again. "What do I really know about you, Graham? All these years and I would never, never have expected you to cheat on me, to lie and continue lying until you were caught." She swallowed more tears. "And now there's a baby in our lives. Not my baby, not the one I wanted to have when you said you weren't quite ready. Yours. The one you decided to have without me. But you know what? Even if I send you packing, I'll worry about this little guy. He's already getting diaper rash. And that's your fault, too."

"The worry or the rash?"

"This isn't funny."

"Tell me about it. I would willingly do another year of chemo rather than face what I've done."

He was silent so long she assumed he was finished, but he finally spoke again. "You have to know something else."

She realized how little she expected now.

"Not done with the surprises?"

"I love him. I don't know why. He squirms when I hold him. I've never seen him as quiet as he is now unless he's sleeping. And nothing I do makes him happy. I'm so tired I can't see straight, but I would jump out a window if I had to save his life. Without thinking."

"You realize Marina could come back for him anytime."

"Carrick started the paperwork so I can have legal custody. She has to be notified and respond or default."

"Even if Carrick waives or seriously reduces his fees, all the legal fees are going to add up. But what's another ocean to cross when we're already swimming in debt?"

He winced. "I know a year ago I made the worst mistake possible, but Lilia, that's not Toby's fault, and he has to come first now. I want to be the kind of father I never had, the kind *you* had. That's the least I can do for giving this little guy such a rotten start."

"You may be raising him alone."

"I want to raise him with you."

"It would be easier, wouldn't it?"

"That's not why. I can't ask you to stay and take this on. I know how difficult it's going to be. I can't even imagine how you'll explain his sudden appearance in your life to your readers."

"That's the least of it."

"I know. There are so many parts to this,

but one of them is *not* making things easier for me. I want you because I love you, not because I need a mother for my son. I've loved you since the day I met you. I've never wanted anybody else."

"And yet . . ."

"I thought I was dying. Everything else was eclipsed."

A sigh caught in her throat and turned into a sob. "Me, most of all. I was eclipsed. The love you say you feel? How deep could it be?"

"I want to spend the rest of my life proving it's a bottomless well."

"I'm not ready for that."

"I understand."

"I'm here for now. You and Toby can stay. That's all I can do at the moment. We're in no position for a separation. And I'm not selling my home to fund the results of your infidelity."

"We can work out finances. Can we work out the rest?"

"I have no idea. I really don't. But I'd like you to sleep in my office for now. I don't want you in my bed."

"Okay."

"And Toby is your responsibility. I'll do whatever I feel like and not one thing more. Don't think you can hand him off."

"I don't want to hand him off."

She nodded. "Good."

"Do you want me to take him now?"

She realized whatever she said was crucial, that she couldn't set a precedent. She debated. "I'll finish this because I started it. That's the only reason."

"You have a magic touch. He looks right at home."

"That's the kind of thing I don't want to hear."

He got up. He didn't spring to his feet, the way he would have before his diagnosis. Then his energy had been boundless. Now he had to push himself off the floor and take time to straighten.

Despite herself, despite everything, she felt a tug of sympathy.

"I'll move my things," he said.

"You can do that tomorrow. It's enough that you sleep downstairs tonight."

"I'll take the baby monitor. You won't have to take care of him again."

"You do that."

"Thank you. For coming back. For not kicking me out tonight. For taking care of Toby."

"My choices were limited. Don't read more into them than you should."

She watched him disappear into the hallway. She looked down and saw that Toby's eyes were closing. She stroked a finger across his silky forehead before she lifted him over her shoulder to burp him.

"Some family you got, huh, little guy? But

somebody will always keep you safe and warm. You'll be okay. No matter what else, I promise you'll be okay." She closed her eyes and began to hum.

■ ■ ■ ■

Part II

■ ■ ■ ■

Cliff swallows are just one of the bird species that practice brood parasitism. Instead
of raising her own clutch, the female will
sometimes lay her eggs in another female's
nest and turn the job over to her.

"Our Songbirds, Ourselves:
A Tale of Two Species,"
from the editors of *Ornithology Today.*

12

THE SWALLOW'S NEST

FEATHERING YOUR NEST WITH IMAGINATION AND LOVE

June 3rd:

Redesigning the interior of the heart isn't as easy or fun as redesigning the interior of a home. As you know, in March I learned my husband has a baby son who is suddenly ours to raise.

You aren't shy about your opinions, and I have read them all. I've nodded at your anger while at the same time I've considered the well-meant advice that I should forgive and forget. Please believe me on this. Feelings that are buried erupt like Kilauea on the Big Island. In their own time and in the worst ways.

But forgiveness? In my home state we sometimes practice *ho'oponopono,* an ancient ritual to get to the root of problems in ourselves, and in our families. *Ho'oponopono* tells us to practice love, and not to hold tightly to fault. We look inside ourselves for ways we may have contributed to a problem. Each of us has a chance to speak our pain. Forgiveness and reconciliation come afterwards.

    I am trying. I try every day. I want the comfort, the ease I had before illness and distrust entered my home. But strangely, I don't want a life without the baby who came with both. He is a gift. From sorrow has come joy. I can only try to practice love and open myself to life. Can we do that together?

                               Aloha! Lilia

Lilia looked down at her feet and at the baby pulling himself into a sitting position by grabbing the hem of her skirt. A moment ago Toby had been lying in the corner of her office on his back, playing happily with plastic measuring spoons. He wasn't yet crawling, although he liked to try. He'd gotten to the desk by rolling on the cotton area rug, back to stomach, stomach to back. Toby wasn't easily stopped.

She bent down and lifted his wiry little body to her lap, ruffling the pale blond hair that was as wispy as dandelion fluff. "You're way overdue for a nap. You know that, don't you?"

He grabbed her finger and began to gnaw. He wasn't hungry. He'd had cereal for breakfast and a bottle. Today she'd even introduced him to strained applesauce. She'd made a friend for life.

"Teething, are we?"

When she positioned him so she could see his face, he stopped gnawing and favored her with a slobbery grin. "Ma-Ma-Ma-Ma . . ."

Her heart did a familiar little skip. Toby was vocalizing. She knew that. Graham was treated to Ma-Ma-Ma-Ma as often as she was. But she beamed a smile back at him.

"You got that right. I'm sure acting like your mama." She kissed his forehead and thought of Toby's birth mother, something she tried not to do. According to her husband, Marina had never contacted him. And she knew from Carrick that Marina had chosen not to respond to the court's petition. Graham now had legal custody.

But distrust was a wily creature. After everything that had happened, almost anything seemed possible now, even that Graham and Marina were sneaking in a little afternoon delight on a job site somewhere. Graham certainly wasn't getting any kind of delight, not morning, noon or night, at home.

She forced her thoughts back to the baby on her lap and inclined her head to the mesh-sided Pack 'n Play in the corner. "I say it's time for bed. If you're good I'll tuck you in here."

Toby often took his afternoon nap in her office. She'd found it easier to have him with her so she didn't have to carry the baby monitor from room to room or run upstairs to check on him. If she made noise or talked on the phone he rarely woke. Unlike the first month after he'd been left on her doorstep — and that's how she thought about his arrival — these days he slept through almost everything, as if the early months of colic and sleeplessness were finally catching up with him.

Now she lifted him so they were face-to-face and laughed, as he tried to bounce on her thighs, although his little legs kept curling into a baby version of the lotus position. "If you go to sleep now, you'll be awake when Dolores comes, and you know how much you like to play with Dolores."

He yawned, tiny fists lifting as he stretched. He fussed a little when she settled him into her arms and carried him to the corner, because by now he understood the drill.

"You know what you have to do," she said, kissing his fat little cheeks, "and now you have to do it. Sleep tight, baby boy."

The house was warm, so she didn't bother zipping him into the little bat-wing blanket sleeper Regan had bought for him. Since she was going to stay right here while he fell asleep, she gave him a stuffed dog to cuddle and turned her back when he started to fuss.

He was asleep before she was fully settled back into her desk chair. The dog was safely on the floor.

She read what she'd written and decided she should probably post it, despite how personal the message was. After Graham's diagnosis her blog had grown increasingly intimate. Until that time her own perfect marriage and life had been almost boring to write about, and she had tried to avoid anything except funny anecdotes.

Her blog had always been a way to draw people to her website, where they could arrange for telephone or in-person design consultations. They could also buy products, for the most part small items like embroidered napkins, signed prints and posters from her favorite Hawaiian artists, colorful serveware for entertaining. Some things she distributed, these days with the help of part-time staff and a large storage unit, some she simply sold on commission when a reader clicked a link to another website. Before Graham's illness she'd had big plans to expand her inventory, but like so much of her life, those were on hold.

From the beginning *The Swallow's Nest* had done well. She'd started blogging during her first job as an in-house designer for a furniture showroom. Her posts on the company website had been surprisingly well-received, but she had quickly tired of touting their products and yearned to be more creative and personal.

When she had decided to go out on her own and share office space with two other local designers, she had inaugurated *The Swal-*

low's Nest, and many of her former readers had found her.

A California designer with Hawaiian sensibilities was unique enough to draw people to the website. Along with shopping and consultation she offered recipes, lessons, tips, along with plenty of decorating advice. Each week she answered questions posed by readers about their own decorating crises. Eventually she and Graham had teamed up to make videos, showing the work they'd done both inside and out on their home, sharing disasters along with triumphs. Her design colleagues had moved on, and Lilia had begun working from home, since the increasingly successful website was now the largest part of her income.

But nothing had drawn people to *The Swallow's Nest* like Graham's illness. She'd begun by explaining there might occasionally be weeks when she disappeared from the internet. Questions were asked and eventually answered, and readers who were going through their own crises shared what they'd learned. As she'd described the progress of Graham's illness her posts became more and more intimate. The more details she provided, the more people visited. Their continued presence, and the items they bought, had helped financially at a time when she couldn't travel any distance to the homes of clients.

At some point she had realized that an

authentic blog about nesting had to include the problems that came with making a marriage and a home. Others were learning from her mistakes as well as her triumphs. She couldn't advise anyone else, but she could share her own story.

The blog had given her the opportunity to share her feelings about Graham's illness, something she hadn't been able to do with him. When she had tried, too often her husband had closed all doors. At the time she'd thought that cancer was a journey he had to take alone, no matter how much support she offered. She hadn't realized he'd had *other* things on his mind.

She had never considered there might be a bigger crisis on the horizon, something more riveting for her readers than the impending death of a spouse. She had never considered that she or Graham might do something that would challenge even their most loyal followers. Something like a secret affair and a baby.

Now she was left to tell the story, just enough of it so readers would understand why there was suddenly a child in her home. Just enough to make it possible to understand that the marriage that had looked so solid, so nearly perfect, might end any day. *Not* enough to expose the true state of her heart or, worse, details she didn't want Toby to read on the internet someday.

She walked a tightrope.

Now she pushed "publish" before she could change her mind and went to the kitchen where she started water for tea. Her appetite had never really returned. She had to force herself to eat three meals a day, and since she liked cooking, most nights she prepared dinner for Graham, too. Usually, though, they didn't eat together. If he went to work, something he did more often each week, she ate before he came home and left his in the refrigerator. If he was home she took her share into her office and worked.

Not a habit she would ever recommend to her readers.

While the water heated she checked for lunch possibilities. She was rummaging through the refrigerator, considering yogurt and fruit when the door to the sunroom opened suddenly. Her head snapped up to see Graham carrying a white paper sack.

"Wow." She went back to scanning the refrigerator.

"Did I startle you?"

"I thought you were Dolores."

"Are you communicating with the refrigerator spirits? You look very focused."

She closed the door and faced him. "I thought you planned to be gone all day."

"I had to pick up blueprints, so I picked up lunch on the way home. I'm hoping to entice you if the refrigerator spirits haven't already worked their magic."

He looked better than he had the day she returned from Kauai. Last week he'd actually needed a real haircut, and he was neither puffy nor skeletal, although he'd been one or the other during much of his ordeal. When he could sleep he slept like a dead man, still tired too easily, still suffered side effects from all the drugs they'd poured into his system. His feet burned, and walking any distance was painful. He caught cold easily and had too many upset stomachs and fevers. But even the side effects were diminishing. Removing the ports was still a task for the future, as were more scans, exams and drugs. But Graham was clearly on his way.

She kept her voice neutral. "Lunch was thoughtful."

"There's a hole-in-the-wall Vietnamese restaurant not far from the house in Santa Clara we're remodeling. Their banh mi sandwiches are the best. I knew I had to bring you one."

"I'm making jasmine tea. Would you like some?"

In answer he reached for the canister. "Toby's asleep?"

"He'll stay that way for a while. Hopefully until Dolores gets here."

Dolores de la Rosa, middle-aged and endlessly patient, came three afternoons a week to watch the baby and clean. Lilia handled the mornings, because so far she'd been able to work or shop with Toby in tow. Graham took the other afternoons and most of the weekend. Occasionally Toby went out on jobs with his father, but more often the two holed up in the tiny study off the master bedroom. The space was just large enough for a desk and chair, but the two males spread out, and when Lilia finished for the day she often found baby toys beside the bed or tucked under dressers.

Now Graham added tea bags to pottery mugs. "How was he today?"

"He loves the swing." She and Toby had found the baby swing at a garage sale on one of their walks, and she'd hauled it home, mostly under one arm while she pushed Toby's stroller with the other. Everything they had, equipment and clothing, had been bought at sales or dropped off by friends whose children had outgrown them. Nobody, most especially not Lilia, had figured out the etiquette for this situation, but it certainly hadn't included birth announcements or giggly baby showers.

"You always seem to know what to do with him," Graham said. "When I've got him I know the possibilities, but I don't have a clue which to try."

She poured steaming water and set the timer with her voice, another piece of technology Graham had added to their lives before money was as scarce as love in their home.

She leaned against the counter and crossed her arms. "He's a different baby these days."

"The doctor promised he would be. But I didn't believe it. My mother —"

She waited, but he didn't go on. "Your mother what?"

"The day she came to see him? She said I was the same kind of baby. I screamed and stiffened when she held me. Which from what she said wasn't all that often. But she did say he would improve. Even I improved. Although she certainly didn't think so when I reported my father's top executives to state authorities."

"Or when you married me." She went on because she couldn't help herself. "Has she been back in touch?"

"Not a word. She wanted me to dive back into the bosom of the family. She discounted the fact my father would have booted me right back out. She actually said he had a sentimental side."

"We all delude ourselves, don't we? All those years with Douglas, and she still thinks he's at least a smidgen admirable."

"I don't want Toby near him. Not ever." He caught her gaze and held it. "You'll remember that?"

For a moment she didn't understand. When she did, she frowned. "It's not going to be an issue, Graham. He's your son. Nobody's going to ask me if I think Douglas should have a role in his life. I'm just your wife, not Toby's mother."

"You're his stepmother."

"Which means I probably have as much say in his future as a string bean."

Graham got plates and unwrapped the sandwiches. "They had Sweet Maui Onion chips. I got some."

"Graham, don't assume I'll be around to see Toby grow up. We aren't there yet."

"Not even after banh mi and your favorite chips?" He smiled, but his eyes were sad. He still slept in her office on the daybed. They lived in the same house, passed each other and sometimes had conversations like this one. But in the important ways, they were strangers. They weren't sharing their bodies and certainly not their hearts.

"Not even then." She started to turn away, but he caught her hand, surprising her. For months he'd been careful not to touch her.

"Do you have any idea how much I miss you?"

She didn't pull away, although she considered it. She discarded all the things she could have said. He should have thought of that before he slept with another woman. He should have told her about Toby the moment he learned he had fathered a child. He should have given her the choice whether or not to support his lying, cheating self during all the months of his illness.

178

Instead she looked down at his hand. "I don't know what you miss, Graham. The sex? Being waited on? Being worried over? Planning the TV show that never came to pass?"

"Building a life together. I hate that we're just going through the motions."

"Anytime you need to leave, you know where we keep the suitcases."

He released her hand. "I can't take back what I did, Lilia. No matter how badly I want to."

"No, you can't. And you can't give me back all the love and time I lavished on you, either."

"Marriages survive, don't they? Even after huge mistakes."

"Did you tell yourself that the night you slept with Marina?"

"I didn't tell myself anything. I was sunk in despair. I couldn't hear my own voice. I just . . . was."

For months now she had tried and failed to put herself in Graham's place. Denied the one thing he wanted, the one thing he *believed* might help him cope with his gravely uncertain future, a beautiful woman had offered it to him. Not the wife he claimed to love, but another woman whose company he enjoyed.

One who could give him a child who looked like *him.*

If a thought could be a physical reality, she

felt this one in the region of her heart. And why should she be alone with it? Who was she protecting? The time had arrived to let Graham know what she suspected. Still the words were impossible to force out.

"Does that make any sense to you?" Graham asked when she didn't respond.

The words came. "You knew that if you got Marina pregnant —" She watched him wince. "You knew that if you *did,* the baby would look like you."

"Well, he does look like me, but I don't understand. What's that got to do with anything?"

"I saw the way you stared at little Jonah the last time we were in Kapa'a together, Graham. You were astounded how much he had changed. Apparently you don't know a lot about genetics or how children take on characteristics, as they grow, they didn't seem to have at birth. Like dark skin, dark eyes."

He stared at her, clearly perplexed. "What are you trying to say?"

"I think it occurred to you on that visit that if you and I had a child, not only might he or she look more like *me* than like you, our child might look like my brothers' children. And I think you weren't sure you wanted that."

"I have no idea what you're talking about."

"We came home. I wanted to try to have a baby. You made up excuses not to. Until the cancer diagnosis changed your mind, of course."

"And you think that was because after the trip I didn't want a child with dark skin or Asian eyes? You honestly think that?" His voice rose.

"The timing was suspicious, don't you think? You wanted a baby, then we went to Kauai, you didn't want one anymore."

He dropped to a stool at the small island. "I can't believe you thought that. And you think I had Toby with Marina . . ." He shook his head.

"Enlighten me, then. And don't tell me after the trip you suddenly thought some more about how busy we were going to be and wanted to protect us both. We could have had a baby and done everything. Look how well we've worked it out since Toby arrived."

"Lilia . . ." He ran a shaky hand over his cheek. "How wrong can you be? After we spent that week with your family? I was eaten up with my inadequacies. Your brothers, especially Kai with little Jonah? They're such good fathers, and Jonah absolutely adores his dad."

"Of course he does."

"Everyone in your family knows what to do with babies and every age after that right through to adulthood. Look at Eli with his kids? They're practically teenagers, but he knows just how to handle them. It's natural to all your brothers. Everything is so damned easy! Afterwards, all I could think about was what a terrible father I would be, and how unfair it was for you to do double duty because I would be so inept. I don't know how to love a child. I've never loved anybody but you and Carrick, and now you know how bad I am at that. What if we had one and suddenly you loved him more than you loved me, and I was out in the darkness somewhere not knowing where to go and what to do to claim either of you?"

His eyes shone with tears, and despite a new history of lies and deceit, she believed him.

She believed him.

A weight dropped from her heart, and when it did, she realized how burdened she had been by this secret. "It wasn't because you didn't want my child? A child who might look like me or my brothers?"

"When I look at my son, I wish with all my heart that he looked like you, Lilia. He's beautiful. He's perfect. But he wasn't born to you. And that's always there for me, in the same way it's there for you. Only I know whose fault it is, and I have to live with my shame."

"Toby *is* perfect. You're right about that much. You grew up thinking you weren't good enough, but Toby can't grow up that way. You can't ever let him know you regret a thing about him."

"Can you say the same?"

So much hinged on her answer. A little boy's self-esteem. Her own happiness. And Graham's.

She drew a ragged breath. "All children are God's creations. All children are God's *gifts.* I was taught that. I honestly believe it. Whether he's God's gift to me?" She slowly shook her head. "I guess we'll have to see. But there's nothing about Toby that's imperfect or unlovable. No matter how angry I am at you, I'm not angry at him."

"I don't deserve you."

She bit her lip, then she rested her fingertips on his shoulder. "Neither of us deserves that child. But right now he's ours. And every time he smiles at me, I can't say I'm sorry."

He covered her fingertips with his. She closed her eyes, and when he put his arms around her and brushed his lips over the tears on her cheeks, she accepted that, as well.

13

Marina was nearly finished packing the last of her clothes and jewelry so that tomorrow, a mover could take her personal belongings to Blake's villa and her larger items to storage. Two weeks ago after a wild Vegas trip, she and Blake had tied the knot. On their second day in Sin City, they had strolled by a wedding chapel, and he had proposed, emerald-cut diamond and all. Just like that. She hadn't prompted him, although the idea had certainly occurred to her — occurred often enough, in fact, that she'd already decided to say yes.

Of course, Blake was old enough to be her father. Of course, he was lonely and probably willing to settle for less than love just to have someone to warm his bed and wake up to. Of course, if she was truthful, she supposed she was lonely, too, and probably had been all her life. She'd learned the hard way that romance was for movies and novels. She was ready to settle, too.

Since they'd been in Vegas, arrangements had been simple. They'd booked an informal ceremony, and he'd given her his credit card to shop for a dress. She'd chosen something sexy enough to convince him not to change his mind. Somehow he'd been able to score a fabulous suite with a view of the Strip for the remainder of their stay.

So now she was a married woman, but life had taught her to hedge her bets. She wasn't ready to let go of the furniture she had so carefully selected and purchased over time, even if Deedee did have her eye on it. She could imagine the way her mother would care for her precious possessions. A climate-controlled storage unit made better sense. Just in case.

Using the same logic, she had decided she wasn't ready to let go of her job. Her boss had agreed to let her go part-time, and she had jumped at the opportunity. She was too recently married to be certain Blake would be as generous a husband as he'd been a lover. And spending those two days away each week seemed like a good idea.

No matter how advantageous this marriage might be, she wouldn't have said yes if she hadn't liked Blake. He was easy to live with, undemanding and generous. He paid attention to her in ways she wasn't used to. Still, she didn't want to learn bridge, and her interest in golf was marginal. For now Blake's wanderlust was sated, so while she could, she planned to add to her personal savings.

After she taped all but the final box, she returned to her dresser for one more look. Toby's blanket was now its sole inhabitant.

The reminder of the baby was crazy, and she knew it. Nobody had forced her to give Toby to his father — or more accurately, his father's wife. But having him was the biggest mistake of her life, and she'd done what she could to rectify it.

Still, in the moments when she couldn't avoid thinking about him, she missed her son, or at least the idea of him. Not the inconsolable screaming. Not the spitting up, the utter rejection of her when she held him. Not the lack of sleep, the meals she'd gulped. She didn't miss the way the pediatrician had barraged her with questions or the way onlookers scowled at her when she couldn't quiet him.

What did she miss? Watching Toby when he slept. The sweet curves of his cheeks, the tiny lips pursed to suck, the wisps of silky blond hair. Against her better judgment she had created another human being. And now she wouldn't be with him as he took his first steps into the world, babbled his first words, smiled at her in genuine recognition. They lived in the same city. They weren't separated by thousands of miles, but by thousands of doubts, thousands of hours when she had been an unwilling caretaker. Thousands of resentments.

Graham had been her knight in shining armor. Now both Toby and Graham were lost to her, the latter because he'd never been hers, and the former because she had abandoned him.

She opened the drawer and removed the blanket, drawing it through her hands. Late in her pregnancy, when she'd finally been forced to shop for the baby, her disillusionment had been complete. The knight had only wanted a broodmare. No love had gone into selecting this blanket, just as no love had gone into the pregnancy. The baby's kicks had been affronts. She'd watched her body grow and change in ways she'd never wanted it to. Just weeks before the impending birth she'd finally gone to the store with a list from the internet to buy the most minimal supplies.

The blanket was all that was left now. Three months had passed but she knew her son was okay. A chubby smiling Toby had been with Graham on a job site two weeks ago — one of her fellow employees had made certain to let her know. And the pediatrician's office had called to ask if it was okay to transfer Toby's records to another practice.

And then there were the court documents. Graham establishing himself as Toby's father. Graham making sure he had custody. Had he really expected her to come to the court hearing with her own lawyer and protest? Did he think she'd just dropped off the baby because she wanted to take an extended vacation?

As annoying as it was to have the court involved, she supposed it was a good thing. At least he had Toby's best interests in mind, even if he'd never had hers.

Blake still didn't know she'd had a baby, and while in the future she might have to tell him, for now she had no reason. What would he think of a woman who had let go of her child so easily? They needed to settle in together, to strengthen what bonds were between them, before she made that confession.

For a brief moment she held the blanket to her nose and inhaled. Traces of Toby's scent still lingered, and the memories it evoked were bittersweet. This was the right time to let go of everything to do with her son, but in the end, still unable to part with the last souvenir of the baby's months in her life, she added it to the last box she'd packed and sealed that one, too.

Finished for the day, she locked the door behind her and consulted her watch, a wedding gift from her new husband. Consultations were frequent because she liked to savor the diamond that marked twelve on the dial and each of the eleven semiprecious stones around it. After the wedding ceremony she'd admired the watch at the Via Bellagio Promenade, and Blake had bought it for her without hesitation. Maybe the display was a little gaudy, she wasn't quite sure, but it was clearly expensive. She hoped to get used to expensive.

Six o'clock was right around the corner, and she had promised Blake she would pick up Chinese food on the way home. He wasn't picky as long as he didn't have to shop or cook, and she had found she could pick up or make whatever she wanted, including dinner reservations. He managed money wisely, careful to be certain he didn't spend too much. But the amount he was comfortable with was so generous, she didn't have to worry about anything except large expenditures. And she'd had no time to make many of those.

Not yet.

She took the three flights of stairs at a rapid clip, anxious to call the restaurant from the car so the food would be waiting when she got there. Hungry and tired she didn't notice the man leaning against her Mustang until she was almost on top of him. She stopped and squinted. He was familiar, but for a moment she couldn't place him. Until he spoke.

"I figured you'd come down pretty soon."

This was one of Blake's sons, Wayne or Paul, and she wasn't quite sure which since she'd only met them once. Then she remembered that Paul was overweight, and this man wasn't. So much for becoming a good stepmother.

"Hello, Wayne." Her smile was perfunctory. "I would have been happy to tell you where I lived."

"Past tense being correct, huh? I hear you're moving in with my father."

"I *married* your father."

"And did it without consulting Paul or me."

"That was up to Blake. If he chose not to, that was his business."

"What did you do to convince him?"

Neither of the Wendell sons possessed any tact, but if this one could ask pointed questions, so could she. "I'm curious why you dislike me so much." She flipped one hand palm-up in question. "I make your father happy. He makes me happy. We're both better off for it."

"And what makes a young woman happy with an old man?"

"Fifty-two isn't old."

"Of course not. It's the new thirty-two, right? You married him because he's so smart, so handsome, so *rich.*"

She forced a smile, as if this really were a friendly conversation. "Right now he's so *hungry,* and I need to get home so he can eat. Will you excuse me?"

In answer he positioned himself more firmly in front of the driver's door. "Do you know

190

Dad turned over his company to Paul and me? That we're in charge of it now? We *could* monitor every single penny he takes out of it. Right now we only monitor the big purchases. Like trips out of town. Or *jewelry.*"

"It's hard to believe a court would agree. I mean, this is his company and his money we're talking about, right?"

"*Our* money. We took over a business he left in shambles. We're barely out of the red because of his mismanagement. I don't think a court would be impressed with his ability to handle money."

"What court would hold financial problems against anybody these days? This is the Silicon Valley. Start-ups have the life span of a moth, and established companies go bankrupt every day."

He narrowed his eyes. "Do you know why he let us take over?"

"Because of your sparkling personalities?"

"Because he knew he was losing it."

"He could have hired others to help him hold on to the company. Different management —"

"He wasn't losing the *company,* woman! He was losing his marbles."

"Come on, he's only fifty-two."

"His *own* father died young, and *he* had dementia before he croaked."

"Listen, I have a mother who's showed signs of dementia since she was born. You're talking to a pro. Get out of my way, please."

He didn't move. "When my mother was sick he started forgetting things, and he never got back what he lost. He returned to work after she died, but he was that much worse. He made a couple of choices that were so bad we had to jump in and rescue him. He realizes he wasn't making good business decisions, but apparently, he doesn't realize he's not making good personal ones, either."

She felt just the tiniest sliver of doubt. "Grief affects every part of life, including work. Blake lives on his own. He manages his money. We have good conversations. He plays bridge —"

"Not like he did. He was a silver life master."

"I assume that means something?"

"It means he was better than good. A lot better. And now if he plays at all, he plays with beginners."

"So he's relaxed and doesn't care. But I've never seen any signs —"

"Sure you have, but you weren't paying attention because you were after something else entirely. So I'm here to tell you you've made a bad bargain. Dad signed over the business to us. Isn't that ironic? He wanted to protect his estate from himself. It's too bad he didn't remember that when he married you. Was it spur of the moment? Was he really thinking or did you manipulate him?"

192

"Move away from my car."

"Does he ask you to repeat things? The cleaning woman reports to us, and we pop in every couple of days to make sure everything is running smoothly."

"Everything *is* running smoothly. Your father is thrilled to be married to me. And I'm not doing any more than any wife. He's fine, and I want to go home and give him dinner."

"If we'd been more alert, we would have seen there were real problems, even before Mom died. She wanted to go to Europe, and she finally persuaded Dad to make the trip. Only she said when they got there, he was like a little kid. Confused. Unhappy. Disoriented. He wanted things the way they always were. She had to bring him back early. To this day he pretends coming home was *her* idea."

She didn't know if she should believe a word he said, but she did know she had to leave. "And maybe it was. How would you know? You weren't there."

"You're burying your head in the sand."

"I'm leaving. Get out of my way."

"We'll be watching Dad's expenditures even more carefully now. Before he didn't spend much. He's never cared about things. But now we'll be looking over your shoulder. Don't turn around or you'll see us."

"And if I find you spying on me? I'll hire a lawyer."

He stepped away. "I almost feel sorry for you. You thought you were on the easy road. But you made a bad bargain, Marina, and it's going to come back to haunt you. I don't know what motivated you to go after Dad, but I'm going to do a little digging. If I were you, before you let me dig too far, I'd think about ways to get out while the getting's good. When you're ready, you come to me. I can make it easy."

14
THE SWALLOW'S NEST

FEATHERING YOUR NEST WITH
IMAGINATION AND LOVE

August 9th:

When does a parent begin to love a child? At the moment of conception or birth? At the first smile, the first belly laugh? Or later, much later?

When a man and a woman fall in love, we say it was love at first sight, or their love grew steadily with time, or even that love went unrecognized for years until one day, there it was, standing right in front of them. Why are we surprised when mothers and fathers fall slowly in love with their children, too?

And when a man and a woman fall out of love, or believe they have, why are we even more surprised when they realize that love has only fallen dormant, but most miraculously, it can be revived?

Aloha, Lilia

Toby had been fussy all day, and Lilia made excuses. He was eight months old now, crawling like a world champ and determined to walk. If set on his feet with something to hold on to, he edged along, his little legs bowing as he went. Only he wasn't quite ready to do more. Every time he reached the end of the daybed in her office and plopped to his fat little backside, he was furious at the universe — and at her. In his baby world, Lilia solved every problem, and he took it quite personally when she refused to solve this one.

Nor was she able to solve the problem of a tooth that just wouldn't erupt.

She gave up trying to work for the day and got up to retrieve her office companion, who was wailing inconsolably after another butt plop. "Let's try a little dinner, partner."

Toby quieted, but he was restless as she carried him on her hip into the kitchen where his high chair rested against a small table in the corner. She slipped him in and buckled the harness. Toby was an independent soul, and happiest when he fed himself. She kept an assortment of foods he could manage on his own, and now she put soft peas on one corner of the tray, tiny cubes of cheese in the middle and Cheerios beside them.

Usually that would have kept him happily busy while she fetched more substantial offerings, but tonight he swept the food and began to bang on the tray with both hands.

"Well, okay. I can see that's not making you happy."

She tried a spoonful of mashed banana,

usually a favorite, but apparently not tonight. He turned his cheek to the spoon and wailed. Mashed salmon, another favorite, sparked the same performance.

"Not hungry then." She slid the tray forward and unbuckled his rigid little body, lifting him back into her arms. "A bottle? A new diaper? Speak up. I'm at your service."

He was crying harder, and she had to hold him extra tight with one arm as she made a bottle. While it was only six, early for bed, he seemed ready. Although he wasn't wet, upstairs in the nursery she changed him into an overnight diaper and settled into the rocking chair to feed him. At first he seemed happy enough, and they rocked as she crooned to him.

In the months he'd been in residence the nursery had been transformed. She had inherited the nautical theme, but she'd made good use of it. A quilt with twelve sailboats in shades of red, white and blue hung next to the closet. A string of flags spelling out "Welcome Aboard" hung along the wall high above the crib, which was decked out in nautical stripes. She'd created a valance from an extra set of the same sheets over the windows. The Roman shades below the valance were depictions of sea creatures, and the rug was patterned with ships' anchors. She intended to paint the walls a deep blue, but while she had auditioned possibilities on poster boards she taped to the walls, she hadn't yet settled on the perfect shade. She was a firm believer in doing things right, not doing them quickly.

One of Toby's favorite toys was a bright gold octopus she'd created from velvety Minky fabric — and she was pleased enough with her masterpiece to share it on her blog. She reached for it now so he could cuddle with it, but he thrust the toy away, and immediately afterwards he knocked the bottle away, too, and began to wail.

He wasn't warm, and he didn't seem congested. Her best guess was a new tooth, although none of the ones that had come before had created such a fuss. She decided to give him a small dose of children's Tylenol before she put him in his crib.

The drug might dull the pain enough that he could get to sleep. But she was afraid she had a long night ahead. Graham had flown to Seattle to attend a design-build expo, mostly, she thought, to show the professional world that he was still alive and kicking. He would be home tomorrow afternoon, but for tonight, Toby was all hers.

In his crib at last the baby seemed to settle, and crossing her fingers, she left the door open so she could hear him if he awoke.

The telephone rang as she was heading for the stairs, and she turned and raced for the master bedroom to catch it.

Graham was on the other end. "Hey, I'm on my way to dinner. I just wanted to check in and tell you to forget the room number I texted. My air conditioner was leaking, so I moved out, and they're looking for another place to put me. Just call the front desk if you need to find me."

She perched on the bed they were now sharing again. "I was just about to make something for myself. Or I guess I could eat what your son refused."

"He's not hungry?"

During the past months as they reconstructed their marriage, they'd talked about Toby more than they'd talked about themselves. That seemed to be the best way to feel their way back to each other, even better than their lovemaking, which sometimes felt forced and uneasy. The baby, rather than being an obstacle, had, in a funny way, become the glue that was holding them together.

She kept her voice light because she didn't want Graham to worry when there was nothing he could do. "He's just fussy. In fact I don't expect him to stay asleep for long. It may be a long night."

"I'm sorry I'm not there."

"How's the expo going?"

"I've sat through some helpful workshops and made some good contacts. People seem surprised I'm still alive."

"Sometimes I'm surprised, too." And not

just because he'd had cancer.

He began again. "Lilia, I don't know if you were worried that I might run into Marina here."

One of the ways she hoped to save her marriage was to be honest and not pretend the past was firmly behind them. "It crossed my mind."

"There's no way you have anything to worry about. But today I heard something. She got married a couple of months ago. And she's only working a day or two a week. Mostly developing sales presentations and collecting overdue accounts."

"Who told you?"

He hesitated just a second too long. "I asked one of her coworkers."

"Why would you do that?"

"Because I don't want her showing up on our doorstep demanding to see Toby, or worse, insisting she wants custody again."

She thought that over. "And what would you say if she did?"

"I'd tell her I'm going to consult my attorney."

For a moment, just a moment, she wondered what their lives would be like if Marina took back her son and raised him herself. Graham would probably see Toby a couple of times a month, have him for two weeks in the summer and maybe for a holiday or two. The little boy would become a visitor who already had a real mother, and Lilia would be, at best, an occasional stand-in.

But if that happened? She and Graham would, for the most part, be free of responsibility. Then, in the future when he had recovered fully, they could try for a child of their own.

A child who would not be little Toby. Toby, who held his arms up to her when she came into the room and cried when she left. Toby, who tried to sing along when she warbled lullabies.

"Lilia?"

"I'm sorry. I was just . . ."

"Do you want Marina to have custody? Is that what you're thinking?"

He sounded insecure, as if that would make sense to him, even though he didn't want it to.

She wasn't ready to answer directly. "I don't know what I want for *myself,* Graham. But I want Toby to have the best life possible. He deserves that."

"I can't ask you to give up what *you* need because of what I did."

"I'm not giving up anything but time." She heard her own words and knew they were true. "Please, stop thinking he was just a bad decision, because if you think that, you might say it out loud someday. He's a wonderful little boy. That's it."

"Thank you."

"Marina's husband may not want children. Maybe that's why she gave him to us to raise."

"I don't plan to ask. You know what they say about sleeping dogs."

She thought of something her mother always said. *"Mai ho'oni I ka wai lana mâlie."*

"Which means?"

"If the water is still, don't make waves."

"I hope Toby sleeps well and wakes up in a better mood. You get some sleep, too. After dinner I'll see if they've given me a new room. The battery on my cell is low, but try it if you need me. Hopefully I'll have a room where I can charge it before long."

"Good night."

"Aloha au ia 'oe."

She had to smile. *I love you* was the only Hawaiian phrase Graham knew — and mispronounced — but it was enough.

"Me, too." She hung up and started downstairs when she realized that Toby was still awake and whining.

It *was* going to be a long night.

By midnight she knew that something was wrong with the baby other than a new tooth. He hadn't slept more than a few minutes at a time, and in the last hour he'd spiked a fever of 103. She'd used every trick she knew, bathing him in tepid water, cooling his room with a fan, giving him sips of cold water when he

202

was willing. When he began to pull on his ear, she realized what the problem was.

She called the pediatrician's emergency number and left her own for a call back, explaining who she was and what Toby's symptoms were. Then she walked the floor with the wailing baby until the telephone rang. She lay him in his crib and dove for it.

The nurse practitioner was brisk and efficient. Lilia explained the problem, but there was a deafening silence on the other end as she accessed his records on the computer.

"You're the baby's stepmother?" she asked at last.

Lilia assumed she was just reaffirming what his chart said. "Lilia Swallow." When the silence extended, she added, "I kept my last name, but I'm married to Graham Randolph, Toby's father."

"Is Mr. Randolph there? May I speak to him?"

"He's in Seattle. He won't be home until tomorrow."

"And you're not the baby's biological mother."

Lilia wondered what part of the word stepmother the woman didn't understand. "I'm married to Toby's father, and Toby lives with us and has since he was three months old. Do you think I ought to take him to the emergency room or urgent care? I'm assuming you don't want to prescribe antibiotics over the telephone? But I could have a friend pick them up if you're willing."

"Do you have a document authorizing you to make medical decisions?"

Toby was screaming now, and Lilia was anxious to get back to him. "I'm sorry?"

"I can't do a thing and neither can anyone else without proper authorization. He's not your son."

Anger shot through her. "Not my son? I take care of him. His biological mother abandoned him on my front porch!"

"We wouldn't prescribe over the phone anyway, but it sounds like he needs to be seen. And the minute you fill out the clinic paperwork, they'll refuse to treat him."

Lilia realized she was near tears, although whether from worry, frustration or exhaustion, she couldn't say. "What if I have his father call and authorize it?"

"I don't know details. Maybe if he faxes a form? You could ask."

She thanked the woman, got the address of the recommended urgent care clinic, and hung up.

Graham didn't answer his cell phone, which went immediately to voice mail. As Toby screamed in the background she left a message, and then called the hotel, explaining that she needed to speak to her husband.

The clerk was sorry, but nobody by that name was registered.

She explained that there'd been a problem with Graham's room, and the clerk, who disappeared for nearly ten minutes, came back and told her that yes, they had found him, but no one was answering. When she asked for the room number, the clerk wouldn't give it, but when she recited the number of the room with the leaking air conditioner, he said yes, that was the room they had listed.

She repeated *her* phone number twice until she was certain he had copied it correctly, then told him she needed to speak to the manager the minute he was available, because clearly the hotel had lost her husband.

Back in the nursery Toby would not be comforted. She was fairly certain the problem was an ear infection, but she wasn't willing to wait until Graham arrived home to get help for the baby. He needed to be seen now.

As late as it was, she knew she could call Regan. Her friend's years as a nanny had left her particularly well equipped to give advice. But when she tried to reach her, with Toby screaming in her arms, Regan didn't answer. Lilia considered and discarded the names of other friends. Some had children, which made them more likely to be helpful but less likely to be awake. Some had no children and probably wouldn't have any idea what to do.

Carrick answered on the second ring.

"What's wrong?"

"Are you out of town?"

"At home."

She said a silent prayer of thanks he wasn't backpacking in the wilderness. She knew she could count on him. There was little they couldn't talk about, and even silence on that was a mutual, if unspoken, agreement.

"Toby's sick. Graham's out of town, and the nurse practitioner I spoke to claims no one will treat him if I take him to a clinic because I'm not his real mother."

He didn't argue; he didn't sympathize. This was Carrick in full attorney mode. "Did she recommend a place to take him? Give me the number."

She did. Then she told him about her conversation with the hotel clerk. "When we spoke at dinnertime he was waiting for a new room. It's a big hotel and a big event. Somebody screwed up."

"Give me that number, too."

She did. "The manager is supposed to call me."

"Take care of Toby. I'll get back to you."

She hung up. Only then did it occur to her that maybe Graham hadn't been telling her the truth about the leaking air conditioner. That maybe he was sleeping with someone else tonight, even possibly Marina, while Lilia took care of his screaming son. Maybe her husband was a serial philanderer and pathological liar.

"No." She wasn't sure where that word had

sprung from, but she was sure she believed it. Maybe some part of her still didn't trust Graham, but the largest part of her believed he had been telling the truth tonight. And that was another corner turned.

Staring at the wall she realized that earlier, Graham had texted his room number. With Toby still wailing in her arms she went in search of her cell phone.

His second text had been sent an hour before. Room 6742. Sleep well. With a grateful heart she forwarded Graham's message to Carrick. Then she called her husband and was put straight through.

The exhausted baby was sleeping at last, but Lilia was too keyed up to join him. In the kitchen Carrick fixed her a cup of herbal tea. He'd made himself coffee, since it was three in the morning, and he still had to drive back to his condo in Professorville, a historic section of Palo Alto.

"You're beat." He leaned against the counter after he handed it to her, jean-clad legs stretched in front of him. "Your mother's brew?"

She took her first sip. The taste of mint, chamomile and kookoolau, a flowering plant from her mother's garden, were a welcome reminder of home. "She keeps me supplied. I don't think there's really anything magical about it, but I do save it for moments like this. She had to send it often when Graham was in the hospital."

"I miss your family. It's been a long time since I was in Kapa'a."

"You should visit them. You know they'd love to have you. I'm sure you haven't hiked every inch of the island, have you?" Carrick got along with her parents and brothers nearly as well as she did. He never held himself back, unlike Graham, who smiled and watched her family's interplay from the sidelines.

Of course the lawyer Carrick was a different matter.

She held her cup up in toast. "For such a friendly, down-to-earth guy, you can be scary when you haul out your credentials."

While he looked tired, his smile was as warm and genuine as always. "They teach us that in law school. Polite and terrifying. I'm a fast learner."

Carrick had arrived at her house, forty minutes after their phone call, with a Caregiver's Authorization Affidavit for her to fill out and sign, plus, as backup, a fax from Graham stating that Lilia had his full permission to make all medical decisions for Toby. He had also printed out Part 1.5 of Division 11 of the California Family Code, in case anyone at the urgent care clinic was misinformed about the law.

She had filled out the form, but she was

still infuriated she'd had to seek permission to arrange medical care for the baby *she* was raising.

The clinic had taken the papers, riffled through them and told them to have a seat. Minutes later Toby had been placed in an examination room, and after a careful check, the doctor had concurred that his eardrum was visibly inflamed, and all signs pointed to the type of ear infection that would respond to antibiotics. He'd given a prescription, recommended acetaminophen and anesthetic eardrops, and sent them home by way of a twenty-four-hour pharmacy.

She wasn't sure why Toby was sleeping now. Exhaustion, most likely, and the new dose of painkiller combined with the eardrops. The antibiotics wouldn't kick in right away, but at least she felt better knowing what the problem was. In the car on the way home she'd texted Graham, and she hoped he was sleeping soundly, too.

"I don't know what I would have done without you." She smiled sleepily at him. "I guess we'd have figured it out at the clinic. But driving him there, getting him in and out, trying to fill out the paperwork with a baby screaming in my arms?" She shook her head. "You're always there when I need you, Carrick."

"The affidavit's good for a year. Put it in a safe place, along with Graham's fax."

"And then next year I'll need another one. And the year after that." She set down her cup because her hand was trembling. She was suddenly more furious than weary. "Graham does his share, don't get me wrong, but I'm with Toby more than anybody else. He counts on me. And I have to get permission to authorize treatment? Because I'm not his mother? While Marina could scoop him up tomorrow and take him to a hospital or clinic and nobody would blink. Even if she hasn't seen him in months."

"That's the law. And when he gets old enough for school, without permission you won't be able to register him by yourself or authorize medical care at school, either."

"It just seems crazy. I guess I understand it, but in this circumstance? I'm the only mother that baby knows."

"Where's this coming from, Lilia? You're not one to complain because something's not fair. If things were fair, none of this would even be an issue. No cancer. No Toby."

As always, he had his finger on the problem, carefully applying pressure.

She didn't answer. Instead she watched him run a hand through his dark curls before he set his cup on the counter. "That should get me home," he said. "I'd better go."

"I love that baby." Tears sprang to her eyes. "I can't figure out how I can love him so much, considering everything. But when he was screaming tonight I felt like I was being torn in two."

"Yeah, I know."

"How do you know?"

"Because I know your heart."

They stared at each other until she looked away.

"Do you want to pursue adoption?" he asked at last.

"I don't know. Things with Graham are better. We've salvaged a lot of what we used to have. But this year has been hell. If I file for adoption, that's a huge commitment to our future as a family."

"It would be."

"I don't think I'm there yet."

"The easiest way to pursue it would be to wait a full year from the time Marina left Toby with you. Then abandonment would be easy to prove, and the adoption would be a formality, not a fight."

"She may be happy to let me adopt him anyway. Graham told me tonight that she's married."

"Maybe yes, maybe no, but if she comes back into his life because we show our cards too early, adoption will be harder. You need some time to figure out what you really want anyway. So my advice? Make this easy on yourself. And be sure you know what you're doing."

He straightened to leave, and she got to her

feet. "Thank you doesn't say enough."

"You know I would do anything for you."

She went into his arms and stood close as he hugged her. Then she stepped back. Like everything else about the night, moving away felt wrong.

"I'll let you know how things go," she said, not quite meeting his eyes.

"Good luck. And sleep well while you can."

He disappeared into the front of the house, and in a moment she heard the door open and close behind him.

As she followed his path to lock up, she knew that even if she finished her mother's tea, sleep would still elude her tonight.

15

Ellen wasn't particularly introspective. As her life had unfolded she'd spent little time thinking about the events that had made her the woman she was. Lately, though, she'd thought of little else.

She was the second of three daughters. Her father, Eugene Graham II, had been the president of a chain of banks, and her mother the descendant of railroad tycoons. She'd grown up in an Italianate mansion in San Francisco's Cow Hollow, on the edge of Pacific Heights near Union Street. The house was huge, but she and her sisters had taken up three of the seven bedrooms, and prestigious guests often occupied the others.

Since both parents were only children, and *their* parents died young, she'd known little extended family. Growing up she had noticed that people of her mother's class saw child-bearing as beneath them, an idea that firmly rooted before her youngest sister, Rosamund, was born. One morning Ellen heard her mother apologize to a roomful of other society ladies for her visible pregnancy, like a child who'd been caught reading comic books in church. Not one of her guests had tried to reassure her.

Now as she finished an early morning phone call with Rosamund, who was visiting New York, their past was an unvoiced obstacle between them. Twenty years ago Rosamund had moved permanently to Rome where she'd performed with several opera companies until she'd retired to teach. She rarely came to the US and never to the West Coast. Since at one time Rosamund had been the toast of the San Francisco Opera, Ellen thought this was just another of her sister's affectations.

Rosamund spoke in a slow, sultry voice tinged these days with an Italian accent. Inevitably, the conversation turned to their oldest sister. "Have you heard from Phyllis recently? I'd hoped to see her while we were in New York, but she seems to be missing." The *we* referred to Rosamund's Italian lover, Gian Carlo, who was as much a fixture in her sister's life as any husband.

Ellen allowed herself a small laugh. "I don't even get Christmas cards from Phyllis."

Phyllis, a controversial newspaper columnist, believed greeting cards were a contrivance of the capitalist system, as was every holiday. Ellen sent cards anyway, at least partly to annoy her. In return her sister sent books on politics and religion that she knew Ellen would find objectionable, sometimes highlighting the worst passages.

"Well, I thought she was here, but she's not," Rosamund said.

"The last I heard she and Kay were living in a yurt in Mongolia." Phyllis and Kay had been lovers for decades.

Both Ellen's sisters had chosen to live unconventional lives. Ellen was the filling in an exotic family sandwich, the American cheese between two slices of delectable artisan bread. Rosamund's musical talents had been apparent as a young child. Phyllis's razor-sharp intellect had surfaced early, as well. Ellen had always been the ordinary daughter, the B student, the honorable mention, the child who learned that to be pleasant, to serve at parties, to encourage conversation on any topic and listen as if she were really interested, was her one talent.

Yet it was Ellen who had snagged Douglas Randolph, a marriage that made her parents deliriously happy. And she was the only one who had produced a child — and now, a grandchild, albeit an illegitimate one.

Rosamund finished their duty call, and they both hung up. Her sister had remembered to ask about Graham's health, and Ellen had reported on his recovery, but she hadn't mentioned the baby. Rosamund wouldn't have lifted an eyebrow, but Ellen had been well-schooled by her husband, who believed the less said about Toby to anyone, even family, the better.

As if the thought conjured him, Douglas came into the room. "I hope she's finally ousted that sleazebag, Gian Carlo."

"Gian Carlo's a world-famous filmmaker, hardly a sleazebag."

"He's a sleazebag until he finally decides to marry her."

In Douglas's mind, all important decisions were made by men, even if he had to pretend otherwise in business transactions. In reality Rosamund was the one who thought marriage was too conventional.

Douglas checked his watch. "So we're agreed you'll meet me at Picán at seven. We'll be in the Bourbon Room, and of course, you won't be late. I'd like you beside me to greet our guests."

There was no "our." This was simply another of Douglas's many business dinners, and she would be expected to display her only talent, making people she didn't want to know comfortable.

And wasn't it odd that she'd never been able to do the same for her own son, or now, for her grandson? Toby was growing up without her, and Graham had certainly never been comfortable in their family.

She favored her husband with a thin smile.

"Of course I'll be on time. When am I anything but?"

"The rest of your day?"

She was never certain when he asked her to account for her time if he was playing the role of an ordinary husband or making more calculations. He didn't orchestrate her every move, but he did weave her activities into his own, and often her friends and their husbands became business allies. He could be charming when required, and while nobody had ever said they envied her marriage, she doubted that most people realized how manipulative he was.

She kept her answer simple. "I thought I would do some shopping, then meet friends for lunch."

"Generally after you speak to one of your sisters, you get all starry-eyed about family."

"We're really quite alone in the world, Douglas. In case you never noticed."

He must have recognized her slight frown, because his eyes narrowed. "I hope you aren't planning to visit Graham and that child of his now that Rosamund has you all stirred up. He'll disappoint you every bit as much as your sisters have."

"It's kind of you to be worried." She allowed no trace of sarcasm to color her voice. Douglas had seen the bill for the nursery furniture, and his opinion of that extravagance had been crystal clear.

"But you're going to see him anyway, aren't you?" he demanded.

She hadn't intended to. Maybe after Douglas had left for the day it would have occurred to her, but now she mentally jettisoned the planned shopping trip in favor of one to San Jose. Almost six months had elapsed since she'd seen her grandson. That day Graham hadn't wanted her in his home, and seeing the baby hadn't been enough of an inducement to weather his scorn a second time. But Douglas was correct. Her conversation with her sister had brought home, once again, how few real connections she had in the world. And one of the few was growing up without her.

"I don't know." She met and held Douglas's gaze. "But if I do see him, you don't have to know or hear about it."

He was clearly annoyed, but he knew better than to forbid her. Everything she did for him she did willingly, and the day that changed, their house of cards would collapse. She wasn't under Douglas's thumb, and he didn't abuse her, but they might as well have signed a contract. She trusted him to make the right decisions about his growing empire, and he trusted her to stay at his side and lend the Graham name to social interactions. They were perfectly suited, and they should have raised a son who would fit neatly into the puzzle of their lives.

Instead they had raised one who had so badly humiliated his father there would likely be no reconciliation, unless Douglas had a religious conversion or a lobotomy.

After he left, and she showered and dressed for the day, she thought about the events that had brought them to this place. They had never been a close family, but the rift had begun once their son became an adult.

Despite strife during Graham's adolescence, Douglas had been pleased with his son's decision to pursue an undergraduate degree in architecture, a possible asset for the family business. He hadn't agreed with Graham's rekindled romance and later his marriage to Lilia Swallow, but even Douglas knew some battles weren't worth fighting.

Out of college Graham had entertained several job offers, but in the end he had agreed to work for the Randolph Group, moving among four different units to gain an overview and experience. While he never said as much, Graham probably realized that whatever he chose to do afterwards, his days at Randolph Group would be invaluable.

Looking back now she could see those had been their best years as a family. Douglas wasn't fond of praising their son, but even he didn't find much to criticize in Graham's performance, not until Graham made his final move.

The Randolph Group had many wings, and

one of them bought and developed land for the use of innovative projects. Douglas knew that if he had any prayer of keeping Graham there, this was the unit that most closely matched his son's interests.

Several months into his new position Graham stumbled upon a scam. Two Randolph Group officers, in charge of a multitude of tenants-in-common security offerings held by investors all over the country, were slyly withholding payments. The men deposited the money in cleverly designed special operations accounts and covered their tracks with misleading and falsified financial reports.

Graham wanted to go to his father directly, but he needed proof and legal advice, so Carrick had helped him with both.

In a classic case of blaming the messenger, when presented with all the evidence, Douglas had been furious at everybody, but most of all at Graham for discovering what he had not. After a weekend of putting out fires he had called their son into his office and told him the problem had been taken care of. There would be absolutely no publicity. Graham was not to leak a word, and he was to warn Carrick not to say anything, either. The perpetrators had agreed to pay back what they'd stolen, and in return Douglas had agreed to let them quietly resign.

Graham had disagreed. The men were guilty of fraud to the tune of millions of dollars. If they walked away and started their own investment company, who was to say they wouldn't steal more? And who would guarantee that those who had lost so much would be adequately repaid? Of course when Graham expressed his doubts, Douglas repeated that everything would be taken care of. If Graham breathed a word to the authorities, he would fire him.

Ellen had envisioned what might happen. In secret she had gone to her son and pleaded with him to back away. But in the end Graham hadn't trusted his father or his colleagues to bring justice to the investors. He took all his documentation to the proper authorities who launched an investigation that went to the top of state government and later to the FBI.

The repercussions had been extraordinary. In the world in which they operated, the fact that nobody at Randolph Group had seen or reported the scam for so long was a black mark that could never entirely be erased.

Ellen wasn't certain where Graham had gotten the backbone to stand up to Douglas, or the conviction that doing the right thing was worth living with the consequences. And there had been consequences. No matter how much praise he received in public for exposing the scandal, in private no company of consequence wanted to hire a whistle-blower.

Of course Graham hadn't seemed to notice

or care since, by then, he'd started his own design-build firm. But the fallout for their family? That had been devastating.

By the time she navigated the streets of Willow Glen and parked in front of Graham's house, the sun was high overhead. Once again she hadn't called, which might have been foolish, but she hadn't wanted to hear she wasn't welcome. She knew Lilia was living with her son again because she forced herself to read her daughter-in-law's blog. But she hadn't been able to read between the lines or decide how she felt about a reconciliation. Without Lilia in residence, maybe Graham would have needed his mother, just a little.

Lilia answered the door, and Ellen tried not to show her disappointment. The baby was nowhere in sight.

"Ellen." Lilia nodded, but she didn't smile.

"I could say I was in the neighborhood, but you'd know it was a lie."

"Come in." Lilia stepped back and Ellen entered.

The house looked better, much better, than it had on her last visit. Surfaces weren't littered; no dirty dishes were in evidence. Six months had passed. Her grandson was nine months old now.

And somewhere in the house, clearly unhappy.

"Toby sounds upset."

"He's fussing. We visited the pediatrician

this morning, and he got a shot."

"Is he okay?"

"You can see for yourself." Lilia started back through the house, and Ellen followed. They ended up in the sunroom where she had fed Toby his bottle on her first and only visit. He was sitting in a bouncy chair, wailing intermittently.

Again she was struck by his resemblance to her son, and she wondered about the baby's mother. Possibly Graham's affair had been with someone as blond and fair as he was.

She nodded to the bouncy chair. "He's safe in that?"

"Perfectly for the minute it took me to answer the door. Of course he'd rather be walking."

Ellen was afraid to approach her grandson without Lilia's permission, and that annoyed her. "He's walking?"

"He's trying hard. It won't be long."

Toby was examining Ellen now. He didn't seem to like what he saw. Suddenly he began to cry in earnest and hold out his arms to Lilia. She picked him up, settling the baby on one hip.

"I'm sorry, but he reacts to strangers these days. It's normal, and he'll get over it."

The word *stranger* stung. Ellen retaliated. "Of course he reacts if you never let anybody else hold him."

Lilia seemed to consider her words. "He's

comfortable with several people who hold him, Ellen. But he doesn't know *you,* and he's not feeling great at the moment."

She felt the rebuke. "If I'm a stranger it's because I wasn't particularly welcome on my last visit."

"I'm sorry you felt that was true." Lilia motioned to a chair and sat on the sofa with the baby.

"It *was* true. It was during the time you left my son alone with Toby."

Lilia stared at her, as if she couldn't believe what Ellen had said. After a long moment she shook her head, dark hair swishing over her shoulders. "He's not alone with him now."

Nothing was going as Ellen had hoped, but then she wasn't sure exactly what she *had* wanted. That Graham and Lilia would welcome her presence? That they would view her as a fountain of wisdom when it came to caring for Toby?

She swallowed her annoyance. "How's he doing?"

"Toby or Graham?"

"Toby. Graham can speak for himself. He's not here?"

"He's at a job site for the afternoon. Our helper will be here in a little while to take Toby while I work."

"I'm sorry I missed him."

Lilia looked skeptical, but she nodded. "Toby's doing well. He's in the normal range for height and weight. Except for an occasional ear infection, he's healthy. He's developing quickly in every way. He recognizes words, loves to be read to —" She shrugged as if that finished the report.

"You seem to be getting along with him."

"I am."

"I'm sure it's not easy, considering everything."

"Yes, considering."

"He looks so much like his father."

"We don't have Graham's baby pictures, so I'll have to take your word for it."

Ellen was contrite. "I'll send copies to you. I'm sorry. Of course Graham should have them."

Lilia softened a little. "That would be nice. It would be fun to compare."

Ellen was trying to remember Graham at nine months. She wondered how often she had seen him at that point in his development. She and Douglas had flown around the world frequently after their son's birth and missed major milestones. They had been in Bali when Graham took his first steps. She'd only seen the video.

Sadly most of the time she hadn't been sorry to leave. Usually by the time she returned, he'd seemed a more amiable creature.

"I don't think I was a baby person," she said out loud, without thinking first.

225

Lilia softened still more. "Not everybody is. What was your favorite age?"

Ellen couldn't remember. "When he could talk and behave. When he listened and didn't whine."

"There is a lot of whining that comes with the territory."

"I'm glad to say our nannies nipped that in the bud. They started early." She wasn't certain, but Lilia seemed to grasp Toby tighter at her words.

"Babies can tell us so little," Lilia said. "Whining's part of it. Especially when they're feeling bad."

"If you pick him up every time he wants you to, you'll end up holding him for the rest of your life."

Lilia tried to laugh that off. "Have you ever seen an adult carried around in his mother's arms?"

"No, but I've seen adults who can't handle any problem life throws at them without somebody else's help."

Lilia wasn't laughing now. "I think that's usually because nobody helped them when they needed it as children."

"I've come a long way, Lilia. I would like to hold my grandson. Would you mind?"

Lilia debated; Ellen could see it. To hasten her daughter-in-law's decision, she got up and held out her arms, knowing that Lilia would not deny such an obvious cue.

The young woman stood and positioned Toby so Ellen could take him. The baby began to scream.

"I'm sorry, but this really isn't a good time." Lilia stepped back.

"He'll be fine. He'll settle right down." Ellen reached for him and pulled him close.

Toby screamed louder. He began to kick. Ellen took him to her chair and tried to settle him on her lap, but he would have none of it.

As she attempted to calm him and things grew worse, she finally remembered Graham at nine months. She'd come home from an out-of-town trip of several weeks and gone into the nursery to see her son. He had reacted just this way.

She had been devastated then, and she was devastated now. To make matters worse Lilia was watching this failure, and success wasn't going to be an option. Apologies were in order. She knew a quick admission that she'd been wrong would go a long way toward making things right.

But she just couldn't say the words.

Lilia got up and lifted Toby out of her arms without asking. Then she began to walk back and forth. "I'm sorry, Ellen," she said when Toby began to quiet. "You came a long way, but it's just not a good day. He'll feel better tomorrow. At least by then the shot will have worn off. Could you come back?"

Ellen saw Lilia was trying. The young

woman was attempting to tolerate her mother-in-law's unwanted presence and, yes, her rude behavior. But Ellen just felt angrier. She didn't want to be tolerated. She wanted to be respected, to be wanted, to be all the things she'd given up without a fight when Douglas evicted Graham from their lives.

She got to her feet and gathered what she could of her dignity. "I think you're making a mistake with him. Babies have to be told what to feel and how to act. You're letting Toby make all the decisions."

Lilia took a deep breath. "Babies need love and a gentle hand. It's the way I was raised. I think my brothers and I turned out well."

"Did you? My standards are a little different, I suppose. This isn't Hawaii, and you're not Toby's real mother."

Lilia stopped walking, faced Ellen and then, as if she just couldn't control herself another moment, exploded. "Tell me about real mothers, then, Ellen. Does a real mother visit her dying son when he's in the hospital? Does she stand up to her husband when he fires his son for telling the truth? Does she help out by babysitting or bringing food when things are in turmoil or even by just telling her son she loves him when he needs her the most? Is that what a real mother does? Because, by God, I don't ever want to be Toby's *real* mother if that's *not* the way things are supposed to go!"

Ellen gathered whatever dignity remained around her, which was very little. "Quite obviously that won't be a question you'll have to worry about. He's not your son and he never will be. He's Graham's."

"I would like you to leave."

"I'll let myself out." Ellen walked through the house and closed the front door quietly behind her.

In the car she sat for a moment collecting herself and staring at nothing. Who was the woman who had just destroyed what little chance she had for a relationship with her grandson? Which woman in that house had proven how little she understood or cared about anybody else's feelings?

Sadly, *Lilia* wasn't the answer to either question.

16

THE SWALLOW'S NEST

FEATHERING YOUR NEST WITH IMAGINATION AND LOVE

September 7th:

Families come in different sizes, shapes and colors. Same sex parents welcome children into their homes. Parents with little money, and those with a lot, wait excitedly for new arrivals. Foster and adoptive parents welcome children who others couldn't love. Parents who lost children find their way back to them for another chance.

In historical Hawaii, adoption, or "hanai," was both informal and encouraged. Sometimes children were presented to a relative to raise as a sign of love and respect. Today families still help each other by sharing resources or fostering each other's children. When I was young, cousins often came to stay with us while their parents sorted out events in their lives. One of my brothers spent as much of his adolescence with our maternal grandparents as he did with us.

No child is ours. No child belongs to us. Children belong to themselves. But there are so many ways to make a family, to be together in love. I am learning one of them.

Aloha, Lilia

Graham was late, but while Lilia was out taking Toby for a stroll, he left an apology on their house phone and told her he hoped to have good news when he saw her. Well warned she managed not to wonder where he *really* was until he walked in at seven o'clock holding a bottle of white wine in one hand and a shopping bag from Milk Pail Market in nearby Mountain View in the other.

"I'm sorry I'm so late. Will Danish fontina and a little Saint Agur Bleu get me off the hook?"

Her husband's job schedule was erratic and always had been. For years Graham had come home at odd hours, and she'd never thought the worst. Someday that might be the case again, but at least trust was becoming a little easier every day.

She sent him a smile to let him know she was okay. "Great cheese is a good start. And here's a little boy who's all ready for bed and would love his last bottle in his daddy's arms."

Graham set down his purchases and grabbed his son, kissing him loudly on both cheeks. Toby laughed with delight, and Graham danced him around the room to prolong it.

"Just so you know," he said, as he and Toby

231

whirled by when Lilia returned from the kitchen with Toby's bottle in her hand, "I got that project I bid on, the small cottage complex? That's where I've been. Finalizing plans. Four houses to start, Lilia, and they want *you* to design the interiors."

For a moment she felt as if she'd sprung back to an earlier time, when success had been as common as failure, and she and Graham had worked at each other's sides to create a life.

She slipped into his arms, and the three of them danced together. She finally stepped away and handed him the bottle. "That's awesome, but Toby's had a tough day, and he's finally tired enough to get some sleep. Feed him in the nursery and I'll get things ready in the kitchen. I made a salad and I can warm up last night's chicken. We'll have a party to celebrate. Just us."

"It's beautiful outside. Let's sit on the patio with the wine and cheese first. There's some garlic herb bread in the bag, too."

In the kitchen she loaded the dishwasher. Then as Graham settled and fed Toby upstairs she took her time plating the cheese and opening the wine as she hummed *Manoa I Ke Ko'i'ula,* a favorite of hers, and one that Kai's band liked to perform. As a child she'd taken hula lessons before she moved on to activities she'd liked better. She put down the knife she was using to slice the bread and did a few swirls of her hips, lifting her arms over her head.

"Wow, what did I do to deserve that?"

She turned and saw naked desire on Graham's face. She swirled her hand palm up until it was at her mouth where she blew him a kiss. "I liked to surf better than I liked hula. But I did learn a few things."

"You learned more than a few. You're so beautiful when you dance."

They slept in the same bed now. They even made love. But the last time she'd felt real desire for her husband was before he became so terribly ill. Then just as she'd believed their life and their lovemaking might return to normal, she'd learned about Toby.

For the first time in what seemed like forever, she wanted him. She really wanted him. That was their past, and tonight was their future.

She glided barefoot to him and slipped her arms around his neck. "I like hearing I'm beautiful."

"Every moment of every day."

"I can *show* you just how beautiful after dinner."

"I'll eat fast."

She gave a low laugh and pointed to the patio. "Maybe cheese and wine will be plenty."

"I feel full already."

She kissed him slowly. Then she broke away

and went back to the counter and picked up the bread knife. "I didn't really get a chance to tell you how happy I am about the new contract."

"I knew you'd be thrilled. And we can work together again. It's perfect."

"Toby's asleep already?"

He held up the half-finished bottle. "It must have been a tough day."

"Hepatitis B shot. They last for a while. Next time he needs a shot you take him to the pediatrician."

"Thank you for doing it."

Sobering, she wondered if he would thank her for the part of her day that had included his mother.

Graham exchanged the baby bottle for the wine. "Let me pour." She gathered napkins and small plates as he did, and followed him outside, balancing everything on a bamboo tray which she set on one of the surf board tables.

They settled on an old metal glider she had repainted a deep turquoise. The cushions were brightly flowered, and they fluffed pillows and moved close together, lifting their glasses in toast.

"To better times ahead." Graham clinked his against hers.

"Tell me about your day. Then I'll tell you about mine."

He examined her, then he shook his head.

"I think we need to hear yours first. Mine for dessert. All good news."

"You can tell mine wasn't quite as promising, huh?"

"Afraid so. Other than Toby's shot, what happened?"

Walking in tonight he had looked so much younger, so much healthier, and obviously so much happier. Now he looked worried, as he had so often in the past year.

She set down her glass and cradled his cheek. "It's not about you, okay? It's something I did today." She reconsidered. "Well, I guess that's not true. Actually it was about you. And me. And Toby."

"Our family."

Her smile was sad. "Not according to your mother."

"My mother? Phone? Here?"

The smile disappeared entirely. "Here. And I'm afraid I finally told her what I think about her parenting skills."

He gave a long, slow whistle. "What brought that on?" Before she could answer he held up his hand. "Stupid question. I'm sorry. Here's a better one. How long have you wanted to unload on her?"

"Let me count the days. Or let's not bother. I've never liked her, and she's never liked me."

"But you've been polite, and you've tried."

"I guess we both did. Until today when she

235

told me that California is not Hawaii, where my family's parenting standards are as low as the belly of a snake, and I am not Toby's real mother anyway. Therefore I can't possibly know as much about how to raise him as she does by the sheer accident of her birth. Despite the fact that she couldn't be bothered to raise *you* or support you when you most needed her."

Graham was silent so long she was afraid she had alienated *him,* as well. But finally he shook his head.

"Thank you for standing up for me. But mostly for getting that out in the open, so we don't have to pretend."

"I shouldn't have said anything."

"In her own way I think she's jealous, Lilia. You're everything she isn't. Maybe you're everything she thought she would be, and instead she just . . ." He turned his palms up helplessly. "She just gave up and gave her life over to my father."

"She told me I had to teach Toby what to feel and how to act, that I was letting him make all the decisions. All that because he didn't want her to hold him. It's her fault she's a stranger, but I tried anyway, and he screamed his little lungs out. She blamed that on the way I'm raising him. Because, as she said, I'm not on his birth certificate. So he's not mine."

"Nobody loves him better."

She sat back, tears threatening to spill down her cheeks. "You can tell, huh?"

He moved closer and slipped his arm around her. "Yeah, I can tell."

"I want my name on the birth certificate, Graham."

"I wish —"

She silenced him with a finger against his lips. "No, we *can* make it happen. I can adopt him. And then legally I will be his real mother. My name *will* be on the birth certificate, and the original will be sealed. Toby will always know I adopted him, we can't lie to him. But he'll also know how much I loved him, and how much I wanted him to belong to me that way."

He pulled her even closer. "You've considered this for a while?"

"Carrick and I talked about it last month, when you were in Seattle."

"The night you couldn't get medical care without a fuss? When I didn't even give the legalities a second thought?"

"He told me to think it over, to be sure."

"He would have."

Graham felt warm and solid against her, his arm a comforting weight. "I have thought it over," she said. "And when Ellen hit me with the real mother remark, I realized I only need one court document to make what's already happened to all of us legal. Because in every other way, Toby's my son as well as yours. Now I want to make sure there aren't any problems in the future." She spaced her next words for emphasis. "Because we are a family."

"If we're a family, I come with the deal. You've thought about that, too?"

She turned so their eyes met. "Constantly. Since the moment Marina placed him in my arms."

"There's nothing I want more."

"You've never mentioned adoption."

"Haven't I already asked too much? How could I ask you to adopt him when every day together is a challenge after . . . well, everything."

"Yeah, you have asked too much. I'm not a pushover, but I'll take it on. I'll take *you* on, too. It's time to put what happened behind us. No more talk about mistakes or apologies. We need to pull together and be the family Toby needs. And maybe, someday, we can create a brother or sister for him. When you're well. When we're on our feet again. When Toby is legally my son."

He cupped her face in his hands. "I love you, Lilia. I never stopped. I never will."

She kissed him and threaded her fingers through his hair, something she had once worried she might never be able to do again. "I think we ought to take the cheese and wine upstairs. To our bedroom."

"The perfect place."

"To eat later."

"Definitely later."

"Unless Toby wakes up."

"Quick. I'll beat you up there."

She laughed, turned and leapt to her feet, grabbing the cheese tray off the table. "We'll just see who beats who."

■ ■ ■ ■

PART III

■ ■ ■ ■

Scientists aren't certain what differentiates a parasitic swallow from the host who hatches her eggs and raises her young. Is laying an egg in another bird's nest the result of a difference in genes? Is the behavior of the parasite related to the environment in which she finds herself?

Also unclear is whether parasitic behavior can actually improve the health of the colony or doom it to a slow decline.

"Our Songbirds, Ourselves:
A Tale of Two Species,"
from the editors of *Ornithology Today.*

17
THE SWALLOW'S NEST

FEATHERING YOUR NEST WITH IMAGINATION AND LOVE

December 3rd:

One year ago, a beautiful little boy was born. Through the months our special gift has blossomed. While he has another given name, here at The Swallow's Nest he is Keiki, which in Hawaiian means child. Keiki is walking now, and I thank all of you who have emailed to caution me about the dangers in his path. In fact last week I did a special post with your suggestions.

Since Keiki is especially happy when he's going places he shouldn't, Graham built a custom baby gate from Plexiglas for the top of our stairs. You'll find a link to those instructions at the bottom of this post, in case you're feeling handy yourself.

And for my contribution? Well, Plexiglas is boring. I decided to paint a beach scene with palm trees and dolphins leaping through waves to turn the gate into a work of art. Here's a pattern you can use on your own, or perhaps as a mural on a child's wall. Just expand it at your local copy store to the size you need, and let your inner beach bunny play.

For now, I'm off to finish frosting cupcakes for Keiki's party this afternoon. Since he's recently developed a passion for puppies, we're having a puppy party. Just the stuffed kind for now, although a real one will probably be part of his future if his father has his way.

Next week I'll post recipes, decorations and snapshots from today's big event. In the meantime . . .

Aloha! Lilia

Toby's first birthday party was going to be a small affair. Lilia had instinctively known small was the way to go. Over the years she had made lasting friendships with other home and lifestyle bloggers worldwide, and research on their sites had proved she was correct. No child needed to be frightened by a crowd on his first birthday.

She ran down the guest list for Regan, who was helping spread the last bit of white frosting on two dozen cupcakes.

"We're having you and Carrick. Dolores, his babysitter. Sally, a mom down the street with her little girl, Fleur, who's Toby's age. Then Mike and his family." Graham's foreman had two children older than Toby and the little boy worshiped them.

With the frosting finished Lilia brought out

two pastry bags and tips, and, of course, her camera. She and Regan divided the cupcakes, and Lilia snapped a photo of her friend's face as she explained that Regan was required to pipe paw prints on her dozen. Then she handed her a sketch to follow.

Regan tried to hand it back. "I was studying calculus while you were mastering Art 101. I save corporations gazillions with tax shelters. Specialization is a good thing."

"So is broadening your horizons." Lilia was already settling in to do puppy faces. Oreo cookies sliced in half would stand in for ears, and she planned to add silly little eyes and smiles complete with lolling pink tongues.

Regan picked up her pastry bag and wrinkled her nose. "I'm glad there's a sketch so you can see how far off I'll be."

Lilia couldn't resist another quick shot of her friend's expression. "It doesn't have to be perfect."

"If it did, you wouldn't have chosen me." Regan squirted an unsteady practice line on the parchment paper where the cupcakes rested.

The telephone rang, and Lilia left Regan to practice alone. She told the caller she wasn't interested in a new lawn service and hung up, but before she turned away she saw the phone was blinking. She pressed the code to play back whatever messages were waiting and listened to someone from the office of

Graham's oncologist chide her husband for canceling his last two appointments.

She'd known about one cancellation, but not the other. She jotted down the woman's name and extension before she hung up. Graham was busy, yes, but definitely not *too* busy to follow up with doctors' appointments and CT scans.

Back in the kitchen Regan looked up from blobs of practice icing.

"Graham's canceling doctors' appointments," Lilia said.

"That can't be good."

Lilia knew how little her husband wanted to think of himself as a patient these days. "I'll talk to him. He needs to get the next official all clear, even if he's feeling better every day. He'll see reason."

"You left somebody off the guest list."

With effort Lilia traveled back to the earlier part of their conversation. "Who?"

"Ellen."

Lilia halved a cookie before she answered. "Between us?"

"The guys aren't listening."

Carrick, Graham and the birthday boy were outside on the patio setting up a game of puppy toss. Bean bag puppies were already in place to be tossed, then taken home as souvenirs. Toby was dropping anything he could lift off the ground into the "dog house," and Graham and Carrick were patiently removing sticks and leaves whenever the baby's back was turned. Although the temperature was only in the mid-sixties, Graham had stripped off his sweater, and as she watched he wiped his brow, as if after colder days last month, so much sun was affecting him.

"I invited her." Lilia met her friend's eyes. "Because I can't believe she doesn't want to be here."

"But apparently she doesn't, because you didn't mention her. Does Graham know you asked her?"

Lilia's long braid flopped against her shoulder as she shook her head. "Let's not tell him, either. Okay? When I brought it up a few weeks ago he said not to, that I had no reason to grovel, and if she wanted to celebrate with us, she can call and apologize first."

Regan gave a soft whistle. "He's that angry?"

"I don't know if he's angry — after all, he's had a lifetime of being treated like a second-class citizen by his parents. He was probably just trying to protect me. But it's a much bigger deal for him than for me. She's not my mother." She didn't add "thank God," because there was no need.

"What did Ellen say?"

Lilia could recall the conversation in gruesome detail. The long pauses fraught with dislike, the tone that said Ellen really felt she was too busy, or too important, to have to deal with her substandard daughter-in-law. Regan had heard plenty of Ellen stories to feed her active imagination.

Instead she gave as factual a report as she could manage. "She was stunned. She was so off guard she actually asked how I was before she realized it really *was* me calling. Then, when she recovered her balance, she asked if Graham had told me to try to clear the air."

Regan snorted. "And you said?"

"I told her Graham never tells me what to do, but I decided to call because, for his sake, I wanted the two of us to get along. Then I invited her to Toby's birthday party."

Regan took a moment to digest this. "Well, apparently she said no?"

"She asked if Graham had insisted I invite her, like I hadn't just told her I'd decided to call on my own."

"Wow, she doesn't really get this, does she?"

"I said Graham would be happy to have her at the party, that he knows she belongs in Toby's life."

"And?"

"She asked if Graham even knew I was inviting her. So I gave up and said no, he didn't."

"And then she said she wouldn't come."

"You got it." Lilia continued slicing cookie ears. "All this resentment, Regan. Why do people do that to each other? We fight in my family. But the air's cleared pretty fast, and we're crying on each other's shoulders and at the end laughing at how crazy it all was. But not the Randolphs. It's like they keep score of everything that's ever said to them, every social faux pas, every perceived slight, every way somebody doesn't measure up to their high standards. I'm not sure what prize is reserved for the winner, but I sure don't want it."

"Did you actually think she would come?"

"I hoped. The best thing I can say about Ellen? I don't think she's hateful to the core like Douglas. When she forgets to be the person she thinks she has to be, I see a softer side, a sense of humor, even insight." She remembered all the many slights she had endured through the years, before she shook her head. "I guess I'm delusional."

"Or a martyr."

"Wow!" Lilia looked down and saw that the Oreo ear she'd planned to place on her first cupcake was suddenly nothing but a handful of crumbs. She dusted her hands. "Did you really say that?"

"You're too good to be true. Look at everything you've taken on. Toby and now his grandmother."

"I didn't take on Toby. Toby is the light of my life."

"I know, I didn't —"

"I'm just trying to be a good mother, that's

all. Won't he be happier if he has more people who love him? My mother's a million miles away, but Graham's is right here. Yeah, she's a pain in the ass. I've never been wealthy or white enough to suit her. But she's still Toby's grandmother. And family means everything."

"Not when they're toxic."

Lilia was glad they could both speak frankly. "Well, I tried to bridge the toxicity gap, but even if I'm a *martyr*, I'm not a masochist. The rest is up to Ellen and Graham. But I guess she did me a big favor. She pointed out that I'm not Toby's real mother, and she helped me realize I want to be."

At that moment Carrick stepped inside with Toby on one hip. The little boy was always delighted to be with his "Uncle Carrick" and looked thoroughly at home, his head resting against Carrick's chest.

"Wet baby coming through," Carrick said.

Regan sprang to her feet. "You take over here. You're more artistic than I am. I'll change the goober."

Carrick looked like he'd gotten the raw end of that deal, but obediently passed Toby to Regan and watched them disappear into the hallway. "I really have to do this?"

"Absolutely. Ever use a pastry bag?" Lilia held hers up. "There will be photos, just so you know. Behave and wash your hands."

Once he had he settled across from her, and picked up the bag.

"Try a line." She demonstrated once more. His was perfect. "Good job. Now do this on that." She pointed to the sketch, then a cupcake.

They worked in silence until he'd gotten the hang of it. Regan hadn't lied about who was the more artistic one. Carrick's paw prints were, at the very least, recognizable.

"You and Regan were talking about the adoption," he said after he was on his way. "I overheard part of it."

"It's been nine months since Marina left him here."

"I'm keeping track."

"I still wonder if we ought to move ahead now. If she hasn't contacted us or tried to see him all this time, surely she doesn't want him. With her okay we could get this finished."

They'd had this conversation before, but Carrick seemed to know she had to hear facts again. "Waiting is hard, but losing the chance to adopt Toby would be harder. If she doesn't materialize in the next three months, the whole thing is almost a slam dunk. But if you approach her, and she refuses to give up her rights and then asks to see Toby? It's going to be a much bigger battle, with no assurances you'll win."

Lilia rolled her eyes. "Yeah, yeah. Or she might agree to give him up, but only if we pay her off. And how would we do that?"

"How would you?"

"We couldn't. We have a stack of bills a foot high."

"Graham's back at work and you're working more."

"But chemo year he didn't work much, and he's still not able to do a full week, although he tries harder than he should. And with Toby, even if I work around the clock I'm still getting less done. There were a million little things our insurance didn't cover. There's no money to pay Marina."

"I wish you'd let me help."

She looked up and their eyes met. For a moment neither of them looked away. "You know I can't let you," she said. "And you know how much your offer means."

"I love you both."

"Yes." She sighed. "I know that, too."

"Just remember I'm here."

"When have I ever forgotten?"

His expression was answer enough. They went back to their cupcakes and finished in silence.

Regan returned with a dry baby, and by the time Lilia lined up the cupcakes and the puppy bean bags for one final photography session, guests began to arrive.

Half an hour later she was chatting with Mike and his wife when the doorbell played a chorus of "Happy Birthday." As suddenly as if that terrible day was right in front of her again, she remembered Graham's remission

252

party and the life-altering surprise waiting on her doorstep.

"Someone's at the door," Graham told her. "I've got my hands full, will you get it?"

He didn't look particularly busy to her, and Lilia wondered why he thought greeting guests was her job. Clearly he wasn't thinking about that other party, that other trip to the front door and the way their world had changed forever.

Toby was clinging to her legs, babbling happily to entertain Mike's children, and she picked him up and slung him into her arms. Then she realized what a bad idea carrying him with her might be. This was Toby's first birthday, a very special day for everyone who loved him, and even, possibly for the woman who had given birth to him.

God help them all. Marina might be on her doorstep again.

"Happy Birthday" rang loudly once more. Graham cocked his head in question. She deposited Toby in his arms and started through the house. "Keep him here, Graham."

All the way to the door she wondered what she would say or do if the visitor *was* Toby's mother. Close the door and lock it? Tell her if she wanted to see Toby she'd have to take them to court? Call the police?

And what would *they* say? What legal right did she really have to keep Toby away from his birth mother?

She cleared her throat and took a deep breath. Finally she opened the door.

Her parents and youngest brother, Jordan, shouted "Surprise!"

Lilia launched herself into her mother's arms.

"They adore Toby. My mother could hardly make herself let go of him." As she brushed out her hair Lilia thought about the way the baby had greeted her mother compared to the way he'd reacted to Ellen. Of course the day Ellen had visited he'd been cranky because of a shot, but she wondered if Toby had also picked up on his grandmother's tension. Her mother, on the other hand, had so much experience with babies she was completely relaxed. He'd cuddled up to her right from the start.

Graham was lying in bed watching her. "He saw how happy you were, so he knew he could be happy, too. She was teaching him to call her *Tutu* before I had to put him in his crib for the night."

Lilia smiled at her own reflection. All the Swallow grandchildren called Nalani *Tutu,* and in her family's eyes, Toby had joined the cherished band. "How long have you known they were coming?"

"Two weeks. And it's been hard to keep the secret."

"Jordan didn't seem surprised when Regan offered to let him camp at her place while they're here. He's not much of an actor."

"You didn't know there was something going on there?"

"Well, she told me she went down to San Diego to watch him compete in the Hurley Pro, but I figured if it was anything important, she'd mention it to me. And she didn't."

"He's your brother. That automatically sets limits on what she'll share."

Lilia couldn't blame Regan for her interest. Jordan was, even to his sister's jaded eye, gorgeous. And all the surfer groupies in their skimpy bikinis who gathered around him at events thought so, too.

This was the first time she and Graham had been alone since her parents had arrived. The elder Swallows were now comfortably installed in the small room off the kitchen that Graham had insisted on fixing up as a guest room. Now she understood why her husband had been so determined to finish everything last week.

She remembered the phone message. "Listen, there was a call from Dr. Grossman's office. They're concerned you've canceled two appointments. What's up with that?" She swiveled to look at him when he didn't answer. "Graham?"

"Things came up, and I . . ." He shook his head. "I guess I wanted to just forget about being sick for a while. I didn't intend to cancel for good. I'll call tomorrow and reschedule. I'm supposed to have some tests this month, too. Might as well do it all at once."

Relieved, she brought up the second thing they needed to discuss. "You're probably wondering how *your* mother knew today was Toby's birthday."

About halfway through the party a delivery van had pulled up to their house. But the driver and his assistant hadn't simply dropped off a package. They'd carried in five boxes and asked where the items inside were supposed to be set up. Then, while Lilia watched, they'd unpacked a Toby-sized table and chairs and carried each item up to the nursery, explaining, when she resisted, that the gift came with white glove service.

This evening she'd finally gotten a good look at Ellen's present. The navy blue table was hand painted with an ancient map of oceans, and each of the spindle backed chairs was carefully outlined in gold leaf. As an interior decorator she had a good idea what the set cost, and she never would have bought or recommended anything that valuable for a child's room. Finger paints. Play dough. Ordinary crayons and markers. Cars and trucks screeching from end to end. Nothing fun was compatible with the beautifully crafted table. Toby could stand to one side and admire it. Exactly what a little boy would never do.

"I didn't wonder," Graham said. "I guess you called her, after all."

"She wouldn't come because I was the one to issue the invitation."

"Stop trying, Lilia. You can't make her love you."

"I don't care if she loves *me*."

"Then don't worry. I stopped trying a long time ago. Or stopped expecting her to show she loved me, if she happens to. I'm just grateful I didn't turn out to be like her or, worse, like him. Even after they tried all those years to make me chips off the old block."

"Toby's always going to wonder why his grandparents aren't around. Couple that with figuring out somebody else gave birth to him, and what do we get? A confused, hurt little boy."

Graham opened his arms, and she padded across the floor and lay down on her side facing him, entwining her legs with his.

"Toby will be fine," he said. "He adores you now, he'll adore you always. When he's old enough to hear it we'll explain what happened. But no matter what, he'll always think of you as his mother."

Lilia thought that was one conversation she didn't want to be part of, except to reassure Toby afterwards that she was thrilled to have him in her life, no matter how he first came into it. "And how will you explain your parents?"

"I guess we'll tell him the truth. My parents just aren't people who love or understand children, and they can't change."

"You're such a good father, Graham. You're nothing like Douglas."

"He was a good teacher. I know exactly what not to do."

She kissed him, and he made a low noise in his throat and kissed her back. She wasn't surprised when he slipped a hand under her short gown and began to edge it up her back, and she lifted herself high enough to help him remove it entirely. With her breasts against his bare chest, she realized how hot his skin felt.

She drew back a little. "Graham, are you feeling okay? You're warm. Are you getting sick?"

He laughed softly. "My temperature always rises around you."

She wanted to believe him. She kissed him again and helped him slip off his boxers. She circled his neck and pulled him on top of her, savoring his weight, the slick feel of his skin.

Skin that was too warm.

Before she could insist he had a fever, he went slack against her, then he pushed up, rolled to his side of the bed and left quickly for the bathroom. She heard the too-familiar sound of vomiting, one she hadn't heard in months, and suddenly her skin was as icy as his had been warm.

She went into the bathroom and found him sitting on the edge of the tub, his head in his hands.

She knelt at his feet. "How long have you been sick?"

"Not sick, just feeling a little strange. Since this morning? Last night? I thought it was just something I ate. I bought lunch from a taco truck yesterday."

"Maybe you caught something. But you know you shouldn't just ignore —"

"I've gotten a clean bill of health every time I've gone in for tests. People get normal viruses, and they recover."

She stayed where she was. When he lifted his head she asked again. "How *long* have you been feeling sick?"

He shook his head, and then she knew.

"Is that why you didn't keep your last doctor's appointment, Graham? Are you afraid —" she hesitated, then she said the word "— the *cancer* is back?"

"I want to live a normal life. I just want some time with you and Toby with nothing else in the way."

"Even if the worst is true, the chemo brought you this far. They're always making advances. There's more chemo —"

"I would walk through fire to stay with you

and Toby, but if I'm really sick it's unlikely more chemo will help. It's always risky, and the prognosis after a failed remission isn't stellar. But my heart might not take more, Lilia. The latest doctor I saw made that clear. Getting me to this point was a gamble, and we all knew it. But my heart sustained damage."

"Damage?" Then she realized what else he'd said. "The *latest* doctor?"

"My internist wasn't happy with my last visit, so he set up an appointment with a cardiologist. I went to see her alone. You've heard enough bad news in the past year. I didn't want to alarm you. The cardiologist said I'd never be perfect, but if I don't need more treatment, I'll probably live a normal enough life."

"And you were going to tell me when?"

"When I was sure the cancer wasn't back."

She got to her feet. She couldn't be angry because she knew he had been protecting her. "I think you're overreacting. You need to make an appointment with your oncologist right away to be sure, but this could be a million things, none of them as bad as what you're afraid of."

He stood, too. "It could be. And I'll find out."

She wet a washcloth and ran it over his face, the way she might have if Toby was flushed. "Do you feel well enough to get some sleep?"

He gave a weak smile and nodded.

"It's flu season, Graham. That's all this is."

"I'm sure you're right."

She tossed the cloth in the sink and put her arm around his waist. "We'll resume where we left off when you feel better, okay?"

"I love you."

She hugged him hard, but the lump in her throat kept her from replying. Right now Graham didn't need tears. Despite everything she had said, she had a terrible premonition there might be too many in their future.

18

Marina knew something was wrong with her marriage, and she was fairly certain what it was. In the past month Blake had turned into a silent, preoccupied man who stayed away as often as he stayed home. The most likely explanation? Either, as Wayne had predicted, he was experiencing the onset of dementia, or he was disappointed in her and sorry they'd married. If the last was the case, she was sure she knew why.

Wayne again.

In the months since his oldest son had threatened to dig into her past, she had waited every day for her new husband to confront her. By now there were so many things Wayne could have discovered.

What surprised her most was how much she cared. From the beginning she'd known better than to think of their marriage as anything more than a bargain with mutual benefits. Blake had traded away his loneliness, and she'd banished her financial insecurity.

Naturally she didn't want to lose the creature comforts she'd gained, but there was more to it. She had liked being appreciated, had liked being asked questions about her day while Blake listened raptly to her answers. That kind of interest had been new to her, and she had just begun to count on it when suddenly it disappeared. These days Blake was too preoccupied for former pursuits. He'd dropped out of his bridge group and rarely played tennis or golf. While they still had sex, he was preoccupied then, too, as if he was going through the motions.

She wasn't sure for whom.

Online research hadn't completely reassured her. While Blake never seemed *confused,* many patients with dementia developed ways to cover their deterioration until it was so pronounced they could no longer manage. As they sank deeper they stayed away from social activities and old friends, *and showed a marked inability to concentrate or stay in the present.*

Those parts of Blake were growing too familiar.

Maybe tonight whatever was bothering him would come out between dinner and bed. If her past was the issue, with luck she could convince him their future could be something else entirely.

Tonight she was determined to make a splash in the kitchen and another in the bedroom. For the bedroom she'd bought a sexy new bra and tap shorts. Quite possibly all that lace and satin might not be comfortable to sleep in, but she hoped sleeping was going to be the last thing on Blake's mind.

For the kitchen she'd made a special effort on dinner, and the house already smelled heavenly. Salmon was marinating in lime juice and garlic, and she'd baked a risotto-style casserole with wild mushrooms and Parmesan, her most advanced recipe to date. She hoped he would be pleased.

She was tearing lettuce for a salad when the doorbell rang. Blake had called earlier to say he would be home soon. She wondered if he had forgotten his key. That stopped her a moment. If he'd forgotten something as basic as a house key, what would he forget next? Would she wake up one morning and find he couldn't remember who she was and why she was there?

Wiping her hands on a dish towel she crossed the living room, planning to greet him with a kiss to see if that ignited sparks.

When she opened the door Deedee stood on the welcome mat, and when she saw her daughter, she thrust out a wilting bouquet of daisies and a small package covered in wrinkled wrapping paper. Her mother liked to Dumpster-dive in back of the florist closest to her apartment, and clearly today had been no exception. Marina could only imagine what was under the wrapping paper.

Deedee sounded breathless, as if she'd run all the way from the other side of San Jose. "I guess I ought to have called, only I wasn't far away."

Marina hadn't realized she was holding her breath. She took the flowers but left her mother with the gift. "How did you get through the gate?"

"I gave them my name. You didn't put me on a list or something?"

She hadn't, but Blake must have seen to it. A month ago Marina had introduced her mother and husband at a local restaurant. Days before she'd threatened Deedee with every possible consequence, and for once Deedee had taken her seriously. Not only had she arrived sober, she had proven that, in a pinch, she could screen most of her thoughts, so only the least objectionable were voiced. She'd even paid a visit to the hairdresser and bought a simple shift dress for the occasion. So what if the fabric had been a turquoise and silver leopard print dotted with sequins? At least the hem had stopped just short of her knees.

Blake had been a complete gentleman, pulling out her mother's chair, consulting her on a wine to choose, listening as she described her "restaurant" job. Deedee hadn't lied,

265

exactly. She just hadn't clarified that the job was behind the bar, and then only when a substitute bartender was needed. She had been caught drinking on the job again, and now her hours hovered between few and none.

Marina wasn't surprised Blake had added Deedee to their official visitors' list. He was that kind of thoughtful. Or had been.

"Come in." She stepped aside and hoped Blake would take his time coming home.

"Some place you got here, Rina Ray."

"I was going to invite you. You didn't have to invite yourself."

"I just figured this might be a tough day. You know . . ."

Marina did know. "I don't want to talk about that, okay?"

"I know you can't talk to *him* about, you know. But you can talk to me. I mean, who knows you better?"

Who knew her better? Everybody who'd ever passed her on the street, bumped her cart at the grocery store, called her cell phone by mistake.

Marina went into the kitchen and pulled a vase from a cupboard, filling it with water before she stuck the daisies inside. "I don't want to talk to anybody, Deedee. So leave it, okay?"

As always, Deedee ignored her. "Toby turned one yesterday. You know that, right? I would have come then, only it was Jerry's turn to have Brittany, and he had stuff to do so he asked me to babysit. I figured you wouldn't want me to bring her here." She lowered her voice as if Brittany were in the room. "She's not at a good stage."

Jerry's daughter was six, and so far no stage had been a good one. The little girl was slammed back and forth between disinterested parents like a human tennis ball, and in response she bordered on obesity and depression. What her parents couldn't give her emotionally they made up for with sweets.

Marina felt sorry for her niece, but every suggestion she made fell on deaf ears. In an odd twist Deedee, who carted her granddaughter to garage sales, who painted her nails and trimmed her straw-colored hair, was probably the best influence in Brittany's sad little life.

And how could Marina fault anybody else's parenting when she had refused that job herself?

"I know when Toby was born." Marina managed one calming breath. "I was *there,* remember? Alone. And that's pretty much the way the next three months went. Everybody's better off, and I'm not going to wallow."

"He's my grandson, and I don't think you're as blasé about this as you pretend."

Deedee pronounced *blasé* like *blaze.* Ma-

267

rina pointed a finger just inches from her mother's face. "Stop it. Since when do my feelings matter anyway? You know I haven't told Blake about Toby. I want to do that my own way in my own time. So don't you dare say a word if he gets home before you leave. Not one word."

In response Deedee thrust the package at her. "I thought you might want this. You know . . ."

Marina was sure her mother wouldn't leave until she opened it. To hurry that departure she ripped open the paper and stared. Deedee had blown up a snapshot of Toby, probably one she'd taken with her cell phone, and stuck it in an acrylic frame. Toby looked just the way Marina remembered him, three months old with his tiny face screwed up between screams.

Hopefully not the way he looked now.

She thrust the photo toward her mother. "I don't want this."

"You keep it. He's your son. Sometimes you'll want to remember —"

"What? That I didn't sleep for three months? That I gave birth to a baby I didn't want, a baby whose father tossed me out of his life like a cheap double-breasted suit?"

"He's got your genes."

"Like that's a good thing? For all I know he's doomed to turn out like my no-good brothers!"

"Don't get pissy with me!"

"Deedee, pissy is as close to love as I can get right now, okay? Take it for what it's worth."

"Your brothers didn't have the opportunities you had."

"I made my *own* opportunities, and I tried to help them. I even went to a couple of Petey's teacher conferences to see what I could do —"

She realized this was falling on deaf ears. The only thing that surprised her was that she'd tried, yet again, to make her mother listen.

"Neither of them has your brains." Deedee turned toward the door. "I'll go. Invite me sometime and I'll stay more than two minutes."

Before her mother could cross the room, the door opened. With dismay Marina realized Blake was home. She looked for a place to stow the photo, but she was standing at the island, not close enough to a cabinet where she could shut it away. She turned the photo facedown and slid it on top of the cookbooks that took up the shelf below the countertop. The collection had been lovingly assembled by Blake's first wife, Franny. The risotto recipe had come from one of them; in fact the book had fallen open to that page when Marina first set it on the counter.

"Deedee." Blake smiled and held out his

hand. "A nice surprise."

Deedee crossed the room and took it, then dropped it quickly. "I was on my way out. So it's hello and goodbye." She looked over her shoulder at her daughter. "I was just in the neighborhood. No special reason to be here, right, Rina Ray?"

Marina nodded. "Nice to see you, Deedee. Tell Pete and Jerry I said hello."

"They'll feel the love." She swept out the door, and Blake, with a raised eyebrow, closed it after her.

"Feel the love?"

"An old joke."

"Why didn't you invite her for dinner?"

"She'd already eaten." Marina smiled and went to kiss him before she returned to the island. "How was your day?"

He didn't smile in return. "Busy. I could use a drink." He went to the liquor cabinet and pulled down the gin. "Want one, too?"

She wasn't a fan of gin and tonic, but apparently, Blake's mind was elsewhere — the most positive explanation.

She went back to tearing the salad greens, only now she realized the correct word was *shredding*. She forced herself to regroup. "I'll pour myself some wine in a minute. You go ahead."

He was silent as he poured his drink, but she thought his hand was shaking. And then there was the amount he poured. More than a double. Maybe even more than a triple.

"Your day?" he asked.

Between trips to Victoria's Secret and Safeway her day had been spent worrying. She gave him the fantasy version. "Good. I spent some of it planning dinner. Can you guess what?"

He looked as if food was the last thing on his mind, but he sniffed the air, then he wandered over to join her. "That smells good. Familiar." For the first time since his arrival he looked as if he might be starting to relax a little. "I bet I know."

Before she could stop him, he reached under the countertop for a cookbook and pulled out the one she had used.

With it came Toby's photo, which clattered to the floor.

She watched as he bent and picked it up to stare at her son's scowling little face. Blake tilted his head in question.

She couldn't think of a thing to say, or rather she couldn't think of a way to say the things she needed to.

"Does this have anything to do with the baby blanket you keep in your dresser?" he asked, frame in hand.

"How do you know about that?"

"You asked me to get you a sweater for the movies the other night. You were loading the dishwasher. I saw it then."

Mentally she kicked herself. For bringing

the blanket to the villa. For not hiding it better. For not telling Blake right from the beginning about her pregnancy, and then about her son.

Although if she had, would they even be standing here?

"It's a long story," she said at last.

"I'll pour you some wine. Can dinner wait?"

"The risotto will get cold."

"It reheats nicely. The recipe is one of my favorites."

She was glad something about the day had been a good idea.

Blake poured a glass of pinot grigio, and she took the risotto out of the oven and set it on top. Then she followed him to the great room sofa and settled beside him. But not too close. She needed to see his expression. The wine sat in front of her, untouched, and he'd set his gin and tonic beside it.

She had to start at the beginning. "I never wanted children. I was always so careful not to get pregnant. Then I met a man I thought I loved. He was married, but I thought he loved me, too, and I knew he wanted a baby. It was the worst mistake of my life."

Meeting his eyes was hard, but she made herself do it as she told the rest of the story. She could tell he was surprised everything had happened in the recent past, but she plowed through to the end, the hardest part, and looked away.

272

"I couldn't keep him. I expected to. The father promised to support us, but then he got sick . . ."

"And his *wife*?"

She winced. "Blake, you don't know how many times I've kicked myself for everything. Not just for Graham's part in it, but for my own. Sleeping with a married man is stupid and hateful —"

"Although not unusual."

She tented her fingers together, almost like she was praying. "I was punished big-time. Toby was a difficult baby. He cried all the time. I can't tell you how many times I took him to the pediatrician. Nobody helped. They claimed the screaming would ease, that it was just colic, but three months later it hadn't. I was at my wits' end. And I didn't have anybody to help or give me advice. Graham rarely saw us, and a lot of the support he'd promised didn't materialize. I had to go back to work, but I couldn't afford day care, and who would take a baby like Toby, anyway? In the end I did what I thought was best for all of us. I gave Graham custody and stepped out of Toby's life."

She realized how virtuous that sounded, and she wished her motivation had been that pure.

Blake was shaking his head, which she knew she deserved, then he stunned her. He slid close and put his arm around her, nudging her head to rest on his shoulder. "You poor girl."

Suddenly she was crying. After all these months. She tried to talk through her tears. "I don't know what part of it was the hardest . . . But after I left Toby with Graham . . . I mostly felt relief. That makes me a terrible person, doesn't it?"

"It makes you human. Nothing about the pregnancy was happy or fun. Then you drew the short straw with Toby. Trust me, I'm not just saying that, because I know from experience. Paul was colicky, too. For years afterwards, every time he opened his mouth I expected to hear him screaming again. Franny and I made it through those months, but there were two of us, and we had money to hire help so we could have time away. And believe me, we hired a lot."

She sniffed. "You said you were glad your children were grown. I can see why."

"I had very little to say about the way mine turned out." He spaced his next words. "So no, I did not like raising children. And frankly, I still don't."

She wasn't sure what he meant, but she felt comforted. The feeling was new. She wiped her eyes on the hem of her shirt and looked up at him.

"Wayne —" She stopped abruptly.

"What did my son do now?"

"He said he was going to dig into my past

and tell you who you really married."

"I *know* who I married. Wayne's mostly talk." He frowned. "Nobody wishes that last part wasn't true more than I do."

She was mystified again, but she went on. "There's more he could dig up. You might as well know it all. I have no father. Never did. My mother can't even remember all the men she slept with the month I was conceived. My home life was shit. Deedee is a step away from becoming an alcoholic. One of my brothers well and truly is, and the other is his own kind of deadbeat. I have a niece who's pre-diabetic, and my family still feeds her candy and soft drinks, like they're trying to prove the doctors are wrong. I got out of that life by studying and working hard, but they drag me back whenever they can."

"And the baby must have made you feel like you were sinking again."

He understood. And he wasn't judging her. She put her hand on his cheek and turned his face so he met her eyes. "How can you be so nice about this?"

"Marina, I don't expect you to be perfect. Most of this you couldn't help. The baby? You paid a huge price for your mistake. I just wish I could make it all go away."

"You've been so distant . . ." She tried to read his thoughts. "I thought . . . I thought you'd discovered some or all of it, and you were wishing you'd never married me."

"When I told you I was glad my children were grown, did that have anything to do with giving Toby away?"

"Maybe I factored it in, but not much. You don't need to blame yourself. I liked you. I wanted to see what we had together."

His voice softened. "Did you, now?"

She smiled a little, but it disappeared quickly. "I can't lie, though. I would have found another excuse. Toby was a little stranger. Nothing made him happy. I guess the word I'm looking for is bond. We never bonded. I only hope he's bonding with Graham and his wife."

"You don't know?"

"He's safe, but, of course, I knew he would be. I don't know if he's happy." Her voice caught just a little. She didn't know if he noticed. "I haven't seen him, and I don't talk to Graham or Lilia. After three miserable months I turned my back and walked away. It was the only way I could do it."

"Do you want to change that? Do you want access, if not custody?"

She had asked herself this question a thousand times. She still didn't have an answer. "I don't know. Maybe he'll be happier without me."

"You kept the blanket."

She shrugged.

"There's no right or wrong in what you did," he said. "You were in a bad place, and you saw a better way for both you and the baby."

She wished her actions had been that noble. Some part of abandoning him — and she didn't know how much — had just been about payback.

"You don't want a baby in your life," she said, and it wasn't a question.

He looked regretful. "I have so much on my plate right now, Marina. And I've already proved what a lousy father I am."

"How?"

He held up a hand, as if to make it clear he wasn't going to say more about that.

"Then it's not worth discussing, is it?" she asked.

"It is if you're really unhappy. If you need something other than what we have now."

She wasn't happy, no, but it wasn't because of Toby — or at least she didn't think it was. She was afraid to put into words what was really bothering her, Blake's sudden lack of concentration, his withdrawal.

The possibility he was sinking quickly into dementia and might not even realize it.

"Can you live with things the way they are?" he asked. "At least for the moment?"

She thought about Blake's kindness this evening as she'd told him about Toby. She thought about the endless cups of coffee in bed each morning — still exactly the way she liked them — about the way he made absolutely certain she found pleasure in their lovemaking, and his surprising generosity in the first months of their marriage.

She formed her answer carefully. She wasn't ready to make a change. Not yet. Not until she understood more about what was going on with him. "I think we both said 'for better or for worse.' "

" 'For better' could be shorter than 'for worse.' "

She thought he was talking about Toby, but she wasn't sure. And better would surely turn into worse if she tried to bring the baby here, where Blake clearly didn't want him.

She got to her feet, held out her arms, and when he slipped his around her waist, she kissed him. "There's a special dinner waiting for us. Come talk to me while I finish the salad. Do you want to grill the salmon or let me broil it?"

"I'll heat the grill. I'll be back in a minute."

She watched him go. Her world was in upheaval again, but it was strange how much easier that was when somebody else was there to share it.

Back in the kitchen she saw the photo of Toby on the counter. She lifted it to shove it in a cupboard. Then she thought better of it. She carried the photo into their bedroom and carefully slid it into the drawer of her nightstand. Faceup.

19

THE SWALLOW'S NEST

FEATHERING YOUR NEST WITH IMAGINATION AND LOVE

January 15th:

I came home from the post office box this afternoon with two mail bins filled with get well cards. There aren't enough words in any language to let you know how much I appreciate your generosity and kindness. But in Hawaii we say *mahalo nui loa,* or thank you very much, and so I say that now to each and every one of you. From the bottom of my heart.

With the help of one of Graham's carpenters we've repurposed and installed three window shutters side by side on a wall where he can see them from his bed, and we've filled each slot with your bright messages of hope and recovery. I was inspired by the photos and directions I've listed below, and you might be, too, if you want to do something similar.

Every day I read the new cards and add them to the shutters, temporarily retiring the others so the display changes. After his last treatment Graham asked for the extras and felt well enough to enjoy them up close.

When I began *The Swallow's Nest,* my vision of what this blog would be was very different. I expected to reach out to you, to help you find ways to make your life more colorful and comfortable. Instead, for the past year, you've reached out to me, over and over again.

In the coming weeks I'll be devoting all my time to my family, so I won't be posting often. You can still order from the website, and my staff will be certain you receive your merchandise quickly and efficiently.

Please know that we're doing everything we can here to achieve a miracle, but even if that doesn't happen, the love our family shares at this difficult time is a miracle in itself. And for that, and for your support, I'm grateful.

Aloha, Lilia

When she opened the door Lilia expected to find Regan and Toby on the porch. Her friend had taken the baby for the afternoon so Lilia could spend it at the hospital, but Lilia had texted to say she and Graham were home. Regan and several other friends had stepped forward to help when Graham was rehospitalized. After a somber Christmas and a definitive diagnosis that the cancer had returned, Lilia's parents had gone back to Kauai to settle things there, but they were flying in tomorrow to stay as long as they were needed.

Instead of Regan, Lilia found Carrick on the doorstep. She fell into his arms for a hug and remained there for a long moment before she finally pulled away.

He was the first to speak. "When I got to the hospital they said he'd already been discharged, but they wouldn't say more. You should have called."

She smiled, or thought she did. "Come in. I'll explain."

She closed the door behind him. Afternoon sun was still streaming through the three narrow windowpanes at the top, and for just a moment she inclined her face toward it before she turned and followed Carrick into the living room. He was sitting on the love seat, and she chose the sofa.

"Is he upstairs or down?" he asked softly.

"I don't think he'll be up again." Her voice caught, and she cleared her throat. "Thank God for the guest room down here. The hospital bed my parents rented for us fits perfectly."

"Why did they send him home?"

She needed something in her hands. She grabbed a pillow and began turning it over and over. "The new rounds of chemo weren't working, Carrick. I think you figured that out, too. This morning his doctors sat down and told Graham his heart won't stand any more.

They might chance it if the chemo was working. But it's not."

"The stem cell transplant?"

She'd been hanging on to that final possibility so long that it took courage to answer. She felt the way she might if she were reading Graham's obituary out loud. "The transplant is out of the question without a better chemo result, and unfortunately it was always a long shot. So unless a clinical trial comes up that he can take part in, there's nothing else his doctors can do. And a trial is unlikely." They had also been warned it was unlikely Graham would be well enough for the necessary travel if a trial came up. Unchecked Burkitt's lymphoma was aggressive and fast-acting. Graham had very little time.

She knew better than to soft-pedal the truth. Carrick had been beside them every step of the way, and once Graham's lymphoma had recurred, he'd known the almost inevitable outcome, although he hadn't voiced it. None of them had.

"What now?" he asked after a long pause.

"Now that they've stopped chemo and increased his supportive therapy, he may feel better for a little while. Before things go downhill quickly . . ." She cleared her throat. "They suggest we work with hospice. They made a referral."

Tears filled his eyes. "How's he taking this?"

This second bout was worse for Lilia than

the first. After the initial diagnosis she'd been filled with confidence. People survived this type of lymphoma, and treatment was available. Of course, Toby's very existence was proof that, right from the beginning, Graham had feared the worst, and now his reaction had surprised her again.

"He's more upbeat than I expected," she said.

"He's already gone through so much."

"The first time around, he was willing to do whatever he had to if the treatment gave him a chance. But now that his chances are . . ." She couldn't say the word. She skipped it. "I think he's relieved. Nobody can ever say he didn't face this head-on. He can give up gracefully, knowing he fought as hard as he could." She hesitated. "But he's worried, Carrick. If he dies before I can adopt Toby . . ."

She didn't have to continue. They still had six weeks to go before she could begin proceedings to adopt Toby, six whole weeks before they could prove that Marina hadn't contacted or supported her son for a year. And even if Graham was still alive in six weeks, it was unlikely he would live long enough to see the adoption to conclusion. Once he died, the statutes guiding stepparent adoption became irrelevant.

"Did you ask the doctors for a time line?" Carrick's tone was kind, but the words were an attorney's.

"I asked his oncologist. He said not to put off saying or doing anything, because I'll regret it if I do."

Carrick didn't respond, but no words were needed.

"I don't want to lose Toby, too," Lilia said.

"We can seek guardianship instead of adoption. We can still make a case Marina abandoned him to *you*. She put Toby in *your* arms. And you've been Toby's de facto mother. That's important."

"If Graham dies . . ." She wondered at what point she would begin to say *when,* not *if . . .* "Marina will assume Toby is slated to be his heir. She must know how many billions Douglas and Ellen are worth. She may think a whopping inheritance could come Toby's way. If she's the gold digger I think she is, then she'll want custody again so she can get her hands on whatever his grandparents leave him."

He didn't argue. He had probably considered the possibility of inheritance, too. "There's no way to keep Graham's condition a secret. They work in the same industry. They know the same people."

"I don't want to be Toby's *guardian.* I want to be his *mother.* Isn't there anything we can do immediately? Before she realizes how sick Graham is?"

"She probably already knows, Lilia. He's

not showing up at job sites. Mike's taken over Encompass Construction, and he's making all the decisions. Word gets around."

"Then she could show up any day and try to take Toby, couldn't she? And you can try whatever mumbo jumbo you want in court, but she'll still get my son."

She heard a noise from the hallway and turned quickly. Somehow Graham had made it out of bed and was standing in the archway leaning on a cane. In the past weeks he had lost all the weight he'd regained after the initial rounds of chemo, and he no longer bothered to cover his bare scalp with a baseball cap. He was an apparition, as pale as any ghost, and so thin she could almost see his bones.

Carrick leapt to his feet and went to him. The two men clumsily embraced, and Carrick put his arm around Graham's shoulders to guide him to the sofa.

The contrast was profound. Carrick was the picture of vitality and good health. He settled his friend beside Lilia, and she tucked an afghan over him. These days Graham was always cold. Always cold, never hungry, often asleep, frequently in pain. Hopefully that last would be more controlled when hospice took over, but for a moment she squeezed her eyelids shut so she wouldn't cry.

"I heard your conversation," Graham said, after he'd had a chance to catch his breath.

He wheezed when he spoke now, and it took him longer, so he was developing a verbal shorthand. "Custody. Toby."

"We're just trying to figure out the best way to work out everything." Carrick was nodding, as if this was just a simple conversation, like which car they were planning to take to the movies that night.

"Lilia wants to keep and raise him," Graham said.

"I know. And we'll make that happen." Carrick reached over and squeezed his friend's hand.

"It . . . has to."

"We're going to do everything we can."

It was clear Graham was struggling to frame his next sentence. "Do you remember . . . the first time we met?"

"You were such a prick."

Graham managed a smile. "I thought that was *you.*"

"Both of you were pricks." Lilia moved closer to her husband and put her hand in his.

"My father wanted us . . . to be friends. A rare good decision."

"The best."

"And then . . . we went to Kauai, and you met . . . Lilia."

"We had good summers together, didn't we?" She rested her head on Graham's shoulder, without putting the full weight

286

there. "Every year I waited and hoped you'd come, and you always did. Until you didn't anymore. And then, presto, you appeared in my life again. Right here in California."

The past was safe, and they talked a little more, with both Carrick and Lilia filling in when it was clear Graham was having problems keeping up.

Still, at the next significant break, he was the one who broke the silence, going back to the subject of custody as if they'd never left it.

"Carrick. Will it help if I make a video with . . . my wishes about Toby?"

"Everything's in your will."

"More is better."

Carrick nodded. "It certainly can't hurt."

"Now's good."

Lilia was surprised and sat up to look at him. "Aren't you exhausted? It's already been a long day. Everything at the hospital, and then settling back in here?"

"I heard what the doctor . . . told you. Not to put off saying or doing anything."

Tears filled her eyes. "I didn't know you could hear us."

"I already knew. If you ask . . . they tell you."

"I'm still praying for a miracle." She kissed his cheek. "And a clinical trial with very good drugs."

"I had my miracle. You and Toby." He

rested a moment, then he shook his head again. "And now . . . we need to make . . . another."

Carrick seemed to know she was too choked up to respond. "My smartphone takes good video. We don't have to drag this out. Lilia, why don't you come over here so it's just Graham on-screen. Otherwise it might look like you're prompting him."

She kissed Graham's cheek. Then she got up and went to stand beside Carrick.

Carrick moved around until he got the best angle. "This looks right. I would tell you to comb your hair, but it's already perfect."

Graham's grin was as close to normal as any Lilia had seen in the past weeks. That, too, made her want to cry.

Graham cleared his throat. "Roll it."

Lilia took a chair off to the side so she and Carrick together wouldn't be looming over her husband. She listened as Carrick instructed him.

"Say your name. Today's date — it's the fifteenth — and maybe the time. Then try to explain that making this video was your idea, that you wanted any officials who are charged with deciding where Toby will grow up to know exactly how you feel about it. It would also be helpful if you explain why you're doing this, the state of your health, etc. But be sure they understand you're thinking clearly, and no one has influenced you."

"Let's go."

Lilia knew how exhausted Graham was, and she was sure that, while he didn't complain, he was also in pain. Once they finished here she was going to put him to bed and give him a real dose of the painkiller his doctor had recommended.

Carrick nodded. "You're on."

"My name is Graham Randolph, and I'm sitting in my living room at —"

She listened as he slowly and carefully identified himself, the date and time, and then explained that while he was terminally ill, he was still thinking clearly.

"This video is my idea, and Carrick Donnelly is acting as both photographer . . . attorney and best friend. But neither he nor my wife asked me to do this."

Graham turned a little with difficulty, but now he was looking at Lilia instead of at Carrick's phone.

"My wife, Lilia, is sitting here. She and I have talked . . . at length about the future of my son, Toby Randolph. Lilia has been Toby's mother since his birth mother, Marina Tate, put him in her arms and disappeared on March 3rd of last year. Lilia has wanted to legally adopt him . . ." He paused and took shallow breaths for a long moment before he continued. "Marina hasn't contacted us since leaving Toby here. The few times I tried to get information about him that we needed,

Marina didn't respond."

He closed his eyes, but Carrick kept the camera focused on him. Lilia guessed he was afraid someone might think editing had occurred if they stopped and restarted.

Graham opened his eyes and took another series of breaths before he began again. "We planned to wait until a full year had passed, so Lilia could adopt more easily. But I am afraid . . . I won't live that long. So I want whoever is watching, whoever has control over the fate of my little boy, Toby, to understand that Lilia . . ." He began to cough, and relentlessly, Carrick continued the video.

"Lilia, can you get me some water?"

She leapt to her feet and went into the kitchen. When she returned he had begun speaking again, but she handed him the glass, and he took a few sips before he held it back out to her.

He began again. "No one else deserves to parent Toby. Lilia took him under the most difficult circumstances. I was unfaithful, and Toby was the result. But . . . she learned to love him almost immediately, and she has been an exceptional mom. She and Toby adore each other. She should not be parted from him. Not ever."

Lilia's eyes filled, and tears spilled down her cheeks as Graham went on.

"When Marina got pregnant I asked her to have Toby. I wasn't fair, and she . . . deserved better. But she gave him up and has never expressed interest in him since. She doesn't deserve to parent him."

Carrick was nodding, as if he expected Graham to quit now, but Graham held up his hand.

His voice was halting, with frequent pauses, but his message was strong. "One more thing. Just as important. Both my parents are still living. Some things are worse than abandonment, like having a child . . . when you dislike children. And my parents do. My father has never shown a moment's interest —" he coughed again "— and would not want my child in his home. He would be cruel to my son, and . . . my mother couldn't stop him. No matter what, under no circumstances, should they be allowed to have custody . . . no matter how much money they have or how much legal help they obtain. I don't think they'll try . . . but if they do, please, please, don't be swayed."

He stopped. Carrick inclined his head in question, and Graham finished by saying again that he had made the video of his own free will. "Please, allow the only real mother my son has ever known to raise him. She'll have help. Our friends Carrick and Regan, and many other friends, too. Her own devoted family. Toby's future couldn't be in better hands."

Carrick tapped his phone, then he put it in

his pocket. "I'll download that right away so we can keep it safe. And now, can I help you back to bed?"

But Graham wasn't finished, even though the camera was no longer running. "Both of you, please, listen."

Lilia sat forward. His voice was pleading now, as if he was on the verge of complete exhaustion. "Do you need me to get you something?"

"I need you to know . . ." He took a deep breath, then he looked straight at Carrick. "It's okay. I want you two to be happy."

Lilia waited, but he didn't go on. "Carrick and I will remember you always," she promised.

He turned to her. "Lilia, I know you loved me. Don't ever . . . think I doubted that."

She didn't know what to say, but she knew she had to respond with a nod.

"But I always knew I wasn't . . ." His words trailed off and he was finished.

She didn't need clarification. Graham was talking about something larger than moving on after his death. He was talking about the one thing the three close friends had never discussed. She hung her head and began to cry.

■ ■ ■ ■

PART IV

■ ■ ■ ■

Swallows' nests may fall prey to parasites, but the birds are not defenseless. In North America barn swallows sometimes build their nests below those of an osprey, and in the bargain are protected from other birds of prey that the fish-eating osprey willingly chases away. In return the swallows become feathered intruder alarms, alerting the ospreys to the presence of predators.

"Our Songbirds, Ourselves:
A Tale of Two Species"
from the editors of *Ornithology Today.*

20
THE SWALLOW'S NEST

FEATHERING YOUR NEST WITH IMAGINATION AND LOVE

February 14th:

Because you have cared so deeply and shown your concern in so many ways, I must share with you the sad news that last week we lost our beloved Graham. None of us expected him to pass so soon, but we did know his death was inevitable. We were as prepared as anyone ever is, and he died peacefully here in the home he loved, surrounded by the people who loved him most and will mourn him forever.

In the end nothing mattered but love, not mistakes we made, or sadness we brought into each other's lives. We remembered the joy, the laughter, the shared exuberance of a life well lived, and a marriage that was strong enough to survive, even when faced with challenges.

Graham was only thirty-one, but he lived those years with courage and enthusiasm. He'll be missed by many, and today we celebrate his life in a light-filled sanctuary that he designed and built two years ago for a local church. I can't imagine a more fitting place for a tribute. More than anything Graham wanted to leave the world a more beautiful place.

Mahalo and aloha, Lilia

The house felt different and had since the moment of Graham's final breath. No matter how many people were there, the rooms seemed to echo. Lilia was sure the walls had expanded. Even the air was different without Graham's favorite soap and aftershave scenting it. And the everyday sounds she'd never even thought about? The way he hummed under his breath when he was deeply involved in a project. His favorite playlists as a muted background to every conversation. The soft whisper of his lips against her hair.

He had died in the early evening. She had been lying in the bed beside him, holding his hand, just the two of them. Regan and Carrick had already spent time at his bedside, and they had just taken Toby for a walk. Her parents, brothers Kai and Jordan, too, had been nearby, perhaps in the kitchen making dinner — she couldn't remember now. But Graham had opened his eyes and looked right at her for the first time in a week.

Then, suddenly, he was gone.

Afterwards a hospice nurse, who had been their lifeline in the final weeks, told her that sometimes people stopped fighting to live when everything they needed to accomplish was finished. Graham's downward spiral had begun almost immediately after filming the custody video. Lilia had hoped for a reprieve as palliative care took the place of chemotherapy. While nobody had promised good days before his life ended, they had promised the possibility.

Instead the end had come swiftly. For a week Graham was well enough to spend what time he could with Toby, although the little boy was baffled by this father who looked and acted like a stranger. Eventually he had resisted being with him. Graham even spent most of an hour with Ellen, who came at Lilia's request, insisted on being alone with her son, and left after questioning decisions Lilia had made about his care and, almost worse, the funeral arrangements.

The second week Graham slept almost constantly, only waking when Lilia tried to feed him, or the nurse took care of the hundred and one little things that had to be done. By then he could only manage a sentence or two, and by the end of the week, only occasional words.

Then he had stopped responding at all.

Since his death, in the darkest hours of the night, she had wondered if he'd been in terrible pain, or if he'd needed to say more and hadn't been able to find the strength. In the light of day, she rejected both possibilities.

She had stayed at Graham's bedside almost every moment, unless Carrick or her family were with him so she could sleep. She would have known if either were true. The drugs had helped one, and filming the video the other. That afternoon on the sofa with Carrick recording every word, he had bared his heart.

And now she had to live with the aftermath.

"We have about an hour before we need to leave."

She looked up from the pan of brownies she was taking out of the oven and realized Carrick had come into the kitchen. He was dressed for Graham's memorial service, and she realized the time had come for her to do the same. "I'll be ready."

"You're working too hard."

"It helps me take my mind off . . . everything."

Following his wishes Graham's body had been cremated almost immediately after his death. The church was organizing a reception for guests. The minister had told Lilia it would be a privilege to preside, and his members wanted to pay tribute for Graham's beautiful work on their behalf. Afterwards, though, Graham's closest friends were coming here to laugh and cry together. Lilia and Nalani — who understood her daughter better than anyone — had cooked and baked for two days, concentrating on Graham's favorites.

Carrick leaned against a counter. "You have enough going on now, but when things settle a little, we have to talk."

They had so much to talk about she wondered how he would know where to start. Graham had died on a Monday. On Tuesday morning Carrick had gone to the probate court to petition for *ex parte* temporary guardianship, and to ask that Lilia be granted emergency custody while temporary and later general guardianship were decided. *Ex parte* meant that the guardianship procedure could commence without first notifying Marina or other significant parties. She would be notified sometime in the next weeks, and then she could respond if she cared to.

When he'd returned from the courthouse he had gone over the details. When notification would likely occur and to whom. When a reconsideration hearing would be scheduled. What was likely to happen then. Most of it had flown out of her head. All she remembered was that the judge had issued the order, and for the moment Toby was hers.

Lilia set the pan on a rack and faced him. He was wearing a dark suit, appropriate attire for church. As well as he wore a suit, she always preferred him in jeans.

"Talk about Toby?" she asked.

He nodded. "Toby, your finances, the work

Graham left unfinished."

She had known a conversation about finances was coming. She hadn't billed a single client since the cancer recurred, and without Graham's income, they had rapidly sunk into a crater a mile deep. Then there were new hospital bills, out-of-network specialists who hadn't yet been paid, tests that hadn't been completely covered by insurance.

"There aren't enough words to thank you and Regan for taking over so much while . . ." She shook her head. "While I just couldn't."

"We wish we could have done more."

She tried to smile, but wasn't sure she succeeded. "None of us had miracles in our pockets."

"In our last conversation Graham told me to take care of you." His expression was grave. "And in line with that, there's something we need to talk about right now. It can't wait."

She wasn't surprised that Graham had talked to Carrick about her future. At the same time, if anything else had passed between the two men, she didn't want to know about it now.

"As my *lawyer.*" It wasn't a question.

"You're still planning to have Toby with you today?"

"It's a memorial service. He'll see photos of his father, hear beautiful music. People will laugh and maybe cry. My parents or Kai

300

will take him out if he gets fussy. Someday I want to be able to tell him he was there, and people loved seeing him and knowing that Graham lived on through him."

Both of them were silent as the impact of what she'd said hovered between them.

"Yes, that's what Graham wanted, wasn't it?" she said when Carrick didn't. "That awful night when he decided he had to father a baby. And now, it makes a terrible kind of sense, doesn't it? Because he will live on through Toby."

"You've had too much going on to do any thinking, Lilia. I need to be sure you still want to go forward with the guardianship."

"If anyone else had asked that, I would be furious."

"I know you love Toby."

"I would give up everything I have for him. Does that say it all? Toby is mine!"

"The courts won't see it that way. Especially not if Marina reestablishes contact and wants custody."

"Why are you bringing this up now?" She turned to get a second pan out of the oven. Brownies, just plain homemade brownies, had been Graham's biggest culinary weakness, probably because nobody had baked them for him as a child.

Carrick waited until she straightened. "Marina could be at the service today."

She gripped the pan so hard her hand rolled

over and landed on the edge.

"Ouch!" She dropped it on top of the stove and strode to the sink to run cold water over the burn. "Damn!" Tears filled her eyes, and not from the sting.

Carrick got a bowl and filled it with ice from the chute on the refrigerator, setting it on the counter beside her. "Bad news and cooking don't mix. Got it."

She added water to the bowl and plunged her hand inside. "Maybe you can write a guest blog for *The Swallow's Nest*. Things lawyers should never say in the kitchen."

"You haven't thought about this, have you?"

"If Marina hasn't come to my front door, why worry she'll show up today?"

"She had feelings for Graham."

"Why are you doing this?"

"Because I want the petition for guardianship to go through without a hitch, Lilia. I promised Graham I would do everything and anything to make that happen."

She wanted to snap at him again, but Carrick wasn't the problem. Her stress level was at an all-time high under the weight of grief so heavy that sometimes she found she couldn't move, that she was too weak to drag it from one place to another.

Then there was anger. At Graham for dying. At Graham for leaving a life filled with fragments he was no longer able to put together. At Marina, who might be at today's service. At the debts she owed, the clients who expected her to carry on despite the upheaval of the past weeks, the developer who had backed out of the cottage community the moment he heard Graham was sick.

And could any of them be blamed? Life went on. Only, not hers.

She waited until she could speak calmly. "So when he's a teenager do I tell Toby that we didn't take him to his father's memorial service because we were afraid we might run into his birth mother?"

"I don't think Toby will ask."

"I want Graham's friends to see him, Carrick. I want them to know he's okay, that he's with me and even after everything that happened, I love and want him. This may be the last time I see any of them. I want them to know that little boy and I are going to move on together."

"That's a good thing, but for the record, you need to start calling Toby your *son*. You need to use the word from now on. You are his *de facto* mother, and that's worth everything to you. You need to make it clear that's how you see Toby, even if Graham is gone now."

"It's funny. I was saving that word until the day his adoption was final. I guess I can give that up now."

"Down the road it's always possible Marina

will let you adopt, especially when she finds out Toby won't be inheriting anything from the Randolph estates."

She lifted her hand from the ice water. The burn stung and would probably sting more in a minute, but she doubted it would blister. She patted it gingerly with a dish towel. "Anything else for now?"

"Your family will be glad to help with Toby at the service?"

"Dolores offered, too. She'll be at the church with her family. Just like I'll be there with my *son.*"

She saw him shake his head. "Dolores has to go, Lilia. At least for a while. In case somebody challenges you for custody."

"I can't have help? Half the mothers in America have children in day care, Carrick. Would a judge fault me for having a babysitter right here in our home? I was going to ask her to take over full-time. I can't manage a home business without child care."

"It's not that you can't have help. You can't have *Dolores.*" He held up his hand to let her know he wasn't finished. "She was fired from her last job. You told me yourself. And yes, you checked, and everyone said firing her was unfair. But the family she worked for claimed she didn't take good enough care of their daughter."

"They wanted her to work more hours than they paid her for. They've fired another nanny since and one before Dolores. It was a bad experience. That's why she's working part-time for a couple of different families now, so she won't be at anybody's mercy."

"I believe you. I believe *her.* But you don't need a situation you have to explain. You need to find somebody else, at least until everything is settled."

"You think Dolores will just stay around hoping I take her back? Toby loves her. She's beyond reproach."

"Apparently she's not."

She squeezed her eyes shut for just a moment. "Why tell me this today?"

"So she won't be seen taking him out of the church."

"Please, tell me this whole custody fiasco will be over soon, Carrick. So Toby and I can find a life and live it together. Without interference."

"I wish I could."

"What do you know that I don't?"

"That bad things happen to good people. It's my job to be a roadblock and send bad things in another direction. Nothing more than that."

She heard him say "not yet" as clearly as if the words had actually passed his lips.

The front door opened, and she heard Toby's laughter followed by her father's. Her parents were so good with the baby, but since Graham's death they had kept him out of the

305

house as much as possible, and when her brothers had arrived they'd followed suit. When Toby was home, he searched for Graham. He didn't have the words to explain himself, but Lilia knew. And when he seemed to be crying or fussing for no reason, she understood that, too. In some ways he would look for his father for the rest of his life.

"I need to get ready." She untied the dish towel apron she'd once featured in a how-to post. She supposed women all over the country had their own versions. She hoped none of them had to wear theirs on a day like this one.

"What can I do?" Carrick asked.

"Just what you're doing. I'm sorry, and thank you."

"Nobody expects you to be at your best. Especially not me."

"I'm sorry your parents couldn't be here." The elder Donnellys had both succumbed to the flu and hadn't been able to travel.

"So are they."

"You and Regan will sit at the front with my family and my *son*? You were his best friend."

"What about Ellen?"

"If she comes, I don't think she'll sit with us."

"She'll be there. In her own way, she loved Graham. She was just very bad at showing it."

"And Douglas?"

He grimaced. "Doesn't love anybody. Especially himself. He lives in a prison of his own making."

"Doesn't everybody?" As her parents came into the kitchen with Toby, she rose on tiptoes and kissed his cheek.

Nalani handed Toby to Lilia. "This is a dirty little boy. I'll give him a quick bath and get him ready." Lilia nestled her cheek against his hair and wrapped her arms around him, squeezing until he screeched with laughter.

"Thanks, Mama. I needed a Toby fix."

Lilia handed him back and wondered what she would do when her parents went home to Kauai next week. Eli hadn't been able to make this trip. Kai and Jordan were leaving tonight, and her parents had offered to stay as long as she needed them, but she knew they both had to get back to work. Her brother Micah, who was now in partnership with her father, had stayed behind to manage the security firm, but Lilia was sure he was working day and night.

"I laid out clothes," she told her mother. "And I have a bag of toys to occupy him. Snacks. Juice. A change of clothes and diapers."

"When you bring Toby home to meet his Hawaiian family, we will celebrate Graham's life again."

"He was happy on Kauai." In his last days

when he could still speak, Graham had asked Lilia to scatter his ashes off the shore off Kapa'a. In his death, he would belong on the island he loved.

"He was happy when he was with you, with Carrick and his other friends, with Toby. He had a good life."

Lilia told herself to remember that and be glad for it today. Or at least to try.

21

Thirty-one years ago Ellen brought her baby son home from the hospital to a wood-sided Colonial near Montclair Village in the Oakland Hills. The house wasn't the first she and Douglas had owned, but it was the one she had loved the best. Not because it was the most extravagant — it wasn't. Not because it had a fabulous view, gardens that needed professional care, enough bedrooms for everyone they had ever met. The house, painted a dusky blue and sporting random eucalyptus and pine trees in the front yard, had none of those things. There were better sections of Montclair, higher in the hills on curvy roads with larger yards and exceptional views.

But this was the house where, as a brand-new mother, she had brought her infant son.

Standing at the edge of the front yard today she remembered those first weeks with a new baby in residence. She hadn't known what to do, but that had hardly mattered. Douglas had hired a briskly efficient baby nurse who eased her out of Graham's nursery and life. In the end Ellen had seen very little of her son. Those were the years when Douglas was building his empire one exotic property, one contact at a time, and she had been expected — and willing — to help him do it.

Still, she could see the ghost of her baby boy, running across the grass, falling over his own feet to her laughter and his father's scornful grunts. She'd had no right to bring any child to this house. With a little thought she should have realized how everything would end. She must have known what kind of father Douglas would be. She should have looked deeper into her own heart, too, into her own insecurities and weaknesses, before she threw away her birth control pills and let nature take its course.

But she hadn't. And today she would bury the result.

Of course that wasn't quite true. *She* wouldn't be allowed to bury her son. Lilia had decided on cremation, not a grave in the Graham family plot in the San Francisco National Cemetery overlooking the Golden Gate Bridge. In the last visit she would ever have with Graham, the last time she would see her son alive, Ellen had told him how much she wanted him to be buried in the historic cemetery with her family, and he had said, in a halting whisper, that Lilia would

310

follow his wishes.

She wasn't surprised Lilia had made other arrangements. God knows what the new widow would do with Graham's ashes, but Ellen was sure it would be something casual and inappropriate. And there would be no place for Ellen to mourn her son.

Except here.

"Like I've been telling you, it needs work."

Surprised, Ellen faced Hank Gleason, the real estate broker who lived three houses away, and whose company had managed this house as a rental since the Randolphs had moved. He was as pleasant to look at now as he'd been all those years ago, just as slim, and while his hair had grayed, he still had all of it. His eyes seemed an even more electric blue against tanned, creased skin.

"I parked in front of your house. I was planning to ring your bell, but I was a little early," she said, extending her hand. He didn't shake it; he raised it to his lips and kissed it.

"I was remembering," she admitted. "Graham here. On this lawn."

His eyes were filled with sympathy. "He was a beautiful little boy. Everyone thought so. Sally tried hard to give birth to a daughter for him to marry."

Ellen managed a smile. "Too bad you only had sons."

"She wanted a girl until the day she died. Well past an age to have one."

She rested her fingers on his arm. "You still miss her, don't you?"

"We managed to celebrate our silver anniversary. I was rooting for gold, but the years we had were good."

Four years ago Sally had died of a massive stroke, and Ellen had helped Hank and his sons make the funeral arrangements. Douglas had abandoned his friendship with the Gleasons years before, but Ellen had remained close to both. As a side benefit their friendship had given her an opportunity to come back to the neighborhood.

She and Douglas had lived in this house almost five years. After finding a larger, more elaborate home higher in the hills, her husband had wanted to sell it, the way he'd eventually sold every other house they lived in. When he decided it was time to move up, he always found a more prestigious property in a more prestigious neighborhood and took the leap, sometimes without consulting her.

Just before the house was to be put on the market, Ellen had put her foot down. She explained the property would be worth more in the future. When he'd been both skeptical and dismissive, she'd simply taken the matter into her own hands, paid off the mortgage with Graham family money, and told him she planned to keep the house as an investment.

Of course she'd been at least half right. Today the house was worth at least six times what it had been all those years ago, but decades of renters had taken their toll. For the past year Hank had warned that serious updates were needed. Now the latest renters were moving out, and she could see he was right.

It was easier to talk about the house than the upcoming church service. She swept her hand in front of her. "It needs everything, doesn't it? New roof. New paint. New landscaping."

"The inside's worse. It's so dated nobody's going to buy it without work."

"But I'm not selling. Why did you think I was?"

"It's probably time, Ellen. The market's strong, and you don't have to do everything. You can do cosmetic fixes, reroof, paint, maybe update the kitchen, and it will sell immediately."

"I'm not selling."

"This is the worst possible time to talk this over, isn't it?"

"That doesn't change anything. I'm not like Douglas. Occasionally I get attached to things. And this is one of them."

"No, you're *not* like Douglas." He angled to face her. "He's not coming today?"

"He's in Hong Kong. Nobody expected Graham to die so quickly. Douglas couldn't get home in time." She supposed on some level that much was true. There was no point in admitting Douglas wouldn't have come anyway, no matter how his absence looked to anybody at the service.

Hank didn't bother to ask if Douglas had seen Graham before traveling across the world. "I'm sorry. I know he'll regret not saying goodbye."

"Douglas has very strong ideas about how to live, and one of them is without regrets. By the time regrets appear, it's too late to do anything about the past, and a waste of his time."

"Then thank you for asking me to accompany you. You shouldn't be alone."

Ellen had needed to walk through the door of the church with somebody. She knew what lay ahead; she didn't expect to be welcomed. In their last conversation her son had made it clear she was not to override Lilia on anything. Now with Graham gone, her daughter-in-law had little reason to maintain even the most fragile peace.

"It felt right. Graham always liked you," she said.

"Do you know he finished a number of projects for me after he went out on his own? He was one of the first people I called when any house we listed south of here needed work. Renovation, redesign? He was very talented."

Ellen was surprised, but then after Graham had left the Randolph Group, she'd had few heart-to-heart conversations with her son.

Now, for some reason, she thought she needed to explain. "After Graham and Douglas parted ways, I honestly thought we'd all be better off if I didn't take Graham's side. I thought that might give us a chance at reconciliation. Why didn't I realize Douglas would never change his mind? And Graham would never apologize? That the upheaval was permanent?"

Hank didn't reassure her. "Douglas isn't the only one who has strong ideas about how to live."

"Me?"

"We all see ourselves a certain way. When that image is challenged, we do everything we can to shore it up."

"How do I see myself?"

"As keeper of the status quo."

"That's an awful thing to say."

"And an awful day to say it. But remember, how you see yourself and who you really are can be different. Sometimes we act as one, sometimes the other. I think there's a more important voice deep inside we can listen to if we want."

She remembered now why Douglas had never liked Hank. For Douglas, pondering anything but his next acquisition was ludicrous. "Please, tell me you're not doing astrological charts for potential home buyers or meditating in the lotus position while they tour your houses."

He laughed. "I *have* become more introspective with age. That's all." He glanced at his watch. "Come back when you're feeling up to it, and we'll tour the inside. The renters should be cleared out by then."

They walked to his house and took his car, even though she had expected to drive. They could have gone separately, but she hadn't wanted to stand outside the church by herself, waiting for him to arrive.

They chatted about people they both knew, his children, his grandchildren. She told him about Toby and just enough about the circumstances of the baby's birth to forestall questions. They fell silent about halfway to the church and didn't speak again until they were almost there.

"You didn't say where your grandson will live now," Hank said.

She shrugged.

"It's not unusual for grandparents to seek custody these days."

"Douglas hasn't even met Toby."

"His feelings about Graham extend to Graham's son?"

She realized Hank was the only person living who could get away with a question like that. For some reason, even when they were young and starting families of their own, they had always been able to say things to each other that nobody else could. It still puzzled her.

"Douglas wasn't a good father, and there's no reason to think he'd be a better grandfather," she said.

"I'm better. As a grandfather, I mean. I was making my way through the business world when our children were growing up, but now if one of my grandkids needs me, I drop everything. I lost a big deal last year because I went to a soccer game instead of a meeting with a developer. Not Douglas, by the way. One of his competitors."

"If you'd done that to him, Douglas would have blacklisted you for the rest of your life."

"That must be hard to live with." He pulled into the lot where she'd been told she could park, found a spot and turned off the ignition.

"Why were we friends?" she asked before he could get out. "Your family and mine? You never liked Douglas, and he never liked you."

"But Sally and I liked *you*."

"Douglas claimed you just wanted to ride his coattails."

He whistled. "That was the last place I wanted to be, Ellen. I was competitive, sure, but I didn't need or want everything Douglas was after. Nothing he's gained has made him happy. And me? I *am* happy."

"You're lonely."

"You would understand that." He opened

his door, and by the time he came around to hers, they were both ready to stop analyzing and just get through the next hours.

Inside the church she stood with her head held high, but that didn't stop her from looking around. She should have been seated with the family. They should have come into the church together and sat on the same front pew. In all fairness Lilia had asked her to join them, but she had said no. Her own life was built on pretense, and somehow more of it had seemed wrong today. They were not one close, grieving family, and everybody would know that. She was puzzled her daughter-in-law had even tried to pretend. Graham, as sick as he'd been, had made it absolutely clear that Ellen was to stay far away. Lilia had probably insisted on it.

Graham had also done everything he could to make sure securing permanent custody of Toby would be easy for his wife. He'd as much as warned her not to interfere. Or else? She couldn't imagine what her son believed he could do from the grave. Perhaps, in that way, he had inherited some of Douglas's desire to make the world obey him.

As they walked up the center aisle, she saw that Lilia and her parents and two of her brothers, Carrick and his sister, and Toby were already in place. She signaled to Hank that she wanted to sit several rows behind them on the other side of the aisle, and although he frowned, he escorted her there.

Lilia was already accepting condolences from mourners, on her feet and shaking hands and kissing cheeks. When she glimpsed Ellen she squeezed through the aisle and came back.

"Ellen, please, sit with us."

Ellen got to her feet. Hank was already on his. "Lilia, this is a friend of mine and Graham's, too, Hank Gleason."

Lilia looked exhausted but lovely in a dark dress sprinkled with tiny gray flowers. Ellen was relieved she wasn't wearing bright colors, and that her hair was tucked into a knot.

"Hank and I have met. There's room for you both," Lilia said.

Ellen knew better than to broach this now, but she refused to be manipulated. She lowered her voice and angled away from Hank so that only Lilia could hear. "Graham made it clear I'm to stay away from his little family."

The other woman drew a ragged breath. "He didn't mean it the way you're implying. He wants me to have custody, but I've tried to make you welcome in Toby's life. I'll continue."

"Not today." Ellen gave a sharp nod. "I think the service is about to start."

"I'm sorry we're burying your son today, Ellen. We both loved him. I hope you'll come to our house after the reception here." She

319

turned and started back up the aisle.

"You can change your mind," Hank said, when Ellen sat down again.

But Lilia's words were echoing through her head. Maybe they were true, but she didn't believe her daughter-in-law really wanted her to spend time with Toby. She would never forget how angry, how dismissive the young woman had been on the day that Ellen had tried to hold her grandson, and the way Lilia's real feelings about her had risen so quickly to the surface.

Lilia found Graham's mother just as wanting as Ellen found *her*. Was she just putting on a show for the mourners? Or did she have another reason? After all, Graham was no longer alive to inherit any part of the Randolphs' wealth. But Toby was.

"She's a beautiful young woman," Hank said. "I hope the two of you can find common ground in that baby boy. He does look just like Graham, doesn't he?"

Toby would not have looked like Graham if he was Lilia's child, and now he was living proof that Ellen's son had been unfaithful. At the moment of conception, had Graham begun to see that Lilia wasn't the right woman for him? Had he finally realized he had married an outsider who'd led him away from his real family and all they'd expected?

She didn't know. But as the minister came to the front and asked everyone to rise for a prayer, Ellen decided that she owed it to her son and her grandson to find out. Toby was part of his grandmother in a way he would never be part of Lilia. And she deserved to be more than an inconsequential part of his life.

22

Marina arrived late to the memorial service on purpose. Even then she parked on a back street and took her time walking to the church until she saw everyone was inside, and her arrival would no longer arouse curiosity. To remain inconspicuous she had chosen a dark pantsuit and pulled her hair back from her face with a wide beaded headband. Until she crept inside the sanctuary and took a seat in the back row, she hid her eyes with oversized sunglasses. The service was already well underway. Someone Graham had worked with was in front droning on and on about what a great boss he had been.

"Graham had the best ideas," the man was saying. He looked familiar, and Marina thought she'd probably met him on a job site. "But ideas were only part of who he was," he continued. "He had an amazing work ethic."

She tuned out. None of this seemed real.

Graham is dead. She silently formed the

words with her lips, but even then she felt little. Two years ago she'd thought she loved this man. She'd even loved him enough to give birth to his son. Now he was gone, but for her? His death hardly mattered. How could she miss what had never really belonged to her in the first place?

There might be someone here, though, who had belonged to her for a few short months. She had come to catch a glimpse of Toby. She'd made a calculated guess that Lilia might want him with her, because memorial services were more about celebrating life than death. And Toby was Graham's son. His only son and bid for immortality.

At Marina's expense.

The church was small, but the soaring wooden ceilings and the high rows of windows that let in light without distracting views of the street, made the sanctuary feel larger. A woman sitting on the aisle had slid over to make finding a seat easier for her, and now Marina had a view all the way down the center to the front.

She immediately recognized Lilia on the end of the first row, but she didn't see a child. There were other adults, possibly Graham's parents? Lilia's? She thought she recognized the back of Carrick Donnelly's head, but he was too far down to tell for certain.

Then, as she watched, there was movement, and a child's face popped up to stare at the rows of people behind him. A child with a head of blond curls and a cherubic smile.

Her son.

Marina hadn't guessed how she would feel. Nearly a year had passed since she had seen Toby — if he was still called Toby. He'd been a wailing bundle of raw nerve endings, hardly a human at all. But this child? The one now banging his palms happily on the back of the pew and making certain everyone knew Graham lived on in his tiny form? This child was someone entirely different.

"That's Graham's son," the woman beside her whispered, as if Marina was a stranger and couldn't possibly know. "Isn't he adorable?"

Marina gave a quick nod without looking at her.

"It's such a shame Graham didn't live long enough to raise him," the woman said before she sat back. "He was crazy about that little boy."

Marina realized she needed to answer, unless she wanted to draw more attention to herself. "Who wouldn't be?" She realized the irony immediately.

"He — Graham, I mean — did renovations on our house and sometimes he brought Toby if he was just stopping by."

"Clearly devoted," Marina said and leaned farther toward the aisle, hoping that would silence her seatmate.

So her son still carried the name she'd given him. Who would make the important decisions and raise him now? Despite his infidelity and the result, Lilia had stayed with her husband. Most likely she had assumed some of Toby's care and possibly grown fond of him. But legally? She hadn't adopted him. Marina was sure she would have been contacted to sign papers if that had been the case. So what were Lilia's rights? Or wishes?

Of course Graham's parents were probably in the picture. They shared bloodlines, but while Marina didn't know details, she did know that Graham had been estranged from them at one point. Impending death changed everything, of course. Surely the estrangement had ended, and now? Perhaps Graham's parents wanted to take the baby and raise him.

At the front the man finished droning, and a woman with pale red hair moved to the microphone. She nodded and said, "The first reading is from Second Corinthians."

Marina didn't care where the Bible passage was from or what it was about. Her gaze was riveted on the little boy who was now trying to climb over the pew.

As someone pulled Toby away and settled him on a lap, she continued to go over possibilities in her mind. She wanted her son to have a good home. She wanted all the things she had never had for herself. Parents who could afford to raise him. Parents who didn't leave him to his own devices and expect him to take care of them once he was older.

Toby deserved all the good things his father had grown up with. Wholesome food on the table, and a room of his own in a house with a yard. The best schools. Vacations to exotic places. Maybe summer camps and tennis lessons.

Was Lilia teetering on the verge of poverty? Graham must have left a mountain of debt. He'd certainly never attempted to pay Marina the rest of what he'd promised. Of course Graham's illness had undoubtedly wiped out whatever savings he and Lilia had accumulated anyway. Even if Lilia wanted to keep Toby, could she afford to?

That left Graham's parents. Perhaps they would help Lilia now, but perhaps not if the estrangement from their son had never wavered. And if that turned out to be true? The Randolphs were probably in their fifties or older. Who wanted to start another family at that age? Of course they could hire help. From the little she knew, they could afford to give Toby anything he required and everything else besides.

And finally? There was Marina herself.

The young woman finished her reading, and the minister came forward to announce an anthem by the choir. The organist began to play, and the small choir rose.

"Was Graham a friend of yours?" The woman sitting beside Marina seemed to take the music as a signal to chat.

Marina wished the organist would turn up the volume. She glanced at her seatmate, probably in her fifties with wide streaks of gray in her hair and a ruffled blouse. She looked eager to continue.

Marina searched for a conversation stopper. "I didn't know him at all." She paused just long enough. "And from what I've heard about him, frankly, I'm just as glad I didn't."

The woman's eyes widened, then she slid away from Marina and turned her face to the front.

With relief Marina went back to thinking about her son. Maybe if her marriage were happier, if she could have a heart-to-heart with Blake and ask him to reconsider his position, then she could try to be a mother again. But Blake became more preoccupied every day, and more watchful of every penny. He'd canceled several credit cards, and these days she cooked almost every meal. No real explanation had been forthcoming. He'd said this was a tough time for most companies in the Valley, and tough times meant everybody had to be tougher, too.

She wondered if this was a slogan one of his sons had coined. Were Wayne and Paul trying to squeeze their father financially so he would squeeze her out of his life? It seemed preposterous, but she wasn't sure Blake would even understand what was happening. Half the time she wasn't sure he understood the things she said to him. The most recent bonus to disappear was morning coffee in bed. Most of the time Blake was gone when she woke up, and when she finally saw him in the evening and asked about his day, he was vague, as if he didn't really remember.

The woman beside her began to hum along with the choir, then tap her foot. In a moment she was singing under her breath. When she saw Marina glance at her, she narrowed her eyes and sang a little louder.

She had been on her own for so long she knew she needed to return to working full-time so that when everything blew up — as things had so often in her life — she could take care of herself. She'd asked her boss to reinstate her former schedule, but he'd told her he had to let her go entirely. He had waved pages of statistics to prove her dismissal was the result of an economic downturn.

Of course the statistics also meant that finding another job in the industry was going to be challenging. Since then she'd learned that marketing jobs of all kinds were scarce and applicants plentiful.

Toby was old enough for day care, but what kind of life would he have in the off hours if she could even find work? If she could convince Blake that Toby had to live with them, what would it be like for the little boy to be raised by a reluctant father old enough to be his grandfather, and a mother who'd already proven she didn't want him?

Everyone stood for a responsive reading, and reluctantly Marina stood, too. A hymn was sung, and while she fidgeted, hoping for another glimpse of her son, Carrick Donnelly came forward to eulogize Graham.

Sitting again, she half listened. Carrick told funny stories about growing up as Graham's friend, and then moved on to how much those who had loved him would miss him. He was a striking figure in his dark suit, and the church fell silent as he continued, listening raptly. Like any good lawyer he knew how to play to the jury.

And who would judge Graham now? Marina supposed each person sitting there would have to do that for themselves.

Near the end, a man in the family pew got up and started down the side aisle with Toby in his arms. Marina was too far back to know if there'd been any commotion, but she imagined the little boy had finally tired of good behavior. The man, who resembled Lilia, was probably her father.

And Lilia's father wouldn't know Marina from any other well wisher.

Her chance to see her son up close had arrived. She waited until the man and child disappeared, and then she discreetly got up and headed out the center doors.

In the vestibule Toby and his escort were nowhere to be seen. When a door banged somewhere to the left she realized there must be a corridor leading off the side aisle exit.

Another woman was standing nearby, and when Marina tried to move past her to look for her son, the woman cocked her head, then frowned. She put a hand on Marina's arm, surprising her. She was an attractive blonde, middle-aged and expensively dressed, but the frown looked as if it wasn't the first of the day.

She examined Marina through narrowed eyes, then she nodded. "I know who you are," she said softly.

Marina shook off her hand. "Excuse me. I need to leave."

This time the woman clamped her hand on Marina's wrist and her fingers tightened. "Don't make a scene." She nodded to emphasize her words. "Believe me. It's not to your advantage, but talking to me might be. I promise I can make our conversation worth your while."

"Who *are* you?"

The woman nodded toward the front door. "I'm Ellen Randolph, Graham's mother. And hearing what I have to say might be the best thing that's ever happened to you."

23

The reception for Graham's closest friends was quiet but not subdued. Everyone had a favorite story to tell. Tears were shed; wine and beer flowed freely, and despite the reception at the church, Graham's favorite foods quickly disappeared.

By the time the only guests remaining were Regan and Carrick, Toby had been passed around and gushed over so much that now he was exhausted and fussy.

In the dining room Regan bounced the baby on her hip like a pro while she gathered up the last of the paper plates and napkins. "This guy's getting sleepy. Would you like me to put him to bed for you? I know where all his things are."

Lilia's parents had left a few minutes before to take her brothers to the airport for their flight home, and Lilia realized that as Regan made the offer, she had almost looked for Graham to see what he thought.

She took a moment to recover. "I think I'll

do it. He's had quite a day. We probably need to fall back on our normal bedtime ritual."

"I'll say good-night then." Regan moved closer and kissed her cheek. "Kitchen's in pretty good shape. Leave the rest of it. After Toby goes to bed, you should, too."

Lilia took the baby and then hugged her. "*Mahalo.* I don't know what I would do without you."

Carrick had been clearing the last of the dishes from the patio, and he didn't leave when his sister did. Instead he ended up in the kitchen while Lilia made Toby's bottle. He only got one at night now, since he was drinking well from a cup, but so far she hadn't been able to wean him completely. She suspected *she* was the problem, not the baby, because she loved to hold and cuddle him before bed.

"The service was perfect." She opened the refrigerator and took out a container of grapes she'd sliced to keep Toby busy while she worked. The baby loved the slimy texture on his fingers and tongue. "Graham would have loved your eulogy."

"I know how hard today must have been for you. It was hard for me."

"Rationally I know it was an ending, but I'm not sure I've really digested it. I keep expecting Graham to walk into the room."

"You will for a long time."

"The church was packed. A lot of people

needed to say goodbye."

"Ellen didn't stay for the reception."

She knew he'd been paying close attention, just in case. "If I had to guess? I don't think she wanted to talk to my family or me. And most of Graham's friends wouldn't even know who she was."

Had Ellen stayed, despite the rift between them, Lilia would have been required to introduce her mother-in-law and make certain she felt comfortable. With everything else about the day, she was grateful Ellen had departed.

"Lilia, I know you're beat. I know what an awful day this was. But there's something you need to know. Because we don't have time to spare."

She measured powder into Toby's bottle and filled it with warm water, shaking it to be sure it was mixed. The grapes were still a hit, but she knew the bottle would be a bigger one very soon.

"I need to get Toby upstairs. This can't wait?"

She saw Carrick didn't want to tell her what she already suspected, not any more than she wanted to hear it. But Toby wasn't going to let them talk for much longer.

"Marina?" she asked.

"She was at the service. I saw her in the back when I was giving the eulogy."

Nothing she could think to say was appropriate with the baby balanced on her hip. So she said nothing.

Carrick filled the silence. "You have custody for the moment, and we'll move on to permanent as soon as we can."

"What would I do without you?"

"At least she didn't show up at the reception. I stationed myself by the door to be sure, but she didn't appear. Maybe she just wanted to catch a glimpse of Toby."

"Or maybe she just needed to say goodbye to *my* husband."

"A possibility."

"I could have done without this."

"Like I told you before, we can't put things off until you're back on your feet. We need to make sure everything goes through without a hitch, and your behavior has to be exemplary."

Toby had spotted his octopus on a kitchen stool, and she set him down so he could rescue it. "What should I do if she shows up here?"

"You'll need to be careful. California law favors communication and cooperation among parents, and if you look like you're keeping Marina from seeing her son for no good reason, it won't look good in court."

"She can just walk up to the door and make demands?"

"She did once before, didn't she?"

Lilia's heart was pounding too fast. She

steadied herself against the counter. "Can she just take him and never bring him back?"

"No judge would look favorably on that, not after everything else she did and certainly not while you have emergency custody. Tell her you want to settle final custody amicably, and you hope you don't have to go through the courts, but you will if necessary."

"She's married now. She may have the money to hire a good lawyer."

"He won't be as good as I am, or as devoted."

She wanted to cry. Carrick looked as if he were one step away from taking her into his arms, but neither of them moved. She swallowed, then she nodded. "We'll see what happens."

"That's all I really had to say."

"Thank you, as always."

"I promised Graham I'd see this through. But you know I would anyway. For you. For Toby." He nodded, then without another word, he bent down and kissed the baby's cheek and headed for the door.

Toby was whimpering now, and for once she was glad for the distraction. She scooped him up, bottle tucked against her chest, and he immediately relaxed against her.

Upstairs she gave him his favorite board book while she undressed him and changed his diaper. Then she found his Spider-Man pajamas and managed to slide them up his legs. The book went into his mouth for just seconds before he tossed it to the ground and began to rub his eyes. She worked at top speed and managed to finish dressing him despite epic squirms and escalating screeches.

In the rocker she settled him in her arms and gave him the bottle. He tried to hold it himself, but she held it, too.

"Hey, you're my little boy, kiddo. Let me do the honors."

At first he sucked as if world peace depended on it, but eventually he slowed, and his eyes began to close.

"You need a story, so tonight I'll tell you the story of you." Lilia brushed his cloud of curls off his face. "Once upon a time you were born to a daddy who wanted you very badly. You came to live with him when you were just a tiny baby, and that's where I come into the story. Because even though you were a big surprise for me, I fell in love with you, Toby. And before very long, being with you became the best part of every single day."

His eyes opened, and he gave her a sleepy smile, as if he really understood what she was saying. Then, without warning, his hand shot up and he touched her cheek. "Mamamama!"

Her eyes filled with tears and she kissed his tiny fingers. "You're still my favorite part of every day, and you were your daddy's, too. He wanted to stay with you forever, but sometimes we can't do exactly what we want, no matter how hard we try. And your daddy tried and tried, believe me. Nobody ever tried harder. So now he can't be right here with you anymore, but he'll watch over you the rest of your life from heaven. He loved you so much, Toby. I'll never let you forget that. We'll both miss him forever, but we have his love. He left that for us to share. And there's so much of it, neither of us will ever go without it."

His eyes closed. He was still sucking but slowly. And after a minute, he stopped. Fast asleep.

She continued to rock him, but now she was whispering.

"There are all kinds of mommies, Toby. But there's one kind little boys need most of all. That's the kind who will love them forever, no matter if they make mistakes, or don't want to do their homework, or even if they say bad things they really don't mean. I'm one of those kinds, and no matter what happens in your life or mine? From this moment on, I'll love you every way, anyway. I want to stay with you forever, just the way your daddy wanted to. And I'm going to try to make sure I can."

She rose slowly and carried him to the crib and settled him there, covering him with a light blanket. She watched him sleep. Then she nodded.

"But, Toby? No matter what happens? I

hope you'll always know how much I love you. We were meant to be together, you and me, no matter how it happened. And I promise, whatever I have to do, I'm going to make sure we are."

24

On the Monday afternoon after Graham's memorial service, Marina still wasn't sure why she'd agreed to meet Ellen Randolph for lunch. By the time Ellen had conveyed where to meet and when, Marina had run out of time to look for her son. And there hadn't been time to question Graham's mother, either. People were exiting, and the last thing Marina had wanted was to have conversations with any of them.

The café Ellen had chosen was tucked away on a side street in the south end of the city. Now, as she waited for the other woman's arrival, Marina went over possible reasons for being here. Perhaps Ellen wanted to pay her off so she would stay out of Toby's life for good. Or maybe she was just on a scouting mission so she could tell Lilia why Marina had attended the service Saturday.

A third possibility? Maybe Ellen thought that her job, lifeguard patrolling the family gene pool, was to check out Toby's mother in person and decide if her only grandson might be worthy enough to become the new Randolph heir.

If that was the case, she wasn't going to like what she found. Marina's gene pool was more polluted than some of Southern California's beaches.

As Ellen walked in, Marina pretended to consider the menu for the third time. She had seen the older woman approach through the windows overlooking the sidewalk, but she didn't want to appear overeager.

She looked up when Ellen's shadow fell across the table, and she nodded. "I ordered a glass of wine. I'm sure our server will be right over to see what you'd like."

As Ellen seated herself, Marina made mental notes. She was dressed more casually than she'd been at the service, in a pale blue cashmere sweater and matching cardigan over darker trousers. A long strand of silver beads topped off the outfit, and she carried what had to be a genuine snakeskin handbag. Her makeup was understated and her hair the blond of her son's. Marina saw Graham in Ellen's nose and eyes.

The older woman had carefully chosen their meeting place. The dining area was nondescript, with gray walls and black lacquered tables. Even at dinnertime there probably wasn't much of a wait here, but at this time of day only half the tables were full. Better yet, they were set far enough apart that conversation was possible.

Their server appeared immediately, and Ellen asked for an old-fashioned. Then she folded her perfectly manicured hands and leaned forward. "I'm glad you came. I wasn't sure you would."

"I'm intrigued." Marina considered whether to say she was sorry about Graham's death, something she hadn't had time to say in church, but she decided against it. Ellen obviously knew who she was, and how Graham had treated her.

"I wasn't lying in wait for you in the vestibule. I wanted to leave before everyone else did, and the friend I came with had just gone to fetch his car. Maybe it was fate we would run into each other."

"How did you figure out who I was?"

Ellen was perfectly composed. Her hands didn't even twitch.

"I'd seen your photograph," she said after a long moment. "When I found out about the baby, about Toby, I wanted to know who his mother was. It's not a well-kept secret. And there were pictures of you online."

"I'll make an educated guess and assume you learned more than just what I look like."

Ellen raised one eyebrow in answer. "It's very hard to keep secrets these days. You have social media accounts."

"And you probably have professionals who

can look in other places, too."

Ellen didn't deny it. "You're the mother of my grandson. And my son wasn't forthcoming about details."

"Graham would have been perfectly delighted to forget I existed."

The bar wasn't busy, and their drinks arrived quickly. Neither of them was prepared to order, but Ellen asked for bruschetta with an assortment of toppings to share. They sipped in silence, and Marina decided Ellen was preparing for the next round.

"I'd like a few answers," Ellen said after a while. "I'm sorry this is so personal, and we are, after all, strangers. But we are connected to the same little boy."

Marina gave a slight nod.

"Graham claimed the two of you spent just one night together? That you never had a real relationship? That's true?"

Marina knew if their conversation started with something so private, it would go swiftly downhill. She deflected. "Would you believe anything I told you? I'm just the other woman, and you know what *we're* like."

Ellen tried a different approach. "How devoted were you to my son? It takes devotion of a sort, doesn't it, to have a man's child? A married man at that."

"A foolish devotion. Graham and I were attracted to each other at our first meeting, and obviously attraction escalated. Disastrously or fortunately, depending on how you view the result."

"Toby."

"Yes. Toby."

"Why did you go through with the pregnancy? You must have realized my son wasn't going to leave Lilia. And later you must have learned about his illness."

"Graham begged me to have the baby. In fact I think he used me like a surrogate. Pretty desperate, wouldn't you say? Anyway, I agreed to go forward when he promised to support us."

When Ellen didn't respond, Marina decided to be even more honest. "At the beginning I also hoped a baby would lead to more. I hoped when Lilia found out what he'd done, she would ditch him, and he'd come straight to me. When it was too late to change my mind, I realized how wrong I'd been. The support fell through, or at least a lot of it. By the time Toby was born I realized Graham might shoot a few bucks my way now and then, but I would be pretty much on my own otherwise."

"So you gave him the baby. Because he didn't *pay* you?"

The bruschetta arrived, and they waited for their server to leave. Marina leaned forward, the way Ellen had at the beginning of the conversation.

"You are filthy rich. I don't know exactly

how rich or care, but you've probably never, in your entire life, tried to balance rent, child care, food and all the other expenses a single mother manages alone. I grew up in a home like that, and I can tell you nothing ever balances. We were dirt poor, and I saw history was about to repeat itself."

"And Toby was a difficult baby." Ellen sounded like she knew what that meant.

"Yes, the worst possible kind. Or at least the worst possible *healthy* baby. Because nobody could find anything wrong with him. They just patted my hand, and that was that."

"Graham was the same way."

"I bet you had help."

"More than I should have." Ellen didn't elaborate. "I'm not here to skewer you, Marina, or criticize choices you've made. Just to understand them."

"I don't see why. What's done is done."

"Toby's future is lying in the balance."

The other day in the church Marina's thoughts had traveled the same path.

"Are you wondering what Lilia plans to do with him?" Ellen asked when Marina remained silent.

"When Graham was alive I knew Toby would be well taken care of. I might not think much of your son personally, but I knew he would be a good father."

"And Lilia?"

"If she decided to stay with Graham, I

figured she'd try to be a good mother. And if she wasn't, Graham wouldn't stand for it. But leaving the baby with them was the best I could do for all of us. I really didn't have much choice. I had to work. Can you imagine Toby in day care screaming all day?"

"It was more than that, though, wasn't it?"

"I'm not ashamed. I wanted my life back. With support, not just financial but in other ways, maybe Toby and I could have made some kind of life together. But I didn't have that, so I figured it was time Graham learned what it really means to be a parent. After all, Toby was his idea."

"And then you got married."

"I didn't expect that."

"It would have been hard . . . impossible?" Ellen turned up her hands. "How could you pursue a husband if Toby was around?"

Marina realized she was smiling, although nothing about the conversation was funny. "Look at me, Ellen. You might not love what you see, but do you actually doubt I've had marriage proposals before? Men *like* me. More than a few have loved me. I didn't have to pursue Blake. I just had to be in the vicinity when he decided he wanted to spend the rest of his life with me."

"He didn't want Toby?"

"He didn't know about Toby. Not until after we married."

The bruschetta hadn't been touched by

either of them. Marina picked up a baguette slice and added a tomato topping, popping it into her mouth, chewing and swallowing, before she went on.

"You said Toby's future was lying in the balance. What did you mean?"

"Surely you've considered who'll take custody."

"I have."

"Graham wanted Lilia to adopt Toby. He told me so in our last conversation."

Marina finished another slice. "That's the first I've heard about adoption. I'm sure someone would have consulted me."

"I spoke to my attorney. Have you seen Toby since you left him with Graham? Have you communicated with him?"

"He's really not old enough to hold a telephone."

Ellen looked pained. "Birthday cards? Gifts? Have you contributed to his support?"

"With what? And no, I gave Toby to Graham, and I figured that anything else I tried to do would be unwelcome interference."

"Didn't you care what was going on?"

"I *knew* what was going on. Graham and I work in the same business. Occasionally I heard about Toby through the grapevine, and I knew Graham would find me if he really needed my help."

"Here's what my attorney says. Because this was a stepparent adoption, if you *hadn't* initiated contact in a year's time, the courts would have ruled that you abandoned your son. Most likely you would have lost all rights, and Lilia could have become his mother."

Marina digested that along with another piece of bruschetta. She had wondered if lawyers would step in, but when nothing had happened, she hadn't seen any urgency to act. She had wanted to see how the baby did, how *she* did, before she got embroiled in legalities. She'd assumed that when the time was right, an agreement could be worked out.

"Wouldn't somebody have to inform me about an action like that?" she asked.

"My guess? They decided waiting a year was a gamble, but if it paid off, they would reap the rewards."

"A year from the day I left him with them?"

"A year from that day. Of course it didn't pay off because Graham died before they could file the paperwork."

Ellen signaled their server and ordered another round of drinks. "The Cobb salad is good," she told Marina while the server waited.

Marina's appetite had fled, but she nodded and Ellen ordered two.

"This doesn't really seem like your kind of place," Marina said. "How do you know what's good?"

"We're just a few miles from Graham's

347

house. I came here once to recover from an encounter with my daughter-in-law. I ordered the salad because I needed a reason to take up a table."

Marina was surprised Ellen was admitting to weakness. "I don't suppose you'll tell me about that encounter?"

"It's irrelevant." Ellen made a face, another surprise. Marina had thought Botox or a lack of real emotion had rendered her incapable.

Then Ellen surprised her again by adding. "Only it's not, I suppose. It's not irrelevant. That day Lilia made it clear she wanted me out of Toby's life. And I'm his grandmother. His only real grandmother —"

"My mother would be surprised to hear that."

Ellen bit her lip. Then she waved her hand. "The only grandmother he ever knew. I'm sorry."

"For the record not *that,* either. My mother tried to be a good grandmother when Toby was with me." Marina was surprised to find herself defending Deedee, but as far as it went, it was true. Her mother, as flighty and clueless as she was, had done her best.

"Lilia wants me out of Toby's life," Ellen said. "Advice annoys her. My presence annoys her. And that baby needs me. I'm the only link to his father. Lilia would sever that completely if she had her way. She claims otherwise, but I know who she really is."

"Who *is* she?"

"Lilia's family is very happy being who they are. Believe me, I'm not prejudiced because they're Hawaiian. They're good people, just not ambitious. They're happy where they are, but she's not like them. She told me once that as long as she could remember, she wanted to leave Hawaii and move to the mainland. She met Graham when they were still children. I can't say she decided right then that Graham would be her ticket to a different life, but I can't say it's not true, either."

Marina knew she was often unfair to people. Mostly she didn't care. Her entire life had been unfair, and spreading a little around didn't bother her. But Ellen's view of Lilia surprised her. She didn't like Lilia. How could she when Graham had chosen his wife over the mother of his baby? At the same time, she couldn't imagine the young woman as a schemer or manipulator.

"So you're saying that Lilia married Graham just to get ahead?"

"Can you imagine anyone more able to give a girl like Lilia everything she ever wanted?"

Marina wondered how much Ellen knew about *her* background. Because Lilia might be from a culture Ellen clearly didn't value — no matter what she said — but Marina came from a family with no culture at all.

"I'm not sure where you're going with this,"

349

Marina said. "Do you want me to support a bid for custody? Do you want me to say I think you'd be a better mother for my son than Lilia would?"

"It can't be that direct."

"Why not? A lot of grandparents are raising grandchildren."

"Because my husband doesn't want Toby. He's never seen him, and he doesn't want to." She bit her lip again, as if she was searching for words. "He and Graham were estranged, so Douglas wouldn't have been happy to hear about any grandchild. But . . . ."

Marina finished for her. "The circumstances of Toby's birth make it less likely he'll come around."

"Douglas rarely changes his mind about anything. Maybe in time, he'll come to accept Toby, I don't know. Maybe someday when it's clear that Toby is a child to be proud of."

"How clear? Straight A's? Eagle Scout? Developing a billion dollar start-up before he's twelve?"

Ellen waved that away. "I'm not counting on Douglas. Graham was never good enough for my husband, and unless age softens him, Toby won't be, either. In the meantime no court would give us custody, not when one of us doesn't want it."

"So what do you want from me?"

"I want you to get custody yourself."

Marina finished her first glass of wine and waited to speak until the second was in front of her with what was obviously a pre-assembled Cobb salad.

"You dislike Lilia that much? You want me to raise Toby to spite Lilia? I've heard of tension between in-laws, but that's extreme, wouldn't you say?"

"You've missed the point."

"Apparently."

"I want easy access to my grandson. In fact I want him with me whenever it makes sense. Douglas is gone more than he's home. He travels frequently to view property, and he can be away for weeks at a time. Toby could be with me whenever Douglas is away."

"You don't think your husband would figure out that something was going on?"

"He'd know, of course. I'm not delusional. But as long as Toby wasn't in sight, he'd just have to live with it. He's not going to divorce me. I'm too important to him and everything he's built."

"And I would have Toby the rest of the time?"

"Yes."

"What kind of percentages are we talking about?"

Ellen looked annoyed. "We would just have to work things out."

"Uh-uh." Marina shook her head. "You might be able to *work things out,* but on my end? I'm looking for a full-time job, and I'll be back to square one with a child. When Toby was with me I'd have to plan day care, if any reputable center would even take him on such an erratic schedule. And what about weekends? I would never be able to take trips out of town with my husband. You're asking me to manage doctor's appointments and play dates. My husband didn't sign on for any of that, and most of the time he's gone during the day, so he couldn't help."

"Of course all those things would be problems if you needed a job."

"I *do.*"

"I see raising Toby as a job, Marina. Even as part-time as Toby would be for you. I couldn't ask you to plan all the things you just named around my schedule. But if you weren't working, wouldn't everything be much easier? If I paid you so you could afford to raise my grandson? Why shouldn't I? I'm asking you to bend your life around mine and his. And you'll be paid more than you would be for a full-time job in your profession, but most of the week you'll only be part-time. What I'll give you won't depend on the hours you spend with my grandson."

"*My son.*"

"Yes. *Your* son."

Marina tried to imagine the scenario Ellen was describing. Some weeks she would rarely see Toby. Others she might have him most of the time. How would Blake feel about that? He hadn't signed on to be a father.

And what about Toby? How would traveling between his mother and grandmother affect him?

Ellen read her mind. "Maybe it's not ideal for a baby to go back and forth, but children of divorce do it all the time. And isn't this better than being raised by a woman with no biological ties? This way he has his real mother, his real grandmother, and every financial advantage. And we can make the transitions smooth. He would have a room at my house, and one at yours. We could furnish them in similar ways. Each of us would have whatever he needs right at our fingertips, so he didn't have to pack more than the favorite toy of the week. Children adjust to whatever situation they're in, as long as it's healthy and tension free."

"He'll be in school by the time he's five. I'm sure you and I don't live in the same school district."

"We'll choose a private school somewhere between us, so we can both have easy access."

"Don't you travel with your husband? It seems to me Graham said you were gone most of his childhood."

Ellen didn't wince — at least not exactly. "I was gone much too much, but I won't be going on extended trips anymore. I'll be in town to take my grandson as often as I can."

"What's different?"

"I can't make up those lost years to Graham, but I can be a good parent . . . grandparent, an exceptional grandparent, to his son. *Your* son. Whatever Graham claimed he wanted for Toby — and he was too sick to make good decisions by the time custody came up — this is better."

"And Lilia?"

"Adoption seems out of the question now, doesn't it? She's not Toby's stepmother anymore, and nothing she planned is the same, including the law. I wonder, don't you, if she'll be relieved? Toby's not really hers. She's taken care of him, of course, but Graham was in the picture, doing his part. Now she can start a new life, not weighed down by a child she has no real ties to. If she wants to see Toby occasionally, we could allow that, as long as it didn't upset him."

"You think she'll agree?"

"Oh, she'll put up a fuss at first. But she's under a great deal of stress. Finances alone must be a drain. I'm sure the medical bills are overwhelming. When she's able to see the entire picture, she'll probably agree without much of a fight."

Marina tried to imagine that. She didn't know how Lilia felt about Toby. How could she? But she did know Lilia and Ellen had clashed over Toby's care. And didn't that indicate a strong attachment? Or had it simply been a power struggle?

She felt her way. "I'm sorry, but I'm confused. You just said she's probably under a lot of pressure *financially*?"

Ellen nodded. When Marina waited she gave a small sigh. "My husband is adamant we can't pay whatever bills came with Graham's illness. Graham made choices, and he needed to live with them."

"Of course he didn't, did he? He didn't *live* with them. It's hard to teach a dead man a lesson."

Ellen's tone was icier. "I think you can see that stepping in and helping after all our unpleasantness would look like I'm trying to control her. Lilia would dig in her heels. And besides, financial uncertainty might make it simpler for her to give Toby to you without a fight. Perhaps later, when custody is resolved, I can pay the last of whatever she owes for my son's final care."

Marina didn't want to pursue this, but she knew she had to understand even the undercurrents. "You've fought. Will she want you raising Graham's son?"

Ellen shook her head. "She won't know."

"I'm sorry?"

"Lilia will know that *you* have custody, and that'll be that. How much time he spends with me will no longer be her business. So there'll be no mention of our arrangement. And you'll win. I guarantee it. What court would rule otherwise, particularly because you'll have good representation, which I'll pay for."

Marina realized Ellen's reason for this meeting had finally been revealed. "How can you be so sure?"

"I'm sure because you'll tell the judge what you told me. You were more or less forced to turn Toby over to Graham by circumstances and finances. But now, with Graham's death and your marriage, you're the best choice to be his mother."

"Really? And what if nobody else thinks so?"

Ellen leaned forward. "Who would think otherwise except Lilia? You *are* Toby's mother, Marina. And that means that, going forward, you hold all the cards."

25

Marina was rarely confused. As a child she'd figured out that doing anything was better than doing nothing, and acting as if she'd made the right decision was nearly as helpful as making one.

This evening, though, she was off her game. After lunch with Ellen, she was light years from making a decision. On the surface the other woman's offer was golden. Marina wouldn't have to find a job, and she would only be a part-time mother. Ellen might have a lot to say about raising Toby, but Marina's name would be on the custody documents.

Of course the offer *seemed* golden, but it might be, at best, gold-plated. Problems rimmed the horizon. Blake might not agree to any of this, and Marina would have to deal with Ellen until Toby was an adult.

Finally? If Lilia lost custody now, would she be willing to resume it in the future if she was needed?

The last seemed unlikely. As sad as it was,

Graham and Lilia had provided a safety net, but who would be her safety net if Ellen died or lost interest in her grandson? With the passing of time, wasn't it likely Lilia would move on to a different life, and Toby would become a stranger she was no longer invested in?

Marina had known Graham's parents were wealthy, although she'd also known they were estranged. This afternoon, though, she'd done a little online research, and she had been blown away by exactly how wealthy the Randolphs were. In fact Douglas Randolph seemed to be ruthlessly focused on accumulating property and power, and wildly successful at both. Obviously Ellen could afford what she was proposing. And in the future, if Toby didn't blow his chances — the way his father obviously had — Toby might be a wealthy young man indeed.

With a headache and too many possibilities, she made her way to the kitchen to open another bottle of wine, having already finished part of one from the refrigerator. Blake wasn't yet home. He usually remembered to text her to say when he would arrive, but it was almost seven, and she hadn't heard from him all day. If he arrived at some point, ready to eat, she had leftovers she could warm. But even though she'd barely picked at her salad this afternoon, she wasn't hungry.

She was cursing the wine cork, which had

broken off before she could get it out, when Blake walked in. She noticed he forgot to lock the door behind him.

"I apologize for being so late."

She watched him hang up his coat by the front door and waited until he joined her in the kitchen. "Have you eaten?"

He took a moment to answer, as if that required focus. "I had a late lunch. I'm not really hungry. I hope you didn't go to a lot of trouble."

"When I didn't hear from you I thought we'd just have leftovers."

"Good. Want me to get things out of the fridge?"

Normally she would have said no, but now, teaching him to share the kitchen chores made sense. If she accepted Ellen's offer — or even if she simply found a job — she would become a breadwinner, too.

"Put everything on the island. I'll get the plates. I think everything can go in the microwave."

He gestured to the bottle in front of her. "Looks like a cork mishap. Want me to get the bottle open first?"

"I mangled it. Sorry."

"Easy to do."

She let him take the corkscrew as she got everything they would need from cabinets and drawers. He quickly removed what had remained of the cork, and as she watched, poured them both a glass.

While she took her first sip he removed a couple of plastic containers from the refrigerator, then one more, lifting a corner of the lid. "Last night's broccoli looks good."

She was encouraged he remembered when they'd had the broccoli. She took the containers as he handed them to her and opened them, adding serving spoons. Then she dabbed food on a plate, added a small chicken thigh and put it in the microwave.

"Like I said, I did hope to get home by five. But time got away from me."

She was perplexed. "Like you *said*?"

"In my message."

She'd had her cell phone with her all day, and there had been no message. "Something must have gone wrong. I didn't get one."

"Were you out? Did you check the machine when you got back?"

"The home phone?" She realized that, this time, she'd been the one who was preoccupied. "I never thought to look at the answering machine."

"I figured if you had gone somewhere you might not want an interruption. So I didn't call your cell."

She put her hand on his shoulder and her lips on his cheek. "You're a thoughtful man. And I'll check next time."

"Want to tell me about your day?"

She didn't. At least not until she figured

out how to tell him. "I did some shopping. Groceries," she hurried to say, since that was one thing he couldn't complain about spending money on. "I worked out, then I cooled down on a walk through the rose garden." The municipal rose garden, a showstopper on any tour of the city, hadn't been far from the restaurant Ellen had chosen, and she'd had it largely to herself, since February wasn't the right time for blooms.

Now she wondered what it would be like to take Toby there in the spring. She imagined a slightly older version of the baby she'd seen yesterday trying to climb into the fountain in the middle.

"How about you?" she asked, smiling.

"Same old."

"There's a lot of that going around."

He warmed up his plate when hers came out, and they took them both to the small table in the breakfast nook. They never used the larger table by the French doors leading to a patio. At the beginning she had thought it might be fun to host a dinner party, but who would they invite? They weren't making friends together, and Blake had cut himself off from his old ones. Neither had family they wanted to entertain.

What would it be like for Toby in this community of mostly singles and retirees, where children were accepted but not welcomed? A lone playground stood behind the clubhouse, and it was small enough that it might as well have a sign: "For the Occasional Grandchild."

Dinner passed in silence, and afterwards Marina cleaned up their few dishes while Blake went into his office. An hour later she gave up on a television sitcom and decided to get ready for bed. If Blake ever stopped working, maybe there would be a chance for another conversation, although she didn't know what she would say. She was as confused now as she'd been earlier.

Once in bed she tried to read, but the chapter went the way of the sitcom. Ready to turn out the light, she opened her nightstand drawer to put away her reading glasses and saw her baby son staring up at her. She drew out the photo that Deedee had given her on Toby's birthday and held it up to the light.

Blake chose that moment to come into the bedroom. She knew that making a fuss and trying to hide the photo would draw more attention. She opened the drawer wider and slid it back inside, closing it. She was about to turn off her bedside lamp when Blake spoke.

"He's a beautiful baby. He looks a little like his mother."

She wondered if Blake had checked out the photo when she was away. "He looks more like his father."

"Maybe, but I see you in him, too."

"His father died." She wasn't sure exactly

where that had come from. Sometimes, even though she'd schooled herself from childhood to be cautious, she was afraid she'd inherited at least a few bad habits from her mother.

"When? Did you just find out?"

She told him the basics, ending with: "His memorial service was Saturday."

"Did you go?"

"I did, but only to see my son. I thought he might be there, and he was."

Blake sat on the edge of the bed and faced her.

"How was he?"

"Adorable. I didn't see him up close. Just from a distance."

He looked surprised by this news. "When were you going to tell me?"

"I don't know, Blake. I'm still trying to figure it out."

"Who has him now?"

"Graham's wife. Lilia."

"Your son's stepmother?"

"Is she still Toby's stepmother if she's no longer married to his father?"

"It probably depends on why you're asking. And who."

"Toby's grandmother — Graham's mother — took me out to lunch today to talk the whole thing over."

"In between the rose garden and Safeway."

"I did both those things, too." Mentally she paged through what she could tell him now and what she probably never would.

"You'd met her before?"

"No, but she recognized me at the service. We both left a little early. She asked me to meet her today."

"And?"

She felt her way. Omission was bad enough, and she didn't want to lie outright. He waited until she had explained Ellen's concerns about Toby.

"Why doesn't Ellen ask for custody then?" he asked.

Marina embroidered. "She and her husband travel for his business. That, and possibly their age, would be a hindrance, and a judge wouldn't look favorably on giving them responsibility for a child as young as Toby. But she wanted me to know that if I get custody, she would like to have Toby sometimes. Like any other grandmother."

"If *you* get custody?"

"I *am* his mother."

"But you haven't been for a while, Rina."

"Did I stop being his mother because Toby's father was taking care of him?"

"His father *and* his father's wife."

"At the time I thought a clean break was better for all of us. But now? Things are so different, and there's an added element. If Lilia doesn't want Graham's own mother involved in my son's life, not only is that unfair, what does that say about her? Even though I'm his mother, is she going to keep me away from him, too? She could go to court to terminate my rights, may already have done so, and I just haven't been notified yet. And if that happens, I might be left out of future decisions. For all I know if she decides she doesn't want Toby, after all, he could be adopted by strangers."

She rested her fingers on his arm. "I think it's clear I need to consult a lawyer."

"It sounds like you're seriously considering it."

He hadn't told her to forget it. She was encouraged. "I have to think it over. And you need to do the same. Just remember there are two grandmothers ready and willing to help when we need them. We won't be without resources."

He looked skeptical, but he didn't challenge her. "No wonder you seemed so far away at dinner."

She'd gone as far as she could for now. The time had come to change the subject.

"That's my story. Now why have *you* been so distant?" The question emerged abruptly, once again, straight from her inner Deedee.

"Let's make this a national holiday and call it Confession Day."

Something was very wrong. Her warm feelings evaporated. Was this the moment he was going to admit he was starting to forget things, that he was finding daily life confusing, and she needed, at the very least, to prepare? Had he spoken to a doctor and gotten bad news?

She tried to sound as normal as possible. "You have something to confess, too?"

He got up suddenly and began to pace. "MeriTech Network Systems is on the skids, Rina. It's that simple and that complicated."

Since this wasn't what she'd expected, she was startled. MeriTech, the company he had founded, had sounded solid in every conversation they'd had about it. "Since when?"

He stopped pacing and looked at her. He suddenly looked older, at least a decade older than his fifty-two. "I told you I let my sons take over when Franny was so sick. It was a mistake. I even knew it at the time, but I didn't really care. I'd been through so much, and was still going through so much. Franny didn't die easily or well. Even at the end she insisted on staying at home instead of in a hospital or hospice, where they were set up to help her. I told you how she fell apart when we were in Europe?"

She remembered Wayne's version of the trip, but she nodded.

"As the illness progressed she was less and less able to handle change. She fell into a deep depression when she was away from the house, and later, when she was away from her bed. The doctors finally suggested round-the-clock nursing care. So that's what we did.

366

But if I tried to leave, she fell apart again."

She believed him. About this much, at least, Wayne had probably been lying. Blake was too emotional for this to not be true.

"I let the boys take over MeriTech. We're tiny in comparison to the big players like Cisco, but we have a niche we've managed to hold on to. I thought we were safe enough, so I gave them control. Things weren't fabulous. It's a tough business, but we seemed to be in a holding pattern. Both Wayne and Paul had been involved in administration for some time, and while neither was a brilliant manager, they were solid enough. I thought they could provide steady leadership."

"Were you planning to take over again after . . . everything settled down?" She paused, then decided to push on. "Were you worried about your *health*?"

He looked puzzled, but he answered. "If I thought about it at all? I thought I wouldn't have the heart to go back to work full-time in such a demanding position. I was completely exhausted. I had very few reserves left. My own father died young —"

"I know."

Now he looked puzzled. "I don't think I've ever mentioned that."

"You must have."

He searched her face, then he shook his head. "Wayne. The day he threatened you. What else did he tell you?"

She couldn't find a good way to say this. "Wayne told me that your father suffered from dementia."

The statement took a few moments to sink in, but then he understood. He said a few well-chosen words about his son. "My father didn't receive decent medical care at the end of his life, so I'm not sure *what* was wrong with him. He was working overseas for a nonprofit setting up refugee camps, but I saw him whenever he came back to California for R and R."

She was sorry she'd brought this up. "You don't have to explain."

He waved that away. "After a while he stopped calling, and then he stopped writing. I thought he was just busy, and by the time I realized it might be more, it was too late. Maybe he had dementia, strokes, a metabolic disorder? I just know at the end his colleagues say he grew confused and increasingly incoherent, and then before anybody could convince him to come back here for help, he died. Familial Alzheimer's, which sets in early, was just a theory because he was still young, but probably not the best one."

"I'm so sorry. That must have been horrible for you."

"Have you been worried all this time that I'm sinking fast? Watching for signs?"

She shrugged.

"Rina . . . Do you think I would have mar-

368

ried you if I thought something like that was hanging over our heads? My doctor doesn't feel I need genetic testing, not unless I show signs of slipping, but I have physicals every six months just to keep tabs. My brain scans, mental status are all perfectly normal."

"Wayne certainly didn't put it that way."

"My son has a lot to answer for. I should have warned you. Neither son wanted me to marry again. They're protecting their inheritances, although that's a moot point these days. I should have taken their weaknesses into consideration when I put them in charge. But I thought new responsibilities might make them stand taller and work harder."

"I'm guessing that didn't go as you hoped."

He was pacing again. "The figures they showed me, the work I witnessed, looked okay. Not stellar, but okay. Then I got the real story from a group of high-level employees who finally went over their heads. To make the story shorter, unless I can get control again and turn things around, we'll be lucky if *anything's* left."

She wasn't sure what to say. "What are your chances of saving it?"

"Iffy. I don't want to mislead you. We have tough times ahead. I won't be able to take money out of MeriTech for some time. You and I'll be living on savings, and we'll have to tighten the purse strings even more than we have these past months. If it gets to the point there's nothing more I can do at MeriTech, I'll probably start looking for work as a consultant." He gave a wry smile. "And this is the Silicon Valley. Who'll want an old guy who drove a perfectly good company into the ground?"

"But you *didn't*."

"I let my sons do it instead, Rina. A bad decision is a bad decision."

She was quickly considering her options. Leaving Blake, even if she *had* married him because he offered a stable, carefree lifestyle, didn't feel like one of them.

"I want to help," she said, "but a bunch of people at work were let go last week, me among them. I've been scouting for something elsewhere, but it's not going to be easy."

"You should have told me. Don't do that. Things are in too much flux to make those kind of commitments."

Was he talking about MeriTech? Or Toby? Was he really considering everything she was asking of him? She thought about the other sons who had brought them to this place. "What about Wayne and Paul?"

"Right now they're fighting my efforts to take control again, so they're still in place. I'll win in court if it gets that far, but only after we spend even more money uselessly. Then?" He shrugged. "They're still my kids."

She hoped the two "kids" looked for work

far afield. She had a suspicion he hoped the same.

He stopped pacing. "Their mother spoiled them, and they got everything they ever wanted. Everything came too easily. I was gone a lot, and when I was home she went behind my back if I handled them with a firmer hand. If it comes down to ousting them, finding and keeping jobs on their own is going to be a rude awakening."

"That's why you said being a parent had so little appeal."

"It still has very little. If you get custody of Toby, I won't be much help. I'll be busy trying to earn a living. It's not going to be easy."

He was considering her plan. She felt a surge of warmth. He was open to staying with her, even though this meant a change of lifestyle. "I have a lot to think about."

"Start with what's best for that little boy, though. He's lost a father. He needs a stable, happy future. Who can best give that to him?"

After Blake had gone into the bathroom for a shower, she thought about his parting shot. What *was* best for Toby? And once she figured that out, what was best for her, for Lilia, for Ellen, for Blake himself? Suddenly she was making decisions for people she hardly knew. And all of them centered around a tiny boy she had given away.

One thing was for certain. If she did pursue custody, with their newly reduced financial situation, Ellen's wealth would be a godsend. Eventually however, once Toby was living with them, Marina would have to explain the extra income. Right now if she told Blake that Ellen wanted to pay her to raise Toby, he would be appalled, but by then, she might be able to convince him that Ellen felt supporting her grandson was a duty.

She couldn't imagine how she would decide everything. But she did know that, this time, if Toby came back to live with her, it had to be for keeps.

26

In the two weeks since Graham's death Toby's world had changed, but the little boy was adjusting. Lilia had not taken Carrick's advice to fire Dolores, but when asked to go full-time, she had said no anyway. Her other clients depended on her, and she couldn't let them down. Luckily she had a younger sister who was looking for work, and Lilia and Toby liked Valencia right away. She was taking college classes at night, but Lilia had no desire to go out in the evenings without Toby anyway.

In her three days as a full-time housekeeper, Valencia, a pretty dark-haired woman in her early forties, had already proven she was worth everything Lilia was paying her. Still, finding the money wasn't easy. Lilia's financial situation was in complete disarray. When Graham's life insurance check arrived, the top layer of medical debt would disappear, but the bottom was likely to weigh her down for a long time.

She had to work. She'd taken so much time off that there was none left now to mourn her husband.

Regan, who had been going over bills and bank statements, pulled all the documents into one file and neatly stacked them. "So that's where you stand. These belong to you. I have copies of everything at the office."

Lilia accepted the folder to file later with several others equally as troubling. "The insurance company says, barring a problem, their check will be mailed at the end of next week."

"Good. I'll keep after them if I have to."

"I have four appointments with clients in the next week. I'm doing a round of guest blogs next month to drum up business online. Meantime my internet store is holding its own, but I need new items to sell. I'm attending a trade show in Sacramento next weekend."

"With Toby?"

Lilia gave a wry smile. "This one's focused on kids. Toys, furnishings, decor. At least he'll have a lot to look at." She glanced up at the clock. "It's about time for Valencia to bring him home for lunch, but he'll probably give her a hard time about leaving the park. Why don't you join us when they get here?"

"You don't need to play hostess, and besides, I need to get back to the office." Regan rested her hand on Lilia's arm. "You're exhausted. I know you're worried about finances, but I wish you would hold off on doing so much until you've recovered a little."

"Am I going to? Recover?"

"A little at a time."

"You would know."

"If you just keep trying to plow through, eventually you wake up and realize the furrows are crooked and the mule's nowhere in sight."

"Toby's a big help. I don't know what I would do without him."

Regan looked as if she wanted to speak but was thinking better of it. Lilia knew what her friend wanted to say. "No. Not a word from Marina. Not a phone call, a note, an email. It's been four days since Graham's service. In thirteen more days, a year will have passed since she left him with me."

"You must feel like you're waiting for a bomb to go off."

"I thought about taking Toby somewhere for these last few weeks, maybe even home. That's part of the reason I decided we should head to Sacramento. But Carrick says now that won't make a difference since I'm seeking guardianship instead of adoption and everything has changed. Of course every day she delays is a day in our favor. A judge will take the length of her absence into consideration when deciding where Toby will live."

"You deserve easy."

Lilia didn't know about that, but she woke up every morning sure this was the day that Marina would come to her front door again.

"I have copies of the order giving me temporary custody in a folder in the coat closet, all ready to give her. But I'm not giving her my son."

Regan rose and stretched. "I've got to go, but I'm just a phone call away if you need me. I'll be at my office, where I'll be every day until April 15. But I can abandon tax documents for you and Toby."

The two women hugged, and Lilia walked her to the door. When she opened it, Marina was coming up the walk.

Her breath caught in her throat, and her legs no longer wanted to move. For a moment she wondered if agonizing about this moment had somehow set it in motion.

"Is that who I think it is?" Regan asked.

"Yes."

"Maybe I'm not leaving, after all."

Lilia squeezed her friend's hand and realized her own was trembling. "Go make tea. I'll yell if I need you. Call Carrick and let him know."

Regan started toward the kitchen. Lilia stepped out to the porch and closed the door behind her. She folded her arms and waited.

The last time she and Marina had been in this same place, the other woman had been seething. Lilia remembered feeling afraid Marina might attack. She was even more afraid now, although not of physical violence, but she knew better than to show it.

"Marina." She nodded.

Marina's face was expressionless, but as Lilia watched, she thrust her hands in the pockets of skinny black jeans, as if she wasn't sure what to do with them.

"I know about Graham. I'm sorry."

"Thank you." Lilia saw no reason to admit that she knew Marina had been at the memorial service.

"His death changes things. When I left Toby with you . . ." She cleared her throat. "I thought Graham would stay in the picture. He wanted Toby. I'm sure he told you that much. I knew he would take good care of our son."

Lilia winced, but she didn't say anything.

"He's not alive to do that now, and my situation is stable and happy. I can take Toby and be the kind of mother he needs. I want him back. This probably doesn't seem fair to you, but I'm his birth mother, and we both know any court will give me permanent custody. I'd like to do this the easiest way. You can just let me take him without all the legal hassles. Later after he's adjusted, maybe we can arrange for you to visit him. To satisfy yourself everything is fine."

"One visit, huh? You think that's payment for a year of raising him?"

"I really didn't have any choice except to give Toby to Graham. Your husband was supposed to support us, that was the deal we made. But you know how that turned out. I didn't have the money or the right situation to take care of him."

"And you were furious. I was here on this porch, remember? A year ago you practically threw that baby at me. And you were so delighted to be the one to tell me that Graham had been unfaithful, you could hardly contain yourself."

"Not a year."

"You abandoned him to me almost a year ago. And I don't think a judge will quibble if I'm a few days off."

"Here's what he'll see. Graham was cruel to both of us. He convinced me to have the baby, then he more or less abandoned me."

"He was sick. He was in and out of the hospital."

"Whatever the circumstances? It's still true. Then he convinced you to take his son and help him raise him."

"My son now. Because you left him on *my* doorstep."

"Neither of us were treated well by your husband, Lilia. I can't take back what I did. I didn't think I had any choice, but Graham's gone, and I can take Toby now."

"You think it'll be that easy? Do you honestly think I've taken care of that little boy for a year, and he's just going to forget I exist? Or that I'll just go on my way after he's gone? I'm Toby's mother, Marina. I'm the only one he knows and loves. He's already upset Graham's gone. But at least he's in the same house, and he still has *me*. Don't you understand what this will do to him?"

"He's almost fifteen months old. He'll have the rest of his life with me. The first few weeks might be rough, but he'll settle down. The longer you drag this out, though, the older he'll be and the harder moving will be for him. So do what's best, okay? Let me take Toby home with me."

"I have papers giving me custody while we work this out. That's what Graham —"

"Who is *dead*."

"That's what Graham wanted. It's better for Toby not to be moved, and the court agreed. For now my son is going to remain where he is."

Marina didn't seem a bit surprised, and Lilia wondered if the court had finally notified her. Or she might have consulted counsel and learned where things stood.

"I want to see him."

Lilia remembered Carrick's warning. It wasn't in her best interests to be rude. But thankfully Toby wasn't yet home from the park. She prayed he wouldn't appear in the next few minutes.

"You don't have a legal right to visit him.

But for the record, Toby's not here."

"Is that why you closed the door behind you?"

"I closed my door because I don't want you in my house. He's with his babysitter at the park."

"What park?"

"Nice try."

"You're keeping him from seeing his mother."

"I'm the only mother he knows, and I am not keeping you from anything. You've waited a year —"

"Not a year."

"It might as well be. You've waited all this time, and now you just expect me to produce him out of thin air? Really? With no warning? No communication in a *year*?"

"Not a year!"

"Honestly, that's all you can say about this? That you're still a caring mother because it's not quite a *year* since you walked out on him? Give me a break, Marina. I've been that child's mother, and I wanted to adopt him. That's what Graham wanted, too."

"It doesn't matter what he wanted. He's not here to throw his weight around again and decide what happens. But I am."

"Why did you get pregnant in the first place? Didn't you know it could end like this? It was a one-night stand. As one woman to another, what in the hell were you thinking?

He was a married man. Did you think one night —"

"My God, is that what he told you? He told you it was *one night*? Wow, he was an even bigger liar than I thought."

Shocked, Lilia fell silent.

"We'd been having sex on and off for *months* before the night Toby was conceived," Marina said. "You think I would have been stupid enough to have that baby if I hadn't believed there was a chance everything might turn out in my favor?"

Lilia searched frantically for proof that Marina was lying, but she had none. She only had Graham's word, and she had learned the hard way what Graham's word was worth. Now she was so stunned, so shaken, she could only repeat the obvious.

"He was a married man!"

"Yes, and sleeping with him was wrong. But I loved him, too. And I thought he loved me. I fell for the same freaking line women have been falling for since time began. He was unhappy in your marriage. You were too demanding, too determined to be a success. You didn't have time for him. You didn't want a real marriage, a child. You didn't understand him!"

When Lilia didn't answer, Marina cocked her head. "You don't believe me? You really thought Graham and I had a one-night stand? Wow, did he ever do a number on you.

You knew he'd lied all that time about the baby, and you still didn't think maybe he was lying about that, as well?"

Lilia finally gathered herself to speak because she had no choice. "I would like you to leave now. Please."

"I want to see my son."

"You have no right and he's . . . not . . . here!" She heard the slam of a car door, and her eyes followed the sound. With a sinking heart she saw her statement was no longer true. Valencia had driven Lilia's car to the park because that was easier than moving Toby's car seat to her own. Now the woman was walking around to the passenger side to open the back door and get him.

Marina followed her gaze. "Well, at least you weren't lying."

"I have a court order."

"It sounds like you want to go the whole nine yards, instead of settling this between us. I'm sorry that's your decision."

"I will fight you with everything inside me."

"Your babysitter will testify I was here today to see my son. And my mother's waiting in my car as a witness." She nodded her head to the other side of the driveway. Then she gave a humorless laugh. "Not waiting, actually. Here she comes."

Lilia saw a frowsy-looking blonde heading toward Toby, a huge stuffed elephant in her arms. Marina sped down the sidewalk, and

Lilia followed close behind.

Valencia was already saying something to Marina's mother that Lilia couldn't hear. Valencia held up her hand in protest when the woman offered Toby the toy. Marina's mother began waving the elephant, grape-colored with flopping plaid ears, back and forth in ever widening circles. Toby puckered up, and he began to whimper.

"Deedee, don't scare him, for heaven's sake." Marina moved between her mother and the little boy, but Lilia moved faster. She pulled Toby out of Valencia's arms and held him tightly against her.

"You're okay," she told him. "Did you have fun at the park?"

He stuffed his fist in his mouth, something he always did when he was hungry. Usually, if he wasn't fed immediately, screams came next.

"It's lunchtime," Lilia said, looking up. "He's tired and hungry. I'm sure you can see what a bad time this is for a reunion."

"He's just so cute," Deedee crooned. "I knew he would be. I just knew it. He looks like you, Rina Ray, only not exactly." She held out her arms, but Toby nestled closer to Lilia, and began to wail.

Marina waited, clearly undecided what to do. Then she shrugged. "Don't think you've won. Think of this as the opening skirmish."

"Please, leave. Please."

383

Marina took her mother's arm and started toward the car, but Lilia wasn't fooled by the retreat.

The war had begun, and Marina might have all the ammunition.

■ ■ ■ ■

Part V

■ ■ ■ ■

Male swallows are active in raising their young, often defending an area around their nests like feathered warriors. They've even been seen to grab intruders with their feet and hurl them to the ground. Both individuals and groups of barn swallows will gang up on predator birds that draw too near their nests.

Both parents take turns with feeding, not a simple task since nestlings must be fed every 20 minutes for more than 12 hours each day. If one parent dies and the other must feed the young alone, fewer baby birds survive.

"Our Songbirds, Ourselves:
A Tale of Two Species"
from the editors of *Ornithology Today.*

27

The Swallow's Nest

FEATHERING YOUR NEST WITH IMAGINATION AND LOVE

May 8th:

How do you prepare your young child for an afternoon away? I've been giving this serious thought, since Keiki may be spending days and then weekends with someone else in the coming months. I've packed his favorite snacks, his sippy cup, toys he likes — for now the most beloved will stay here, just in case. I've printed out what passes for a schedule with a seventeen-month-old. I've explained what his favorite words actually mean. He talks all the time now, although understanding his opinions takes a little patience and a lot of careful listening.

I found this delightful pattern for a baby backpack online, and I've put Keiki's things inside the one I made. His favorite color is green, and he's still crazy about puppies, so I made a few alterations. Keiki has filled his with toys and he'll carry it along with him today.

I'm not sure how I prepare myself for

watching him walk away. That will be the hardest part of all.

Aloha, Lilia

"When did you have time to make *this*?" Carrick had dropped in to be with her this morning, and now he held up the backpack with floppy puppy ears and a big puppy smile. "Toby" was emblazoned in bright gold letters on the back.

Lilia leaned against her kitchen counter and sipped a cup of the fresh coffee she'd made for both of them. "You don't actually think I'm getting any sleep these days, do you? I sew after I put Toby to bed."

"And worry."

She worried all day, and considering the dreams she had when she finally did fall asleep, apparently she worried all night, as well.

Since Marina had come back into their lives, Carrick had been in and out of the Santa Clara County courthouse making certain Lilia continued to have custody while guardianship was decided. Despite the objections of Marina's attorney and several delays and postponements, he had been successful, but during the last hearing the judge had granted Marina supervised visitation.

For the past six weeks Lilia had taken the little boy to the offices of a local charity on Wednesday mornings and left him there, where for forty-five minutes he supposedly interacted with his birth mother and several other children and parents in a well-equipped nursery under the watchful eye of a trained volunteer.

Now, in fifteen minutes, for the first time, Toby's birth mother would have her son all to herself, and this time she was allowed to take him wherever she wanted until six o'clock.

Lilia just hoped she remembered to return him.

As worried as she was about what the day would bring, she was also seething. She had managed to avoid contact with Marina since the day she'd shown up to reclaim her son. Now Lilia had to hand over Toby like a sweater or a purse Graham's lover wanted to borrow for the afternoon.

She knew this was the wrong time to fall apart, that she had to keep her temper, be polite, even helpful, so Toby would suffer as little as possible, but she wasn't just angry at Marina; she was angry at the man standing in front of her. In the past weeks she hadn't told Carrick everything Marina had said the day she'd come to claim her son. She had been too upset, not just at Graham, who was no longer here to defend himself, but at Carrick, too.

Because surely, he had known?

"You don't think I'm going to end up with

389

him, do you?" She banged her mug on the counter so hard she realized she might have cracked it. She picked it up again, relieved to see it was still intact. Unlike her life.

"I'm going to do everything I can to make sure you do."

"Please, just be straight with me this once, okay?"

"This once?" He set down his mug, but not with the same force. "I know you're upset Marina's taking Toby today, but I'm not the enemy."

Carrick was her lawyer, and needed to know everything *she* did, but she had counseled herself to wait until there was a lull in the battle. She'd told herself not to upset him, not when he was negotiating her son's future. But the real reason? Early this morning as she'd stared at the ceiling, dreading the sunrise, she had faced the truth. She hadn't confronted Carrick because she hadn't wanted to confirm her suspicions.

Now she couldn't wait. She prepared to do battle. "You want to know what *else* is bothering me? Apparently Marina and Graham had a real affair. Not a one-night stand, but something long-standing. And you knew, didn't you?"

He didn't confirm or deny. "Who told you that?"

"When were *you* going to tell me? Didn't you think it would come up at some point?"

He finally shook his head. "I hoped it wouldn't."

And there it was.

She had known. She hadn't been sure, but she had known the truth from the moment Marina had told her. Now all the work she had done to trust her husband again seemed like a terrible joke she had played on herself. Her marriage had been a sham, and Graham's betrayal was like a fist slamming against her chest.

She felt Carrick's arms close around her, and she tried to push him away, but he just tightened them. "Don't. Listen. I didn't know, not until the very last conversation I had with Graham."

"I was married to a stranger." She opened her eyes and looked into his. "And you're a stranger, too."

"No, but I'm a fool." He stepped away, but not before he brushed a lock of hair over her shoulder. "If I hadn't been so close to the situation, if Graham hadn't been my best friend for most of my life? I wouldn't have believed him for a minute. Marina's calculating. She's not a woman who would get pregnant without believing she had a real shot with the baby's father. I get paid to figure out what's really going on with people, and I let that slide right by."

"What did he tell you?"

"She'll be here any minute. You want to go

into this now?"

"I want the truth. For a change."

"Graham was afraid the whole thing might come out if Marina wanted custody again, and he didn't want her to blindside me. But he asked me not to tell you unless I absolutely had to."

She was so furious she could hardly push out a response. "How nice he wanted to *protect* me. Too bad he didn't think of that before he unzipped his pants. Over and over and over . . ."

"He loved you. Despite what you think right now."

"If he loved me, did he tell you why he *still* had an affair?"

"He didn't have to. You can't grow up with the kind of criticism and contempt that he did and not take it to heart. Graham put on a good show, but he was damaged. He never felt he was good enough for anybody, especially not you. And sometimes the pressure of trying to be good enough just got to him. Marina's expectations were zero to none, or so he thought."

"I never made demands on him!"

"Lilia, this was about Graham, not about you. But look how hard you work to make things beautiful. You do everything with love. The house, your cooking, your blog and business. Here's an example." He held up the puppy pack.

"Let's see, he cheated on me because I can sew and cook?" She was trying not to cry.

"You're amazing, and Graham knew it, but in his eyes he was a phony who didn't deserve you. With Marina there was no pressure. Just a few drinks, a night away from trying to be the person you thought he was, sex that didn't mean much. He said he just fell into it, that at first he was surprised, then ashamed, but it was too easy to keep going back, because she didn't ask for anything in return. When she got pregnant, that changed. Coupled with his illness, his whole life came crashing down. He was terrified he would lose you, so when you found out about Toby, he came up with the only story he thought might work."

"One meaningless night of sex. A well-crafted pack of lies."

"Everything he told you was true, except that it wasn't the first time they were together. According to him he had broken off any contact with her months before. Then the night you told him you weren't willing to have his baby until things stabilized, he ran into Marina. From the things he told her she apparently believed his marriage was on the skids, and he wanted another chance with her . . ."

"And she saw her shot at happily-ever-after bliss." She was too tired to cry, but tears filled her eyes anyway.

"I think he was finally telling the truth. He was dying. He wasn't worried about saving his reputation or marriage. He was sick with worry about you and Toby. I know this is going to be hard to put behind you, but Graham loved you. He just didn't love himself. He was flawed, no question, but I think most of your life together was exactly what you thought it was. Don't look at everything through this lens."

She was saved from having to answer by Toby's arrival, with Valencia right behind him. The other woman looked worried when she saw Lilia's expression, but she seemed to think the best thing she could do was leave. "He's all ready. Shall I run to the grocery store now? I'm planning to do a good cleaning in his room when I get back."

Lilia wiped her eyes and thanked her, and the other woman left for the store.

Toby held up his arms, and Lilia swung him up to her hip. No matter how she felt, she had to put on a better face. She cleared her throat and managed a smile. "Remember what I told you? You're going to the park today with your friend from the playroom. Then she'll bring you home to have dinner with me. You'll be good?"

Toby babbled happily, and even she, as keeper of his vocabulary, wasn't sure whether he was answering or just vocalizing. She kissed his curls just as the doorbell played the first bars of "California Dreaming." She looked over to Carrick. "You changed the music?"

"Basic theme. No hidden meanings."

"I wish I had a theme with no hidden meaning for my life."

He was wearing his lawyer face, but she could tell he wasn't any happier about Marina's arrival than she was. "I can do this for you," he said. "I can put him in her car."

For a moment she considered, but she shook her head. "I need to do it."

"I'll come with you, then."

She started through the living room, Toby on her hip, his new puppy pack over her other shoulder. She'd already put a canvas bag with all his supplies and information by the front door.

Once there she took a deep breath and opened it, nodding at Marina, who had come alone. "He's all ready for you. Just let me get his jacket and hat."

"It's not that cold. He'll be fine."

Lilia knew he wouldn't be. Toby didn't have much body fat, and he got chilled easily. "The temperature's supposed to drop later. This will only take a minute. Then you'll be all set."

"Just give it to me then. I don't want him to get hot in his car seat."

"I was going to offer my seat. I just got a new one."

"I don't need yours. I have *everything* I need."

Lilia restrained herself from asking if Marina's was new enough to meet safety standards. That, like too many other things, was out of her hands now.

Perhaps sensing the tension, Toby put his arms around her neck and held tight. His head was against her shoulder and turned away from Marina. His grip was growing tighter by the moment. She kept him against her as she got his coat out of the closet, stuffed his favorite dinosaur hat in the pocket, and handed it to Marina, who shrugged and tossed it over her arm. She held out her hands to take him.

"It may take him a few minutes to warm up to you," Lilia warned.

"Especially now that you've said so."

She took a deep breath. "I'm not trying to make this harder. I'm trying to make it easier."

"Give me my son." Marina held her arms wide.

As angry as she was, Lilia could understand at least something of what the other woman must be feeling. "Of course I'm going to give him to you. I was just hoping we could make this as trouble-free as possible."

"The longer you stall, the worse it will be."

Carrick picked up the canvas bag and held it out to Marina. "Why don't you take this, and Lilia and I will get him in your car seat. To spare you a struggle."

"Does visiting with my son, which a judge has *ordered,* require an attorney to be present?"

Lilia answered before Carrick could. "Carrick happened to be here. But letting us put him in the seat is a good idea, don't you think?"

"No, I . . . do . . . not . . . think. I don't know what's in the bag, but I have everything my son will need. Give him to me now."

Lilia tried to untangle Toby's arms from her neck but he was holding firmly to her hair. "It's just his schedule, some hints for understanding what —"

"You don't get this, do you? I don't need your opinion about what's best for Toby. We need to make our way together. I'm not your babysitter. He is my son."

Lilia was now struggling to release Toby's grip on her hair. The little boy was wailing, and his arms were flailing. Carrick moved closer to help and managed to separate him from Lilia, but Toby launched himself back into her arms.

Lilia tried one more time. "Marina, please? If you come inside and give him a little time, he'll go with you once he calms down. You can play with him in his room. He can show you his favorite toys. I won't interfere."

"I'm not stupid. You're trying to prevent

me from being alone with my son." And with that Marina grabbed the little boy from behind and yanked. Without another word, and with a screaming, kicking child in her arms, she marched down the sidewalk.

"Come in and close the door," Carrick told Lilia.

She was sobbing too hard to move. He put his arm around her, pulled her inside and closed the door so she wouldn't have to watch what was surely going to be high drama out on the street.

He held her as she sobbed. "I just wanted . . . it to be easy for him."

"She's going to report you to the judge."

She tried to breathe, but her lungs wouldn't cooperate. He released her and she bent over, hands on her thighs, and finally managed a deep enough breath. "That's . . . unfair."

"I'll tell Judge Garrity what I saw today, but you can't go through a scene like that one again. She has a legal right to visitation. You have to just put him in her arms no matter what he does and walk away."

"This is supposed to be about *him*!"

"And that's what she'll tell the judge. She'll tell him this is all about Toby, who he should be with, and you have no respect for his ruling."

"But you were here. You saw what happened. She didn't want his coat. She refused the bag with his things in it." She slid the puppy pack off her shoulder and held it up. "And his toys, too."

"She saw all that as interference. The bag was evidence that you think you're better suited to be his mother, and the puppy pack? A reminder of life with you, so he won't be able to move on."

"How can you do what you do for a living? It's all about lies. All of this!"

"It's perceptions. She thinks she's in the right. She gave birth to him."

She heard his warning loud and clear. She took another breath. Then another. Finally she straightened and looked into his eyes. "I asked you earlier if you thought I was going to end up with him. You changed the subject."

"I've told you what I think. I'm going to do everything I can to make that happen."

"Am I going to end up with Toby?"

She watched his debate. He finally turned up his hands. "I don't know, Lilia. The courts favor biological parents, but they also look at what's best for the child. You have a good case since he's been with you almost since birth, but she has a case, too. And even if the court decides in your favor, guardianship isn't like adoption. It's almost never final. Marina will probably get visitation, and afterwards she can continue to petition for more and more time, as well as reassessment. The whole situation is going to depend on a lot of things. Most of all how badly she wants to pursue it."

"Should I prepare to lose him?"

"I don't know how you prepare for something like that without damaging both of you."

"I need to do something. I can't just sit around."

"Right now just follow the judge's instructions to the letter, and be as polite and co-operative as you can when Marina comes to the house, and when the court investigator visits. He or she will be looking at every aspect of your life and relationship with Toby."

"All I want is to take care of him and love him, the way I have for more than a year now. I'm his mother, no matter what the courts say!"

He touched her hair. "What can I do right now to help?"

"I need to be alone."

His expression changed subtly, and she wasn't sure if he was hurt or relieved. "Call me if you need anything, or if she doesn't have him back by six."

She heard the front door close, and she realized she'd gotten exactly what she asked for. She was alone, and the empty house felt like a tomb.

28

Toby couldn't care less about the fragrant beds of blooming roses, the brand-new state-of-the-art stroller, or the textured balls Marina had hung from a mesh pouch for him to play with as they walked. With clenched teeth she'd managed to get him into the car seat, despite a full-fledged tantrum, and then on arrival at the rose garden, she'd buckled him into the stroller, too, working around an arched back and tiny hands pounding her. He was quiet, now, which was a relief, but she was afraid to stop pushing him, in case he started screaming again.

"So, we're alone together at last," she said to the back of his head. "And I guess looks can be deceiving, because you haven't changed that much, have you? Still determined to make my life miserable."

As she spoke his head lolled to one side. She paused, despite misgivings, and walked around to peek at him. He was sound asleep.

"Well, at least that's new. Sleeping, I mean."

She squatted beside him for her first good look without somebody carefully observing every move she made.

Her son. That part was still hard to believe, even after six weeks of supervised interaction in a dusty charity playroom where every glance had been scrutinized. In her mind *her* son was still three months old, with wisps of dandelion fluff on his scalp and a way of screwing up his tiny face that reminded her of a famous painting. Something about a scream? *That* was her son.

This one? Now that he wasn't wailing, this child was beautiful. Fat, rosy cheeks, a mop of golden curls, a sweet little mouth. How could such horrifying sounds issue from lips as rosebud perfect as these?

She waited for a wave of maternal affection. Asleep the little boy was adorable. She had to give him that. But she felt no sense of possession, no real connection. He was somebody else's son, somebody else's joy.

Whatever had been wrong with her when Toby was an infant still hadn't been repaired.

Her gaze moved down his body. Lilia had good taste in clothing. Marina had to give her that. Today Toby wore denim jeans and a royal blue sweatshirt with "King of All He Surveys" in white script over the gold outline of a crown. She admired his shoes, black with the same royal blue lining and laces. Of course the laces were just for show, and the shoes closed with practical hook and strap tape.

"Lilia thinks of everything." How had Lilia managed so well in the final months of Graham's illness? How had she dressed and fed Toby, taken care of her dying husband, run a business?

While she knew family had flown in from Hawaii, the majority of decisions and care had probably fallen to her. Despite everything that had happened and would continue in the next months, Marina felt sympathy. After all, who would know better than she what it felt like to be left alone with this guy?

Toby started, then opened his eyes to stare at her. "Hey, kid. You took a nap."

His eyes narrowed, as if to tell her to shut up and go away. But at least he didn't start screaming again.

She got to her feet and leaned over to unhook his harness. "Do you want to get out and run around? You probably hate being strapped in all the time."

He still looked suspicious, but he let her lift him to the ground. Once she let go he held on to the stroller a moment, as if steadying himself, then he took off. She followed right behind.

Eventually he tired, but she had to give him an A for stamina. He plopped to a patch of grass and examined a stick. Marina took one of the balls out of the bag and rolled it to him. She'd tried balls before, in the supervised charity nursery, but he'd only glared at her. This time, when the ball got to him, he examined that, too, but he didn't pick it up.

She lowered herself to sit beside him. "You can throw it to me."

Toby looked at the ball as if he wasn't sure what to do with it. She remembered trying to teach one of her brothers to play catch. She cupped her hands and smiled at him. "Pick it up and throw it to me, Toby."

He picked up the ball, put it in his mouth, and glared at her.

"Or chew it."

He tossed it to the ground and looked around. "Ma Ma Ma Ma?"

"That would be me. I guess you don't remember our all-night love fests."

"Dink?"

Who needed Lilia's translation guide? Marina went back to the stroller and rummaged in a bag with snacks, diapers and a brand-new sippy cup. She would love to know if Toby still took a bottle, but asking Lilia had seemed like an excuse for a lecture. And Marina didn't need lectures on raising children.

She turned with a bottle of water in one hand and the new sippy cup in the other to see Toby streaking down the sidewalk.

She caught him as he started toward the street. Of course choosing the worst possible direction was unintentional, but the escape had been planned. She swung him into her arms.

"Listen, your mother would kill me if —" She realized what she'd said and stopped abruptly. Just what the court needed to hear, Marina referring to Lilia as Toby's mother. "I guess it's time to leave. We have people to meet and places to go. You can have your 'dink' in the car."

He swatted her cheek. Then he laughed, and not as if they were comrades, and this was a game. As if he hoped she'd felt the sting.

As she trudged to the car, juggling Toby and the stroller, she asked herself what she had expected. Of course Lilia was right. She should have taken some time to help the baby get comfortable being alone with her, before she snatched him up and brought him here. She hoped Lilia wasn't giggling or nodding sagely from behind a bed of climbing roses. Suddenly everything about the garden felt off. The scents, the rich colors, the other visitors enjoying the spring air and view. She couldn't wait to leave.

At the car she steeled herself for another struggle, but this time Toby went right into his seat, and he let her snap him in without inflicting bodily harm. She filled the cup and gave it to him. Then she folded the stroller and placed it in the Mustang's trunk.

As she pulled away from the curb she realized that she'd forgotten to check his diaper. She hadn't given him anything to play with in the seat, either. The good news was that if either bothered him, he wasn't letting on.

At the first stop sign she turned to check and discovered why he was so quiet. He had unscrewed the top of his "babyproof" cup, and now he was dunking his fist in what was left of the water.

She slapped her hands on the steering wheel. "When they were sending babies to earth, why were *you* at the head of the line?"

He dumped what was left of the water over his head. Then he grinned at her.

And for some reason, against every rational impulse, she grinned back.

By the time they arrived at Blake's villa, Ellen was already waiting. Marina still didn't think of the villa as home. Her marriage seemed precarious, almost like a play she'd been cast in with lines she couldn't remember. For all she knew the whole production might close after a historically short run.

She pulled into the driveway and opened the garage from her car, aware that Ellen, who had parked in front, was getting out of hers. By the time the older woman joined her, Marina was removing Toby from his seat.

"He's soaked." Ellen, who looked like she'd stepped out of a Bloomingdale's catalog, folded her arms and stared as her grandson was freed. "Did you have a thunderstorm inside the car?"

"He got the top off his cup, and since he seemed perfectly happy wet, I left him that way."

"It's a little chilly for wet, don't you think?"

Marina spared her one glance before she hefted the baby into her arms. "It was not chilly in the car."

"It's a cute car. Does it have anchors for the car seat?"

Ellen had been doing grandmotherly research, and Marina was sorry to hear it. "I had the anchors checked the last time my car was serviced."

"Good. And you had him in the back. I'm glad."

"Of course I had him in the back." Marina started toward the door. "Do you mind going inside this way? It's easier."

Marina hadn't been sure how to handle buying supplies for the baby. She didn't want to clutter Blake's house. She'd solved the problem by clearing out a closet in the guest room and storing her new purchases in plastic bins. The room was almost never used. If all went well, someday it would belong to Toby.

Before leaving this morning she'd converted a corner of the great room into a play area. She knew better than to overwhelm any child with toys. She'd settled on a few plastic trucks, brightly colored blocks to put in them, a few cloth books, a stuffed panda. She'd refused Deedee's elephant, suggesting she keep it for Toby's visits to her apartment. Of course the San Andreas fault would miraculously repair itself before she ever took Toby to Deedee's, unless she went over ahead of time and cleaned. Deedee kept house the way she'd parented her children. Great enthusiasm; little skill.

With Toby in her arms Marina realized he wasn't just wet from the outside in. He was wet from the inside out. And possibly worse.

She wrinkled her nose. "I'll be back. Make yourself comfortable. This guy needs a diaper change and some dry clothes."

In the guest room she spread a towel on the bed and gave Toby a plastic caterpillar with strings to pull and buttons to push. He was more interested in watching her. At one point he puckered up to cry, but he stopped when she began to talk to him.

"You used to listen when I talked to you," she said. "Not often enough, but sometimes. You were a shrimpy little guy. And wow, could you scream."

"S'cream . . ." He frowned. "S'cream?"

He tried to sit up. "S'cream!"

Puzzled, she worked faster. "Screech. Do you like that better?"

"S'cream!"

She couldn't help herself. She smiled, despite the thunderous look on his face. "Oh, I get it. You think I'm talking about something else, something you apparently like to eat. Aren't you a little young for ice cream?"

Suddenly thunder was replaced by sunshine. "S'cream!"

"Not a good idea. Sorry. But I have cookies. Do you like cookies?"

"Keys." He tried to sit up again.

She finished changing him. The clothes she'd bought were a little large, and of course whatever spare clothing Lilia had tried to provide was back in Willow Glen. But she rolled up the sleeves on the camouflage Henley along with the legs of the khaki pants, and left him shoeless.

After she dumped his wet clothes in the dryer, she rummaged through the kitchen pantry and pulled out a bag of toddler animal crackers. "If he doesn't have a cookie immediately, he's going to die," she told Ellen. She presented him with one for each hand.

"I haven't held him since he was an infant," Ellen said.

Marina really didn't want the other woman to hold Toby, at least not yet, and she wasn't quite sure why. She nodded to the play area. "Tell you what, why don't you sit over there with him, and when he's ready, maybe he'll let you put him on your lap."

"You sound like my daughter-in-law. I

always thought babies had to be told what to do."

"Is that how you raised Graham?"

Ellen looked unhappy that Marina had said her son's name. "Yes, it was."

Marina avoided the obvious response: *And look how well that turned out.* She deposited her son on the floor and started piling blocks in his dump truck. "Every generation seems to have a different way of raising children."

"Your generation thinks babies should teach parents."

After making that pronouncement, Ellen loosened up a little. She joined them on the floor, but she was careful not to move right in on her grandson. "To be honest I'm not sure what my generation believed. Not really. My friends and I rarely discussed our children. I listened to professionals who seemed to know more than I did, but I guess they were all from a previous generation. And a lot of them were trained in British nanny schools."

Marina rarely worried about what other people were feeling. Living with Deedee had cured her of that. But she did notice that Ellen sounded wistful.

Did she want to become this woman's friend? She doubted that was possible. They were from different planets. Ellen was using her, and not that differently from the way Ellen's son had used her. Graham had wanted this child; *Ellen* wanted this child. Neither could accomplish their heart's desire without her.

Still, didn't they have to be friendly enough that sharing Toby wasn't impossible? For obvious reasons, Ellen couldn't dismiss her.

"So your husband is willing to cooperate?" Ellen asked.

Toby finished his cookies and zeroed in on a flatbed truck with paneled sides, tossing blocks in, then taking them out. Marina slid back to let him have more room.

"He's not wildly enthusiastic, but he wants me to be happy. I did tell him you would be available if we needed you."

Ellen looked unhappy at that. "I really hoped we could keep that to ourselves. Eventually, if everything goes the way we hope, the court will have to investigate both you and Lilia to make a final determination."

"Well, Blake needs to know we aren't going to be alone. He's closer to your age than mine, and he has two grown sons. He doesn't really want to raise another one."

Ellen still didn't look happy. She scooted closer to her grandson and began helping him put blocks in his truck. He glanced at her, and then he looked away, but he didn't complain.

"I spoke with your attorney," Ellen said. "She's pleased the judge allowed you to have unsupervised visitation. Allowing you to

411

establish a real relationship with Toby is a step toward giving you custody." She made a tower of blocks beside the truck and actually laughed when Toby knocked them over and clapped his hands.

Marina got up to get him milk. She'd bought 2-percent, but she had no idea what he usually drank. She wondered if Lilia would bring up her refusal to take the instructions when the court investigator came for a visit. Next time she needed to be more cooperative.

She sat back on the floor and handed the milk to Ellen, along with some napkins. She had learned her lesson in the car.

"Toby, why don't you sit over here and drink this." She pointed at Ellen's lap.

Toby ignored them both and tried to make his own block pile to knock over.

"We're okay." Ellen began another pile. "But thank you."

"Your lawyer —"

"Not mine, please. *Yours.*"

Marina reined in her annoyance. "*My* lawyer, who you are paying, may think unsupervised visitation is a good thing, but she told *me* I only have a fifty-fifty chance of final custody. Would visiting rights be enough for you? I could make sure you saw Toby whenever I had him."

"I want more than a few hours a month with my grandson. You need to do everything she tells you to and more."

Marina waited for Ellen to add that there would be no point in helping her financially if Toby wasn't living with her full-time. But Graham's mother probably wasn't yet at the point where she was willing to make threats, although she would get there quickly if things didn't go the way she wanted. Douglas Randolph might be the truly ruthless partner in their marriage, but Ellen had likely learned a thing or two from her husband.

Ellen laughed when Toby knocked over his own pile, and then she started a new one for him. "He's going to be an architect, like his father."

Marina hoped that was the only way Toby was going to be like Graham.

Ellen's tower grew. "When I talked to the attorney I detailed all the problems I've had with Lilia over the years. I can't believe she won't leak some of that to the judge."

"Did you and Lilia ever get along?"

Toby tired of block building and reached for his milk, but he refused to sit on Ellen's lap. She handed it to him, although it seemed apparent she was tempted to force the issue.

Her eyes never left him. "I never paid much attention to her as a child. Then as a teenager it became clear she was using her beauty to entice my son and Carrick, too. Years later she somehow ended up back in Graham's life."

"So after they married?"

"She never really fit in. Graham was working for Randolph Group. Certain things were expected. She hung on to her Hawaiian identity, the way she dressed, the long hair. She wasn't interested in becoming friends with the right people. She was invited to work for a well-known interior design firm, one even Douglas was impressed by, but she wanted to do what she wanted to do, so she turned them down."

To Marina, this sounded as if Lilia just wanted to be happy and independent. And while she hadn't ever had a choice like that herself, she couldn't really fault the other woman for the one she had made.

She wondered why she was defending Lilia, even silently.

"I think she was after Graham's money." Ellen tried to wipe Toby's chin and he began to wail. "Toby, hold still," she said, taking his chin in her hand.

The little boy launched himself to his back and began to kick.

"Goodness!" Ellen sat back. "How *is* Lilia raising this child?"

Marina remembered months of misery with the same little boy, well before Lilia came on the scene. "Children are not little adults." She stood and looked at the clock on the mantel as he began a litany of "Ma-ma-ma" again. She wanted to put her hands over her ears. As Toby got louder she could feel every screech crawling along her skin.

She forced herself to sound calm and reasonable. "Let's give him a little space, Ellen. He's tired, and he doesn't know us."

Ellen got up, too, as Toby continued to kick, but his screaming tapered off as they moved away. Marina was glad, but surprised. She'd made a good call.

Ellen folded her arms and looked down at him. "Next visit I'd like to have him at my house. He'll need to get used to being there. I'll make sure I have everything he'll need."

Toby continued to kick. Ellen shook her head and moved farther away. "Maybe it's old-fashioned, but every child has to learn self-control."

Marina wondered what both she and Toby were getting themselves into.

29

Hank Gleason's house was best described as California modern. It featured walls of glass, post and beam construction, an unassuming exterior in the front and a fabulous walled garden in the back. Hank and Sally had chosen to be true to the vision of California architect Joseph Eichler, but splashes of color and richly textured rugs over concrete floors warmed what could have been a stark floor plan. An atrium of tropical plants, with Hank's collection of orchids, spread light into the darkest corners.

Ellen rang the doorbell and almost immediately Hank, in soft faded jeans and a black T-shirt, welcomed her with a hug before he led her into the kitchen. "I'm just cleaning up after dinner. You're sure I can't get you anything? You've eaten?"

She hadn't wanted to stop on the trip from Marina's condo, but at her age missing the occasional meal was a boon for her waistline. She did accept a glass of white wine and sipped as he put food back in the refrigerator. The kitchen was sleek, and she could see he had finally veered away from functional sliding door cabinets and Formica to a whole new kitchen with natural maple, a soft gray subway tile backsplash, and beautiful granite countertops.

"I like this." She ran her fingers over the blue-green granite.

"Costa Esmeralda. That particular piece came from Italy."

"When did you do all this?"

"About a year after Sally died. I never liked the original kitchen, but it took me that long to realize she wasn't coming back, and I could change things to suit myself."

"You made good decisions, but then you would." She looked up. "Would this be good in my house, do you think?"

"Not if you're going to keep renting it. There's cheaper granite, and you can go thinner, maybe tiles instead of a slab. Once granite's installed, it's durable, and you can work through a wholesaler for the best price."

She remembered butcher block and wondered if it was still there. "She's like an old friend. The house, I mean. I've been neglecting her. I'm not sure the best way to make it up to her is to go cheap."

"Who is this sentimental woman?" He smiled, and she smiled back. "I'm finished here. Let's go see what's left of your old

417

place. This last family was as nice as could be, but as renters go, they lived hard. We'll start a list tonight, but I can hire a design firm to come in and make recommendations. If you want me to."

She wasn't sure why that sounded so unappealing. Of course she knew an interior designer who probably needed the work, but she wasn't about to hire Lilia. In fact the more she thought about it, the less she wanted to hire anybody.

She saw she'd emptied her wineglass. "Let's go see."

Outside the sun was sinking, and blue sky was fading to gray. Eucalyptus and pine scented the air, and a neighbor's pink camellias danced in a light breeze. When they reached the colonial, she found she was reluctant to go inside.

She waited on the porch as Hank juggled keys and finally pushed open the front door. "Twilight's probably my favorite time of day. From that moment when the street lamps go on until I really need them to see where I'm going. One part of the day is finished but evening's ahead."

Hank stepped aside to let her precede him. "I always liked evening because it was family time. Of course too many nights I was out showing houses. But when I was home, I loved helping with baths and homework. I had my best talks with my boys then."

She couldn't imagine Douglas helping with either. In fact she'd rarely bathed Graham, even as a toddler, and his nannies had been certain that homework was completed as soon as he returned from school. Later he'd gone away, and faculty and staff had seen to his schedule.

She had missed so much.

"Ellen?"

Hank rested his hand on her back to move her into the hallway so he could close the door. A staircase rose to her left, and the doors closing off the living room were open so she could see that the walnut floors were worn and scarred, and the walls badly needed painting. Still, the living room was spacious, with a corner between windows where she'd always wanted to put a grand piano. Not the largest size, but something still substantial and gleaming. She'd even imagined Rosamund visiting and entertaining their friends by singing some of her favorite arias as Ellen accompanied her.

"I used to play the piano." She realized she was thinking out loud, and she covered it with a small laugh. "When I was a girl. I'd play for my sister's lessons. Not well and not easily, but I did play. I always wanted a piano right there." She pointed to the corner.

"You must have bought a piano in the years since."

She hadn't. Douglas wouldn't have objected; in fact he would have ordered the grandest of grands, even if nobody ever touched the keys.

And maybe that was why.

Their footsteps echoed as they strolled into the connected dining room. The built-in corner cabinet looked worse for wear, but she couldn't imagine the room without it. A designer would open these rooms to create one where now there were two. The cabinet would go, and most likely the wall behind it so the kitchen would also be in full view.

She was still thinking out loud. "I like this the way it is. It's a cozy space, and I love the way these doors open to the backyard. Each room is a surprise. There's something to be said for walls, isn't there?"

"The yard needs everything. Peek now before it gets dark."

The glass-paneled doors were bordered by sidelights, so the view became part of the decor. Hank unlocked one so she could step out to the brick patio. She saw immediately what he meant. Bricks heaved unevenly, and the landscaping had been sadly neglected. Grass and weeds had become equal opportunity ground cover, and one tree, whose shade she had enjoyed all those years ago, needed immediate surgery.

"You can recommend a landscaper?"

"Don't you have to decide a few things first? If you're going to keep renting the house, you'll be looking for low-cost durability. A big-box store and some day laborers will suit your needs. If you've changed your mind and want to sell?"

"Don't you sell enough houses without trying to sell mine?" She laughed at his expression. "I know you're just trying to figure out what's best. The thing is, I'm feeling my way. Right now I want somebody to clean up, trim the shrubs and that tree, if it can be saved, make sure the irrigation system is up to code and working properly, suggest some changes, maybe more flower beds out here to cut down on water usage."

"I can do that."

"Perfect. Let me know when they're coming and I'll be here to talk to them."

"You want to do this *yourself*?"

Ellen realized this was a cockeyed, backwards way to honor her son. Once, she had brought Graham to visit the Gleasons when he was on school vacation, and he had shown no interest in seeing his first home. But even if *he* hadn't heard it, she knew his baby laughter still filled these rooms, and sadly Graham had laughed less and less as each year of his childhood passed.

If she tried to explain that to Hank, he would drop her at the nearest psych unit.

She settled for simple. "I was happy here, and I think it'll be fun to redo it myself. If the house needed structural changes or an addition, I would be in over my head. But it's a straightforward colonial, and it would be silly to try to make it something else. Paint, floors refinished —"

"You haven't seen the kitchen." Hank closed and locked the patio doors and led her there now.

She almost clapped her hands. The kitchen was outdated and needed everything, including new countertops, although somewhere along the way the butcher block had been replaced by ceramic tile. "I can order appliances, sinks, cabinets. These can't be saved. They don't even hang properly."

"I see that."

"I need a project, Hank."

"I see that, too."

"Let's save the downstairs master suite and the upstairs for next time. I ought to get home now that rush hour will be tapering off."

They walked through the kitchen, and Hank pointed out wiring that also needed updates. As they passed she took a peek into the family room, small and darkly paneled, before she walked down the hall to the front door. Her mind was buzzing with possibilities.

She paused on the front porch. "When I come back to meet with the landscaper, I'll check out everything else. I'll visit a showroom or two in the meantime to see what I like."

He told her the names of several he used, and she jotted them on a pad in her purse.

Together they walked up the sidewalk toward her car. "Did you come straight from home?" he asked.

She realized she must look like it. She was wearing an expensive cap sleeve sweater over dark leggings and ankle boots, but everything could be easily laundered. She was still disappointed Toby hadn't gotten close enough to dribble milk down her sweater.

"I spent the afternoon with my grandson. It's been a long time since Graham was that age, but I did remember not to wear my best clothes."

"You look great, and hey, I'm glad you got to see him. Douglas finally got to meet his grandson?"

She unlocked her car door, but she leaned against it. "No. He doesn't know I went."

"So how do you explain away your day?" he asked.

"He has a business dinner tonight, so he'll be home so late I won't even see him."

"Just out of curiosity? If you did see him, would he ask about your day?"

The question was surprisingly personal, but more surprising was her response. "He usually asks. He rarely listens to my answers."

He pondered that a moment. "You know,

I've heard about people living double lives. But sometimes I wonder how many you lead. More than two, for sure. Which Ellen am I talking to now? The one who abandoned her dreams back when she was a girl to become an appendage of her parents? Or the one who emerged as a young woman to do the same for Douglas?"

"Hank!"

"Or maybe the one who wanted so desperately to be a good mother but let her inexperience and an impatient husband override her best instincts?"

She stared at him, wondering what to say. Finally she just shook her head. "We've been friends a long time, but not that long. You have no right to say those things."

"Of course I don't. But I bet what I said is nothing compared to what Douglas says when you're alone. Only his is probably designed to make you shape up to his standards."

"I'll tell you who I am. I'm the woman committed to giving my grandson the good start I thought I gave Graham, only I didn't. But I'm not sitting back and pretending Toby doesn't exist, no matter what Douglas wants. I'm not letting anybody else do the things I should have done for my own son."

"He's not your son, though. You're his *grandmother* and that's special in itself."

"He needs me to be more."

"Ellen, Toby's not Graham. You see that, right? He's a different little boy, and it's a different situation. He has a mother."

She didn't tell him that Toby had two, and if she had her way, they would have very little to do with raising him. Neither Lilia nor Marina had what Toby needed most, the abilities and contacts to help him take a place in a different world from the one they inhabited. Ellen had to be the support and primary influence she had never been for her son. This time she could do things right, and Toby would be the one to benefit.

"I'm working it out. All of it," she said.

"Does this house have anything to do with it?"

In some odd way it did, only she wasn't sure how. She shrugged.

"Two different projects, Ellen. Your grandson and this house. Don't get them confused, okay? And you can't turn back time. Not with either one." He kissed her cheek and left her there.

She drove home slowly, in no hurry to get back to Belvedere Island. With each mile she felt as if she was leaving something behind. She just wasn't sure exactly what.

30

While Toby was with Marina, Lilia kept busy by visiting her storage unit and consulting the women who filled her internet orders. Together they looked at recent history and pricing. The consensus wasn't pretty.

Orders were down and, with them, income. During Graham's final illness she had been forced to find other designers to handle local clients, just as she had when he was first diagnosed. What little time she'd had for work she had put into her website, but analytics still weren't encouraging.

Documenting her trip to the children's trade show with Toby, including photos of her son trying out toys she'd featured in her online store, had produced a temporary spike. Unfortunately she wasn't adding enough home dec items to hold website shoppers' interest, and she hadn't given her staff the required guidance so they could share the load. Her assistants were hampered by limited space and an atmosphere that wasn't conducive to anything other than packing and shipping.

Of course her audience for *The Swallow's Nest* had dropped off, too. These days she certainly wasn't photographing her parties or taking on projects readers might find interesting or helpful for their own lives.

Too often in the past months her blog had been filled with death, fear, sadness. If she didn't take a turn in that road and soon, nobody would log on to see what was new.

At home again, with a glass of wine for companionship, she called one of her favorite fabric artists, a young man in Michigan who silk-screened his own creations and combined them with vintage textiles to make fabulous one-of-a-kind pillows and floor cushions. He promised to send photos of half a dozen nearly completed projects she could feature. His work cost the moon, but even if most of her readers couldn't afford it, occasionally the right buyer came along. He gave her names of fellow craftsmen she might like, and, grateful, she made notes.

Next she emailed Kai and asked him to visit a mutual friend who lived off the grid, to see if he had anything she could sell in her store. His candles scented with Hawaiian flowers and herbs, plus the planters and baskets he made from natural materials near his homestead, were always popular, but she hadn't heard from him in months.

After several additional phone calls she closed her computer and grabbed her camera. Her front yard was awash in blooms. Flowers represented hope, rebirth, love. Those were the messages she and her readers needed, and the golden hour, the best time of day for photographers, was fast approaching.

Taking photos was also a good opportunity to look busy when Marina returned her son, which she was supposed to do in the next half hour.

At the stroke of six the yellow Mustang pulled up in front of her house, and by then Lilia had taken multiple shots of everything in the yard and moved to her favorite neighbor's for a few more.

She remembered Carrick's warnings, and while she couldn't make herself smile, she schooled herself to be polite.

Marina parked in front of the house. Lilia didn't hurry to help or intercept. She placed her camera on the porch and waited. When Toby saw her, his glum little face broke into a grin and he crowed "Ma Ma Ma," until Marina deposited him in Lilia's arms.

She kissed both his cheeks and held him tight. She knew better than to tell the little boy she'd missed him, although she was sure it was apparent. She nodded at the other woman after she'd kissed him again.

"Has he had dinner? Just so I'll know what to do next."

"He has."

Lilia had hoped for a little more, but she nodded. "Good. Anything I ought to know?"

"Like whether I beat him or ran out to the store and left him at home alone?"

"You know, this doesn't have to be so hard. We can make these visits easier on each other by just sharing a little information. Let's just do what we need to for Toby."

"And how does your sermon end?"

"I guess I throw up my hands and go inside." Lilia turned to do just that.

Marina spoke to her back. "His clothes got soaked. He took the top off his sippy cup. They've been through the dryer."

Lilia glanced over her shoulder. "He has amazing dexterity."

"Maybe that was in all those notes you tried to give me."

"He lives to take things apart."

"He looks like Graham."

"Yeah." Lilia wanted to ask if the reminder was as jarring for the other woman as it sometimes was for her, but that was one step too close. They weren't BFFs in a bar, comparing the men who paraded by.

"It doesn't bother you that he looks a little like *me,* too?" Marina asked.

"Considering everything, I guess it was too much to hope he'd look like me."

Marina actually smiled, and Lilia thought that probably surprised them both.

Inside she babbled happily to the baby, but now that their reunion had ended, he started to fuss. She understood why. How else could he let her know he was angry she'd just sent him off for the afternoon with a stranger? She checked his diaper, but he was dry. She offered him food, but he clenched his lips and turned his head. She was trying to convince him to play basketball with the plastic hoop in the corner when the doorbell sang "California Dreaming." While Toby sat on the floor, banging his palms in rapid succession, she went to answer.

Carrick held out a pizza from her favorite Italian restaurant. "Pineapple, ham, grilled onions, green pepper." He held her gaze. "I'll pick off the pineapple. You know it really doesn't belong on pizza, don't you?"

Her stomach rumbled, but, more important, at the sight of him on her porch, the tensions of the day faded away. Not that being with Carrick didn't produce a welcome tension of its own.

She favored him with her most glorious smile. "I may be starving. I have beer."

"Toby's back?"

"She brought him back exactly on time. But now that he's here, he's an unhappy little dude. Cheer him up while I get plates?"

By the time the two males joined her in the sunroom, where she'd set the table for two and a half, Toby was telling Carrick all his troubles. But he definitely looked like he was getting over the worst of it.

She buckled the baby into the high chair and watched as he tried to launch himself at the pizza she'd slid on to Carrick's plate.

"Looks like he needs his own." Carrick took some of the toppings and most of the cheese off half a slice and cut it into pieces on the high chair tray. Toby grabbed one and began to lick it.

Lilia decided it couldn't hurt. "That's a first."

"We ought to get a photo. How old were you the first time you had pizza?"

"Not old enough to remember."

They enjoyed Toby's introduction to what would probably be a favorite by the time he hit kindergarten and laughed when he moved on to a second piece. Lilia recorded the event with her cell phone.

Carrick waited until they had both finished a slice before he asked: "Did she say how things went?"

Sharing her day, sharing this burden, felt natural, although at the same time she knew better than to take his interest for granted. "She finally broke down and told me he took the top off his sippy cup and got soaked."

"That's our boy."

She sobered. "I wonder if she gets custody if she'll agree to let me see him, or if the judge will make her. What if hanging on is

431

worse than just letting go?"

"You don't have to cross that bridge right now. You're on the road to becoming his permanent guardian, and right now he's sitting at this table smearing pizza everywhere."

"He's happier when you're here. You're such a favorite."

"It's a mutual admiration society."

"You never talked about having children of your own."

"That requires the right woman."

"Unless you're Graham."

An abrupt change of subject seemed called for, and Carrick obliged. "After we eat I have something to show you. Do you think Toby can manage another trip away from home? We don't have to be gone long."

"I think it's going to take a while for him to settle down. As long as he's in the car with us, he'll be happy."

"There might be ice cream in the deal."

Toby's eyes lit up. "S'cream!"

Lilia shook her head. "Now you've done it."

"Forbidden word."

"A food I shouldn't have introduced until he was twenty-one."

"Like pizza."

"Za!" Toby held up another piece and slapped it against his forehead.

"There will be a sponge bath before we leave." Lilia started on another slice.

Forty-five minutes later they were finally in her car with a pizza-free Toby in the back, paging through a toy catalog from their Sacramento excursion. Occasionally, as if to make a point, he tore out pages to crumple and toss into the front.

Lilia backed out and waited for Carrick to give instructions.

"Lincoln. Go left when you get there. I'll tell you when to slow down."

Since Lincoln was Willow Glen's main thoroughfare, she couldn't drive fast anyway. Not between stoplights and pedestrian crossings.

Carrick told her when to pull over, and she did, parking on the roadside. The area, which was outside the main business district, looked to be both commercial and residential, and the house to their right was a stucco bungalow, charming and spacious, but in need of updated landscaping, chimney repair and new paint.

"What next?" She turned to make sure the catalog was in no danger of being eaten.

"I'll show you."

Once outside she released Toby from his seat. Then with the baby on her hip she followed Carrick up the walk. He was on his cell phone, but he slipped it back in his pocket when she joined him. The first thing she noticed was the "for sale" sign.

"So, what's up?" She took a closer look at

the house and, even with its cosmetic faults, loved it immediately. Most of the details which would have brought so much pride to its architect were still intact, a courtyard wall with a Mission style arch over the gate, the arch mirrored over a front window, a turret in the front inside corner.

"What can you tell me about it?" Carrick asked.

"Well, it's Spanish Eclectic architecture, cross-gabled style. Most likely built in the 1920s, maybe the '30s. Originally the turret probably had a fabulous carved wooden door or one that was ornate iron, which apparently disappeared somewhere along the way, but the door surround is stunning. She pointed. "Cast stone relief, and I'm so glad they didn't remove it."

"You're a regular textbook."

"This is part of the reason I love living in Willow Glen. We have examples of almost every architectural style." She stepped back and pointed at the risers of the steps leading to the front door. "See those tiles? Another great detail. So why are we here?"

"The house is for sale."

"I see that."

"This block is zoned for commercial and residential. The house is a disaster inside, water damage among other things, but there's plenty of room to work with. I need someone with your skills to accomplish a professional redesign, and I want Mike and Encompass to do the work."

"What am I missing? You *have* a place to live."

He sounded almost too nonchalant. "I want to live in Willow Glen. I like it here, and the price is right because of the condition of the house."

He wanted to live here. Closer to her and Toby. Carrick had never announced he wanted to be a larger part of their lives now that Graham was gone, and he wasn't admitting it now. For her part, telling him how much she liked the idea seemed too intimate. She wondered how long they would slowly feel their way toward each other. Would they be so careful they might pass without touching and just keep going?

She forced herself to sound nonchalant, too. "Why on this street? It's a fabulous house, I know, but it's also zoned commercial."

"I'm looking ahead. I might want an office of my own one day. Meantime I can live here happily. But it makes sense to buy in a place where I can do both, just in case. And this property won't last long."

"How do you plan to pay for it? The price has to be as high as the moon."

"You know my father's been consulting for Douglas for years?"

She was sorry Graham's father had entered

the conversation.

Carrick went on. "He's made a lot of money for Douglas."

"Which the Randolphs *really* needed."

He grinned at her sarcasm. "But Da is surprisingly not interested in money — which, for an economist, is odd, I know — so he quietly invested every cent Douglas paid him in some of his own hunches. For him, it was play money. Over the years his hunches paid off. Now he thinks Regan and I need places of our own, and he's offered to finance them. She's waiting to commit until she's sure she wants to keep the job she has, but I've decided not to. I'd like to put you in charge of renovations."

She finally saw what he was doing. "And I'll charge you enough to pay you back for all the legal work you've done? Right?"

"You can see how well we complement each other."

She had never done a project this size without Graham. This would be a test, but she was excited. She wanted to do it. She was sure she could, and, of course, she loved doing it for this particular man.

Carrick was watching her expression. "I know Mike's finishing up jobs Encompass contracted for while Graham was still alive. How's he doing?"

"He puts his own spin on things, but so far everyone's been happy."

"Would he and his guys do this job? Maybe others? Keep the business going? Could you work with him the way you did with Graham? It could be a good move for both of you. I could work out the legal stuff, draw up a contract."

Lilia had been too focused on Graham's illness and the custody battle to spend time debating that question. But she thought Mike would be willing, and most likely able, especially if she was still onboard as consultant.

She realized then that Carrick had slyly found the perfect way to nudge her into action. She needed the money, but even more so, she needed the confidence. And she needed to make sure she and Mike could move on as a team.

"It's really a mess inside?"

"A disaster. You'll have a great time."

Toby was getting fidgety. Luckily a young woman came striding up the walkway with a smile distorting her narrow face. "Good evening, Mr. Donnelly. You're ready for another look?"

He introduced Lilia and Toby, and the Realtor unlocked the front door. "I'll let you walk through on your own. I'll be in the kitchen. I've brought all the paperwork so you can look it over when you're finished. But take your time."

"Let's go." Carrick put his hand on Lilia's

back to escort her. She set Toby on the floor and let him run ahead.

Afterwards they indulged in frozen yogurt at the Willow Glen Creamery, vanilla for Toby, pineapple for Lilia and chocolate fudge for Carrick. Outside on a bench under the first stars of the evening, they talked about the last time they had come here, when Graham was still healthy.

"I'm eating his favorite." Carrick held up what was left of his cone.

She held up hers. "He was as wildly enthusiastic about everything pineapple as you are. Except my sangria. He liked that sangria. I should write all this down. For Toby. When he's old enough he'll want to know everything about his dad."

Seamlessly Carrick moved into attorney mode. "Everything you *want* him to know. You were careful with Marina today? Careful not to give her ammunition?"

"I got the message."

He finished his cone, then as naturally as if he'd been doing it for years, he reached over and mopped Toby's face with a wad of clean napkins before the toddler could protest. "Have you asked yourself why she's doing this, Lilia? After eleven months of silence, why she's suddenly determined to be a mother again? Of course Graham's death was a catalyst, but was it the only one?"

"It's not like changing a dress because you've decided it's the wrong one to wear out to dinner, is it?"

"Maybe her circumstances *have* changed, and she can finally see herself providing the home Toby needs now that Graham's gone. But all those months of silence? She didn't show any interest then, so why now?"

Lilia wondered, too, and as she'd learned at her mother's knee, she had tried to put herself in Marina's situation. "Maybe it was just too hard to see him again? Maybe she was afraid she would want him back, and she knew she couldn't handle it."

"She's been married awhile. If her life is finally stable, why not ask for visiting rights before Graham got sick again? Or even go back to court and ask for joint custody so they could share?"

"Is there any way to find out?"

"I'm not sure we need to know right now. If the court investigator recommends you as guardian, the judge is almost certainly going to let Marina have visiting rights unless we submit proof she's a danger. Maybe visitation is all she really wants. And if she agrees to that and doesn't push for more, then that's as good as it's going to get."

"Can you imagine me visiting Toby's school some day and introducing myself as his *guardian*? Like something out of a Brontë sisters novel? Can you hear it now? Will he call me by my first name instead of Mom?"

"It's not ideal, but you were his stepmom, and he'll always know that. So you'll still be *Mom*. And nobody needs a lesson on the legal arrangements."

She wasn't simply being stubborn; she knew the truth. "He needs a real mom. A guardian is not the same."

"If you ask the court to terminate Marina's parental rights so you can adopt, you'll probably lose. Unless you hire an investigator and learn something that might convince the judge."

He had been strictly logical and analytical, but now he covered her hand. "I'm going to put out feelers, anyway. Just to see what I can learn. But this is no time to give up."

"My relationship to Toby is so tenuous, and Marina's is cut and dried."

"You mean the relationship where she dropped him off and forgot about him for most of a year?"

Lilia wondered if Marina really had forgotten her son. "I love him too much, so even if it was the best thing, I couldn't turn him over without a fight."

"Good, because you're obviously the best one to raise him, and Graham wanted you to."

"I guess we just take this one day at a time."

Toby had been patient long enough. Ice cream mostly gone, he started to rub his eyes and struggle to get down. Bedtime was overdue. They strolled back to the car, and the ride home was mostly silent.

Carrick saw them inside, and then Lilia and Toby watched from the doorway until his Prius pulled away.

She didn't want him to leave. But then, she never did.

Bedtime was accomplished quickly. Toby snuggled more than usual, as if convincing himself he was home, and all was well. She knew the little boy was bewildered by the changes in his life. He still searched for his father in places where they'd always spent time together. Today he'd had to contend with Marina, being away from home, being away from *her.* When she finally laid him in his crib and gave him a small stuffed toy he liked he watched her for a while before he finally closed his eyes.

She stayed until she was sure he was asleep. Then she went to get ready for bed. Once there she stared up at the skylight overhead.

Almost from the beginning Carrick had been more to her than Graham's best friend. Both she and Carrick had recognized it, and separately, both of them had decided to ignore it.

Had her life been a play, and she could have cast all the parts, she didn't know which of the two friends she would have chosen to love, honor and cherish. But as children she and Graham had been friends before Carrick came on the scene, and Carrick and Graham had been roommates, friends and the sons of two men who conducted business together. The choice between them had been made before anyone put it into words. And she had loved them both. Differently, perhaps, but she'd never let herself wonder what *differently* entailed. It was as much a distraction as a reality.

She and Carrick had only brought their attraction into the open one time. Now, as she stared at the stars, she thought about that night.

She and Graham hadn't yet married, but despite his family's disapproval, they had been heading for the altar. After completing his undergraduate degree in Washington state Carrick had just been accepted to Stanford Law, and the three old friends had planned to have dinner together at Lilia's favorite sushi bar to celebrate being together again. She was just finishing up her degree in interior design, and Carrick was in town to visit his new alma mater. At the last minute Graham had canceled, and they'd decided to go to dinner without him.

The restaurant had dark walls and subtle lighting, and Carrick had joked that at a sushi restaurant, not being able to see clearly was a leap of faith. They had ordered a variety of rolls and laughed and chatted easily as they tried each one.

She remembered introducing him to sake, quite a lot of sake. The evening had moved languidly toward the moment when he had reached over and taken her hand.

"Did you wonder why, all those years ago, I didn't continue emailing you?"

She had laced her fingers through his so he wouldn't pull away. "I know why Graham never emailed or called. He was embarrassed at the way his father treated him in front of me."

"That was vintage Douglas."

"I think maybe you guessed Graham had feelings for me. You didn't want to poach."

"He talked about you a lot. You were never just a ghost from his past."

The sake had made her both sad and brave, brave enough to ask. "If I had been? If he'd just forgotten about me?"

"Our lives would be very different." Then he had raised her hand to his lips and kissed her fingertips. And she had been forced to admit the one thing she'd never wanted to think about, that despite talk of soul mates and one-true-love, she had been in love with two different men since she was a teenager.

Carrick had placed her hand gently on the table. "We both love him, Lilia. Neither of us could live with ourselves if we hurt him."

Only twenty-one, still trying to figure out who she was and what she felt, she had been grateful he hadn't asked her to choose. But she had gone home that night and shed tears for what could never be.

Since then, she and Carrick had never talked about their feelings. She had filed hers under friendship, and even after Graham was unfaithful, she had known she couldn't run to Carrick. Despite Graham's own lapses, neither she nor Carrick would have been able to forgive themselves if they had reacted any other way.

Now she knew that, despite tiptoeing carefully through years of friendship and never veering off their chosen path, Graham had realized what they felt. The day he'd made the video he'd as much as said it out loud. *But I always knew I wasn't . . .*

He hadn't finished, but he hadn't had to. She had finished silently: *. . . the only man you loved. Perhaps not even the one you loved the most.*

She was old enough to understand that feelings can rarely be controlled, but actions can. She and Carrick had been careful to act honorably, and still, Graham had seen and recognized the truth.

That same day in that same sad conversation, her husband had assured her that he knew she loved him. Tonight, lying in the bed they had shared for almost ten years, she thought those words were as close to a

444

benediction as any man should ever have to
come.

31
THE SWALLOW'S NEST

FEATHERING YOUR NEST WITH
IMAGINATION AND LOVE

June 25th:

I'm delighted so many of you wrote to say you're already planning what to work on during our "Just One Room" project. I promise you'll have help. Together we'll explore the best ways to change your room and maybe change your life a little, too.

Today to begin I've decided to redo my bedroom, and tomorrow I'll make a list of everything I plan to keep. Nothing more. Right now I know my Hawaiian applique quilt, a gift from my parents, will remain on my bed and I'll work around it as I plan. Another day I'll decide whether my discards will be moved, given away, or sent to the landfill.

Just remember, start small and decide what you like before you decide what you don't. Visit some of the wonderful companies who advertise here to see what's new.

Think of the first step this way. What

memories can you fondly put away to make room for new ones?

Aloha, Lilia

Lilia fell to her sofa, pulled off her jacket and kicked off her heels. Unlike Regan, who had a closet filled with expensive stilettos, Lilia still channeled her island childhood, preferring to go barefoot at home, and only grudgingly wore low-heeled pumps when she was with clients. Today, on her initial visit to a home where she was redesigning the children's quarters, heels had been called for, and now her feet were protesting.

Her newest client subscribed to *The Swallow's Nest,* and while she wasn't a do-it-yourselfer, she was committed to creating a casual beachy feel in the west wing of her Los Gatos home. There was nothing casual or beachy about the seven-bedroom contemporary, but today Lilia had suggested a different way to structure the children's space, along with ideas for furniture and paint colors when the construction was complete. The mom had been so enthusiastic, she had signed a contract on the spot and paid a healthy deposit.

Business was picking up. Traffic at her website had improved with this week's launch of the "Just One Room" project, along with an influx of new items in her store. She'd found an interior design student at San Jose

447

State who was now spending several hours each week combing craft and design websites for likely items, and then contacting the artists or companies once Lilia approved. Like any small business owner, Lilia knew she couldn't afford to hire help, but she couldn't afford not to, either. The young man had a good eye for what she wanted, and the gamble was paying off.

The wolf might still be at her door, but for now, she'd fashioned enough weapons to keep him at bay.

She was just closing her eyes for a mini-nap when she heard baby chatter outside. Valencia had taken Toby to have lunch with Dolores and her two high-school-aged daughters who were home for the summer.

In the doorway Valencia set Toby on his feet and he ran to Lilia, climbing up in her lap to finish his one-sided conversation. Of course he didn't stay. Toby never stayed anywhere for long these days. He was a streak of lightning, here, there, everywhere. His vocabulary seemed to double every time he opened his mouth, and his favorite toys were inevitably things he could take apart and put back together. She would love to know if Graham had been this way, but even if Ellen had been willing to speak to her, Lilia couldn't imagine she knew the answer.

Lilia hadn't seen her mother-in-law since Graham's service. And that was more than three months ago.

Valencia lingered in the doorway. She nodded her head, indicating someone behind her. "Somebody's coming."

Lilia was expecting a box of office supplies, but the man who appeared was no deliveryman.

"Eli!" Lilia flew to the front door to grab her brother as Valencia, satisfied all was well, took off after Toby, who had already disappeared.

Lilia thrust Eli away for a good look. He was wearing a tropical shirt and khaki shorts, and his hair was long enough for a ponytail. "You look fabulous! You're making me homesick. What are you doing here?"

"Visiting dealers to see new equipment. And an old friend farther south's building a solar-powered beach buggy, and he's promised me a test drive."

"Farther south?"

He grinned. "San Diego."

"A *lot* farther south. You're here to check on me, aren't you? Jordan's been in and out a couple of times. Who's next?"

"You need to come home and convince everybody you're fine."

She tried to imagine a world in which she could just hop a plane with her son and take him to Kauai to be with the people she loved. "There's so much going on. It's going to be a while."

"Have you had lunch? I could take you out."

"Let me introduce you to your nephew. Then I'll make us something while Toby wears himself to a frazzle. He can nap while we eat."

Toby was so delighted to have Eli to play with that most of an hour passed before Lilia could get him into his crib. Valencia left to do the week's shopping, and she and Eli lounged in the sunroom over ham and cheese paninis and vegetable soup.

"He's something else," Eli said. "A beautiful kid."

"I'm holding on to him by my fingernails. I don't know how much longer he'll be with me." And even though she'd faced the possibility of losing Toby over and over, Lilia's eyes filled.

"They made you his guardian?"

She wiped her eyes with her fingertips. "For now. We've been in and out of court. The court investigator came, apparently liked what she saw well enough, and recommended I keep guardianship. But on Tuesday at the hearing Marina — Toby's birth mother — objected. And even though we had a meeting afterwards to try to work out details, we couldn't. So the judge ordered a full-fledged custody evaluation, and that's going to take weeks, even months, and cost a fortune."

"Doesn't it seem like maybe things are going your way? Until she objected the court said you could have him."

"But she *did* object. And this time the judge told her she can have Toby for one weekend a month until this is settled, starting this Friday. He's going to be so confused."

"He's visited with her already?"

"Weekly." She made a face. "Sometimes longer than he's meant to. She's gotten sloppy about bringing him back. Excuses are thin. Traffic. Last-minute diaper changes. Problems getting him in the car. The last time she brought him home almost an hour late, and he hadn't eaten anything but an afternoon snack."

"The judge knows?"

"I hope it will come out in the new evaluation. I'm keeping notes and sending them to Carrick. I try to have somebody here to verify what time she returns him, so it won't just be my word against hers."

"Is she taunting you?"

Lilia wished it were that simple. But while Marina never seemed overly penitent, these days she was better about sharing information Lilia might need, and she'd taken Lilia's notes and apparently read them, because sometimes she referenced a fact Lilia had detailed for her.

She pushed her plate away with half the sandwich intact. "I don't know what she's doing. He's always so glad to see me. Then

451

he whines and pouts because I made him go. He'll be a mess after the weekend." She didn't voice a worse fear, that Toby would bond with Marina and not want to come back to the woman he called Mama.

"Are you going to eat that?"

"Are we home? You used to eat half my dinner when I wasn't looking."

"A growing boy." He exchanged his empty plate for hers and demolished the rest of her sandwich.

They chatted about family, his and theirs. He gave her the most recent photos of his kids, and while she cleaned up dishes, he went out to his rental car and brought in a suitcase filled with pillow tops with Hawaiian applique designs, some which cleverly used fabric from vintage aloha shirts.

"These are fabulous!" She lifted them, one at a time, from the suitcase. "Who did this?"

"Amber."

She looked up. "*Our* Amber?"

"She took a sewing class to relax, and now I can't get her away from the machine. Mama taught her how to create the patterns, and she took it from there."

"She really wants to sell these?"

"She keeps anything she can't live without."

The pillow tops were perfect for her online shop, and Amber was probably going to be amazed at how much Lilia was already planning to charge. "Tell her I'll take as many as she wants to give me. And ask if she'd like to branch out into place mats and lap quilts."

"She'll be pleased." Eli looked pleased, too.

Somebody knocked, and Lilia thought Valencia probably had her arms filled with grocery bags. Instead when she answered the door, Carrick was standing there. She stepped forward for a quick hug.

"Eli's here. He just showed up on my doorstep so he could eat me out of house and home."

The two men greeted each other with handshakes and grins.

Carrick followed them back into the sunroom. "I wanted to see if Lilia was willing to come over to my new house to show me her latest ideas."

She stacked the dishes on the table. "Would you like to see what we're doing there, Eli?" As if on cue, Toby woke up and started calling "Mama."

"My fan club." She went to get him, and after a new diaper and change of clothes, he launched himself into Carrick's arms as soon as he got downstairs.

"I'd like to see the house," Eli told her. "Carrick just told me the whole story."

"How about the part where we found asbestos and had to back off while a special team came in to remove it. Oh, and the part where the sale hung in midair for weeks because the title company ran into one snafu after another."

"I think she loves solving these problems," Carrick said. "She would hate doing a simple house."

They smiled at each other.

Thirty minutes later they were standing inside. Eli was carrying Toby, who was already at home with him. Mike's crew had carried out all the construction refuse and swept. Lilia could see all the possibilities now.

She began the tour. "We started by consulting with the building department. Then Mike and I drew up a design. We didn't want to lose any interesting architectural features, so that had to be figured in. We're keeping the fireplace, millwork, wood floors."

She gestured and paced off areas to show what they were planning. Eli asked if he could put Toby down, and they followed the little boy through a hallway as Lilia explained what would happen there.

"Carrick wants as open a floor plan as —"

A shriek cut off the rest of her sentence. Toby was just ahead. She'd been keeping her eye on him while she talked, but now he had fallen to the floor and was tearing at his shoe.

Carrick reached him before she could. He swung Toby into his arms and pulled the shoe off for him. Or he tried to. It was held in place by a nail that had gone up through the rubber sole and was now implanted in the little boy's foot.

"You're going to have to yank this off while I hold him." He held the little boy firmly. Eli glimpsed the horror on his sister's face and moved before she could. With one sharp tug the shoe and the nail were removed.

Lilia cradled her son's foot and removed his sock. Then she folded it and held it against the wound, which was bleeding freely. Toby tried to kick her away, but she held his foot firmly.

"ER," Carrick said. "They'll need to clean it and do whatever else they think best."

"I shouldn't have let him run ahead, but I thought he was safe. I was here yesterday when the crew was cleaning up. They were so thorough." She could hardly hear herself over Toby's screams.

"He's a kid," Eli said. "This won't be the last injury."

She clasped Toby in her arms, while still holding the sock against his foot. "I can't believe I let this happen."

Eli lifted the sock for a better look. "The bleeding's slowing now. He's going to be okay. We were all here, Lilia. We were all watching. It was an accident."

She shook her head. *"I maika'I ke kalo I ka 'oha."*

"And that means?" Carrick asked.

Eli answered. "A taro plant is judged by the little plant it produces."

"Lilia, nobody's going to hold this against you."

Lilia started toward the steps. "Marina gets Toby for the weekend starting on Friday. When she picks him up, I'll have to tell her what happened so she can make sure no infection develops." She didn't have to follow that to its obvious conclusion. This, and any other mistake she made in the next weeks, would be paraded in the final report and possibly the evidentiary hearing.

In the end could she really lose her son because of a nail the crew had missed? Was the whole procedure so unfair that this one mistake could tip the balance in Marina's direction?

She was nearly asleep that night when Carrick called to check on Toby. Eli was already on his way to San Diego, his visit much too short. She lay in the room she was planning to renovate. She couldn't erase Graham's presence in the house, nor did she want to try, but this room would have to be her sanctuary and refuge in the years ahead with a small boy, then a teenager, just down the hall.

If she was fortunate.

"He's doing fine," she said, settling against the pillows. "I gave him ibuprofen."

"The wound wasn't deep. Thanks to the thick soles of his shoes."

A nurse in the ER had examined and cleaned the puncture wound thoroughly and given instructions for aftercare. Lilia had already made an appointment with Toby's pediatrician for follow-up.

"I can't keep this from Marina. She'll have to check his foot when he's with her."

"I'm glad you got to see Eli. Your family's great."

"I'll never be able to move back to be near them. Not if . . ." She looked up at the stars, the way she had as a child on the family lanai. "If I have Toby. I'll have to stay close to Marina so she can see him."

"Do you want to move back?"

"In a perfect world I'd like a little cottage or condo there, but we both know how likely that will be. I'll be lucky if I can keep this one."

"You're down tonight."

"I keep thinking about the weekend."

"That's the other reason I called."

She hesitated. "As my lawyer or *friend*?"

"I want you to get out of town. There's nothing you can do at home except worry."

"I plan to work."

"You won't."

She gave a low laugh. "You really do know me."

"There's an inn down the coast that you'll love, and there's something near it I want you to see. Come with me."

She didn't know what to say.

He filled the silence. "I know what you're thinking, but don't worry. We'll have separate rooms. Nothing will come back to haunt you in a custody fight. Not that it would anyway."

"Isn't this above and beyond your duties as my attorney?"

"What do you think?"

She tried to imagine being with Carrick. Just the two of them. Was this an added complication in a life about to overflow with them? Or was this what a hidden part of her had strained against for years?

One of them had to speak the truth out loud. "I'm at my most vulnerable."

"The rules changed, and not because either of us asked for what happened. When rules change, it's important to move slowly. I'm not suggesting anything except a weekend out of town and a hike you don't want to miss. Please, come with me."

The answer was easy. "You know I will."

"I'll pick you up tomorrow evening. We'll eat on the way down to Monterey."

She hung up and stared at the skylight Graham had placed above their bed because he'd wanted to please her. He had done so many things to make her happy, and a few that had nearly destroyed them both.

"You did please me," she said softly. "Whenever you could, you did. Wherever you are, Graham, I send you my love. But it's time now for you to move on in peace."

When she couldn't fall asleep she got up, took a legal pad out of the small desk in the corner, and started a list of everything in the room she wanted to keep.

In the end there was very little.

32

Marina packed carefully for her upcoming weekend at Deedee's apartment. She hadn't spent the night under her mother's roof in years, but very little had changed. Deedee still refused to throw out anything with print on it. Yesterday, in preparation for the weekend, Marina had spent the afternoon trudging back and forth to recycling bins.

Why Deedee subscribed to *The Mercury News* was a mystery. On Sundays her mother read *Family Circus* and *Garfield,* as if they were repositories of universal truth, and then pored over the TV section so she could save esoteric educational programs to her DVR — where they languished until they disappeared. As she'd cleaned and cleared, Marina had discovered months of daily papers that had never been unfolded, along with mountainous stacks of advertising circulars and junk mail.

Deedee swore she was saving every scrap of paper to read when she had time, but Marina had gotten rid of the whole mess anyway. Toby deserved better.

Now she added another pair of jeans and comfortable sandals to her backpack and zipped it closed. She already had a suitcase of Toby's clothes, toys and other necessities in her car, and she planned to pick up diapers and baby toiletries on the way to Lilia's. In the time it took to pack and plan for a weekend with a toddler, she could have organized an extended European vacation.

As she lifted the backpack Blake wandered in. "You're sure you need to stay overnight at your mother's?"

"I'll just feel better if I keep an eye on her and Pete. You know how miserable summer colds can be, and both of them are probably going to need somebody to take care of them through the night. With those coughs they won't get much sleep."

Blake didn't appear overly concerned, and as usual, he seemed preoccupied. She knew very little about what was happening at Meri-Tech. She did know that the issue of who was going to be in charge had ended in his favor without going to court, but for now his sons were still working there. Blake claimed he needed his home to be a sanctuary where MeriTech wasn't under discussion, and she'd been glad to give it to him.

Apparently, between them, they had enough secrets to fuel a reality show.

"Since you won't be home I'll probably go back and work this evening." Blake reached for the pack, as if he planned to carry it outside, but she slung it over a shoulder. She didn't want him asking about the suitcase in her car with Toby's things.

"I've got it, don't worry. It's not heavy. I left dinner in the fridge. All you have to do is put it in the microwave, but you'll be on your own tomorrow."

"I'll probably work tomorrow, and grab a sandwich somewhere. I'll make a weekend of it."

She leaned over to kiss his cheek. "You just be sure you're home on Sunday afternoon. I'll be back no later than five thirty." She had to be since Toby was due at Lilia's by five.

"We'll go out for dinner."

"I would like that."

"Good." He walked her to the door. By the time she turned around to wave goodbye, he was already gone.

She wondered if it was a mistake not to bring Toby here this weekend, but she'd already told the necessary lies, so there was no turning back. She had worried that the little boy wouldn't be on his best behavior. This was his first entire weekend away from Lilia, and he was bound to be unhappy until he adjusted.

She didn't want Blake's introduction to her son to be a weekend with a screaming toddler. She also didn't want him to wonder why she was spending so much of it at Ellen's. She'd told him very little about the custody battle, mostly that she was working with an attorney to preserve her rights. He knew she spent time with the little boy, and even asked if she wanted him there when Toby visited, but in the end she'd said no. First she wanted Toby to get used to *her*, so when Blake met him, he saw a happier, easier child.

She spent most of the drive to Lilia's trying to ratchet up her enthusiasm for the upcoming weekend. She supposed Toby was a typical eighteen-month-old. Into everything. Demanding. Obstinate. Viewing him as an outsider, she knew he was a cute kid, smart and already something of a clown. As an adult he was probably going to be as good-looking as his father, and every bit as good at getting his own way.

Viewing him as a mother? Nothing she had done, nothing that had happened in all the weeks of their reunion, not one bit of it had helped her feel closer to her son. No matter what she learned about him, and no matter how hard she tried, he was still a stranger.

Women were supposed to have maternal feelings. Deedee gushed with love, although it hadn't spurred her to be a better mother. But maybe Deedee had cornered the market for their family, and Marina had just been given the burdens that went along with it.

She would never tell Ellen, but the snail pace of the custody battle was a blessing. The attorney Ellen had hired was whip-smart, ruthless and undoubtedly expensive. Fifty-something Glynnis Jacobs was using every ploy, and between that and the difficulties of scheduling court time, Toby's fate hung in the balance while everyone involved was closely evaluated.

All she could feel about the delay? Grateful.

She parked down the street from Lilia's cottage and took her time walking back. She had to get through the afternoon and evening. Douglas was going out of town tonight, and tomorrow she was taking Toby to Ellen's, where Graham's mother expected to be alone with him. Marina would pick him up tomorrow evening, spend one more night at Deedee's and drop him off here again on Sunday. Surely she could find enough things to do that the weekend would fly by.

She wished it already had.

Lilia took a few moments to answer the door, but she smiled politely when she did. "I have everything ready. I'll get him. Would you like to come in?"

"I'm fine out here."

Lilia left the door open, returning in a few minutes with Toby and the silly puppy backpack the little boy treasured. Toby took one look at Marina and clung to Lilia, turning his face away.

Lilia stroked his hair. "I'm going away for the weekend, but you have my cell number, and I put my contact information in Toby's backpack. There's just one other thing."

Marina waited for one of Lilia's mini-lectures. But instead the other woman removed Toby's shoe. "He stepped on a nail. He's been to the emergency room, and everything looks fine, but they told me to check the site a couple of times a day, keep it dry and covered. I gave you a copy of their instructions with the phone numbers and some Band-Aids. You won't mind checking to be sure it doesn't get infected?"

Marina peered at a round adhesive bandage with a happy face on it. "A nail?"

"He was wearing shoes. Luckily it wasn't deep."

"He's had tetanus shots, hasn't he?"

"I gave you a copy of his medical records."

"Which I don't happen to have with me at the moment, Lilia. I don't carry them in my pocket."

"He's had all his shots, all his checkups. Actually, he started his shots with you. Remember?"

Marina did. The shots had made a perennially fussy baby that much worse. She probably hadn't gotten an hour of sleep for days afterwards. "How did it happen?"

"We were touring a house under renovation. The crew did a great job of cleaning up before we got there, but they missed a nail."

Marina knew her son was going to be fine. But a perverse part of her raised an eyebrow in question. "Isn't that the kind of thing you should have checked for? Safety's a big issue with toddlers."

Lilia paused before she spoke, as if she was schooling herself not to react. "It certainly is. Which is why I'm so careful with him."

"But not . . . when did it happen?"

"It happened yesterday."

"But not *yesterday.*"

"I try very hard to be everywhere and see everything. I plan to continue. Nobody saw the nail."

"Nobody?"

"I had two men with me."

"Maybe you were busy talking."

"Here you go, Marina." Lilia leaned over and placed Toby in her arms. He began to whimper. Marina stepped back quickly.

Lilia turned to go, as if she couldn't stand to watch Toby fall apart again. "I hope everything goes well. Let me know if you need anything."

As the little boy struggled to get back to Lilia, Marina turned away, too. She knew better than to back down. They were battling for custody. She couldn't give an inch, and no matter what, she was going to report the nail incident to her lawyer.

Then some part of her, maybe some better part, made her glance over her shoulder. "It could have happened to anybody." Before Lilia could respond, Marina strode down the walk and up the street to her car.

She didn't want to end up at Deedee's too early. Deedee had found a new gig and was working part-time at a dive bar not far from her apartment. Marina hoped, if she waited long enough, she would miss her mother entirely. Of course Pete might be home, but when she'd asked Jerry if she could use *his* room, he hadn't argued, which was a sure sign he planned to spend the weekend with his new girlfriend.

As she was snapping Toby into his car seat, she realized she had forgotten to ask Lilia if he had eaten. These days the other woman didn't volunteer anything. She supposed even if he had, he probably wouldn't balk if she bought him a kids' meal while she ate a fast-food salad.

She had problems starting her car and wondered if Lilia was inside watching. By the time the engine finally caught, and she had negotiated Friday rush hour and gotten him out of his seat again at the restaurant, she abandoned healthy for calories.

Inside she ordered a chicken nugget meal for Toby, smiling politely as the woman at the counter exclaimed how cute he was, and then asked for a double hamburger and fries for herself. She managed to negotiate her way to a window table with Toby in one arm and the tray in the other and strap him into what looked like an insecure high chair.

She decided to blame her son for her food choices. "If you come to live with me permanently I'll probably turn into a blimp."

She pulled him closer to the table and opened his box, setting his food in reach. She remembered to tear the nuggets into smaller pieces and break up the apple slices. Then she poured chocolate milk into his sippy cup, which she'd had the foresight to bring along. He stared at the food as if he had never seen anything similar and had no idea what to do with it.

She shrugged and unwrapped her burger. Toby leaned forward and made a grab for one of her French fries. She pulled the carton farther away, but he leaned farther until she wasn't sure the chair would remain upright.

"Hey, stop that. You have your food, I have mine."

He began to squawk. "My . . . my . . . my . . ."

"You think?" She debated. What was a French fry other than a potato? A potato was a vegetable, and this vegetable was cut just right for a little boy's fingers. She put several with his dinner and went back to her burger.

By the time she was finished Toby had eaten a dozen fries and only one bite of nugget.

The apple hadn't been touched, but the chocolate milk had vanished.

Chocolate and French fries. Epic bad parenting. She pretended to eat a slice of apple, then offered it to him. She could tell from his expression he was hoping he hadn't inherited her IQ.

"I hope Lilia fed you something better." She remembered the haphazard way Deedee had fed her brothers when Marina hadn't cooked. And now, look at them both. They had survived and grown. Well, and grown and grown . . . Jerry was easily a hundred pounds overweight. These days Pete survived on beer and cigarettes.

She would have to remind him not to smoke in the apartment while Toby was with her.

Six o'clock hadn't yet rolled around, and Deedee didn't leave for work for another half hour. Marina wasn't afraid to let her mother see Toby; she was afraid to subject Toby to the tornado that was Deedee getting ready for work.

She settled on a trip to the Valley Fair mall, which wasn't far from Deedee's apartment. With Toby in his stroller they wound between cars to a side entrance. For the next hour they explored, although every time she stopped, Toby fussed. Finally she let him get down and run. At one point she left the stroller to keep up with him and turned just in time to see someone eyeing it with more than casual interest. She grabbed Toby and sprinted back. The young man shrugged and went on his way.

As she was putting Toby back in, he hung his head and with one explosive burst left absolutely no doubt that French fries and chocolate milk were not the best possible combination for dinner.

By the time they made it to Deedee's, Toby was still pale and whining, and she was afraid the next round of vomiting might be scheduled for her car.

She hauled him out quickly and grabbed his suitcase to roll along beside her. The apartment complex passed muster on the outside, spartan but neat. A few trees rustled in the evening breeze, and they passed a swimming pool with tables for picnics. Luckily Deedee's apartment was on the ground floor.

At the mall Marina had only done a cursory cleanup of Toby's clothes, and she hoped Deedee's tub was still clean. Chances were good. Yesterday she had scrubbed it thoroughly herself, and nobody in the house showered daily. "Home run for my intuition," she muttered as she unlocked the front door.

The apartment wasn't much to look at, but since the complex qualified as affordable housing, Deedee was lucky to have it. Inside two bedrooms sat side by side behind the living, kitchen and dining combination. The only bathroom was at the end of a short hall that passed in front of the smaller bedroom.

The apartment wasn't large enough for three adults, but that hadn't motivated Marina's brothers to move out. The smaller room was officially Jerry's, but Pete either slept there or in Deedee's room depending on who was gone for the night. Otherwise he slept on the pullout sofa, most often, without bothering to pull out the bed. Small as it was, the apartment was still head and shoulders above the one they had shared when Marina was growing up.

She rolled the suitcase into the bathroom and ran a bath, stripping off Toby's clothes and settling him in the water. She knew he still wasn't feeling well because he didn't protest as she washed and then dried him with a clean towel she'd hidden under the bathroom sink. He looked miserable, and he shivered, even though the apartment was uncomfortably warm. She wiggled him into a new diaper and pajamas and took him into Jerry's room. She had asked her brother to retrieve Brittany's old crib from storage and set it up in here, but apparently he hadn't gotten around to it.

There was no way she could wrestle the crib into the room by herself.

"You'll have to sleep with me tonight, kiddo." While Toby sat on the floor and closed his eyes, she stripped the sheets off the bed and remade it with clean ones which, like the towels, she'd hidden after washing them. Then she picked up her son and placed him in the bed against the wall. She didn't relish sleeping with a toddler, but she had to lie down beside him to keep him in place.

"Won't this be fun?" She pumped enthusiasm into her voice. "You, me, a double bed? Wow, can't wait."

He was no longer pale. Now his skin had a greenish tint, and his lips trembled. "Mama?"

"*I'm* your Mama."

"Mama!" He turned away from her.

It was too early to go to sleep. She lay still, listening to him whimper. This was almost worse than Toby's earliest months. Then she'd had a real place for him to sleep. Now she couldn't even go out to her car to retrieve her backpack. It was only a little past seven, and she had the whole night ahead of her.

She got up and replaced the overhead light with the softer glow of the bedside lamp.

"Doggie?"

The word was clear, the meaning behind it wasn't. "Doggie?" she asked.

"Doggie. Now."

His puppy backpack was still in the car with hers. And unless she took him outside with her, there was no way to get it. If the mysterious Doggie was there, he would remain in Mustang exile until someone came back to the apartment and babysat.

She tried to sound firm but kind. "Doggie's not here."

"Doggie. Now."

"Hey, you're speaking in sentences."

He began to cry. Not scream. Just cry, a sad little sound she'd never heard before.

She turned to look at him. His eyes were wide open and tears dripped down his cheeks. Her heart sped up a little. "Toby, I'll get Doggie later. I promise. Why don't you close your eyes and go to sleep? Doggie will be here soon."

"Doggie."

"I used to sing you a special song when you were a baby. It helped you sleep." She thought about that. "At least it helped a little."

He whimpered louder.

She decided to give it a try. "It was your favorite," she said, hoping that would entice him.

She cleared her throat and began. "Ninety-nine bottles of beer on the wall . . ."

He turned to his side and faced her, his little face screwed up in a frown. But he was no longer whimpering.

"Do you remember?" She had to smile. He actually looked as if he was trying to. "Take one down, and pass it around . . ."

"Beeh?"

"Right, beer." She started on the next verse. It was going to be a long night.

"Beeh."

"Please, don't tell your mother, okay?" She realized what she'd said. "Your *other* mother."

He looked puzzled. She started to sing again.

By the time they were on the seventy-seventh bottle, Toby's eyes began to close. By sixty-two he was sound asleep.

With his face in repose he was impossibly beautiful, but then he always had been. He was sucking his thumb, but since she had seen him do that before, she wasn't worried. He needed comfort. She felt a pang of sympathy. She could relate.

What was she doing with this child? Pour all her warm feelings for Toby into a cup and there would probably still be room for one of those bottles of beer that had lulled him to sleep. On top of that her maternal instincts had apparently been chopped off at the root. Tonight she'd fed him French fries and chocolate milk just because he'd wanted them. And now she remembered that she hadn't checked his foot before putting him in bed.

Add up all that, and then take a look at where they were sleeping tonight. And *how.*

"I left you on a doorstep once," she said softly. "Maybe I ought to do it again."

He sighed and turned over and suddenly he was cuddled against her, his curly head brushing her arm. Rolling to her own side was a simple matter. She pulled him a little closer and lay her arm over him, not to weigh him down but to give comfort.

She could feel his heart beating against her palm. She could feel the gentle in and out of his breathing. She reached behind her and clicked off the light. The room was silent.

She had not loved this child at birth, and she had convinced herself love would never be possible. Fury with Graham and later herself for going along with him had eaten at her. By the time Toby was born he had become nothing more than a burden she was forced to carry alone. Even after their "reunion" she'd still viewed him as a burden. Witness tonight.

But maybe all those months ago, in her own screwy way, Deedee had been right. Maybe she had suffered from postpartum depression. Hormones in disarray. Lack of sleep. Lack of help. How many nights after she'd brought Toby home from the hospital had she thought what a relief it would be just to sail over her balcony into the parking lot below?

Now she faced something else she had tried to suppress. Even after giving Toby to Graham and Lilia, she hadn't been able to forget him. And she hadn't taken Ellen up on her offer just so Graham's mother could help her financially.

"I left you on a doorstep," she whispered

after a long time. This time she knew, as she said it and her heart flooded with something she didn't want to name, that she wasn't going to leave Toby on a doorstep again.

Not ever.

33

Carrick couldn't have chosen a more perfect inn for the weekend. Just down the coast from Carmel-by-the-Sea, the Seascape had been designed to nestle into the outstanding scenery with the lowest of profiles. In addition to three rooms in the main house, six charming cypress cottages were snuggled along a ridge in pairs, with walkways that both connected them and provided a porch so guests could sit and watch extravagant sunsets over the Pacific. Native poppies, hawkweed and sky lupine adorned the bed in front of Lilia's cottage tucked around an elf garden of quirky houses and figurines produced by one of the inn's owners. She was ready to move in permanently.

While each cottage was large enough for a small family, Carrick had reserved the one connected to hers for himself. She was as grateful as she was sorry. She needed to put her life with Graham behind her before she committed to another relationship.

Of course telling herself that didn't lessen the temptation of having Carrick a stone's throw away for the weekend.

As she unpacked her suitcase, she pushed temptation away and thought about Toby. Marina was a puzzle. Lilia knew she should despise the other woman. Yet every time they were together, Marina surprised her.

In the strangest of ways Graham was the two women's common denominator. Linked forever by a man who had tricked them both. In his own charming, thoughtful way, Graham might have been as ruthless as the man who had sired him.

A soft knock at the side door was a welcome distraction. She set the suitcase on the floor and crossed the room to let Carrick in. He had slipped on a dark green pullover that dramatized the changeable sea-green of his eyes. Since he paid almost no attention to clothes, she wondered which of the women he'd dated had picked it out for him.

"You chose a perfect place." She had a mental list of exactly what was appropriate for the weekend, and she put her arms around him for a hug, but stepped back quickly. "I even have a fireplace."

"Then we'll need a fire. In the meantime if you're getting hungry I've got restaurant recommendations from our host."

She didn't want to dress up, and she didn't want to leave the cottage for long. "It's too pretty here to spend the evening away, don't you think? We have time to run out for cheese, hummus, olives, fresh bread."

He looked pleased. "I brought wine."

"Of course you did. This is California. I brought white, and it's already chilling in the fridge."

"Then after we shop let's sit on the porch and watch the sun set."

"And if it cools down later, we can come inside, light the fire and make s'mores."

In an hour they were back at the cottage, having found plenty for dinner as they strolled through the picturesque town.

Without even discussing it they ended up in her cottage. His was every bit as charming, but smaller. He had an overstuffed love seat; she had a sofa. He had a queen-size bed. Hers was a king.

A king that was much too large for one and, like its name, ruled over everything in the vicinity.

They assembled dinner as efficiently as if they'd always put meals on the table together. Graham had designed church sanctuaries and restored historic houses, but he had been a hindrance in her kitchen. She and Carrick seemed to waltz around each other, never getting out of step, never treading on each other's toes. When they touched it was casual and natural.

It also sent her heart into double time and

was impossible to ignore.

The sun was sinking toward the horizon when they took plates outside and set them between their chairs. She had poured a glass of Carrick's Napa Valley red blend that was so perfect she wanted to savor it forever. He was drinking the Sonoma Valley pinot grigio she had chilled.

She clinked her glass with his and met his eyes. She tried to make her question sound like an afterthought. "How did you find this fabulous place?"

"I did some work for the owners, a particularly sticky lawsuit. It's as wonderful as they promised."

She was ridiculously glad he hadn't been here with another woman.

"Missing Toby?" he asked.

"Oh yeah."

"If you weren't worried about him, would it be nice to have a break?"

"Oh yeah." She offered a cracker with a slice of Brie. "I love him, but he is a drain. Sometimes —" She caught herself and stopped.

"Sometimes you understand why Marina couldn't handle everything by herself and gave him to you?"

"How do you always know what I'm going to say?"

"Because we've been friends so long. And I understand it, too. A baby's scream is quite an invention. It's so horrifying his caretaker figures out what's bothering him and fixes it fast. But some babies don't come with an off switch, or an explanation. Then the magnificent invention becomes torture."

"I really don't want to empathize with her. She's trying to take him back."

"Yep."

"We should talk about something else."

"You choose."

There were so many things they shouldn't talk about she had to think before she started. Then while they were awed by a perfect sunset and a scrumptious mushroom and lentil pâté, they talked about everything except the things that really mattered. Later they made s'mores and popcorn and lounged together on the slipcovered sofa to watch *Young Frankenstein.*

When the movie ended he got up to leave. "We'll be busy tomorrow. We should both get some rest."

She didn't want him to go. She knew he shouldn't stay. She saw he understood her turmoil, and that he had decided the decision had to be hers. They'd both lost Graham, and while months had passed, they were both still suffering from everything that had happened before and after.

He gave a brief nod, then without fanfare, he pulled her close a moment and kissed the top of her head. Before she could phrase a response, he was gone. She stayed up another hour watching the glowing embers in the fireplace and wondering exactly what curve ball life was going to throw next.

In the morning they met in the main house for an elaborate breakfast buffet. She didn't tell him that she'd woken before dawn, sure she heard Toby crying for her. When she realized where she was and why, she'd been so worried she had almost called Marina, although she'd had the good sense to put her cell phone back in her handbag.

"So . . ." Carrick crossed his arms over a full stomach. "Are you up for this?"

"You have to be more explicit. *What* should I be up for?"

"Eight miles? Quite a bit uphill? Spectacular views, a beach to splash around in, and something special I want you to see."

"I brought hiking shoes, a hat, sunscreen."

He nodded approvingly. "I asked our hosts to pack a lunch. We'll be gone most of the day."

She couldn't imagine a better way to try to put Toby out of her mind.

They drove to the Andrew Molera State Park. She was impressed when Carrick showed his annual park pass. "I'm with a pro," she said as they got out of his Prius.

"I've been here a couple of times. Two weekends ago with a friend."

She schooled herself not to ask for details.

"Then I'm in good hands."

"He's a birder, a guy I know from law school. He's trying to get me hooked."

She wondered if he had added an explanation to make sure she understood, or if it was simply an afterthought. "Has he succeeded?"

"I like knowing what I'm looking at when I'm wandering through backcountry. But I'm not much for lists or notes. I do enough paperwork as it is."

They gathered their supplies into day packs. He took water, their lunches, binoculars, and she carried extra socks, snacks, her camera, and their lightweight windbreakers.

The day was nearly perfect, warm but with a light layer of clouds. They started across the lot. He took longer, faster strides than usual. "Let's work up a sweat, because we might get a chance to cool off."

The *chance* was a rock-lined stream. Following Carrick's example Lilia removed her boots, stuffed her socks inside, tied laces together and slung them around her neck. Then she rolled her pants mid-thigh.

"Part of the year there's a bridge," he said. "But they remove it when the steelhead are spawning. I thought it might be in place already, but we're too early."

"I don't know whether I'm happy or sad we missed it."

"You're about to find out." Carrick extended his hand. The water was icy cold, and she yipped as he laughed at her.

By the time they got to the other side, her pants were soaked, but she was laughing, too. "That would probably have been more fun after a long, hot hike."

"You'll find out. All trails lead back here."

They trudged along together, drying off in the sun. She asked about his job, and he described some of the work he was doing. "When I joined a large firm I knew I'd get some broad experience, and I have. I've learned a lot, but this isn't how I want to spend the rest of my working life."

"You mean you want to go out on your own?"

"I may have to one day, or else join a smaller firm. I've begun working toward certification as a child advocate attorney. I did the course work in law school, and I've just about completed the hours of specialization I need."

"You never said a word."

"I knew I needed to round out my experience first. Then when the whole deal came up with Toby, I realized this really is where I want to put my energy."

"What will you do exactly?"

"Investigations, coordinating services with the court, representing minors in criminal cases. Everything in between, like advocating for children with special needs."

"You'd be happy doing that."

"I won't ever be rich, and I'm fairly certain I won't make partner where I am. My colleagues have larger ambitions."

She wondered if he was warning her. Then she decided he knew her better than that. "You're your father's son. You really don't care, do you?"

"I had a bird's-eye view of how happy being filthy rich made the Randolphs."

"And Graham."

There was nothing he could say to that.

The track was pleasantly shady in places. At one point Carrick pointed. "That path goes to the beach, but we'll hit another later and see where the Big Sur River meets the Pacific. You okay with moving on?"

"I'm going strong."

"You'll need to be."

They walked most of a mile on a wide trail with golden lupine blooming in waves beside them. Treeless hills undulated in the distance, and the sun peeked out from the clouds to bake their bare arms.

"Okay, that's the easy part." Carrick stopped and pulled out water. They sipped as he played tour guide. "From this point we'll take the ridge trail. It's exactly what it says it is, so we have to climb to get to the top. When you get tired, take a break. I think this is one of the prettiest parts of the hike. The ocean, coves, headlands. You can even see the old lighthouse on Point Sur. So we'll take our time."

They stopped for water, pointed out views, snapped photos. Lilia couldn't remember the last time she'd just explored, purely for the joy of it. Before Toby, certainly, but then Toby was a different kind of exploration.

"When Toby's a little older, I'd like to bring him along," she said. "We can take turns carrying him if he gets tired."

Carrick, who was just a little ahead, turned. "I'll consider that an invitation."

They stopped to rest where two trails met, and Lilia bent over, resting her hands on her thighs and breathing deeply.

"That was the steepest climb." Carrick pulled out the water again. "There's more to come, but it's not as rugged. You're okay?"

"I've walked a lot of mountain trails in my day."

"Someday we'll go back to Kauai and you can show me some of them."

She grinned and repeated what he had said earlier. "I'll consider that an invitation."

He laughed, and before she realized what she was doing she straightened, rose on the balls of her feet and kissed him. She hadn't planned it, and she hadn't planned to lean into him when he circled her waist and pulled her closer. She had never kissed Carrick, certainly never this way, but his taste, the feel of his lips were familiar, which didn't make her any less hungry for them.

They finally broke apart. She caught her breath. A moment passed before she could speak. "I know how reckless, how stupid, it is to jump from one relationship right into another one."

He took her hand and didn't let go. Then he kissed her palm. "It's no leap. We aren't strangers."

"This is a difficult time. We're both trying to make sense of everything that happened."

"I never hoped to be more than your friend. But now that both our futures have changed? Do you think I'm going to walk away?"

"I don't think I deserve you." And she knew that no matter how much she had loved Graham, she'd never been tempted to say the same to him.

"You deserve everything." He kissed her lightly on the lips, then turned, as if he knew moving on would be their salvation. "More miles ahead but, Lilia, we'll get there."

She knew he wasn't just talking about the hike.

The Pacific was often hidden now, replaced by ridge views to their east and the distant summit of Pico Blanco. Miles later they stopped for lunch in a thicket of young redwoods and oaks. After they ate she leaned against a tree and Carrick lay down with his head in her lap, enjoying the respite from the sun.

She played with his hair, combing it with her fingers. "Have we seen what you wanted to show me?" she asked after a long silence.

"Nope."

"I love everything so far."

"I knew you would."

"You aren't going to give me any hints, are you?"

"You're wheedling."

"Toby has taught me so much."

He laughed, then rose and held out his hand. "Moving on."

Eventually they descended through rock formations, the last blooms of wildflowers and breathtaking views. They only paused for photos. Hours had already passed.

Carrick finally stopped and pulled out water again. "So below us is the beach."

"It's gorgeous."

"We're going to climb down to the sand. The tide's out, so this is the perfect time to walk back along the water instead of the trail."

"Is the beach what we're here for?"

"You'll see."

The descent was steep, and they were careful. But once they were on the sand, Lilia ran to the water's edge, removed her hiking shoes and socks and waded. The water was almost flat, but she knew to watch for sleeper waves. Carrick joined her, and they ran along the beach and in and out of the water like children.

They finally went back for their boots and packs and strolled hand in hand. About half a mile north he stopped. "Time for the binoculars."

"Are we looking for something special?"

"Your namesakes."

"Lilies?"

"There's a colony of swallows ahead. Have you ever seen one?"

She remembered a drive south with her aunt and mother when she was ten. "On my first visit to San Jose, I went on a car trip with my family down to San Juan Capistrano to see the swallows arrive from somewhere in South America. I don't remember where. Only we were early or they were late that year, and by then they were already nesting in other places. So there was nothing much to see."

"You missed them?"

"A big disappointment for a ten-year-old."

"Like those, these are cliff swallows. You won't be disappointed today."

Now she was intrigued. "Cliff swallows apparently nest on cliffs."

"Or anywhere that has an overhang. And they nest together."

A little farther ahead Carrick pointed. "That's what we're here for. We can get closer. They don't scare easily."

The nests became more obvious as they approached. They were nothing like any other bird's nest she'd seen, or the sweet little nest with three pearly eggs that was the logo for her website. These looked as if they had been sculpted from clay and plastered by some giant's hand to the side of the cliff.

"There are at least five or six dozen nests here. Apparently some colonies have thousands. There probably aren't enough prime spots to expand here."

"What are they made of?"

"The birds gather mud in their beaks. See that stream?" He pointed just ahead where a stream trickled down the cliff side. "Probably from that as well as places farther away. Then they shake the mud until it forms a pellet and add it to the nest. Eventually they create a gourd shape, with a small opening at the top. And my friend says they line the nests with dried grasses. Perfect for eggs."

"Isn't it amazing that a bird knows how to do that?" Now she was close enough that she could see the swallows without her binoculars, but she focused directly on the nests. "I love this, Carrick. What a great surprise. I'll take photos for my blog."

"I thought you might. Take your photos, then let's sit over there and watch awhile. I know something you'll find interesting."

She did, glad she had a zoom lens on her camera, although she wished she could scale the cliff to get closer. When she'd finished she joined him on a rock with a good view of the colony. "The nests are amazing, aren't they? Very practical and clever, but I don't think I'm going to change my logo anytime soon."

"Some people think swallows are pests." Carrick handed her the last of their water.

She fished in her pack for snacks and gave him the last of their trail mix. "I hope they're protected."

"They are when the nest is inhabited. My friend said that in Russia, if a swallow builds a nest in the eaves of a house, that means good people live there. But if somebody destroys a swallow's nest, they'll be doomed to live in misery for a very long time."

"I like that logic."

"There's something just as interesting, and it's absolutely true. Have you ever heard of a brood parasite? They depend on another creature to raise their young. Brood parasitism exists in fish, insects *and* birds. The cliff swallow is a brood parasite."

As she finished her water she considered how that might work. "So what does that mean? The mother bird expects other birds to help feed her young?"

"Much more diabolical. The brood parasite lays her egg in another bird's nest. Apparently she waits until the other bird is gone or even when it just turns away, and the nest is momentarily vulnerable. The parasite swallow lays the egg in a blink of an eye and flies away. She never returns."

"And the bird who's duped?"

"I don't know if the bird *feels* duped, do you? She ends up with another mouth to feed, but she and her partner raise the stranger's egg like it was their own until it's time for the new little bird to fly away."

She let that sink in. She'd have to be clueless not to see the similarities between the cliff swallows and Lilia Swallow.

"Well, at least my situation's not unique in the animal kingdom," she said at last.

"It gets even more interesting. They've actually documented birds laying eggs in their own nests, then carrying them to another nest in their wings. And some brood parasites, like the Common Cuckoo, are so determined not to raise their own young they can actually modify their eggs to resemble another bird's, so the host won't recognize the egg as counterfeit and eject it."

"For the record? I don't regret for one minute that I hatched Marina's egg and I'm raising her baby bird until the day he's ready to leave my nest. I just hope I get to."

He took her hand. "You're the best kind of swallow, aren't you? The kind who takes a situation you didn't choose and turns it into something good. Because if there were no host swallows, I'm sure there would still be plenty of swallows determined not to raise their young."

"And the world would have fewer of these amazing creatures."

"I know you love Toby just because he's an awesome little boy, but you can be proud of yourself. Because not everybody has the strength of character to do what you've done."

She squeezed his hand in thanks, but for a moment she was too emotional to speak. Finally she cleared her throat. "What do the male swallows think about all this, Carrick? Do they complain? Do they refuse to feed the rogue swallow's nestling and teach it to fly?"

"The male swallow treats the stranger's egg and her baby bird exactly the way he treats his own."

"You don't really know that, do you? You're making it up?"

"I'm not making it up. I know for a fact."

"How can you know?"

He placed her hand on his chest. "I know it right here. The only way we ever know anything for certain."

34

Sometime during the endless night of toddler kicks and a thumping bass from the apartment next door, Pete and Deedee finally came home. Toby was an early riser, and with no way to avoid him, Pete grumbled his way into the shower while Marina fixed her son a packet of oatmeal and a banana smoothie in Deedee's blender which, until that moment, had only whirled for margaritas and mudslides.

Toby ate a little oatmeal, which was encouraging, but he was happier when Deedee hobbled to the table and began to feed him pieces of a day-old doughnut.

Marina carried the doughnut plate away, despite her son's protests. "His stomach was upset last night. That's not a great idea."

"It's a maple doughnut. Maple's natural. You look like you got drugs behind a car."

Marina hadn't been able to retrieve her backpack, so she was wearing yesterday's clothes and makeup. She poured freshly brewed coffee for herself and her mother and sat down to enjoy one, if not the other. Toby smeared the rest of his oatmeal on the table.

Deedee leaned over so she was right in the little boy's face. "Toby, give me a big kiss. I'm your grandma."

Toby recoiled, and Marina rolled her eyes. "Back away, Deedee, until he gets used to you. What's wrong with your leg?"

"Just my foot. Something got dropped on it last night."

Marina was afraid to ask how the injury had occurred. Most likely Deedee's new job was on the bottom rung of the bartending ladder. "Tell me it didn't happen during a fight."

"Nothing like that. I finished out the night, but somebody had to drive me home. I probably ought to go over to urgent care today."

"Sorry I can't give you a ride. Maybe Jerry has a friend to help retrieve your car. Then he can take you to the clinic."

"Pete can walk over and get it. It's just a couple of blocks."

"Deedee, Pete no longer has his license, remember?"

"Not for real stuff, but this is just a couple of blocks. Nobody'll care."

Pete came in, dripping water on the floor. He was as blond as Marina was and yardstick thin. His skin was sallow, maybe even jaundiced. She hadn't seen her brother in weeks, and he hadn't looked healthy then. Now he looked ill.

Both brothers knew who their fathers were, but sometimes she thought that not knowing had been kinder. Jerry's was serving time for a liquor store robbery, and Pete's only came around when he needed money. Neither had provided any kind of role model. As a family they were a sorry lot.

"You look awful," she said. "Are you sick?"

"Yeah, good morning to you, too, Sis." He plunked down in a chair and rested his head on his arms.

She made a face he couldn't see. "Let me introduce you to the new guy at the table. This is your nephew, Toby."

"Yeah, I remember. You had a baby. For a while anyway."

"Well, I have him again, and you can't smoke in the apartment while he's here."

He sat up at that. "I *live* here."

"And I help Deedee pay the rent. Do you?"

"Piss off."

"I'm serious. Do you? Last I heard you were taking night classes to get your GED so you could look for a job. Is all that hard work taking its toll? Or maybe it's the drinking?"

"Pete's going to meetings," Deedee said.

Marina didn't believe it. "Are you going with him?"

"Me? I'm just a social drinker."

Pete's driver's license had been suspended

for two full years after his second underage DUI. Marina hoped the suspension, at least, had made an impression, but the earlier conversation with Deedee worried her.

"Pete, you're not driving, are you? Because even if you aren't drinking, if you get caught behind the wheel, you're going to be in real trouble."

"Who appointed you judge and jury?"

"I'm not the judge you have to worry about."

"I walk and I bike. Last time I heard, that was legal."

"How about school?"

"I took the damn test. I'm just waiting to see how I did. Now piss off, okay?"

She sat back and looked at her mother. Deedee nodded to confirm it.

"Hey, that's great," Marina said. "You're plenty smart. I bet you passed."

He got up and went to the refrigerator. Marina had stocked it when she'd come to clean. She hoped he found something that would pack a few ounces on his frame.

While Pete continued to stare at the contents, Marina addressed her mother. "Toby and I have to head out in a while. We'll be gone all day. Could you get somebody to bring the crib in from the storage area and set it up for tonight?"

"That? Jerry sold the crib along with all Brittany's baby stuff a year ago."

"When I asked about it he didn't say anything."

"He likes to yank your chain," Pete said. "Payback."

"Such a happy little family." Marina stood up and got paper towels to wipe down the table. Toby was obviously finished with breakfast, and she knew Ellen would be trying to feed him all day, anyway.

"I work again tonight, if I can stand up that long," Deedee said. "Petey, bring me a bowl and some cereal. Oh, and the milk."

To Pete's credit, he didn't tell his mother to take a hike. Marina accepted that as a sign of hope.

She took her son to the sink to mop his face. "We'll be back sometime after seven." Tonight she planned to take Toby to a restaurant without French fries on the menu.

Deedee sniffed, then once again for good measure. "I might be at work, or I might not. You could bring me some dinner, just in case."

"Good luck at urgent care." Marina grabbed her handbag from Jerry's room and left the apartment in the same clothes she'd arrived in.

Before she headed home to change, Marina called to be sure Blake had already left for work. Once there she managed the quickest shower of her life, shutting Toby in the adjoining bedroom after making certain there was nothing in reach a toddler could get into. When she emerged mostly dressed she found him on the bed she and Blake shared, bouncing up and down. She added climbing to his growing list of skills and caught him as he soared toward her.

"An upset stomach followed by broken bones. Not a great way to return you to Willow Glen tomorrow, kiddo." She squeezed him tight before she lowered him to the floor. "Let's go buy a portable crib, shall we?"

They arrived on Belvedere Island by eleven. Ellen had wanted her to come earlier, but in addition to a long drive, Marina had braved rush hour, a crowded discount store and parking lot, and getting Toby in and out of the car seat. In other words, real life, something Ellen didn't seem to know much about. She didn't look happy when she opened the door, but she had the sense not to complain. She squatted to look Toby in the eye. "Remember me, Toby?"

Toby grabbed Marina's leg and held tight, refusing to look at his grandmother.

Marina defended him. "Everything's new. Just give him a little time."

Ellen stood. "Has he had breakfast?"

Either Ellen couldn't tell time, or she didn't think Marina was smart enough to feed her son. "Hours ago. And he just had a squeeze pouch."

"What?"

"Nourishment for toddlers, all organic. He had peas, broccoli and pears."

"And he ate it?"

"Slurped it."

"Well, I have *real* food for lunch."

Ellen led them into a great room that looked like a cover for *House Beautiful.* The ceilings soared, and the view was indescribable.

"I researched the best toys for his age," Ellen said. "I'm sure he'll enjoy them."

Toys were fine, but as she'd grown to know her son, Marina had pegged him for a get-out-and-run kind of kid, most likely with a fetish for large cardboard boxes, laundry baskets, and kitchen cabinets to crawl in and out of. She had a feeling when he visited the villa, or even moved in, her plastic containers and pots and pans were going to get a workout.

Ellen held out her hand to her grandson, who was still clinging to Marina's leg. "You can stay a few minutes, Marina. Then I would like to have Toby to myself."

Marina had expected this, but still, the idea of leaving him here bothered her. The little boy didn't really know Ellen. And hadn't he already had enough stranger trauma to last the weekend?

"We'll see." She smiled to soften the words. "He might need a little more than a few minutes to warm up to you."

Again Ellen didn't look pleased, but she gave a curt nod. She also dropped her hand. "I'll set out some toys."

Marina was glad to see she wasn't completely clueless about her grandson. She watched as Ellen set out a drum set that guaranteed hours of happy banging. And she had remembered how much Toby liked to build things and bought a toddler version of Legos.

"Great choices. Let's go see what we can do, Toby."

She settled him beside the drum set, then demonstrated what he was supposed to do, handing him the drumsticks when she'd finished. Toby stared at them and didn't move.

"It's really for an older child." Ellen sounded worried.

Marina wasn't fond of Graham's mother. She thought Ellen was calculating and manipulative, but right now she sounded like any grandmother who was afraid she'd chosen the wrong gift. She decided to play nice. "If he doesn't get the hang of it you can give him pots and a big spoon to practice on. He'll figure it out fast."

"I'm sure our cook wouldn't appreciate my grandson banging on her copper cookware."

"Hers? She brings her own?"

Ellen was silent too long, and Marina

thought she'd offended her, which seemed remarkably easy to do. But Ellen surprised her. "You're right. Mine."

"Does she cook for you every night? I can't imagine that."

"No. Two, maybe three nights a week. She cooks for other families, too. She made Toby's lunch last night when she was here."

Marina tried to imagine hiring somebody to slap a cheese sandwich together and cut it into quarters. "That must be some lunch then."

"He won't be able to squeeze it." Ellen actually smiled, and it looked genuine. "What will they come up with next?"

Toby tentatively hit the drumsticks together, then he leaned over and hit one of them on the biggest drum, giggling at the noise. His approach wasn't orthodox, but pretty soon he was banging away.

Marina decided this was a good opportunity to sneak out. She pointed toward the door, and Ellen nodded. But just a few steps into it she was tackled by a small body. Toby began to screech.

She picked him up and frowned. "Don't you want to stay and play?"

He threw his arms around her neck, and the screeching grew louder.

She settled him on the floor beside the blocks and sat beside him so he wouldn't worry she was trying to leave again. "Let's build a house. Ellen, want to help?"

When she finally got up, he was so involved in destroying the house Ellen had built for him, he didn't seem to notice. But when Marina started for the door again, he was right behind her.

She picked him up and kissed his cheeks. "You twerp." She shook her head at Ellen. "I guess I'm staying."

Ellen was standing now. "No, just leave him. He'll be fine after a while, I'm sure."

Marina wondered how it felt to be Toby. Everything he knew was back in Willow Glen. The woman who had raised him, the home perfectly set up for a little boy, the food and toys he knew and loved. His father was no longer living, and now he was being forced to spend time with people he hardly knew. Did he wonder if he would ever go home again? Clearly now he was worried that the woman who had slept beside him last night might disappear, too.

"He won't be fine." She held Toby a little closer. "We're asking too much of him. I need to stay, or I need to leave with him. Which would you like?"

Nothing was going the way Ellen had hoped. That was easy to tell. But at least she didn't argue. "Stay this time. But he'll have to get used to you leaving at some point."

Maybe someday Toby would adore this stranger-grandma, who wanted so badly to please him and didn't know a thing about how to do it. Ellen could read about proper toys, hire cooks, make endless suggestions, but she had as much to learn about her grandson as her grandson did about her.

Marina realized how odd it was that she, who had given this child away, was the one who understood him. "I suggest we see what your cook worked up. Toby's probably hungry. He napped a little on the way here, so that's not going to happen again anytime soon. But maybe the three of us can take a walk down these beautiful streets after he eats."

"If you think that will make him more comfortable."

"I think it will."

"I hoped he would get used to me. Maybe even spend the night here tonight."

"I'm sure that will happen eventually." But even as she said it, Marina wondered if she wanted it to. She had agreed to this arrangement, even championed it. Exactly what had she done?

35

The list of things Ellen didn't know how to do was as long as her list of regrets. This afternoon she was staring at one of them, wondering how she had gotten into this fix.

Toby and Marina had left sooner than she'd counted on, and to fill the rest of her afternoon she had decided to visit the house in Montclair to make sure all the wallpaper in the master bedroom and the bathrooms had been removed, as promised. A crew of painters was scheduled to come on Monday and paint the entire house the warm earth tones she'd chosen.

She had a new appreciation for the difficulties of bringing a house back to life. As it turned out renovation wasn't just picking out pretty countertops and state-of-the-art appliances. Even with Hank's recommendations to guide her, she'd already run into countless problems in the six weeks since she'd begun the project. She'd nearly given up more than once, her finger poised over the telephone to

call an expert at Randolph Group who could recommend a general contractor.

Of course, she could have gotten suggestions from Hank, but she hadn't wanted him to say "I told you so."

Now in the master bathroom, as she stared at just one of many walls still covered with paper, she could read her failure in the bold yellow poppies staring back at her.

She was so unhappy she was actually muttering to herself. "Okay, it's Saturday. You can call somebody from Randolph Group at home, but the word will get back to Douglas."

She wasn't sure why that bothered her. She hadn't told Douglas about this project because it felt too sentimental. Douglas was the kind of man who would sell his mother's deathbed — with her still in it — if the price was right.

She had to smile at that, although it was too close to home to be funny.

"You can do this." Sighing, she pulled the ladder from the backyard storage shed closer to the wall, told herself she was not afraid of heights, and set the pump sprayer she had filled with diluted wallpaper stripper on the ladder shelf. She and her newly purchased scraper knife climbed to the top.

She felt dizzy, which went well with stupid. She should have been here last Monday, just to check and see if the man removing wallpaper had actually done the job. At least she hadn't paid him yet.

Now she, who had paid a cook to make lunch for a toddler, was going to strip off every shred of wallpaper by tomorrow night. By herself.

She leaned back and began to spray the wall. Was she putting too much water on the paper, too little? The clerk at the hardware store had promised this was the best method. And luckily her painter had promised — after a frantic phone call — that if she got the wallpaper off somehow, he and his crew would do the prep work and add a skim coat if necessary. Otherwise she would have to wait almost a month for them to come.

She sprayed a large swath at the top, then set the sprayer on the shelf and watched as water ran down the wall. She wasn't sure how long to wait. She wondered if the solution actually bled through to the wall behind it. The clerk had told her some wallpaper was as easy as peeling a sticker, and some wasn't. Judging by the way her day had gone? The poppies probably intended to bloom here for another century.

"You look amazingly natural on that ladder."

She clapped a hand over her chest, luckily not the one with the scraper. "Hank, I'm going to take away your key."

"I made enough racket coming up the stairs

that everybody in the neighborhood probably knows I'm here."

"Why are you?"

"I saw your car. I wondered what you were up to. I didn't expect this. What's going on?"

She gave him an abbreviated version.

He nodded when she was finished. "He probably got a bigger job and just wrote you off."

"He could have told me."

"If he's the only subcontractor you have a problem with, it will be a miracle."

"Well, I decided to take matters into my own hands."

"Ellen Randolph, of the ever popular Wallpaper Princesses."

She had to smile. "Ever done this?"

"More times than I care to remember. Often for the same reason you're doing it. Because somebody screwed up or didn't show up, and a house I wanted to list needed to be finished immediately."

"An all-purpose Realtor. I never knew."

"You need a scoring tool. A Paper Tiger. I have a couple at home. Want one?"

"What does it do?"

"Scores lines so the solution gets behind the paper."

"I was just thinking I needed something like that. I must have a knack for this."

"I'll bring my ladder, too."

"I'm on a ladder. You can't tell?"

"I'm not busy. I'll start in the bedroom."

She had never been more grateful.

She was lucky. The wallpaper peeled off in long strips, and she managed to finish one entire bathroom while Hank worked on the master bedroom, which was now more than a third completed. He promised to send a neighborhood teenager to help finish tomorrow, and she promised him dinner as a thank-you. His choice.

Now they were sitting in exactly the kind of place she never went, a funky barbecue joint on Telegraph that smelled like a million dollars and looked like a million bad decisions.

"You really come here often?" She wondered if anything that came out of the kitchen in a place like this one could actually be edible. The linoleum floor tiles were peeling up at the corners; the tables were scarred and covered with place mat menus. Old-fashioned circular fans stirred the air, and a screechy AM radio station provided the soundtrack.

"I come as often as I can. Don't let looks fool you. This is the best barbecue in Oakland. Look how many people are here."

She'd been taught not to value public opinion, but she had to admit the place was popular. She and Hank had been given a booth in a corner, and he'd informed her they'd only gotten it because he was a regular.

"I'm having the ribs. The potato salad is

fabulous, and the collard greens have been known to grow hair on a bald man's head."

She perused the menu for salad, which was noticeably absent. "I'll try the chicken. White meat only, no sauce. A baked potato with a pat of butter on the side. Steamed broccoli." She nodded, glad that was decided.

An older woman, who looked like she probably ate here every night, ambled over and pulled a pad out of her apron. "What'll you have?" It sounded like one word.

"We'll both have ribs, potato salad and collard greens," Hank said. "A side of fried green tomatoes and a plate of hush puppies to share."

"Drink?"

"Whatever local's on tap for both of us."

"Got it." She sashayed out of range before Ellen could protest.

She leaned over the table and glared. "Maybe you eat like this, but I don't."

"Good news. You won't be able to say that ever again. Now sit back and enjoy. Nobody's counting calories or fat grams tonight. And the best bread pudding in the entire universe will be your final reward, so leave room."

She was too exhausted not to obey. He could order it, but she didn't have to eat it.

She sat back. "This has been a day like no other."

"Tell me about it."

"Yours first."

"I listed a new house in the morning, a real beauty. I asked the sellers to let us stage it, and they agreed. We'll do an open house in two weeks, and it will be gone in hours. In the afternoon I showed a transplanted executive houses in three neighborhoods. Guess which one he liked best?"

"Montclair Village?"

"I drove him by your house."

"What did he think?"

"I don't know. We whizzed by. It was the straightest route to a house higher in the hills. Almost to Berkeley. He's probably going to make an offer."

She laughed. "I'm glad you caught on and aren't trying to list mine."

"Have you decided what you're going to do with it?"

"I'm going to finish the renovations. That's challenge enough for now."

"So why was your day like no other?"

"I'm finding more and more things I don't know how to do."

"Like strip wallpaper? Maybe you didn't know when you started, but by the time we quit you were going strong."

She was actually enjoying the work. Revealing those bare walls had felt like a new beginning. Time and energy might be needed, but in the long run, the result would be worth it.

She decided to be honest. "It wasn't just wallpaper."

"What else?"

"I spent four hours with my grandson today, and by the time he left he was a quivering, screeching mess. He hated the food I provided, got exhausted on a walk that went on too long, refused to let go of his mother whenever I was around."

"Your son's wife was visiting?"

She'd backed herself into a corner. "That's a long story."

"But a simple question."

"His birth mother brought him to spend the day with me. His *real* mother."

"He's in her custody now?"

The whole scenario was so complicated, she didn't know where to begin. She found, though, that she wanted to try. He knew the basics. She caught him up without mentioning her part in the story. "Marina wants custody now, and she has visiting rights while the court investigates. She has Toby this weekend, and she brought him to see me."

The waitress arrived with their drinks, the hush puppies and a chili-honey sauce to drizzle over them. Hank toasted her with his mug. "You're not getting out of here until you try a bite of everything."

"That's what I used to tell Graham. On the rare occasions I ate with him."

"I love being a grandfather. I'm out of the food lecture business and into the one where I sneak grandkids all the stuff their parents won't let them have."

She'd done exactly the opposite. She'd carefully planned Toby's lunch, and he hadn't eaten a bite of the low-fat cheese and turkey on whole wheat bread, or the cute little stalks of broccoli and cauliflower that the cook had roasted and decorated with minced pimento.

"What do you give them?"

"Nothing awful. I buy natural chicken hot dogs, and they think they're getting away with something, since they never have any kind of hot dogs at home. Multigrain chips? Same things. Cookies from the bakery over on College. I just don't tell them the cookies are stuffed with things to make them grow stronger."

"I guess I have a lot to learn."

"Then it sounds like you think you'll see him?"

"That's what I'm hoping." She picked up a hush puppy to show she was a good sport, dunked it into the honey sauce and took a tentative bite.

"See, I told you," Hank said, watching her expression.

"I'm going to hold you responsible for any weight gain in my future."

He smiled and reached for one himself. "I'd love to see you happy, Ellen, whether you're skinny or fat. Let's work on it, starting tonight."

36

THE SWALLOW'S NEST

FEATHERING YOUR NEST WITH IMAGINATION AND LOVE

August 31st:

I have a special treat today. My friend Regan has invited us to see the results of her "Just One Room" project. Remember Regan's earliest photos? Click here to see where she started. While she's not finished — and judging from my mail most of you aren't, either — Regan's made substantial progress. If you remember, she told us she didn't have a lot of time to devote to renovation, so she chose the smallest room in her apartment.

The closet.

"Just One Room" began nine weeks ago as we each made a detailed list of the things we wanted to keep. At first Regan was reluctant to let go of anything. Then she consoled herself by imagining that the clothes she didn't need were going to delight another woman.

Hangers were just as hard. Yes, hangers. Sometimes the things that seem practical are the hardest to let go of. But Regan and

I hung up all the clothes she was giving away on two dozen wire hangers. Then, to celebrate, we shopped for new ones.

Did you know hangers could be fun? Starting today you'll find some you can't resist in my store. Jewel-encrusted, hand carved, leopard trimmed, decoupaged and, of course, since this is my website, how about those vintage wooden hangers from the Waikiki Sheraton, or the ones my sister-in-law padded with hula girl fabric?

Everything in your home should make you happy. And who would forget to hang up their clothes with these waiting patiently on their closet rods?

Enjoy Regan's photos. She even painted the inside of the closet a deep violet. Her landlord doesn't know, so let's not tell him.

Aloha! Lilia

"I'm taking the whole morning off. You're sure you don't want me to go home with you to watch Toby while the custody evaluator is there?" Regan rinsed out the plastic bowl with banana slices she had given Toby while Lilia was photographing her closet. "The minute she arrives Toby's going to start demanding your attention."

Lilia slipped on her second sandal. "I bet she wants to see me interact with him. I'd better do this alone."

Lilia had never imagined just how long the

custody battle would drag on. The suspense built every day, and most nights she woke up in a cold sweat, heart pounding, hands shaking. Finally today the official investigation began. A social worker was coming to see the house and question her. It would be a more thorough evaluation than she'd undergone the first time, and this time the court would look closely at everybody.

Even then, either party could challenge the decision, although Carrick said that would be more or less a formality.

Regan pointed at her clock. "You'd better get going. You don't want to be late."

"Thanks for prepping me." Regan had spent part of their morning asking Lilia pointed questions provided by Carrick, to prepare her for what might be ahead.

"Toby?" Regan's apartment southwest of Willow Glen was tiny. Lilia found the toddler in the living room, which didn't require many steps. He was fascinated by Regan's new cat, a pretty lilac calico she had rescued a week ago, and he'd spent most of their time following her from room to room.

"Kitty me!"

"You can't take Sherbet home. Sherbet is Aunt Regan's cat. We'll come back and visit her, I promise."

"Kitty!"

Regan was smiling. "How long will he keep that up?"

"Until we get home. Or until I give him his favorite snack, which is the plan."

"You're so good with him."

Lilia hoped the social worker thought so, too.

On the way back to Willow Glen Toby worked on a cookie while they battled traffic. She had hoped for half an hour to feed him lunch and settle him with his favorite toys before the social worker arrived, but an accident slowed traffic to a crawl, and by the time they pulled into the driveway, it was almost time for the woman's arrival.

Or rather it was past time, because the moment she opened the door to release Toby, someone got out of a car parked on the road and started toward the house.

"Terrific." She dusted crumbs off her son's shirt. With all she'd heard about how busy the court investigators were, she had expected the woman to be late.

She intercepted the visitor on the walkway. The woman was in her forties or older, with short dark hair and a ruddy complexion. She wore black-rimmed glasses and peered over them as Lilia approached.

"Weren't you expecting me?" the woman asked.

"Of course, but a little later. Toby and I got stuck in traffic, but I think we're on time, aren't we?"

"Do you generally cut your appointments

this close?"

Lilia drew a breath and it seemed to take forever. At the moment oxygen was not her friend — nor quite obviously was this woman.

She thrust out her free hand. "I'm Lilia Swallow. And this is my son, Toby. And you are?"

"Irene Monte. You should have been given my name."

"Thank you for coming. Shall we go inside?"

"I hope you have more space for Toby to play in the back. This may be a residential neighborhood, but cars do whizz by. I know since I've been waiting for ten minutes."

Lilia decided she would kill with kindness. It seemed to be the only option, although it had never worked with Ellen. "I hate to wait, don't you? I'm sorry you had to."

"The yard?"

"Toby plays in the back. He's never outside unless an adult is with him."

"Which adults?"

"Me. Valencia, our part-time housekeeper and nanny. Family and friends. He has his own play area."

"You have family who helps?"

Lilia entertained a vision of her *helpful* brothers carrying this woman into Kauai's waves for a good dunking. "I come from a large, close family in Kauai, and they visit whenever they can."

"When guardianship is settled do you intend to go back to Hawaii to live?"

"No, my aunt left me this house. San Jose has been home since I was eighteen. But I plan to visit my family often. They already adore Toby, and he has a lot of cousins in the islands to play with."

By now Lilia had covered the distance to the front porch, and she unlocked the door. Toby was squirming and beginning to make ominous noises.

"This Valencia? Would you say she has a lot to do with raising Toby?"

"No, I wouldn't. But when she is with him, she's great. I prefer having Valencia over day care because I'm nearby if he needs me. And I do have to work."

"I'll be calling her. Do you think she'll agree this is a good arrangement?"

"I do." Lilia waited for another attack, but when one didn't arrive she pointed toward the kitchen. "Toby's had a snack, but he really needs lunch. Will you mind if we talk while I give it to him? Then if you'd like to see the house, I can show you whatever you need."

As if to prove he was starving, Toby jammed the rest of his cookie in his mouth.

"I'm curious. What's he eating if he hasn't had lunch?"

"I bake treats because they're healthier than the ones in the store. Those have banana, apple juice, whole wheat, peanut butter."

"You give him peanut butter? Isn't he too young?"

"Thinking's changed on that. His pediatrician suggested we start right after he turned one year. He loves it."

Irene Monte made a disapproving noise in her throat. Lilia thought, if given the opportunity, this woman and Ellen could become firm friends.

"His lunch is all ready," Lilia said. "I'll just get it out of the refrigerator."

"I would like to look around. Will that be a problem?"

"Absolutely not. Would you like coffee or something cold to drink first?"

"No."

Lilia nodded pleasantly. "Just let me know if you need anything."

Toby was tired and not much of a fan of his high chair. After a struggle to get him in, he played with his lunch, tossing shredded chicken on the floor and following that with steamed carrots, usually a winner.

"Kitty." He rubbed his eyes.

She assumed a long memory was a sign of intelligence. Today she could have done without it. "We'll see kitty soon." She lifted him down. "Let's get Doggie. Would you like to see Doggie?"

He rested his head against her shoulder as she stooped to clean the food off the floor.

When she straightened the social worker was standing in the doorway. "Where does he play most of the time?"

"Everywhere. But when I'm working he's either at the park or playing with Valencia on the second floor. My husband built gates for the stairs. So we fasten the gate, then he has the run of it. There's nothing that can hurt him. And run is the right word."

"I understand he stepped on a nail not long ago."

Lilia had known that would come up. "He did, and we went straight to the emergency room to be sure it was properly cleaned and treated."

"Were you careless?"

"I missed seeing the nail, as did the men with me. He had three sets of eyes on him and none of us saw it."

Irene Monte looked as if she didn't believe it. "Toys?"

Lilia felt sure the woman had already checked Toby's closet, but she told her all the places his toys were kept.

"You seem to keep a lot of his things out of sight. Why is that?"

Lilia mopped her son's face, and he struggled to get away. "I like to bring out things to play with in small batches and trade them around. That way he's not distracted. I also like a neat house. It's easier to get things done if there's not a lot of clutter."

"Toys are *clutter*?"

Lilia stifled a sigh. "Have you seen how many pieces children's toys come with these days? I try to keep everything together so he'll have what he needs, and we don't have to waste precious time looking for missing parts. We certainly have days when clutter reigns. I just try for fewer."

"I understand you're an interior designer. Does that make it hard to tolerate messes?"

"I tolerate them fine. I make my own. I just don't think messes make children happy. Toby likes to help me straighten up and toss toys in the right crates. It's a sorting game. Of course I can't guarantee he'll love cleaning up once he's a teenager."

"But you show your house so often on your blog. I've looked through it. Isn't it a strain to keep it that neat? That . . . picturesque?"

Lilia was beginning to fray around the edges, but she spoke slowly, carefully. "I think you mean doesn't keeping it neat interfere with my parenting, right? For the record, I don't keep it that neat unless I've planned to take photos. And that's usually when Toby is out of the house —"

"But he's in some of the photos. And you certainly have discussed a lot of personal details about your life and about him on, what do you call it, *The Swallow's Nest*?"

"I don't use his name, and I'm careful not to show anything overly personal. Things remain on the internet for a long time, sometimes forever. I think by the time Toby goes looking, if he ever does, there's nothing I've revealed that he won't already know."

"Like the fact that you're not his real mother."

"When he's ready to know details, I will tell him details."

"Why don't you tell *me*?"

Lilia set her squirming son on his feet and watched as he ran into the sunroom. She followed. Doggie was on the couch, and Toby climbed up and got him, then he scurried down again and took him to the corner where he plopped down with a basket of plastic toys and began to empty it.

Lilia could have kissed him right then and there for occupying himself. Instead she turned to Irene Monte. "Would you like to sit? What would you like to know?"

The woman sprawled on a chair and took out her notebook. "How did you feel when you discovered your husband had a child you didn't know about?"

Lilia tried not to wince. Undoubtedly the facts were in the court's file. "I was upset. Toby's birth mother came to the door and practically threw him at me —"

"Aren't you exaggerating?"

"No. There was a moment when I thought if I didn't grab that baby, she was going to drop him at my feet. So I did, and she left him in my arms and walked away."

"And you felt?"

"Incredibly angry."

The woman nodded and scribbled in her notebook. "You had no idea?"

"None. Graham had never said a word, not during all the months of her pregnancy or afterwards."

"How do you feel about that now?"

"My husband's dead. I'm trying to work through my feelings about the way he treated me. But a long time ago I realized that nothing that happened had anything to do with Toby. *None* of it was his fault."

"I understand you left for a while."

"I went to Kauai to be with my family. I needed some time to figure out what to do. Then I came back. And I stayed. I took care of Toby because he needed a mother, and later I realized I needed and wanted him to be my son."

The other woman continued to badger her with questions. Lilia struggled to be calm, polite and not to walk across the room and kick her in the shins.

Finally the social worker closed her notebook. "Why didn't you adopt him? Didn't you want to make your relationship legal?"

Lilia explained that she and Graham had hoped to make adoption easy by waiting a full year after Marina abandoned the baby. "But he died before the year was up," she finished.

"Now that Mrs. Wendell wants him back, aren't you tempted? You're alone now and that *close* family of yours is hours away by airplane. Don't you yearn for freedom? Don't you wonder if Toby will hinder you from finding another man, maybe having a real son?"

"Toby *is* my son." Lilia's patience had finally run out. "No matter what you say, what the court says, what anybody says, I have raised this little boy since he was three months old, and he and I know who his real mother is. I truly hope if you investigate adoptions, Miss Monte, you don't tell those families that the child they're adopting isn't going to be their *real* child."

For the first time the social worker smiled. "You have a temper. I wondered."

"I also have the good manners not to show it unless I'm pushed to my limits. Is there anything else you would like to see? Anything else you'd like to know?"

Toby took that moment to abandon his toys and crawl up into Lilia's lap. She put her arms around him, and he leaned against her and closed his eyes.

"He looks comfortable."

"Toby knows he can always count on me."

Irene Monte stood. "Don't get up. I'll show myself out." She didn't say goodbye. She just walked through the house and in a moment, Lilia heard the door close.

She was fairly certain she'd just made a powerful enemy. But even after the fact, she had no idea what she could have done differently.

37

Toby no longer cried when Lilia put him in Marina's arms. He'd caught on that she would bring him home eventually, and he seemed resigned to being away. Sometimes, after a while, he even seemed to enjoy the things they did together.

More surprising, so did Marina.

Today, after retrieving him at noon, she connected to a station with children's songs, and for more than an hour of their drive he napped and listened, which was perfect.

She spent the time thinking about her conversation with Blake that morning. She'd gotten up early to see him off to work and inform him the custody evaluator wanted to interview them on Monday morning. Even though she'd finally introduced her son to her husband, and Toby's visits had gone well, Blake obviously continued to have doubts about what was best for all of them. Still, in their conversation this morning, he had agreed to be supportive when the evaluator arrived.

Toby's silence was too good to last. When they still had at least fifteen miles to go, he started to fuss.

"We're going to see your grandmother today." Marina tried to sound delighted, but truthfully, she was not. The trip to Belvedere Island was long, and when she only had her son for one afternoon a week, they were spending too much of it in the car.

Today she'd asked Ellen to meet them in San Jose, but Ellen had insisted that Toby needed to get used to coming to her house. By Marina's calculation she and Toby would have, at most, an hour with his grandmother. Too many times when she'd dragged him to Ellen's she had been late getting back to San Jose, and her lawyer had warned that the court might reduce or eliminate visitation if that continued.

She tried to sound cheerful. "Can you see the water? This is the Golden Gate Bridge. People come from all over to see it, and you and I are lucky to drive across it."

No fan of historic scenery, Toby continued to fuss.

By the time they pulled into Ellen's driveway, he had moved from cranky to furious. She was sure that would only be worse on the way home. She had years of this drive ahead, and she didn't look forward to them.

Ellen met them at the door, although sometimes an older woman, a Mrs. Beaton, who seemed to do everything Ellen didn't want to, ushered them inside.

"What's wrong with him?" Ellen held out her arms.

Toby screamed louder and clung to Marina.

"Give him a minute. He's just tired of being in the car seat."

"Did he have anything to do?"

Marina had to raise her voice to be heard. "Of course he had toys, and I hooked up my Bluetooth to play an hour of Raffi, which, by the way, is my definition of torture. How much fun would *you* have if you were strapped into a seat without being able to get out for almost two hours?"

"Yes, you've made it clear you don't like the drive."

"Well, today Toby's making it clearer."

"Once custody is final, you can leave him and go about your business. No more short stays."

With effort Marina bundled up her temper and slipped it into her back pocket. She managed a grimace, but Ellen didn't notice. She nodded toward the kitchen. "I thought we could make cookies today."

"Whatever we do, Toby and I have to leave in an hour. I've been late three times returning him, and Lilia's keeping score."

"That's not enough time."

"It's all the time we have. Shall we start?"

Ellen humphed. "Mrs. Beaton's going to help."

Marina followed her into the kitchen and greeted the maid-of-all-trades. Mrs. Beaton was in her early sixties, and today wearing an apron, she looked like a quintessential grandmother, which neither of Toby's real grandmothers resembled. Mrs. Beaton was *going to help,* but she had probably done all the prep work.

"Toby, do you want to help me mix cookies?" Ellen asked.

Marina knew this wouldn't turn out well. Toby wasn't old enough to help, and even if he had been, starting his cooking career when he was grouchy was a bad idea. Ellen held out the spoon and released it when he grabbed it. She picked up a second one.

"Let's stir. Can you stir?"

So far the mixture looked like eggs, some kind of liquid and other things Marina couldn't name. She doubted Toby understood what was going on, since the concoction didn't resemble the finished product.

Clearly a lot of thought had gone into the activity, only no one had taken into account a toddler's short attention span. Toby found a better way to entertain himself. He whacked the side of the glass bowl with his spoon, then again before Marina could pull him away.

"Not like that. Like this." Ellen demonstrated. "Now you try it."

Toby tossed his spoon on the floor and struggled to get down.

"I put three plastic bowls and a variety of spoons in the corner," Mrs. Beaton said. "Let's set him on the floor, and he can play with those while we mix the dough."

Ellen shook her head. "He just needs to understand. Toby, we're making cookies. You like cookies, don't you?"

"No keys!" His face looked like a thundercloud.

Marina tried to lighten the mood. "I know you went to a lot of trouble. When he's a little older he'll love cooking with you. Maybe today Mrs. Beaton can finish the cookies, and we can play in the other room? Then he can take a cookie to eat on the way home."

Ellen looked defeated. Not angry she was being thwarted. Not commanding. She looked just like anybody else who'd lost a battle that really mattered. "I don't seem to be making inroads."

"It's not easy. He doesn't see that much of you."

"I bought some books for him."

Marina was sure her choices had been recommended on every library and award list. "Once he calms down, maybe you can read to him."

"Graham never liked to be read to."

Graham had rarely seen Ellen, too. The pattern was repeating itself.

In the living room Ellen pulled out a plastic house complete with furniture and tiny people. Marina didn't remember it from other visits, but Toby loved it immediately. He flopped down on the floor and set the little sofa on the roof and the family car in the living room.

To Ellen's credit, she didn't correct him. "Let's put Mama on the sofa, shall we?" She laid the bigger female doll on the sofa, and the whole thing slid off the roof. Toby laughed, and put the sofa back, diving next for the family dog who was tossed through a window into an upstairs bedroom.

Ellen sat back when all the furniture and all the people had found homes. "He takes after Lilia. Happiest fixing up houses." She seemed to realize what she'd said and turned to Marina. "Of course that's what he's exposed to."

"Well, his father designed and built houses."

"Of course he did. I didn't mean —"

Marina waved her off. "It's a toy and he's having fun. Let's face it, he's not showing much talent."

"Shall we see if the cookies are out of the oven? Toby, do you want a cookie?" Ellen held out her hand. Toby let her lead him into the kitchen. Despite her own irritation, Marina was touched. Queen Ellen was barely tolerable, but she could get used to Insecure Ellen.

Toby was much happier about eating cookies than baking them. Mrs. Beaton put on music, a CD of silly songs that made him clap. Ellen even picked him up and danced with him, and he seemed happy enough to let her.

An angry male voice put an end to that.

"What's going on in here?"

Ellen whirled around, and Marina watched the color drain from her cheeks. "Douglas? I thought you weren't coming back until tonight."

"I can see that."

Marina took in a suit that had probably been tailored in Italy, a scowling bulldog face and quarterback shoulders. Douglas Randolph wasn't a tall man, but he made up for it by the way he held himself. She didn't see a bit of Graham in him.

"This is Toby. Your grandson." Ellen didn't move closer, but she was standing taller, now, certainly not cowering. Mrs. Beaton had quietly disappeared.

"I know who he is," Douglas sneered. "I just don't know why he's *here.*"

Marina moved forward and rescued her son from Ellen's arms. For a change the other woman seemed glad to give him up. Toby's good mood had vanished, and he was beginning to whimper. Marina picked up another cookie and handed it to him, even though it meant a sugar high on the way home.

"This is Marina, Toby's mother," Ellen said. "I invited her here. I wanted to see my grandson."

"And since I wasn't home, that seemed like a good time."

Marina marveled at his ability to make ordinary sentences sound like threats. She nodded in his direction without smiling. "Delighted to meet you, too, Douglas, and now we're on the way out the door." She faced Ellen. "I was happy to bring him to visit. Have a good evening."

She left the kitchen and started through the house. Douglas didn't make an attempt to lower his voice.

"Another example of the low-class women my son surrounded himself with. And that baby is the result!"

"Stop it!" Ellen's next words were muted. "For God's sake, keep your voice down. She probably heard you."

"Do you honestly think I care!"

Marina couldn't reach the front door fast enough. Toby was crying now. She was learning a lot about her son, and one trait was certain. He picked up tension in a room and absorbed it. For the first time in a long time she felt sorry for Graham, who had probably been the same kind of child. She couldn't imagine any little boy, even the sturdiest, being forced to grow up under the thumb of Douglas Randolph.

Outside the air had a definite chill, and mist was rolling in. She comforted Toby as she got him in the car, but before she could slide in herself, Douglas appeared by the driver's door and held up his hand. "I won't take a lot of your time. But I need to talk to you."

"Funny how that works. I *don't* need to talk to you."

"It's in your best interests."

Toby's screeching was growing louder. He was truly upset. "You have my best interests at heart? That is so touching." She pulled the car door toward him, eyebrow raised.

"Money is involved."

"I'm sure money is involved in everything you do. You're going to threaten me."

"To the contrary. I'm going to make you a rich woman."

Her chest and throat felt tight, so tight she wondered if her eyes were bulging. She wondered why he thought she was for sale.

But, of course, she knew.

"I'm not going to hurt you," he said. "I just want a brief conversation."

She saw Ellen in the doorway, coming down the steps, probably to stop her husband. "Make it really brief, Mr. Randolph. Talk to yourself." She managed to squeeze into the narrow opening between the man and the door, and drove away.

Toby was too unhappy to continue driving for long. She'd learned her lesson about fast food, so she stopped at a family friendly chain, retrieved and cuddled him, talking softly in his ear until they were inside. He sat on her lap instead of a booster seat and picked at a healthy-enough kid's meal.

When she was sure he was calm, they started home and faced one traffic slowdown after another. Toby fell asleep, lulled by soft music and the rumbling of the engine.

Up until this point she'd been crawling, but since they'd left sooner than planned, she'd hoped they would still be on time. Now, suddenly, the traffic flow stopped. Minutes later, somewhere far ahead, she heard sirens and realized there had been an accident. She slapped the steering wheel with her palm.

"Just what I need." Since there was no question she was going to be late, she sent Lilia a text with her ETA.

With nothing to distract her, she replayed the scene at Ellen's. For the first time she'd seen what her son would encounter if Douglas became part of his personal equation. No parenting manual would recommend the way *she* had been raised, but despite poverty and men coming and going in her mother's life, she had never doubted that in her own ineffectual way, Deedee loved all her children.

And now, had Marina become a monster like Douglas, unconcerned about her baby's welfare? Was she willing to subject him to his grandfather's abuse in return for payment? What exactly had Douglas wanted to propose?

Her cell phone rang. "Marina? Are you home yet?"

By now she knew Ellen's voice. "I'm sitting in traffic."

"I'm sorry about what happened. I didn't think my husband would be coming home so early."

"So I gathered."

"What did he say to you outside?"

"Nothing I care to repeat."

"Seeing Toby was a shock for him. But I think he'll get used to spending a little time with him now and then. When things like that happen, I mean."

Marina inched forward, then stopped again. When things like what? Like Douglas showing up unannounced? Like Ellen's best-laid plans going awry?

She was too tired for a real discussion. "It doesn't seem that way."

"If he doesn't soften, I'll find ways to enjoy Toby's company that don't include my husband. But I think I can persuade him to give Toby a chance."

The ridiculously long trip. The traffic. The scene at the Randolph house. Marina could no longer hold her tongue. "I don't believe you. Do you have *any* power in your marriage? Granted, I've seen it in action for maybe two minutes, but it looks to me like your husband pulls all the strings."

"That's not your concern."

"No? Whose kid is Toby again?" She disconnected and tossed her phone on the seat beside her where it bounced to the floor. She was exhausted, angry and not moving. Somewhere behind the headache that was gathering strength, she had a vision of Lilia documenting the minutes Marina wasn't legally entitled to be with her son.

By the time she got to Willow Glen, Toby was awake and unhappy. He was probably wet, possibly hungry and absolutely sick of sitting.

She lifted him out of the car and realized immediately that he was worse than wet. Of course it was too late for her to clean and change him now.

As she walked up the sidewalk Lilia came out to the porch. Marina made the transfer and saw that Lilia, too, had gotten a whiff. "We got stuck in traffic. There was an accident on I-280. Did you get my text?"

Lilia wasn't smiling. "You mean the one that said you'd be here half an hour ago? A text you sent while *driving*?"

"We weren't *moving* when I texted you, which is why I *did*. I didn't cause the accident, and I'm not clairvoyant. I couldn't see what was going on ahead of me. I wasn't lying about when I'd arrive. I was just wrong."

"What were you doing on I-280 anyway at rush hour?"

"I don't have to tell you where I go when Toby's with me."

"No? Well you do have to account to the judge when you're chronically late, which you are. He was supposed to be home almost an hour ago. He must be hungry for dinner. And he sure needs a diaper change."

"Sorry I didn't stop in the middle of the fast lane once the traffic started moving again to change him. And he ate a while ago."

"Something good for him?"

Marina flashed on too many cookies, the tablespoon of applesauce Toby had sucked off his fingers, the three bites of mac and cheese. Her head began to pound harder. "Yeah, it was good for him. Do you think I feed him cotton candy and Popsicles?"

"You really can't see this from my standpoint?"

"It doesn't matter if he ate a hot dog or a tofu wrap. I took excellent care of him. He is my son. And when it comes right down to it? You are nobody. So get off my case."

"Apparently I'm more than *nobody*, or there wouldn't be a *court* case, would there? And you'd better believe this conversation is going in my notes with the time you returned my son." She turned, stomped across the front porch and into the house, slamming the door behind her.

Marina thought of the first time she'd given Toby to Lilia. No matter what she'd said today, she knew by her own actions she had turned Lilia from a nobody into a somebody. And if things continued the way they were going, Lilia might win the right to be the most important *somebody* in Toby's life.

38

While waiting for Toby's return Lilia had distracted herself by whipping up comfort food, Hawaiian comfort food, because she was homesick and needed her mother, even if that only meant Nalani's recipes. She had made chicken long rice in her Crock-Pot, spicy eggplant and pork in her wok, and for dessert, coconut haupia. She'd wanted to make *every* recipe she loved, but even with Carrick's help tonight, anything more would sit in her refrigerator until she threw it out.

Now her son was home with a new diaper, running through the house after spending too much of his young life stuck in traffic. And the house smelled like the one she'd grown up in.

When the doorbell rang she scooped up Toby, and together the two of them let Carrick inside. He bent down and kissed her, something more arousing than a hello kiss, and for the first time that day, she could feel her tension drain away.

She drew back reluctantly when Toby began to slap her shoulder. "I'm so glad to see you."

"I can tell." Carrick lifted Toby out of her arms, then tossed him up and caught him to wild screams of joy.

"Wow," she said, "just what he needs, thanks. More stimulation."

Carrick set him on the floor after two more tosses, and Toby took off for the sunroom where a stack of toys awaited him. "Maybe I should have brought a tranquilizer gun instead of this."

He opened the brown bag he'd brought along so she could peek inside where a wine bottle and a plastic deli container nestled side by side. "Will you settle for tuna sushi instead of poke?"

Sushi wasn't the same as poke, a Hawaiian favorite, a raw fish salad with soy sauce and sesame, but there were enough similarities to make her happy. "This'll be great with dinner." She checked the wine label. "Syrah. Perfect with the eggplant. And I have a really nice chardonnay to start."

"Why does it sound like you're going to drink both bottles before the night ends?"

Talking to Carrick was so easy. In the kitchen, with one eye on Toby, she told him about her encounter with Marina, and the harsh words they'd exchanged.

"You documented everything?"

"What fun that was."

"And she refused to say where she'd been?"

"She said she was under no obligation to tell me what she does or where she goes when she's with Toby."

Carrick was already getting bowls and plates to set the table. "Did it sound to you like she was hiding something?"

Lilia wondered what the truth would sound like. "I can't tell. She's always defensive."

"So why was she stuck on the interstate? Did she jump on for a quick trip to the next exit? Seems unlikely since she was more than an hour late. Did she drive a real distance? I can check traffic and accident reports when I get home. But if she went very far, why? Her family's all in town, and her husband's company's here, over by the PayPal campus. I've been doing a little checking."

"Oh?"

"Most likely the guardianship battle is going to end once and for all with an evidentiary hearing. We'll be allowed to present what we know, backed by facts and experts, so the judge can make a good decision. But it's up to us to learn everything about Marina and the people she's closest to and present it. Knowing what she does when she has Toby in the car could be important, too."

"How do we do that? How do we learn everything we need to know? I'm drowning in work and wouldn't know how to proceed anyway. She'd lose me in traffic. And I'm already taking too much of your time."

"It's not time, it's expertise. You aren't going to like this, but I think you need to hire an investigator. He or she can turn up ten times as much in the same amount of time as I can."

"I can't afford that."

"I have something at stake here." Carrick took her hand and removed the ladle for dishing up the soup. He turned her to face him. "I want Toby in my life, too." He put a finger over her lips when she started to speak. "I'm not asking a question, and I'm not looking for an answer. I'm just telling you why I don't expect anything except a yes on the investigator. Let me do this for you."

For a moment she was too touched to speak. Then she shook her head. "That's not fair."

"Of course it is. Now's the time to firm this up. If you don't hire somebody, we'll always wonder what we missed."

She wasn't worried about being in Carrick's debt, or whether this new act of kindness might pressure her into something she wasn't ready for. She already knew what she wanted.

"I promised Graham I would fight for his son," Carrick said, when he saw she was struggling. "At the end, when we talked about where Toby would live, I told him I would make sure he stayed here with you. And I meant what I said. He was my best friend. I have to follow through."

She blinked away the tears. "Did he want you to take his place as Toby's father?"

He chose his words carefully. She could see he wanted to be fair. "When you left for Kauai, Graham came to me. I was so angry about everything that after you left, I didn't call or contact him. But he came to my office a few days later with Toby. We took a walk." Carrick hesitated, not, she thought, because he couldn't figure out how to explain what had been said, but because talking was suddenly difficult.

He cleared his throat. "He told me he'd made a terrible mistake, but he wanted you back. He said you and Toby meant everything. And he said . . . he'd been warned his remission might not be permanent. He said his body had been through too much with both the cancer and treatment, and he couldn't imagine ever being really healthy again. I asked why he was telling me, and he said he wanted another chance, that he wanted to make this up to you somehow and be the husband he hadn't been. Then he told me he knew you and I had feelings for each other and always had."

Her breath was a sob. "I can't listen to this."

He went on anyway. "He wasn't accusing either of us, Lilia. He just asked for a chance to make things right. Then he added — *while I still can.*"

She could no longer blink away her tears. He pulled her close and spoke softly.

"Before he died Graham made me promise I would tell Toby stories about all the things he and I did when we were growing up. He wanted me to keep his memory alive. Then he asked me to be there for Toby and for you. He said I had his blessing."

"He never said any of that to me. That day, he hinted he knew how close we were . . ."

"Because he couldn't say more. He didn't want to say goodbye to his life with you until he had to, not until the very last second."

She remembered lying beside Graham at the very end, feeling his life slip away one breath at a time. She was glad they hadn't talked about a future he wouldn't share. How much harder would those last days have been?

He framed her face with his hands. "Lilia, to make those memories, Toby has to be in my life."

"We want you in our lives. Both of us do."

"That's the easy part. Let's just get there."

39

Marina's interview with Irene Monte had been surprisingly easy. On Monday Blake, at his most charming, had said all the right things, and after he left for work, Marina had described the desolation she'd felt and the pit her life had become when she was left alone to raise a baby she had expected to share with his father. She'd detailed Toby's colic, her realization that she'd probably suffered from postpartum depression, and her sadness that she'd felt forced by circumstances to give her son to Graham.

When asked why she hadn't visited or tried to see Toby until Graham's death, she had looked away. "It was too painful."

Her eyes had filled as she spoke, although they might have been tears of anger at Graham for what he'd put her through. Whatever had caused them, the tears had been timely.

At the front door the social worker had turned back. "I'm hoping to interview the baby's grandparents, the Randolphs."

Marina had tried to look, at best, mildly interested. "I suppose you have to."

"I'll be interviewing your family, too. To make sure everybody's interest in Toby's welfare is documented."

She nodded, as if that wasn't the worst news she'd heard since a doctor had confirmed the result of her pregnancy test. "I'm sure they'll be happy to help."

The social worker had reached for the doorknob before she turned one final time. "I've already had a phone conversation with Mr. Randolph. I ought to mention that, according to him, Toby won't inherit one cent from his estate. Did you know that?"

Marina straightened to her full five foot eight. "I don't know how that could possibly matter."

"Don't you?"

"I'm just sorry Mr. Randolph felt it needed to be said. It's sad he's determined not to have any part in Toby's life."

"How do you know that?"

Marina backtracked. "Well, you just said he wasn't leaving Toby a cent."

"Hardly the same thing."

"Graham told me that he and his father were estranged. I think it's clear he's not going to be taking his grandson on Boy Scout campouts."

"And you don't care?"

"It has nothing to do with me. But he'll be

missing something special."

"I'll be visiting your mother and your . . . brothers? Early next week."

If Irene Monte could find Jerry and pin him down that long, Marina thought she'd be a miracle worker.

Once the door had closed, she'd given the absent social worker the finger and gone to phone Deedee. At least she had some time to school her mother and Pete in the things they had to say.

Now it was Friday, and she was making Blake a special dinner. He'd called that morning and said he would be home by six, and while he'd sounded distracted, as usual, she had taken the early arrival as a good sign. As the week progressed he'd seemed more and more worried, and she hoped a good meal and an evening together would help.

The last time she'd made beef stew, Blake had eaten like a starving man. Tonight she was debuting a new slow cooker recipe with beer, mushrooms and bacon. She had water ready for noodles, and a crisp green salad waited in the refrigerator.

The special dinner was a thank-you. How many men who were thrown a curveball like Toby would agree to make the best of it? In her experience men were basically selfish. They wanted what was good for them, and a woman's job was to provide it. Graham being a prime example.

In the months of their marriage Blake had been more than a nice guy who was easy to live with and able to support her in style. He was becoming a partner. If he ever stopped working around the clock, she thought their marriage might be a success.

On that thought she heard the front door and the sound of Blake hanging up his coat. While a lot of Silicon Valley executives dressed as casually as their employees, her husband either wore a suit and tie or, on casual days, a sport coat and slacks. She liked to tease him about his old-fashioned ways.

Marina went to greet him. "Let's see if the good smells in this kitchen have reached the great room. Tonight we dine like kings on a serf's budget."

He didn't smile. "I don't have much of an appetite."

Something was wrong. He looked older, haggard, upset. "Hey. Are you feeling okay? Do you need to sit down?"

"If you have anything on the stove, turn it off."

She hesitated, then shrugged. "Shall I bring you something to drink?"

"Just come back. We're going to talk."

She took longer than she needed to in the kitchen, composing herself and racing through possible explanations. She quickly settled on MeriTech. Blake had been hopeful he might be able to turn his company around, at least enough to exit gracefully. But maybe he hadn't been able to. Maybe he was about to lose everything and figured he would lose her with it.

He was wrong.

She'd slowly been coming to the realization that Blake was important to her. They'd been cutting corners for months, and the only money going into either of their bank accounts had come from Ellen. Still, Marina hadn't been tempted to leave him, and not because she was hopeful their lives would return to normal. Because she couldn't hurt him that way. And because she would miss him. She had to reassure him.

Back in the great room she settled beside him on the sofa. He turned so he could see her.

"Blake, whatever's going on at MeriTech, we'll face it together." She covered his hand with hers. "We'll see it through."

He moved his hand away. "I know Ellen Randolph is putting money into your checking account every week."

"I'm sorry?"

"Please, don't play dumb. On Tuesday there was a message on the answering machine from the bank, some problem with a check she sent you, a mistake they made. They said to disregard a notice they'd sent, it was all settled." He shook his head. "You never check the machine. This time you should have."

She played for time and tried to put him on the defensive. "I thought you and I had a deal. I have an account, you have an account. We put what we can into our mutual account. What we do with the rest is our own concern. Why are you questioning me about this?"

"I'm not questioning you. I'm just going to *tell* you what I know. The name seemed familiar, but I didn't pay much attention. I even forgot to mention the call so you wouldn't worry when the bank statement came. Then on Wednesday I went into the office and there on my desk was a folder. Wayne's parting shot."

"He's gone? You fired him?"

"He's taking a job with a company in Pittsburgh, God help them. Paul's going with him. As his formal goodbye Wayne documented lots of things about you to hurt me, but the only one that matters? You're taking money from Toby's grandmother. Weekly. I couldn't figure out why. Why would this woman pay you? So I did some checking. Graham Randolph was estranged from his parents. They disinherited him. When he made his will he specifically stated that he didn't want them to have custody." He leaned back as if he was too exhausted to sit up straight. "Is any of this familiar?"

She couldn't think of a convincing lie. She did her best. "Douglas Randolph is beyond the pale, but Ellen isn't the awful person Graham made her out to be. And when she learned how badly Graham had treated me, she started sending checks. I think she was afraid if she sent one large check, her husband would notice, so she's been paying —"

"This is the right time to be honest. The only time. Will you please do me the courtesy of telling the truth?"

The whole truth was so ugly she didn't dare tell it all. "She's not awful. That part is absolutely true."

"And now the rest?"

"It sounds worse than it is, which is why I didn't want you to know."

"I can decide how bad it sounds."

She had no choice but to tell at least some of it. "At Graham's memorial service Ellen figured out who I was and approached me. We went out to lunch the next day. We talked about how much we wished Toby could be in our lives. She told me, with Graham gone, she didn't trust Lilia to be a good mother. I told her I wanted to raise my son, but I was newly married, our finances had taken a downturn, and I would have to start working full-time. It wasn't the best scenario."

"It wouldn't be. Not put that way."

"She thought Toby should be with his real mother, so she offered to help."

"And what was she going to get from it? What was the price of her generosity?"

"She just wanted to be sure he was in the

best —"

He slashed his hand through the air. "What does she want for her money?"

She had never seen him this angry, not even when he'd learned that Wayne and Paul had run MeriTech into the ground. "She was, *is,* afraid Lilia won't allow her to visit. And she loves Toby. She knows she wasn't a good mother, but she wants to be a really good grandmother."

"So that was her only condition? Seeing him occasionally? That's what she wanted for helping you get custody? For hiring and paying your attorney? Because I know about that, too. That's why you pretended you were still consulting for your old boss, so I wouldn't worry about how you were going to pay those fees. You lied. Why?"

"She's hoping for some good blocks of time when he can stay with her. But, Blake, she only plans to have Toby when her husband is away. Douglas is the reason Graham didn't want Toby to spend time with his parents, and he won't have contact with Douglas. Ellen just wants what grandmothers everywhere do, real quality time with her grandson."

"And your lawyer knows this, and she's made sure that Ellen's assistance in the custody dispute is on the record?"

"There's no reason it should be."

"The *reason*? The court needs to know everything so they can make the best decision for your son."

"*I* am the best decision. I'm Toby's mother. Ellen is helping me, and in return, I'm going to help her be the kind of grandmother every child needs. Committed and involved."

"So why isn't this out in the open? Why all the secrecy?"

"Because Ellen is afraid the judge will put too much weight on what Graham said in his will."

"I could almost believe your story, but here's the thing, Rina. You showed no interest in Toby, not until after that lunch with Ellen. You never mentioned wanting custody. You hadn't seen him for almost a year before his father died. Then, suddenly, you decide to become his mother again. Or, maybe you decided a generous income and blocks of time away from the child you gave away was a bargain you couldn't resist."

And there it was. The part that was so ugly. Because that *was* the way it had started.

If she'd continued to wonder, even a little, if there was any truth to Wayne's insinuations about Blake's mental status, her fears were now completely laid to rest. Her husband was in full control of his faculties and making all the correct leaps in logic, in fact making them to her detriment, because clearly, she could no longer twist the truth, not even a little, and get away with it. Blake was much too sharp.

She put her face in her hands. "Blake, you have no idea how awful those early months of Toby's life were. I was so depressed I couldn't cope. I was at my wits' end. Then Deedee took him a few times so you and I could go out. When we were together I wasn't just somebody's mother. You didn't even know I'd had a baby. I could smile again. I could laugh. And I finally saw if I gave Toby to the one person who really wanted him, I could have my life back."

"I believe that much."

She straightened. "Graham's death changed it all. I heard he was sick again, but I didn't think too much about what that meant. I thought he'd get better. Then the next thing I knew he was gone. I didn't have time to figure out what I should do about Toby. I was just getting to the point where I realized I *could* do something the day Ellen took me to lunch."

"And you jumped on it."

"I *didn't* jump on it. I considered the right path. Even after the first supervised visits, in a playroom with other parents and kids, I was still trying to decide. He was a stranger. I didn't feel much of anything. Then the first day I had him to myself? I sure didn't feel what a mother's supposed to. That went on for a while. You don't know how many times I almost picked up the phone to call the lawyer and tell her to let Lilia adopt him.

Then . . ." She turned to face him. "Then things, well, they changed. He's not somebody else's kid now, Blake, he's *my* kid. I love him." She held out her hands. "I didn't know I was capable of that, but I am."

"And Ellen?"

"She's made so many mistakes. She wants a second chance. It's too late to have one with Graham. But she loves Toby, too, and she wants to be a good grandmother."

"You should have told the truth. Right from the beginning."

"Have you been listening? How do you think a judge would look at this story? Both Ellen and I come off as horrible people. Villains. But in the end? No matter how we went about it? We're just two women who love a little boy and want to be sure he stays in our lives."

"The way we go about things says everything about who we are."

"What does that mean?"

He stood, surprising her. "It means that I'm not going to be part of this charade. If I hadn't been so preoccupied, I might have realized something was fishy. But I didn't, and for that, I'm sorry. But not for the rest. I trusted you. I supported you. I was even willing to be Toby's father."

"Blake —"

He shook his head. "I don't want anyone to think I sanction what you've done. This whole custody thing will come to a head soon. Maybe then we can sit down and see if anything's left. In the meantime, I'd like you to move out. I'll help you find a place if you need one." A note of sarcasm crept in. "Or maybe *Ellen* will. She's been very generous. Maybe she'll be more so."

She stood, too. "I made mistakes, but I'll be honest from this point. You know the worst. Can't we move on?"

"I don't think so. Not now at least. I'm going back to work, and I'll sleep there tonight. When I come home tomorrow, I would like you to be gone." He crossed the room, got the coat he'd hung up earlier, and left.

She was aware of everything, the scent of beef and mushrooms, the cold air that had entered when he opened the door, the ticking of a clock on the opposite wall. Her hands began to shake, and for a moment, standing in the first real home she had known, she couldn't think why she felt so afraid.

Then she began to cry.

40

A week after she moved out of Blake's villa, Marina took the first job she was offered: business development coordinator at a luxury car dealership. She was on the phone from the moment she arrived until she left, setting up sales appointments. Judging from the number of people who hung up before she finished a sentence, at best the "hot" leads she'd been promised were tepid.

In addition to sitting in the same seat all day, oozing warmth and enthusiasm, the downside of the job was the schedule. In order to reach potential customers, she was required to work some evenings and weekends. If custody was decided in her favor, she couldn't imagine how she was going to work out child care. But a job was required. If the courts gave Lilia permanent guardianship, Ellen certainly wouldn't continue to send checks, and Marina had to have a steady income. For now she was watching her savings grow.

Blake hadn't called since she'd moved out, although she'd left a note telling him where she would be. She'd arrived at Deedee's with two suitcases, leaving everything else behind. To her credit Deedee had waved her right in. Pete had argued to keep the room which had, until recently, been Jerry's, but for once Deedee hadn't given in to her baby boy. The room was her daughter's as long as she needed it.

Marina hoped that wouldn't be long. She intended her stay to be short. Her mother was home most of the time, working just a few hours on the late shift while her foot healed, and Marina knew Deedee would quickly drive her crazy. Unfortunately, finding an apartment in a family-friendly unit was turning out to be tough. She had little time to search.

If Lilia retained guardianship, then Marina could live almost anywhere, but she hoped she still had a shot at gaining custody. If she could settle into an adequate apartment and establish child care, her plans for Toby might be acceptable. Maybe her marriage hadn't lasted, but Lilia was a single mother, too. How could the court hold divorce against her?

On Friday she left work at noon to pick up Toby. The previous week Deedee had picked him up so Marina could attend a sales meeting. This week Marina was scheduled to work

Saturday afternoon, and Ellen, who had a luncheon nearby, had agreed to meet them at a local park instead of her home. Marina planned to tell her what had happened and how best they could present it to the court.

In Willow Glen Lilia handed over her son, who went willingly into Marina's arms. "He's had a cold. He doesn't have his usual energy."

Marina adjusted Toby's coat after the transfer. "That's never fun. I'll be sure not to tire him out."

"I don't think you could if you tried. This morning I found him on the sofa staring at the ceiling."

"Please, don't lecture me, but he's seen a doctor? I'm assuming?"

Lilia exhaled loudly, but she didn't sound angry. "Yes. It's a cold. He had a little fever, but it's gone. The cold just wore him out. He might need a nap while he's with you."

Marina was glad Lilia hadn't saddled up her high horse. "Is he on meds? Will I need to give him anything?"

"You know not to give aspirin, right?"

This time Marina took a moment before she spoke. "I do, yes."

Lilia's expression softened. "I'm sorry, but I'm always surprised how many people don't seem to know that. So much advice has changed since our parents' day."

"Babies sleeping on backs instead of stomachs."

"No crib bumpers. No cute baby quilts to smother newborns."

"It's amazing, isn't it, that any of us survived? My mother made me hold my baby brother on my lap in the car. And I couldn't use a seat belt in case we needed to get out fast."

"How old were you?"

"Not even a teenager." They both rolled their eyes.

Marina knew on that brief note of camaraderie it was time to leave. "I'll bring him home on time, unless you think you'll be out?"

"I'll be here."

She had been careful all month to slip in under the deadline. With her marriage on the rocks she had enough strikes against her with the judge.

As she bundled Toby into her car she found herself smiling. Maybe if she and Lilia were eternally forced to trade him back and forth at court-assigned intervals, they might learn to be honest and band together with his best interests at heart. Of course, that wasn't the first fairy tale she'd believed. For years she had wondered when her real father was coming to whisk her away to a mansion by the sea.

While she waited for Ellen to finish planning charity events over rubber chicken salads, she took Toby to Deedee's. Miracu-

562

lously no one was at home. Since all his toys were still at Blake's, she'd bought a few new ones. While he fumbled listlessly with wooden cars, she fed him a Popsicle. He wasn't hot, but his china-blue eyes were bloodshot, and she had to follow him around with a tissue. An hour later, she decided to put him in the portable crib, and he went to sleep almost as soon as she laid him down — or more honestly, after she'd ended his lullaby with eighty-eight bottles of beer.

In the living room she opened her computer to look for rental apartments. Among other things, since her life and Toby's were so unsettled, she needed a month-by-month lease.

She connected to the best site and made three calls to landlords, none with a promising result. She had just started looking through the newspaper when somebody banged on the front door. She was afraid to ignore the summons. Whoever it was might wake up Toby. She checked the peephole first, just to be safe.

Douglas Randolph stood in the hallway, ready to bang again.

41

Ellen wasn't happy. For most of an hour she'd been fuming at a picnic table in an iffy neighborhood playground. Unfortunately she'd had to attend a luncheon, something she absolutely could not get out of. Marina had known that today she had only the most limited time to spend with her grandson.

By the time she saw Marina and Toby walking across the grass in her direction, she was simmering. Marina looked tattered around the edges, but Ellen complained anyway. "I'm not sure how safe this neighborhood is, and you're late."

Marina, dressed in faded jeans and a hoodie, nodded to Ellen's white sheath with its matching shawl draped gracefully across one shoulder. "Next time don't dress for a mugging."

She held out Toby, and he let Ellen take him, although he struggled to get down almost immediately so he could investigate the play equipment.

Ellen tried to resettle him on her lap. "I brought clothes so I could change at the club, but there wasn't time. Because *I* was here precisely at three."

"He wants to play." Marina sprawled on the bench and leaned back against the table. "We can watch from here unless he needs help."

"I have little enough time with him as it is." Reluctantly Ellen set Toby down, and he made his way to the play equipment, but not with his usual zest. He stood at the edge of the mulch examining all the possibilities, then he sat down to investigate the grass.

Ellen started to rise. "He's going to get dirty."

"Yes. He's a little boy. If he starts eating dirt, we'll grab him. But Lilia says he's had a cold, so he doesn't have much energy today. In a minute we'll try the swing."

"You didn't tell me he was sick."

"I didn't know until I picked him up. He's fine, just recovering."

"I need to know these things."

Marina stared straight ahead, as if she was searching the play equipment for a sign. Then she sighed. "In the future, if I get custody, Ellen, and if it matters, I'll try to let you know what's going on with your grandson. I know you care about him. I'll make sure you see Toby whenever we can arrange it. But what I say and do will be my decision."

Ellen frowned. "If I'm supporting you —"

"I've had quite a day, which explains why I'm late."

Ellen didn't want to hear the ins and outs of Marina's life. "I'm sorry, but we made an agreement."

"Douglas came to see me."

Ellen fell silent.

Marina finally turned to look at her. "I'm living with my mother for the moment, but he didn't have trouble finding me."

"You're living with your *mother*?"

"Until I find something else. My marriage is on the rocks, and I've taken a full-time job. In fact I had to promise to work tomorrow in exchange for taking this afternoon off."

"I don't understand."

"Yeah, well, here it is in a nutshell. Two weeks ago Blake discovered your part in the custody battle and asked me to move out. I took the first job I was offered."

Ellen was trying to make sense of this. "What did you mean about Douglas?"

"An hour ago he offered me money to disappear. He wants Toby out of your life. He wants Toby out of *his*. He said he'd make sure I got custody. Then he'd help me start a new life, new name, new place, anywhere, as long as I never contacted you again."

Ellen was stunned. "And you're going to take him up on it?"

Marina narrowed her eyes. "You know, I've

never been a good person. I never had the luxury. I had to fend for myself, so I did. But Douglas made a big mistake today. He thought I'd put myself first again, as always. But it *was* a mistake. Because when he woke Toby with his shouting, and I got my little boy out of his crib, your husband said awful things to him."

"What do you mean?"

Marina continued, as if she hadn't spoken. "From this point on, Douglas can never be in the same room with my son. Never. And the only way I can make sure that happens is to control *your* time with Toby. Because you can't or won't control your husband, and you can't or won't remove yourself from his life."

"I'll make sure —"

Marina shook her head and kept shaking it. "I'm sorry, but I don't believe you. I can't trust you to put Toby first. You never put his father first, and there's no reason to think you've changed."

"You think I would let Douglas hurt Toby?"

"I was at your house the day he came home early, remember? He upset your grandson then, and today he called him a *bastard.* Right to his little face. Plus, he found me at my mother's, although almost nobody knows I'm there. What does that say about how determined he is?"

"I can take care of this. I can —"

"Here's what I think. In your husband's

mind Toby is living proof Graham stood up to him. First he married a woman neither of you liked, and part of the reason *he* didn't is because Lilia's strong, and she does what's right. And that's enough to set his porcelain veneers on edge."

"Are you really going to defend her?"

Marina ignored her. "Then Graham refused to go along with his father when the Randolph Group tried to cover up crimes they had missed. And for that, today, he called your son a misfit and a pariah."

"He was upset. He —"

"And finally Graham had an affair. Granted, that wasn't the most noble thing he ever did, but to his credit? He refused to bury the consequences. He wanted Toby, and even if he almost destroyed two women in the process, he stood up for his son. He loved Toby, and that must be the worst of it for Douglas. Because he couldn't love his."

Ellen wanted to say something, anything to refute what Marina was saying, but the words wouldn't form.

Marina turned away. "If I touched *anything* that belonged to that man, my fingers would fall off. The only reason I'd ever leave town is to get Toby as far away from him as I can. As long as you stay connected to us in any significant way, your husband will try to destroy me, and worse, my beautiful little boy. I'm sorry, but you let him destroy *your* son. I won't let him touch mine."

"What makes you think you can get custody without my help?"

"I don't know, but I won't be taking another dime, and I'll find a way to pay the attorney or get a cheaper one."

"You'll lose him! We'll both lose him!"

Marina executed the slightest of nods. "Nothing is certain. But Ellen, I would rather let Lilia have Toby than you. Because Lilia won't let anything happen to him. And as long as you're married to Douglas Randolph, you have tied your own hands."

Ellen was proud of the way the house in Montclair Village had turned out. She'd made a few mistakes, paint colors that hadn't been as soft or inviting as she'd hoped, Middle Eastern marble in a guest bathroom that had looked cheap when installed, although it certainly hadn't been. Luckily paint could be changed, and she'd caught the tile mishap well before the work was finished.

Hank had approved her decisions. Months ago he had stopped warning her not to spend too much. Instead, the last time they'd been together he'd given her a fake business card. Ellen Randolph, Flipper Inc.

Hank was the only one who'd realized, after a week or two, what she'd really been doing. Even she hadn't, or at least she hadn't admitted it to herself. She had been readying Graham's first home for his son. She had been creating a home where Toby could visit her.

What had she thought? That she would then live happily in two places? That she could continue living on Belvedere Island and come here whenever she had Toby to herself? As if her husband wouldn't know? As if he wouldn't follow her or have a lackey do it? As if Douglas would shrug this off as a passing phase and continue to pretend their grandson didn't exist?

"Hey, where'd you come from?"

She turned at the sound of Hank's voice and attempted a smile as he came to stand on the sidewalk beside her. He had a sixth sense about her arrivals, or more likely, he was outside gardening.

"I was just on my way home, and I thought I'd drop by and see how the yard was coming along."

"What do you think?"

She'd hired the best landscapers, so, of course, the front yard was perfect. She'd demanded the crew leave some of the lawn that Graham had once run across, baby feet barely stirring the grass. The women, from an all-women team, had trimmed the trees, taken out overgrown shrubs and replaced them with hardier varieties. She'd asked for flowers, and after they'd deepened the beds they'd created a swath of perennials. None of it was as fussy as Lilia's gardens, of course.

But bold enough to add color and life.

The front was lovely.

"I can't wait to see the back." She injected the lie with as much enthusiasm as she could muster.

"The painters did a good job, don't you think?"

The house was the same blue-gray, although the man in charge of the crew had insisted that everyone was painting houses in dark earth tones. She had driven nearby streets shuddering at charcoal and slate-colored exteriors that disappeared into the shadows of large trees. Perhaps this shade of blue wasn't the best seller at the moment, but it would be again. And she could wait that long.

Or so she'd thought.

She cleared her throat, and for a moment whatever lump was clogging it refused to disperse. "I like everything. I guess I do have good-enough taste."

"Well, you've decorated a lot of houses in your time."

She glanced at him. As always, Hank was in jeans, topped today by a hand-knit sweater with sleeves that hid his fingertips. As she watched he pushed them up to his wrists. "My daughter-in-law." He grinned. "She chose me as her first knitting victim."

She wondered what that would be like, a daughter-in-law who loved her husband's father enough to make her first mistakes at his expense, and to know, as she did, that he would love her anyway, and the sweater, too.

She turned back to the house. "I haven't decorated a lot of houses. I hired professionals. Maybe that's why I wanted to try this one on my own. I got tired of other people's opinions."

"Want to see the back together?"

She had to say yes. "We can go around or through the house."

"Anything inside you need to take a look at?"

She hadn't seen the family room floors since they'd been refinished, but she shook her head. "Let's go around."

The backyard was fenced, and they passed through the gate on one side. She didn't bother to fasten it behind them. She wasn't going to stay.

The brick patio had been repaired and extended. Now it took up a significant part of the yard. When she had finally gotten around to admitting the truth to herself, she had envisioned Toby here on a tricycle. In preparation she'd demanded every brick be exactly the same height. She'd had a flower bed positioned along one side, raised high enough that a small child could easily dig in the dirt and help plant flowers. She'd left room along the other side for play equipment.

"I like the shrub border along the back

fence," Hank said. "Whoever lives here will have flowers most of the year."

Manzanita, bush anemone, blue Ceanothus, Santa Barbara lilac. She had carefully agreed to them all. She supposed she would never see how successful her plan had been.

She pointed to the edge of the brick and an oval of ground cover. "The plan has a place for a little pond someday. Right there. Goldfish, frogs. For later."

"If this yard were mine, I'd sit out here every night with a glass of wine, soft jazz, a good friend."

She could do all those things. She could invite *him* to share a drink with her, to reminisce, even to talk about whatever the future held for each of them. But she wouldn't.

She was nothing if not a coward. When she'd left Marina and Toby at the park, she'd told herself it was time to take her life in her hands, well past time for a divorce. By trying to bribe Marina to leave, by verbally attacking his grandson, Douglas had stepped over a line she couldn't forgive.

If she had divorced him when Graham was young, how different her life would be now. Without his father's constant criticism, her son's life would have been different, too. Without admitting the truth to herself, she had tried to protect Graham by thrusting him out of sight so Douglas would have less influence. She had protected her little boy, no, *shielded* him, by sending him across the country to school and summer camps. And she had shielded him by not making a fuss over him, too. Because hadn't she known that if she hovered over Graham and stood up for him too often, Douglas would see how much her son meant to her?

Of course, she'd never quite understood any of it. Not in so many words. Not until today when Marina, a woman who seemed to have few maternal instincts, had proven she had so many *more* than Ellen. Now she understood that her choice had been the coward's choice. Because when it came right down to it, staying with Douglas had just been easier.

"Do you ever wonder why I've stayed with Douglas?"

"Because you thought being his wife was what you did best."

"You said that before. That's part of it. But here's the rest. Without Douglas, I'm nothing, Hank. Nobody. On my own I have nothing to offer another living soul. But Douglas needs me and what I can give him."

"Needs?"

She hesitated before she looked at him. "Needs, yes. Being married to Douglas is all I know how to do. I've made such horrifying choices. And now? Maybe Douglas is my punishment."

His expression was kind, and he reached out, but seemed to think better of it. His hand dropped to his side. "You need to talk to somebody. See a therapist for a while to help put your life in perspective."

"That's the California way, isn't it? We look anywhere and everywhere to solve our problems. Inside, up to the heavens, to the latest guru? Perspective? I am the envy of every woman in the world, Hank. I have everything I could ever want. Douglas is rich, powerful and probably even faithful. Why would I need a therapist?"

"Because you're desperately unhappy."

"Isn't everybody?"

"I'm not."

"Then you're one of the lucky ones."

He appeared to choose his answer carefully. "You have a lot of years ahead. You could live them differently. I know you wish you'd been a better mother. You can't change that. But you can be a wonderful grandmother and help raise Graham's son. He would have liked the new you."

She turned away. "I've decided to sell the house."

Hank was silent.

She didn't look at him. "I've had fun. It's been a diversion. Maybe I'll buy every house I've lived in and fix them up, whether they need it or not. While I was doing this, I felt good. I felt like I was creating something. But it's over. I'd like you to put it on the market as soon as possible. You can send me anything I have to sign. You have my address?"

He remained silent.

She finally faced him again. "I can find somebody else if you don't want to."

"No, I'll do it."

"I appreciate all your help. It's been nice to reconnect."

He gave a slight nod.

"I'm too old to reinvent myself." She started back through the gate and didn't wait to see if he followed. On the street again she knew that he had remained in the backyard that had fed so many hopes for a life with her grandson.

For a moment she hesitated. She was poised on a precipice instead of an Oakland sidewalk. In the end, though, she got in her car and drove away without looking back.

42

THE SWALLOW'S NEST

FEATHERING YOUR NEST WITH IMAGINATION AND LOVE

October 30th:

We're approaching our big holiday season here in the U.S. Halloween tomorrow, then Thanksgiving followed by Christmas, Hanukkah, Kwanzaa, the Solstice, all the December holidays you celebrate. And with all that fun? Something added.

It's time to talk about stress. Don't pretend you don't feel it. Life is filled with ups and downs, and we all need a nest to come home to, a place where we feel safe and protected. A place where love can flourish.

As you decorate and redecorate, a stress-free environment should always be a priority. In fact creating a sanctuary should top your list.

What's the first thing you see when you walk in your front door? Chores that must be done immediately? Stacks of papers to take to the trash, mail that has to be answered, fussy furniture that forever needs dusting?

Instead, imagine how you'll feel if what

577

catches your eye is a beautiful holiday decoration. Or the rest of the year? A piece of art, maybe just an inexpensive poster, or better yet, a gallery wall.

Still too much work? How about fresh flowers in an elegant vase? A small table covered by a beautiful quilt and a stack of colorful books? A flourishing green plant — find a variety like philodendron or cast iron plant that doesn't need constant attention.

The options are endless. But so is stress. Luckily, a home that soothes and enriches every moment is the perfect place to combat it. When you walk through your front door anytime of year, breathe a sigh of relief and don't gasp in horror. It's up to you.

Aloha! Lilia

"Carrick says it's not uncommon for guardianship cases to drag on forever." Regan was standing in front of Lilia's oven, her fingers carefully curled over hibiscus print pot holders, which in turn were curled over the edges of a casserole dish filled with sweet potatoes. She was holding so still she looked frozen in place.

Lilia took another photo from a different angle. She'd stopped counting, but she thought this time, with the help of poster board that reflected light to the farthest reaches of the kitchen, she might finally have a good one.

"A decent shot is taking about as long as Toby's court case." She glanced up. "Unlike that, I think we're finished here. Take a break." As Regan set the dish on the stove top Lilia scrolled back through her shots. "Great. I think we finally got one. Are you too tired to keep going?"

"Born to be a hand model." Regan waved her painted fingernails in the air. "What's next?"

"Scooping the casserole on a plate with your gorgeous manicure in full view again. I have the dining room table all set. Before we get to it, let's sit. Tea? Coffee?"

They took cups of jasmine tea to the sunroom, where Regan reclined. "Doesn't it feel odd to be working on Thanksgiving web pages so far in advance? Tomorrow's Halloween."

Lilia had spent most of October featuring Halloween decorations and party menus, so she was well past that, although she was looking forward to taking her son, dressed as a lion, trick-or-treating for the first time.

"I'm planning a big spread to get more viewers and clicks, so I have to start now." Lilia made quotation marks in the air. "Thanksgiving with Hawaiian flare. I'm doing a content swap with some of my blogging sisters."

"If those sweet potatoes are any example, we have a lot to look forward to at Thanks-

579

giving dinner."

The elder Donnellys were coming to California for the holiday, and the whole family had been invited to have dinner at Lilia's house. Today's much-photographed casserole was bursting with coconut as well as macadamia nuts, and Lilia thought her readers and guests would like it. She wouldn't tell anyone that the Swallows had never eaten sweet potatoes on Thanksgiving day. In fact they hadn't always eaten turkey. More often than not her mother had prepared local dishes, including fresh fish steamed in taro leaves, laulau style. Lilia's brothers were all capable spearfishers.

They sat in companionable silence until Regan put down her cup. "Maybe by Thanksgiving, Toby will be yours free and clear."

"If that happens, this'll be a Thanksgiving to remember."

"Carrick seems optimistic."

Lilia was glad he was sending the same message to both of them. "We're just waiting for the official report. Then if both parties let the evaluation stand and settle visitation, it will finally be done."

"And if not?"

"More delays. A hearing, with lots of accusations tossed back and forth, witnesses, tears." She blew out a long breath. "And it's likely that's what will happen."

"The house seems awfully quiet when

Toby's not here."

"Which is why I can take photos." Since her new mantra was *keep busy no matter what*, she got to her feet. "Let's get the rest of the photos. He's supposed to be home by six. If we don't get a good shot with the casserole from the oven, I have spares."

"How many did you make?"

"Four. You're taking one home."

"Carrick's picking me up. We'll share."

Lilia hadn't realized he was stopping by. "He can have his own. And he never mentioned he was coming. Didn't you drive?"

"He dropped me off. He was going over to his new house to see what's happening."

Lilia winced. Late in the week Graham's old crew had finally finished framing new walls and gutting the former kitchen. Because she had insisted on keeping the original details, none of it had been simple. She'd suggested Carrick not view it until she could go with him. Apparently he hadn't listened.

"He'll be a wreck," she said.

"He trusts you. Besides, the house is an excuse to see you tonight."

Lilia and Regan had carefully avoided talking about her relationship with Carrick, even after their weekend in Carmel. Now apparently the moratorium had ended. "For the record, he doesn't need an excuse."

"Yeah, I can tell."

"You're okay with that?"

"I can't think of two people who deserve happiness more."

Lilia gave her a quick hug. "That means a lot."

"And if the two of you ever, well . . . ?" Regan made a face. "We'd be sisters. And that's the only way that'll ever happen."

"What about Jordan?"

"He paddled his surf board into the sunset last month."

"A month ago?" Lilia realized what that said about *her*. "What kind of friend am I?"

Regan draped her arm over Lilia's shoulders and nudged her toward the dining room. "Your brother and I are cool. I never made it to my feet on his surf board, and he never understood he has to stop filing his income tax with the EZ form. Doomed from the get-go."

Lilia wondered how much of the problem had been their differences and how much had been Regan's continuing fear of commitment after what she'd gone through with Devin. She could certainly relate.

By the time they finished the photo shoot on the dining room table with the formal setting Lilia had placed at the end of the table, Carrick was at the door.

While Regan insisted that Lilia had forgotten to turn off the oven and left for the kitchen, Lilia greeted him with a kiss. "The nicest of surprises."

"I had a late lunch with a client."

"And then you went off to see your house. I told you to wait for me."

"Now that everything's framed in?" He looked expectant.

"You couldn't tell a darn thing."

"You could build a maze in there, and I wouldn't know until I tried to move my stuff inside."

"You'll love it, I promise."

She kissed him again, taking her time. She saw Carrick frequently, but after Carmel they had established a silent pact. Their relationship, and all the decisions and intimacy that waited in the distance, needed to remain there until things with Toby were finally settled. Once that fog lifted for good they would be able to see each other and their futures more clearly.

She just hoped, for any number of reasons, that would be soon.

Arms around each other's waists, they strolled into the kitchen where Regan was finishing cleanup. "Is that sweet potato casserole?" He sounded wistful.

"I'm sending a pan home with each of you. Toby and I are heading to a neighbor's barbecue tonight."

"Where is he?"

"Marina's afternoon, remember?"

"Shouldn't he be back?"

Lilia glanced at the kitchen clock, not

583

surprisingly a pineapple. Early in their marriage Graham had given it to her for Christmas, and even now she smiled. The reminder no longer hurt, nor did it stir her to anger. She had loved a flawed man, and he was gone. The good memories would stay; the bad ones would fade.

"It's not quite six. He should be here any minute," she said. "Marina mentioned her mother might return him tonight."

"Oh?"

"Deedee picked him up last week, too."

"You didn't mention that."

"Is it important?"

"Her mother has a problem with alcohol. She's a bartender who shouldn't be, and she's lost jobs because of her drinking."

Lilia's pulse sped up. "I met her at the door that day. She seemed fine, limping, but fine."

"She broke a bone on the top of her foot four months ago when she dropped a bottle on it. A full one. Expensive scotch. The manager suspects she was drinking too much herself and careless, but he can't be sure. The break didn't heal, so they had to do surgery. She's only working a few hours a night because she can't stand up long, but he's keeping his eye on her."

"You know this how?"

He just lifted one brow as if to say, *How do you think?*

She had asked Carrick not to tell her what

584

his investigator had discovered unless it affected Toby's safety. If her guardianship was finalized by the court, most likely Marina would continue to be in her life. She hadn't wanted to know more about the other woman than she had to. Now she knew she had been foolish. Forewarned was forearmed.

She concentrated on the present. "Deedee drinks early in the day?"

"If she's an alcoholic she drinks whenever she can get away with it."

The doorbell rang, and Lilia put her hand on his arm. "Listen, I noticed she headed south last time she left the house, even though there was parking in front of my house. She *walked* south. I didn't see her car. Do you think you can get ahead of her when she leaves while I stall her? Just to see what's going on? Maybe we'll get a better read on this?"

"Chat a few minutes if you can."

"If she tries to leave I'll give her a sample of sweet potato casserole," Regan said.

"Give her a pan." Lilia headed for the door.

Today Deedee looked like a New Age Grandma, diaphanous purple blouse hanging almost to her knees over a sequined skirt. Toby was playing with a pentacle on a heavy chain that was hanging between unfettered breasts.

When he saw Lilia he launched himself into her arms. She held him tightly against her and smiled at the older woman. "Were you a good boy for Deedee?"

"Dee!" He struggled to get down. She let him run inside where Regan was waiting with open arms. Then Lilia closed the door so he wouldn't come back.

"Isn't that great?" Deedee said. "He can say Deedee. Well, almost. He can say Dee. So I tell him to say it again, and he does. That adds up to Deedee, don't you think?"

"I'm teaching him to call my mother Tutu. That's what we call grandmothers in Hawaii. Does he talk a lot when he's with you?"

"Rina and I took him to the park, and he chattered about squirrels. He calls them *quirls.* It's adorable. My granddaughter — her name's Brittany — didn't say her first word until she was two. Nobody noticed she wasn't talking but me."

"Well, she's . . . lucky to have you." The little girl probably was lucky. As eccentric as Deedee was, apparently she cared about her grandchildren.

Unless she was drinking. Lilia stepped a little closer, wondering if she would smell alcohol. With relief she only smelled lavender and patchouli.

She hunted for something else to say. "Do you have a photo of your granddaughter? I'd love to see one."

Deedee was carrying a cross body cloth bag, probably from India based on the embroidery and tiny mirrors sewn across the surface. Now, clearly delighted, she pulled it over her shoulder and began to dig. A minute passed, then another. She finally came up with a pocket album and whipped it out.

"I have photos on my cell phone, too, but I left that in the car for Pete. He had to call a friend."

"Pete?"

"Rina Ray's brother."

"Oh, of course."

"He might have found a job. He needs a reference."

"I hope it works out."

Deedee flipped through photos until she found one of an unsmiling little girl eating an ice cream cone. She looked neither happy nor healthy.

Lilia managed a smile. "She looks a little like you. Do you think?"

"More like Jerry, her dad. He'll eat anything that's not nailed down. Me, I don't eat much." Deedee found another photo, similar to the first, then she put the album back. "I'd better go."

Lilia hoped enough time had elapsed for Carrick to position himself so he could watch Deedee's exit. She had one last thing to check out. "Thanks for bringing Toby back. It must be a struggle to get his car seat in and out of your car."

"We drive Rina Ray's car when we have

Toby. She took mine so we wouldn't have to make the switch. She won't let that child near a car unless he's in a proper car seat. Brittany used to ride in my lap. But not Toby."

If anybody else had gone on that way, Lilia would have suspected they were trying to cover a lie. But after her brief encounters with Deedee, she knew chatter was in character.

"Well, have a good evening. You and . . . Pete?"

"You, too." Deedee turned and hobbled back out to the road. Then she turned south and started up the block. This time Lilia was more aware how odd that was. As before she could see parking places on the street near her house. Was Deedee confused about the location? Had she driven past, parked and then decided to walk back rather than turn around?

Clearly she was in pain. Why would a woman with an injured foot park so far away, knowing she had to walk back with a toddler in her arms?

She raced through the house and asked Regan to watch Toby. In the garage she started her car and pulled on to the side street, turning in front of her house. Deedee was about half a block ahead, still hobbling along. Then as she watched, a car that had been parked another half block farther pulled out, made a U-turn and started back toward her, stopping as Deedee moved around it,

588

holding on to the sides as she went. Finally she got in on the passenger's side.

Lilia watched them speed past. Deedee wasn't driving.

In a moment her own passenger door opened, and Carrick got in. She placed her hand over her heart. "Were you lurking all this time?"

"Up the road a little." He didn't sound happy. "I was taking photos with my cell phone. And video."

"Why?"

"Because Marina's brother had his license suspended for two years after his second underage DUI."

She remembered what he had said about Deedee. "You think the brother's intoxicated now? My God, did he drive Toby here like that?"

"I don't know. I just know he's *driving*. I caught it on camera, and he probably drove Toby here. Maybe Deedee's foot hurt, and she couldn't get behind the wheel."

"I still don't understand the problem. Unless we can prove he was drinking."

"We don't have to. His license hasn't been reinstated, Lilia. And it won't be for another three months. He's driving illegally. I've already notified the police, and with luck they'll be waiting when he and Deedee get home. But Marina sent her son back to you with a driver who has no license and could be thrown in jail for it. I don't think our judge is going to be pleased."

43

Marina made it through Thanksgiving without murdering anyone. She, Deedee and Pete had dined on their traditional rotisserie chicken and canned cranberry sauce, and later Jerry had dropped off Brittany for the rest of the weekend. As holidays went, it had been better than some she remembered.

Now the season of ho-ho-ho was creeping closer.

Christmas had never been special for their family, either, even though Deedee had tried harder. Every year her mother had hauled a bedraggled tree out of a closet for Marina and her brothers to decorate with ornaments salvaged from the roadside. To this day Marina had flashbacks when she saw a tree waiting for garbage pickup after the holiday.

Deedee had always given her children presents, but never anything they asked for. For the most part, presents had been salvaged, too. As an adult Marina had ignored Christmas tradition and gone out alone for Chinese food while her friends celebrated with their families.

This year? She would probably be alone again. Blake had finally called. She didn't know why. Yesterday at the dealership she had been too busy making her own calls to check her cell. Apparently Blake had called around noon, and he'd asked her to call him back.

She hadn't.

Not celebrating Christmas was one thing. Kung Pao chicken alone instead of turkey with family? She was used to that. But having her husband ask for a divorce right before the holidays? That was a low she wasn't ready for.

She hoped her appointment with her new attorney wasn't going to be another.

Gil Braber's office wasn't in the best part of San Jose. This street was at the edge of gang turf, but when she drove into the closest garage, she didn't notice any obvious signs. Still, she chose a slot as close to the parking booth as possible. Someone had draped red-and-green streamers around it, and she could hear tinny carols from the attendant's radio.

Outside she put on her best mean girl face and strode half a block toward the building where Braber's office was located. He wasn't long out of law school, an underling at a small firm that wasn't on anybody's top ten. But he'd been recommended by someone at work, and his fees weren't out of sight. Since she could no longer afford the best, she had to take what she could afford.

Santa's elves hadn't made it into the building lobby, which was bleak and empty. The elevator that carried her up three floors was swathed in cheap carpet, floor to ceiling. She wondered if the carpet was supposed to protect her if the car plummeted to the basement. She decided to take the stairs on the way out.

When she entered the office an elderly receptionist asked her to take a seat. There were two young men in the waiting area, both heavily tattooed. One sported a pound of gold chains, and she wondered if they were decoration or handy for trussing up his next victim. She was just choosing a magazine when Braber arrived to escort her to his office. They shook hands, and once there she settled herself on a chair in front of his desk and refused coffee. Since he charged by the minute she assumed she'd be expected to pay for the time it took him to pour it.

"Chilly weather." He smiled, showing a chipped front tooth. With freckles and a crewcut, Gil Braber didn't look old enough to be taken seriously. She was more than a little nostalgic for Glynnis Jacobs, the shark Ellen had chosen and paid for.

She leaned forward to signal her impatience. "I'm hoping you have some news?"

"I wish it were better."

Now she was sorry she hadn't ignored *his* phone call, too.

"The evaluator's report is in. I have a copy. It's long and involved. I won't go into all of it. But her recommendation is that —" he glanced down at his desk "— *Toby* . . . right? Toby should stay where he is." He looked up again. "I'm sorry."

"I don't get it. I'm his mother."

"The high points? Or rather the low points, I guess. You had to prove that the baby's stepmother wasn't a good parent. There's no proof. Apparently she's exemplary."

"But he's not *hers.*"

"She's been the *de facto* parent now for almost two years. The social worker saw no reason to change that."

Two years. Yesterday Toby had turned two. It didn't seem possible, and even more so, it didn't seem possible he had celebrated the event without his real mother. She was picking him up later this afternoon for the upcoming weekend, and they would celebrate with presents and cake. But it wasn't the same.

It wasn't the same.

The attorney folded his hands and chewed his lip before he spoke. "You had a lot of strikes against you. First and foremost you abandoned your son. And you can't provide any record of contact or support for almost a year afterward."

"I was depressed and practically destitute."

He looked sympathetic but he shook his head. "Now your marriage is in trouble. Your living situation isn't the best —"

"I'm saving every penny to rent a decent apartment once custody is official."

"That's a small part of it. The latest? You allowed your brother to drive Toby to and from his stepmother's house with a suspended license, thereby endangering him."

The "thereby" set her off. "Get off your high horse, okay? My mother said *she* was driving him. I didn't know!"

"So that's a strike against you, too. You made a bad call. You *should* have known, and it came back to haunt you." He gave one shake of his head. "I'm not trying to be the voice of doom, Mrs. Wendell. This is already a lot to take in. But I want you to understand something else and think it over carefully. It's entirely possible that when the judge decides on visitation for the future, he'll insist you be supervised again. Apparently you were late several times returning your son, and then the situation with your brother —"

"Pete wasn't drinking. He's on the wagon. He found a job. He's getting his life together. He drove carefully!"

"Nonetheless he'll go in front of another judge later this month, right? You have to take that seriously."

She ran her fingers through her hair until it

was probably standing on end. "What can we do?"

"You have twenty days to object. The next step would be an evidentiary hearing. But I have to ask, what will you gain by dragging this out? Do you have witnesses who can prove the stepmother isn't taking care of your son? That Toby will definitely be better off with you instead of the woman who's been raising him for almost two years?"

"How can I prove that? I can't be a fly on her wall."

"Have you seen any evidence of abuse or neglect? His pediatrician hasn't. The nanny hasn't."

She had nowhere to turn. And still, she couldn't quit. "I want to object. I need more time to prove I'm the best choice."

He leaned over the desk. "You can do that. But unless something major turns up, you're going to lose this battle. If I were you I would concentrate on just keeping my visitation rights, and then expanding them in the future. You need to convince the judge you can return your son on time, and that from now on you'll do all the transportation yourself. That's going to be hard enough. In the future if that goes well, maybe we can ask for more time. Two weeks in the summer. Maybe an extra weekend every other month."

"It's not fair. I was late a few times because I took him to see his grandmother, and I ran into heavy traffic. His stepmother doesn't make any attempt to take him there." The next part wasn't true, but she added it anyway. "And I wanted Toby to spend time with my mother, too, even though it backfired. Surely somebody will see I was just trying to include the family members who love him."

"It's possible if you explain it that way, the judge may be more lenient. But you'd better hope he doesn't see the statement from the baby's grandfather. Mr. Randolph says his wife was paying you *and* your first attorney so she could spend more time with her grandson. Their son . . . Graham? Graham made it clear in both his will and a video that he didn't want his parents to have custody. And obviously the grandfather doesn't want anything to do with the baby. His statements here are damning." He held up the report.

"Ellen Randolph wasn't asking for *custody.* She just wanted to see her grandson, and she wanted to help me with expenses, since I'm his real mother. But I ended that when it got uncomfortable."

"Spin it that way? Maybe you'll be okay."

He stood, and that was her cue. Chipped tooth or not, he was right. She couldn't fault him. He knew the facts of the case. He was being honest about her chances.

She stood, too. "I want you to object. I want my day in court."

"You have twenty days to think this over. Call me before the holidays if you're still sure that's what you want to do." He extended his hand for a final handshake. "But your chances of gaining custody are slim. And it's not going to be cheap to bang your head against the wall."

In the hallway she took the stairs back out to the street. In the garage she found her car untouched, the first good news of the day. The bad news was that it took her three tries to start it. Apparently she was past due for a tune-up. Something else to worry about.

It was only three, and she had an hour before she could pick up Toby for their weekend together. She had birthday presents in the trunk, and she planned to take him to a family-style Italian restaurant where the owner had promised a small birthday cake. She had invited her mother, and she tried to imagine facing Deedee over the table when *she* had been the one to convince Pete to drive Toby to and from Lilia's. But how could she fault Deedee when, right from the beginning, Marina had made so many mistakes herself?

How many more weekends like this one would she be allowed?

In Willow Glen she parked across from a playground where she'd taken Toby. She turned on the radio and closed her eyes to wait until it was time to see her son. When her phone rang, she fished it out of her handbag and stared at the display. Finally, with a shrug, she answered.

"Blake." She waited.

"You're hard to track down."

"How would you know?"

"I've been working seven days a week. I crash by the time I get home."

"And I'm sure calling your wife would have just pitched you right over the edge."

"I'm sorry, Rina. I needed time. How are things going?"

"Which part? Living with my mother, working full-time or trying to get custody of my son?"

"You're working?"

"How did you think I would support myself?"

"I expected Ellen to do it."

"I told Ellen goodbye in October. I'm doing this on my own."

"Why, when she was willing to help?"

"Because I'm a better person than you think I am."

The silence went on so long she finally broke it. "Why did you call?"

"I want to see you. We need to talk."

She wondered if Gil Braber would handle their divorce. "Now's not a good time. I'm putting in extra hours at work. I have the whole custody thing hanging fire. I'm trying to line up child care and find an apartment so if I do happen to get lucky, Toby will have a decent place to live. I don't need another distraction."

"I'm a distraction?"

"You haven't even been that! You tossed me out and ignored me for two months. I know I screwed up, Blake, but if you had any real feelings for me, you would have tried to work this out. We could have gone to counseling. We could have figured out if we had anything worth saving. Instead you left me in the cold. Well, the good news? I haven't frozen to death, and I'm still fighting. It's what I do best."

"Rina, we need to talk."

"Call me after the holidays. Maybe by then I'll be ready for yet another court case." She tossed her phone back in her handbag. Then she rested her forehead on the steering wheel and wondered exactly when her life had become unglued. The night she slept with Graham Randolph and didn't use birth control? The afternoon she gave her son away? The lunch when she let Ellen talk her into regaining custody?

The night she fell in love with Toby?

Half an hour later she parked in front of Lilia's cottage. It wasn't dark, but she could see lights strung along the eaves and woven through bushes, waiting to be plugged in for the evening. A Christmas tree sat in front of the house, threaded with more lights and adorned with red-and-gold balls. Oversized boxes wrapped in Christmas foil sat in piles beneath. As she'd driven through the neighborhood she'd seen similar trees in front of other houses.

She compared this scene with the one Toby would encounter at her mother's. The tree from Marina's childhood had finally been carted off to the landfill, but this year Deedee had found a tabletop version on sale, and now it stood on a cardboard box draped in the remnants of a salvaged curtain. Even then the tree seemed to take up half the living room.

She wouldn't lose her son because of an inferior Christmas tree. She wouldn't lose him because she was a working mother. She wouldn't even lose him because her marriage had fallen apart and most likely her husband wanted a divorce. None of those things would have been reason to investigate her competency. There were worse parents and far worse circumstances, and the courts let them stand.

No, she was going to lose Toby because she had abandoned him. She had set everything in motion. And how could she ever make up for that in the eyes of the law?

Outside the car she straightened her jacket and took a deep breath. Since the day Pete had driven Deedee here, Lilia had been even less enthusiastic about turning him over to

601

her. Ellen's name had never come up, but the fact that Marina's own lawyer had mentioned her involvement today meant that now Carrick Donnelly probably knew. She wondered if Lilia did, too. If not now, when?

"At some point things can't get worse," she said, as she walked up the path. She hoped that day was coming soon.

She knocked and Lilia took her time arriving. She didn't greet her or smile. She just gave the briefest of nods. "As you asked, I didn't feed him."

Marina nodded. "Is he ready?"

"Valencia's bringing him down."

"How did his birthday go?"

"No problems."

"If anything comes up you can reach me on my cell phone."

"Or at your mother's apartment?"

"We're taking Toby out to dinner tonight to celebrate his birthday." She paused then added, "Since I couldn't be with him yesterday."

"So you won't be at *Ellen's*?"

And there it was. Marina tried not to react. "We won't be at Ellen's."

"Why? Doesn't she want to celebrate, too? How about Douglas? I'm sure he'll be thrilled that his only grandson is now two. I'm surprised he isn't having a party at the country club."

"Really? Wouldn't you know if he was?

You're the daughter-in-law."

"And *you're* the one who let Ellen bribe you into asking for custody after months of absolute silence."

Marina took a step back. "It wasn't a bribe. She offered to help me. She wanted access to her grandson, and you wouldn't give it to her."

"No, she didn't want it if it came from *me.* She disliked me right from the start because her son loved me. I gave Graham what she never did."

"Apparently not everything. Because then he came to me to have his baby." The moment the words were out, Marina was sorry.

"How can you face yourself in the mirror?"

"Really, if I'm that awful, why do you want to raise my son? He has my genes. Aren't you afraid he'll turn into a monster, too?"

"He might if you raise him!"

Marina saw movement in the doorway, and suddenly Valencia was there, Toby clinging to her. Lilia moved to one side, but her eyes shone with tears. She turned and disappeared into the house.

Marina opened her arms, and Valencia gave her the little boy. Then the other woman reached down and got the familiar puppy backpack off the floor and held it out without a word.

"Aren't you going to say something awful to me, too?" Marina demanded.

"Please, take good care of Toby." Valencia handed her the pack, then nudged the door closed.

"Ri—na." Toby smiled up at her, batting her cheek with his hand. "Dee?"

She realized she was trembling. She buried her face in his curls. Toby was happy to see her. *Somebody* in this world, a world she no longer wished she inhabited, was happy to see her. The person she most wanted to be happy.

"I love you, little boy," she whispered.

"Ri—na!"

"Mommy. Call me *Mommy.*"

He gave a big belly laugh, as if she'd told a good joke. She carried him to the car and strapped him into his seat, handing him a plastic truck.

She pulled away from the curb and started up the road to the first stop sign. She was supposed to turn right, go home and get Deedee for dinner. She stopped, but she didn't turn. A car was several blocks behind her, and she could see the headlights gradually drawing closer. For now, though, no one was nearby. From the backseat she heard Toby singing to himself and making car noises.

Sometimes life was just a stop sign at an intersection, and suddenly that simple truth seemed clear. She could turn right, as she had planned all along. Or she could turn left and take her chances with a brand-new life.

44

THE SWALLOW'S NEST

FEATHERING YOUR NEST WITH IMAGINATION AND LOVE

December 4th:

Advent is a wonderful word, isn't it? It signals an advent-ure around the corner, the arrival of something or someone notable. For Christians "Advent" is reserved for the weeks leading up to the birth of Jesus.

For a two-year-old Advent means viewing the world through new eyes. This year Keiki is old enough to notice the lights and decorations. Our community has a tradition of placing decorated Christmas trees in our front yards to welcome the season. Yesterday he helped me hang ornaments, and when the sun went down, we walked through the neighborhood watching other people's trees come to life.

Next week we'll put up an inside tree, and we've already begun making ornaments. We traced his handprint to make a beard for a construction paper Santa. We made snowmen out of foam circles. We'll decorate cookies, too, and hang them high. (I'm not sure he has the self-control not to pull them off and eat them.)

I'm looking forward to the arrival of "something notable." Are you? I know some of you celebrate other holidays. Will you share your favorite traditions of the season?

Aloha, Lilia

By six o'clock Lilia was too tired to do anything more on her website. The argument with Marina had angered and depressed her. After the episode with Pete and Deedee, she had asked Carrick to keep her in the loop with his investigator. She'd already known that Marina and her husband were separated, but a week ago he'd told her that Ellen had funded Marina's quest for custody right from the beginning. Suddenly all the times Marina had been late made sense. Most likely she had been chauffeuring Toby back and forth to Ellen's, and not only had the little boy been forced to endure long drives on California's crowded, even dangerous highways, he had probably been forced to endure Douglas, too.

Her mother-in-law had slapped her so many times that this new attempt shouldn't have surprised her. But for a week now the fresh assault, when Toby's entire future was at stake, had left her discouraged.

Carrick was almost sure Lilia would still become Toby's permanent guardian, but he'd also warned that the aftermath could be a lifetime of back-biting, plotting and legal challenges. With Ellen's inexhaustible funds, Marina could hire the best attorneys. Lilia would have to watch everything she did, not just the way a good mother does naturally, but with an eye to her child being snatched away if she made even one noteworthy error.

And what could she do? She certainly wasn't going to give up custody. But despite what she'd just written on her blog, for her, at this time in her life, the word advent was not a good one. She was afraid the something notable in her future might be the loss of her son.

Tonight she was alone for dinner. Carrick had a deposition in San Diego and wouldn't be home until late. He would probably drive straight back to Palo Alto from the airport, and she wouldn't see him until tomorrow. Regan was visiting their parents in Pennsylvania. Neighbors were having a Christmas party, but not until later. Without Toby's chatter the house was cold and silent.

In the kitchen she poured a glass of wine and pulled out cheese to have with crackers. A few grapes and a tangerine finished the menu. She would do better tomorrow.

She was about to look for a book when the telephone rang. She tossed her hair over her shoulder. "This is Lilia."

A few seconds went by, and then a woman

608

responded. "Lilia? Toby's Lilia?"

She recognized the voice. "Is this Deedee?" She realized Deedee wouldn't be calling just to chat. She gripped the phone harder. "Is Toby okay?"

"Toby?" Deedee sounded confused.

"Yes, Marina came and got him a couple of hours ago. Is he okay?"

"I don't know. I was calling to find out if you'd seen her. We were supposed to go to dinner. For Toby's birthday. She ordered a cake and everything, but she never came to get me. I called the restaurant, and they hadn't heard anything, either. They're not happy because they held the table for an extra half hour and —"

"Did you try calling her?"

"She's not answering."

"Did she leave you a message? Maybe she changed her mind."

"I don't have any messages. No texts. Nothing."

Lilia tried to think. Deedee was, at best, scattered. Could she have gotten the time wrong? Except if she had, apparently so had the restaurant. "Do you know if she was making a stop first? Maybe she got hung up somewhere?"

"She told me she was going to pick up Toby at your house, then come here until it was time to go to dinner. She was going to change her clothes. It's not far away. The restaurant,

I mean."

Lilia's mind was racing. Had Marina been in an accident? Was she in one of the local emergency rooms? Was Toby? If the delay was something as simple as a traffic jam, wouldn't she have called her mother?

"We should disconnect," she told Deedee. "In case she tries to call you. Will you stay by the phone? And will you call and tell me if you hear from her?"

"Maybe she was going somewhere else first, and I just got confused. Maybe she changed plans, and she'll be here any minute."

Lilia hung up. She remembered the evening Marina had returned Toby almost two hours late with a full diaper and an empty stomach. Now she realized the other woman had probably taken Toby all the way to Ellen's.

Ellen.

Maybe Ellen had demanded to see Toby this afternoon, too. Maybe Marina had thought she could make it there and back in time for dinner. On a good day, in light traffic, she might have been able to. But this was Friday in December. There was no chance.

The telephone rang again and she snatched it. "Hello?"

"Hey, were you sitting on the phone?"

She fell into the closest chair. "Carrick, Marina picked up Toby at about four, and they were supposed to go out with her mother to celebrate his birthday. She never made it home to pick up Deedee." She told him about the rest of the call.

"She has a habit of being late."

"I thought of that. I think she was late returning Toby so often because she was probably at Ellen's."

"It's likely."

"I'm going to call her."

"Marina?"

"No, Deedee says Marina's not answering her phone. Ellen."

"She may not realize you know about their connection."

"She will in a minute."

"I'll call around to see if there have been any accidents."

"Please. Call me back when you finish?"

"Better. I'll be there in half an hour. I have news for you, too."

She hung up and rested her face in her hands for a moment. She didn't want to call Ellen at home because she didn't want to risk Douglas answering. Instead she found her cell number. She had called her mother-in-law so rarely that the number didn't look familiar.

She punched in the numbers and waited. The telephone went to voice mail. Rather than leave a message she hung up and dialed again.

This time Ellen answered.

"Yes?"

Lilia knew she could see who was calling. Even so she hadn't bothered to use Lilia's name. "Ellen, I'm concerned about Toby. Is Marina there with you?"

"Why would you think so?"

She wanted to throw the phone against the wall. Instead she took a deep breath. "I'm aware you're trying to help Marina get custody. So please, let's not play games. Is she there?"

"She's not."

"Was she there today? Is she on her way home? She didn't show up for a special dinner, and her mother is worried."

Ellen was silent so long Lilia wondered what kind of story she was inventing. "I haven't seen or spoken to her in six weeks," she said at last.

"Why not?"

"It's really not your concern."

Lilia gave a humorless laugh. "Who does it concern more, other than Toby? Are you helping Marina, and was she there today living up to her part of the bargain?"

"She was not. As I said, I haven't had contact with her in six weeks. And yes, I was helping her, but I no longer am."

"I repeat, why not?"

"Marina decided to do everything on her own."

Lilia found it unimaginable that these two women had ever united. Now she found it even more unimaginable that they had called it quits.

"You have no idea where she might be?"

"No idea in the least."

Lilia could no longer hold in her anger. "Do you have any idea what you set in motion, Ellen? Toby was happy and thriving with me. I told you that you could be part of his life. I bent over backwards to include you, but you refused. And still? Despite that? You went to Marina, who had proved she didn't want him, and persuaded her to get Toby back. And all that for what? So you could get even with me for something I never did? I never, never tried to hurt you. All I did was love your son. And that's what you objected to, isn't it? That I loved him and he loved me. And you were out in the cold."

"That's enough!"

But it wasn't. "Here's the saddest part. All you ever had to do was open your heart and your arms. Not your purse. Not your bank account. Do you know that Graham loved you? Right up until the end. He couldn't tell you. He couldn't tell anybody. But I know he did, and now he's dead and you're trying to steal his son! You're trying to ruin Toby's life just like you ruined his. And tonight *my* son is missing."

There was nothing else to say. Lilia disconnected and began to cry.

Ten minutes later Carrick called back. "No

accidents. Nobody waiting in the emergency room that fits their descriptions. What about Ellen?"

"She claims she and Marina parted ways about six weeks ago."

He whistled softly. "That's why she changed attorneys. She went from someone with contacts and experience to somebody with almost none."

"Why?"

"A promise that came with too many strings? She untangled herself?"

Lilia's mind was racing again. "Or maybe she met Douglas."

"Yeah, that could do it. I'll be there in a little while. Try Marina's number yourself, and anybody else's you can think of." He hung up.

She had tried Marina without success already. But while she waited she tried again, then called Deedee. Deedee said she had called both her sons, but neither had heard from their sister.

She made a strong pot of coffee and poured two cups when she heard Carrick at the door. She fell into his arms. "What's going on?"

He hugged her hard. "Don't let your imagination run away with you. We'll find her. We'll find Toby. It's possible she just decided to do something else and forgot to tell Deedee. Maybe he was in a bad mood, and she realized it would be a tough night for a restaurant. Maybe she took him to a movie, and they'll be home soon."

She wished she could stay in his arms all night, but she pulled away. "Can we call the police? Can we contact somebody at the courthouse?"

"Toby is hers for the weekend. We can't report her. She's allowed to do whatever she wants until Sunday afternoon. I've asked the hospitals and the police to notify me if something comes up. But our hands are tied. They won't search for her just because she missed a restaurant reservation."

"It's more than that. You know it is." She started toward the kitchen. "I made coffee. We need to go over everything and figure out what's going on."

"We can try."

She put out more crackers and cheese, and they took them to the sunroom where he sat beside her. She didn't touch the food, but she sipped the coffee. "You said you had news? Should we start with that?"

"It's good news at a bad time. The custody evaluation is finished, and I have a copy. The social worker who conducted it recommended Toby stay with you. It's thorough. Very well done. You may not have liked her, but she certainly approved of you. And she liked everything she saw here, and everything others said about you. She saw no reason to remove Toby, and she had serious questions about Marina."

"Does the report stand?"

"Unless she objects again. Then it's on to an evidentiary hearing. But even then most of the time the judge pays close attention to these evaluations and abides by the recommendation. She really has very little chance of turning this around. In fact I think she'll have very little chance of continuing to see Toby without supervision. At least for a while."

Lilia didn't know whether to laugh or cry. This was what she had hoped for, but now it almost seemed ludicrous when this weekend Marina was blithely *un*supervised. And missing.

She let her mind spin. Something was just out of reach. Then she knew.

"When did you get the report?"

"I didn't get it until the end of my deposition this afternoon. My office faxed it to me so I could read it on the plane home."

"Do you know when it came in?"

"Sometime after five yesterday. I was already on my way to San Diego."

"Would Marina's lawyer have gotten it at the same time?"

"Most likely. You're wondering if he got it and called her?"

"Or saw her face-to-face. What if he did? And what if she knows about the recommendation? Wouldn't that give her a good reason to disappear with my son?"

"Not necessarily. She still has legal options. This could drag on for months."

"But she would know that we might ask the judge to supervise visitation while everything drags on. And if the evaluation is damning enough, he might do it."

"It's a possibility."

Lilia was trying to put herself in the other woman's place. "If her lawyer told her visitation might change, or he told her she should give up now because she wasn't going to win . . ."

"If Ellen's telling the truth, she's paying the new lawyer herself. She's realized a hearing will be costly."

"Then what's left? Give up gracefully or take Toby and run." She met Carrick's gaze and realized he had already come to that conclusion. "Do you think that's what she did?"

"I think it's too early to jump to conclusions."

"Because there's nothing we can do?"

He gave a short nod. "I'm going to call her lawyer, though. Just to see if she does know about the evaluation."

"Will he tell you?"

"Apparently he's pretty new at this. He may."

"When you've done that, I want to go to Deedee's. Maybe we can get a list of people

Marina might turn to. At least we can make calls."

"We should call Marina's husband."

Lilia hadn't thought of that. They were estranged, but maybe there had been a reconciliation. Maybe Marina was back together with him. "I can get his number from Deedee."

"We can do all that, and maybe we'll turn up something. But if we don't? I'll make sure we'll be ready on Sunday to file a report. Taking off with Toby would be called deprivation of custody. It's either a misdemeanor or a felony, depending on the judge and the situation. But right now it's nothing. Because at the moment there's no crime."

"It doesn't feel like nothing."

He pulled her close and draped his arm over her shoulders. "All we can do is take this one step at a time. Don't jump to conclusions. Don't assume the worst. Most of all, remember Marina cares about her son, and she's not going to hurt him."

Lilia thought of all the news stories about desperate parents taking the law into their own hands with horrifying consequences.

"Maybe she took him to a movie," she said. "Maybe she's spending an evening with her husband that she hadn't expected. Anything but kidnapping."

"I'll call her attorney." He squeezed her

shoulder, and then he got to his feet. "You get ready to go to Deedee's. I'll drive."

45

Marina didn't know exactly why she decided to head for Las Vegas. Maybe it was because she had good memories of going there with Blake, or maybe because it was one of the few places outside California she had visited. She knew there were plenty of cheap motels and restaurants where they could stay and eat while she looked for a job, and she'd heard that a few of the casinos offered day care for employees.

Las Vegas also seemed like the kind of place where she could change her name and find somebody to create new documents. If it was true that "what happens in Vegas stays in Vegas," then it was the right place to disappear.

On the way out of town she stopped at a branch of her bank and withdrew every cent in her checking account. Thanks to the payments from Ellen, her money would stretch awhile. She decided it was safe to use her credit cards before she left San Jose, but after that, it would be risky. So she stopped at a discount store and bought snacks, bottled water and diapers, two changes of clothes for Toby and herself.

Toby hadn't signed on for a long ride in the car, and by the time they were an hour out of San Jose he was hungry and cranky. They stopped at a diner, and while he spread meat loaf and mashed potatoes to the edges of his plate, she checked her phone. Deedee had called several times, and Lilia — most likely alerted by her mother — had called twice.

She debated calling Deedee with a hard-luck story. But while her mother was often as dense as a redwood, she also had a sixth sense when her daughter was lying.

Instead Marina sent Pete an email and asked him to pass on the contents when he got home from work. She claimed she'd tried to phone Deedee with no luck, and texts and emails were bouncing. She hoped her mother wasn't disappointed, but she had run into an old college friend from San Francisco who had invited Marina and Toby to spend the weekend with her. Marina thought it would be a nice birthday treat for her son. She and Deedee would do the restaurant dinner with Toby another time.

She hoped it worked and that Deedee informed Lilia all was well.

Back in the car Toby napped a little, but

after two additional hours of driving, he reached his limit. Foolishly she had hoped to at least get as far as Barstow, but they were still west of Bakersfield. After he threw a full-fledged tantrum from the back seat, she missed a turn and ended up in a one-horse town in cotton country. The only good news? Plenty of cheap motels to choose from. She took a room in the first one, paid cash and carried her son inside.

Happy to be out of his car seat, Toby explored. The room was clean enough, but she stayed close behind him, not sure what was lurking in cracks or corners. The clerk arrived to set up a crib and told her all about the toxic waste dump not far away, and the ever-present possibility of spills from the trucks roaring up and down Highway 5.

By the time he left she was exhausted, but she knew before they could turn in, she had to shop again, this time for night wear and basic toiletries, which she had forgotten. Her best bet was the closest truck stop, and she hauled her son outside again to purchase Bakersfield Blaze T-shirts for both of them to sleep in. They were poorly prepared for their new lives.

Back at the motel she turned on the television, and after another round of exploration Toby crawled into bed beside her to watch the home shopping network.

Once he was asleep she carried him to the

crib. Afterward she lay awake listening to trucks roar by and asking herself what she had done. Was today that much different from all the days stretching ahead? Cheap motel rooms without cooking facilities. Makeshift meals and pinch-penny shopping.

Finding her feet in Las Vegas would take months. In the meantime how long would her cash last? And if she could get by until she had a regular paycheck, what then? Could she find accommodations appropriate for a little boy? If she got new documents and managed to find a job at a casino, what hours would she be required to work? She couldn't fall back on her education or work history. She'd have to take an entry-level job and work her way up, maybe make up a sad story about a husband who had supported her until he was killed in Afghanistan.

Of course she could call Douglas Randolph and let him make all her arrangements in style. She didn't, of course. If she had to choose between the devil and the deep blue sea, diving in on her own was a safer choice.

Throughout the evening Toby had asked for Lilia, but he was used to being with Marina now and trusted she would take him home again. How long before the memory of his stepmother faded? And how many years after that before he noticed he had no family but Marina, and she was gone most of the time?

By the time she fell asleep the only thing she knew for sure was that if she changed her mind, she had to start back to San Jose early Sunday morning or she might lose all rights to her son.

The next morning dawned sunny and cool, and they walked to a nearby Denny's for breakfast. She gave Toby one of his birthday presents, a set of three eating utensils attached to bright yellow construction vehicles. He rolled them over the table and played happily until his pancakes arrived, then he attempted to eat the cakes with his forklift. Having a decent breakfast cheered her, as did her son's happy mood. The doubts of last night receded, and she was ready to push on.

Back at the motel she packed up what little she had brought inside and checked out of their room. With Toby safely in his car seat she turned the key in the ignition. And turned it. And turned it.

Ten minutes later after a tirade of mumbled profanity, she called the truck stop and asked to speak to their mechanic. An hour later a man about Blake's age, balding and weather-beaten, showed up in a tow truck.

"I'm Joey. That's one pretty little car. I like working on Fords." Despite the cheerful introduction, when he couldn't start the car, Joey towed her pretty little car to the station.

While she'd waited for him — and before the crib could be removed — she'd rented the same room for another night and stowed their belongings back inside. The clerk had promised if her car was fixed he'd only charge her for half a day, but the way her luck had gone, she had no illusions she wouldn't be spending another night in the same lumpy bed.

By mid-afternoon, and with nothing better to do, she and Toby walked down to the truck stop to talk to Joey in person, who by now had grease smeared from cheek to coveralls. He'd concluded the problem might be her fuel pump, which would be an expensive repair, but he was waiting for his boss to look at it first. If it was the pump, they would have to order the part from Bakersfield, and Marina knew she would have to use her credit card to pay the bill, even if that meant the payment could be tracked.

Back at the motel Toby was understandably fussy. She'd given him his last present at breakfast, a wooden house with a handle so it could be carried from place to place. There were dolls and furniture, and the house unfolded for play revealing the rooms inside. He'd been so happy with the dollhouse at Ellen's she'd thought he might enjoy this one, too, and he had for a while. Now he was bored, and there was no place to take him and no car to do it in.

"Mama. Want Mama." He rubbed his eyes with his fist.

She knew better than to explain again that the title should be hers. She put her arms around him and carried him to the only chair in the room where she covered him with the blanket from her bed. She settled in with him and turned on the TV. They were rewarded with cartoons.

His little voice trembled. "Go home? Now?"

"Look, the dog's trying to catch the cat."

"Want Doggie."

That she could do. She leaned over and plucked the stuffed toy from his backpack and gave it to him.

"Mama put." He pointed to the backpack.

"I'm sure she did." She pointed to the television. "The cat climbed that tree so fast."

He stuck his thumb in his mouth and anchored the stuffed dog against his chest. In a few minutes he was asleep. She settled him carefully in the crib and was relieved when he didn't wake up.

As she was turning off the television her cell phone rang. She couldn't ignore it since she had given Joey her number, but she checked first. The call wasn't from Deedee or Lilia.

"Blake." She didn't wait for him to speak. "I thought we were going to talk after the holidays."

"Where are you?"

She wondered if he'd talked to her mother, too. "In San Francisco with a girlfriend from college, although why you're suddenly interested eludes me."

"Toby's mother came to see me last night."

So Deedee *had* called Lilia. For once Marina's mother had acted like worried mothers everywhere.

"I don't know why she would do that. I have Toby for the weekend, and I'll have him home on time tomorrow." She didn't like the way the lie felt, but she wouldn't have liked the truth any better.

"You wouldn't do anything foolish, would you?"

"With my history? Why stop now?"

"I don't want to wait until after the holidays to talk to you. I want to *spend* the holidays with you."

She sat on the edge of the bed. "That's a surprise."

"That's what I was trying to tell you yesterday. Before you hung up."

"Funny, it didn't sound like that's where you were going."

"I know I didn't handle this whole thing well. I really thought we needed time apart. You needed time to settle the custody issue and figure out what was best for your son, and I needed time to get MeriTech on its feet again. It worked, by the way. Intel wants to acquire us. It's likely I'll be unemployed very soon."

"Great. So now you have time for me."

"It was never like that, Rina. I just couldn't be part of what you were doing."

She wanted to lash out again, but how could she fault him for not wanting to be part of Ellen's bargain? In the end she hadn't wanted to be part of it, either. Of course, look where that had left her. In a cheap motel room with a child who didn't want to be here, and a future that looked bleak for both of them.

She said the nicest thing she could manage, because this might be their last conversation. "I guess it's never a good thing when two people in a marriage are going through separate crises."

"Can we try to work this out?"

She had always been the mistress of bad timing. Had he asked her earlier? Before she'd made a decision to disappear with her son? She wasn't sure what she would have said. Maybe yes, because she had missed Blake. A lot. Now she realized how much.

She hedged. "I'll call you once I'm back. We'll see."

"Will you call Toby's mother and reassure her?"

"You're *talking* to Toby's mother!"

"I'm sorry. I didn't mean it that way. It's just that she's so worried."

Marina waited to feel pleasure that Lilia was suffering. But it was no surprise when she didn't. She felt sympathy, a surprising cascade of it. After all, who would understand Lilia's feelings better than she? They were united by a common mission. Marina was trying to keep Toby from slipping out of her grasp, too.

She cleared her throat. "My friend's calling. I have to go."

"Please, call —"

She hung up.

The conversation had been too much for her son. He sat up in the crib, rubbing his eyes. When he saw her he began to cry.

She told herself Toby was tired, and he was trying to adjust to new surroundings. Before long he would look forward to waking up and finding her in the room. They would make a life together, and Toby would be happy and carefree. She would find exemplary day care, a nice apartment, and eventually a job that let her spend afternoons and evenings doing fun things together. But right now he was only two, and this motel was one too many bad adjustments.

"Let's go see if there's news about the car." She smiled at him. "After a diaper change and maybe a stop along the way for ice cream?"

The last was a guaranteed Toby pleaser, but he only shook his head and rubbed his eyes again. She wondered if he was sinking into the Terrible Twos. From newborn colic straight to this. Through her own bad decisions she had missed most of the good months in between. But how many more would she miss if she didn't continue on to a life in Las Vegas?

By the time they got to the truck stop, Toby was dragging his feet and whining. She pumped enthusiasm into her voice. "They have Popsicles and ice cream sandwiches. Have you ever had an ice cream sandwich, Toby?"

She was holding his hand, but he stopped walking and fell at her feet. At two he wasn't lightweight, but she swung him into her arms, even though he struggled to get down.

"Listen, I know this isn't fun. But we'll be out of here soon. I promise. Then on to a good life together, sweetheart. Really."

He kicked and cried, and she just kept moving until they were inside. The change of atmosphere worked magic. He sniffled, but he stopped screaming and went limp in her arms.

She asked the clerk behind the counter about Joey, and the woman said he and their boss were examining her car. Glad that at least that much was underway, she decided to stay inside until they finished. She couldn't imagine dragging Toby into the garage.

She set him down in front of a shelf filled with toys, when something at the end of the aisle caught his eye. He let out a screech of pure delight and started forward. She straightened to see what had grabbed his attention. A young woman stood at the end, thin and olive-skinned, with black hair flowing down her back.

"Mama! Mama!" Toby sprinted toward her. "Mama!"

The young woman turned. She had very different features from Lilia's, and the man who was with her began to speak in rapid Spanish. The woman smiled at Toby, then looked at Marina and shrugged.

Marina grabbed him and swung him into her arms. "I'm sorry, he thinks you're someone else."

Toby was wailing now and fighting her. "My Mama!"

"I'm sorry," she apologized again.

The man cocked his head. "You're not his mother? But he's with you?"

"It's none of your business."

He looked at his wife, as if he didn't agree. Marina had to explain, like it or not. "I *am* his mother. He calls his favorite babysitter Mama, too." She didn't stay to see if that satisfied him. She started toward the door, relieved to see her mechanic was on the sidewalk in front now with his cell phone.

She pushed through the door and tapped Joey on the shoulder. He did a double-take and slipped the phone in his pocket. "I was just going to call you."

"My car?"

"A clogged fuel filter. It's all set now. Runs like a top."

She could hardly hear him over Toby's screams. "That's great. What do I owe you?"

"Nothing. I should have figured it out myself and not kept you waiting here in town. I'll bring it around."

"You got to be kidding."

He gazed at her a moment. "You haven't had a lot of breaks, have you?" He nodded, took a rag out of his pocket and started wiping his hands as he ambled toward the garage.

Suddenly she was crying, too. As hard as her son. And she didn't even care that people were watching. She *hadn't* had a lot of breaks, but she wasn't about to get another one. It was time to end this charade.

Toby wanted Lilia. If the circumstances were different, if Toby was screaming for Marina instead, would Lilia take him far away to a life filled with deceit and hardship? That had always been the difference between the two women. Both of them loved the little boy, but Lilia had always put him first. Even when she had no ties to him. Even when Toby had been a constant reminder of her husband's infidelity.

In the worst of circumstances Lilia had stepped forward, perhaps not willingly at first, but she had still done her best for the baby, and before long she'd fallen in love with him.

For months now Marina had only been

thinking of herself. She'd thought about how much she loved her son, how much she needed him. And never, at any point, had she really considered what might be best for *him.*

It was time to make the right decision. Not because Blake had asked for a reconciliation. Not because life in Las Vegas was going to be bleak and difficult. Not because she would always be in danger of going to jail for abducting the child she'd given birth to.

The decision was so simple. Her son missed his mother. His real mother. And even if in time he forgot Lilia, forgot that like the woman inside the truck stop his real mother had long black hair and brown skin, in his heart he would always feel her loss. He would feel it just the way Marina had felt the loss of the man she had believed to be her father. Only Toby would feel it more so, because Lilia had completely devoted herself to him. And that would make the wound deeper and more permanent.

She hugged him tighter. "Toby, it's okay. It's okay. We're going home now. We're going to see your mama. Right now. Let's get you some ice cream, then we're back on the road. Your mama, okay?"

His screams dwindled. She wasn't sure he understood exactly what she was saying, but he understood enough. "Mama?"

"Yes, *your* mama. Rina's taking you home. Can you be a good boy?"

633

"My mama?"

"Yes. Your mama." Pain streaked through her, but it was cleansing, as if it severed and separated a part of her life that was over. She didn't know what the future would bring, and how much time she would be allowed with this child, but the time had come to find out and adjust.

Inside she bought him an ice cream sandwich and broke off a piece for him to try. He smiled a little and reached for another.

When they went back outside she saw her car was at the curb. Joey got out and left the engine running. "You take care."

She leaned over and kissed his dirty cheek. "You're the best. Thank you."

He blushed and lifted a hand in farewell.

She opened the back door and managed to get Toby into his car seat, although he wasn't excited to be there. But when she gave him another piece of the ice cream sandwich, he took it and began to break off smaller pieces to eat.

She was circling the car toward the driver's door when her phone rang. She glanced at the display and lifted an eyebrow. This was one call she had to take.

"Will I have to pay time and a half for a Saturday phone call?" she asked in greeting.

Gil Braber cut right to the chase. "Where are you?"

Clearly Lilia, or more likely, Carrick Donnelly, had called him. She knew about attorney-client privilege, so she told him the truth. "Just west of Bakersfield."

"Why?"

"Because I was going to make a run for it."

"What were you thinking?"

"I was thinking I was going to lose the most precious part of my life. All because I was selfish and stupid two years ago and couldn't cope." She closed her door and walked away from the car because she didn't want the people pulling up beside her to hear the conversation.

He was surprisingly kind. "You're not going to lose him. We won't let that happen. Maybe you won't have all the time you want with Toby, but you'll have some. You won't lose him completely, unless you don't come back by tomorrow. Then all bets are off. Are you going to do that?"

"I just put Toby in the car. We're on our way home." She hesitated, then she asked a question that was hard to form. "I want Toby to have a mother, not a guardian. I know that it won't be me. If I let Lilia adopt him, if we get this whole thing over with once and for all and get the courts out of it, can I still preserve my right to spend time with him?"

"You could. It's called cooperative adoption. We can ask for a post-adoption contact agreement, but don't even consider it if you think Toby's stepmother won't honor it. It's not that simple to enforce."

"She will, because that's who she is."

She heard a door slam behind her. She almost didn't turn, but when she did she saw her car pulling away from the curb.

For a moment she wondered if Joey was moving it. Then her heart began to race. This wasn't Joey. She dropped the phone to the sidewalk and started forward, both hands outstretched. "No! Come back!"

The driver was backing fast, and suddenly he was turning toward the road.

"Help! Somebody's stealing my son!" She ran after him, but she saw immediately that, of course, she could never catch the car. A man pumping gas was just in front of her, and his jaw dropped as she sprinted past.

She could just see the back of the driver's head. He was wearing a cap and crouching low over the steering wheel. There were two entrances to the gas pumps, and he swerved toward the farthest, probably intending to head in that direction. Then he slowed, as if confused.

He couldn't pull out and turn left! She realized, as he apparently hadn't, that there was a concrete median strip running in front of the truck stop, and he wouldn't be able to get across it. Not there. He had to turn to his right and travel forty or fifty feet to make a U-turn. She sprinted toward the road to reach the area in front of the gas pumps before he did. Her legs had never moved so fast.

She screamed as she ran. "He's kidnapping my son!" She ran faster, expecting to see the car streak by before she could reach the road. But she was gaining. The carjacker had been forced to slow in order to make the turn. He was speeding up again, but she was still ahead.

She jumped into the lane and held up her hands as he barreled toward her. "Stop! There's a child in the car!"

The car careened to one side, as if he hoped to miss her, but she kept running forward anyway. When he didn't slow she realized she had to jump to the roadside or risk being hit. But the man had Toby. *He had her little boy.* She knew he expected her to leap out of his way, but she kept running to confuse him, hoping he would see how desperate she was and slam on the brakes.

"Stop! Please!"

Seconds passed before she felt the impact. She rose in the air and flew like a bird toward the ground at the roadside.

Then, blessedly, she felt nothing at all.

46

Under different circumstances the cottage in Bakersfield where Toby had spent the past two nights might have caught Lilia's eye for a quick photo for her blog. She often featured sweet little cottages she saw when she traveled, especially when the owners had done so many things right. Like these owners had.

Today a photo was the furthest thing from her mind.

Carrick pulled into the gravel drive along the side and turned off the Prius's engine. "I'll hang back. I don't think he's going to want to share you. Not at first."

"What can he be thinking? All alone in a strange place. Why did it take the county so long to tell us where he was?"

"The circumstances were confusing, and they had to do this by the book."

She understood the reality, but she still felt as if she'd been separated from her son for weeks instead of days. And how must he feel? After everything that had happened? After everything that he must have seen?

She sniffed and reached for a tissue. Carrick put his hand over hers. "Wait until you're calm."

She gave a brief nod, wiped her eyes, took a deep breath followed by another. "I'm okay."

"You go ahead. I'll follow in a few minutes."

She got out and started for the front door, her footsteps moving faster as she walked. It was still morning, and the temperature was somewhere in the fifties, but by the time she reached the stoop, the desert sun had warmed her hair. The front door was a welcoming cherry-red. The door knocker was — she almost couldn't believe it — a pineapple, a universal sign of welcome. She rapped twice before she took a step back.

The woman who answered was probably close to sixty, plump, dark-skinned, with short salt-and-pepper hair like Lilia's mother's. Lilia nodded, absurdly comforted by the similarities.

The woman smiled. "Mrs. Randolph?"

"Yes, but I go by Swallow. Lilia Swallow."

The woman extended her hand. "I'm Anna Ramirez. I'm so glad you found us."

"This has been a nightmare."

"I'm sure it has. Let me reassure you before you see Toby. He's doing well. He's a charmer. Right now he and my husband are gathering kindling outside to start a fire. He

639

doesn't know he won't be here to see it. But I think that will be okay with him."

"They said he wasn't injured. In the crash." Lilia didn't know why she needed reassurance about that, too, but she did.

"He wasn't. He's fine. They checked him thoroughly at the hospital, and we've been watching carefully, just in case. Apparently the driver wrenched the wheel and slammed on the brake after . . . The car traveled a distance anyway, but the lot where it ended up was sand and scrub. There was no other impact after, well, after his mother was hit."

Lilia knew the carjacker had taken off on foot the moment the car stopped moving. When he'd cleared the vacant lot, he'd fled down a side road. Two men who had seen the whole incident had taken after him in their cars. He'd chosen the wrong town to steal a car and child in broad daylight. The sheriff's deputy who'd arrived a short time later hadn't had to do much except pry the carjacker from the grasp of his captors.

She didn't want to think about that. She just wanted her son. "You have all the paperwork?"

"Everything's all set. I do need to see your driver's license. A formality."

Lilia dug it out of her purse and held it out. "A friend, Carrick Donnelly, will be knocking in a moment."

The older woman gave the license back.

"Let's get Toby."

They walked through a short hallway lined by a dining room on one side and a small living room on the other. In the kitchen Anna pointed to a window. "There they are. He hates to be inside, but you probably know that. Nick's kept him busy. He's happier that way." She rested her hand on Lilia's shoulder. "He's been asking for you."

Lilia opened the kitchen door and started into the yard. At first Toby didn't see her, intent on picking up sticks. His back was turned, but Anna's husband looked up and smiled. Then he moved to one side.

Lilia walked a little closer before she spoke. "Toby? Mama's here."

Toby took a second to turn, as if he wasn't sure what he'd heard. Then he was running as fast as his two-year-old legs could carry him. And he was in her arms.

"Toby! Toby!" She hugged him close. "My baby. I've missed you so much."

"Ma-ma-ma-ma!" He put his chubby little arms around her neck and squeezed.

"I'm here to take you home, baby boy. Back to our house." She didn't add "for good," although she wanted to.

"Mama!" His smile changed to a frown. "Gone! Bad!"

"I know, sweetheart. I know. I didn't want to be gone. But now I'm here. We're together."

He pouted a moment, then he hugged her again.

Carrick strolled across the lawn and waited while Lilia kissed Toby's cheeks. Then she pointed at him. "Carrick's here to see you, too."

"Crick!" Toby grinned, but he stayed where he was.

Carrick came to his side and kissed his curls. "It's great to see you, little guy."

In the house Anna gave them iced tea and cookies, and she let Toby show them where he'd slept. His little puppy backpack was on the neatly made toddler bed along with some unfamiliar clothing and a Bakersfield Blaze T-shirt many sizes too large.

"Are we missing anything?" Anna asked. "This is all we got."

Lilia opened the pack to look for Doggie, who was tucked inside. "It all looks fine."

Toby had climbed up to the bed and was sitting on the edge swinging his legs. She held out her arms, but he didn't jump into them, as she'd expected.

"Rina." He nodded. "Rina?"

The room fell silent.

She turned to Anna and asked softly, "What does he know?"

"I'm not sure. He's had nightmares. But he hasn't said anything I could follow."

Lilia lowered herself to the floor beside the bed. Carrick and Anna left them alone.

"You were with Rina. Do you remember?"

He looked away and didn't answer.

Lilia searched for the best way to say what she had to. "She was hurt. Do you remember that?"

"Rina fell."

"Yes, she did." She bit her lip. "She was hurt. But doctors are taking good care of her. Remember your doctor? Remember when your ear hurts? Remember how he fixes it?"

"Rina fix?"

"Yes, the doctors will help her."

"Want see."

She didn't know what to say.

He frowned. "Want see!"

"You want to see her. I know. But she's in a place called a hospital. They don't let little boys visit."

He folded his arms. "Want see. Now!"

She turned toward the door. "Carrick?"

He hadn't been far away, because he came into the room immediately.

"Crick? Rina." Toby nodded, as if that took care of everything.

Lilia got to her feet. "Clearly you're the man who gets things done. Even a two-year-old can see it."

Carrick guided her away from the bed. "I'll talk to Anna. She may have advice."

Lilia couldn't imagine doing the job Anna and Nick Ramirez did every day, taking in children in trouble and trying to make them feel comfortable and cared for. Clearly they were trained to deal with family emergencies. She went to the bed and picked up the puppy backpack.

Anna arrived and lifted Toby into her arms, as if she'd been hauling him around all his life. "It's time for you to go, sweet Toby. I loved having you here with me. You'll be good for your mommy on the trip home?"

"We're going to try to make it all the way." Lilia was convinced Toby needed familiar surroundings immediately.

The little boy held out his arms to her, and Anna passed him over.

"They probably will let him in for a peek, if you want," Anna said cryptically. Lilia knew what she meant.

She thought of all the challenges of the past days, the recriminations, the fears, the tears. Then she thought about the woman who had nearly died trying to stop the car carrying their son . . . *their* son. Marina must have known she might be killed. But where would Toby have ended up if the carjacker hadn't jerked the wheel and stopped in that lot after he hit her? What would the man have done when he realized a child was in the seat behind him? She had a long road to recovery, but Toby? Toby had been spared so much worse because of his birth mother's courage.

Toby wasn't the only one who needed to see Marina. "We'll give it a try," she said.

"I think that's a good idea." Anna leaned over and kissed Toby's cheek.

As they walked through hospital corridors Toby let Carrick carry him, but he was insistent Lilia stay right beside them. They followed directions to the surgical wing that they'd been given in the lobby. She was surprised how easy it had been to get permission for Toby to visit. Of course they wouldn't be allowed to stay long, but she didn't think Toby needed to, either. She still wasn't sure seeing Marina in a hospital bed was wise, but not seeing her would be less so.

Finding her room wasn't as difficult as it might have been. They turned a corner and saw Deedee sitting in a chair in the hallway. She stood when she saw them approaching, and her eyes grew round.

"Dee!" Toby crowed her name.

"You *came*?"

Lilia nodded. "How are you, Deedee?"

Deedee shook her head. "I can't believe you're here."

"Is the doctor inside with her?"

"No, Blake is. They just brought her here from intensive care. Still one visitor at a time. Ten minute shifts."

Lilia processed that. Marina's husband and mother were both here. Marina wasn't alone. Lilia and Carrick could leave, knowing that Marina would be well looked after.

"How's she doing?"

"They'll do surgery on her leg tomorrow or the next day. They're waiting for the swelling to go down. They think they'll insert a titanium rod, but they'll know tomorrow. She'll have to have more than one surgery on the leg, and one on her shoulder, but when she recovers from the first one, she'll be able to go home. She has a concussion, but no brain injury."

"She's lucky to be alive," Carrick said.

"I'm not sure she's feeling lucky." Deedee's eyes brimmed with tears, and she wiped them with the back of her hand.

"Dee!" Toby repeated. This time he reached out to his grandmother, and Lilia put him in Deedee's arms.

"She made a terrible mistake," Deedee said, stroking Toby's hair. "But she was bringing this sweetheart home. She really was."

"We know," Carrick said.

"She doesn't believe he's all right." Deedee kissed Toby's curls. "She thinks we're lying."

"They need to see each other," Lilia said.

"It'll mean everything."

Lilia tried to prepare herself.

Blake came out of the room. They'd only met on Friday when she'd tried to locate Marina, but Lilia had understood immediately why the other woman had been attracted to him. He was soft-spoken, insightful, kind, and even in her fury, she'd revised her opinion of her son's mother just a little, based on the man she had married.

He shook hands with her and then with Carrick.

"Hey, Toby." He smiled at the little boy, then he focused on Lilia. "It's beyond kind of you to bring him here. Considering everything."

"Will he be frightened inside?"

"Now that she's on this wing the bells and whistles have been removed for the most part."

"Bells and whistles." Carrick nodded at the description. "Things that go beep in the night."

"She had more than a few."

"Do you want to let her know we're here?" Carrick asked.

"It's a private room. I think you can just go in. But you shouldn't stay long. She's ready for some rest."

"She'll rest better after this." Carrick turned to Lilia. "I can do this. I can take him in, assure her he's okay. You don't have to do it yourself."

For a moment she was tempted. Her emotions soared and plummeted with every breath. She didn't know what she would say to Marina, but she knew she had to find out.

"I'll do it. Wish us luck." She took Toby from Deedee's arms and walked toward the door, stopping just in front of it.

"Toby, Marina's inside," she told the little boy. "She was hurt. You know that. But the doctors are making her better. We can only stay a little while. Are you ready?"

She wasn't sure how much of it he'd understood, but he leaned toward the door.

And then she knew exactly what she had to say.

She pushed it open and stepped inside. The door whooshed back into place behind her.

Marina's eyes were closed. Lilia was grateful there really was nothing on display in the room to frighten her son. Her arm looked as if it had been immobilized. Her leg was raised. She was as white as the lovely roses by her bed except for bruises on her cheeks and forehead, but her injuries weren't more obvious than that.

"I brought you a surprise," Lilia said. "Since you already have flowers."

Marina opened her eyes; her head turned, and in a second, she began to cry. "Toby!"

"You're in no shape to hold him," Lilia said. "But I would give him to you if you were."

"Rina!" Toby leaned over the bed, pulling Lilia forward. "Rina hurt?"

She turned so she could see him better, even though it was clear it wasn't easy. "Just a little. I'm okay. The doctors will make me all okay very soon."

"Car hurt."

Lilia's heart lurched. Toby remembered.

"Toby, the car didn't mean to." Marina sniffed, and Lilia reached for tissues and, without thinking, wiped the other woman's cheeks.

"God, this is embarrassing," Marina said.

"This might be the first time I actually have you at a disadvantage."

"He's okay? He's really okay?"

"They took him to emergency foster care. A really nice couple. They were sorry to see him go."

"I was bringing him —"

"I know. Carrick spoke to your lawyer."

"I guess this will do me in with the judge. I'm pretty late getting him back to you this time."

Lilia sniffed. "I was so angry at you."

"Was?"

"Am. Will be. And I'm so, so grateful, too. You . . ." She shook her head. She didn't want to say more in front of Toby about what Marina had sacrificed.

"We can't . . ." Marina started to cry. Lilia wiped her cheeks again.

". . . go on like this," Marina choked out. "I want you to have him. I want you to adopt. He needs a mother, not a guardian. And I know it won't be me."

"That's what your lawyer said."

"But I want him, too. I want time with him. It has to be in the agreement."

Lilia had tried to imagine this a million

times since Gil Braber had relayed his conversation with Marina. How could she share her son with this woman?

But how could she not?

"I love him. But . . ." Marina sniffed and shook her head. "He needs you more."

Lilia needed tissues now and pulled out a wad. "Maybe we can work it out. All of us. Toby will have a big family."

"Deedee comes with the deal."

Lilia laughed through her tears. "I like your mother. How about Blake?"

"We're a work in progress."

"I wish you the best on that."

Marina managed to stretch out her hand and touch Toby's cheek, although it was clear the movement was painful. The little boy giggled, and Marina met Lilia's eyes. She looked wistful. "If we work it out, don't worry, you and I don't have to be friends."

"We probably *won't* be friends." Lilia waited a moment, then she smiled. "But maybe . . . Maybe we can be . . . accomplices."

Marina actually laughed a little. "Accomplices. You do the work and make the decisions. I have the fun."

"Oh no, you don't get all the trips to Disneyland. I get to have fun, too. That has to be in the paperwork."

"Maybe we can work it out."

Lilia stepped back. "Toby, say goodbye to Marina. You'll see her again soon."

47

As Carrick pulled in front of Lilia's house, Willow Glen had never looked more inviting than it did tonight. Christmas lights were coming on up and down the street, and as Carrick turned off the engine, her neighbor's tree suddenly began to twinkle with red-and-green lights.

"Toby's missing this." She peeked at the backseat. "He's still sound asleep."

Carrick smiled, but he looked tired. They'd driven through heavy traffic, stopping only once for a lunch break, and he had been at the wheel most of the time. Toby had been as good as any two-year-old strapped into a car seat too long, but in the hour before he had finally fallen asleep, he had tested everybody's patience.

"I'll get him out in a minute," he said. "Then do you want me to leave the two of you alone?"

Nothing today had come easily, but her answer was effortless. She'd thought about it all the way home. "I want you to come inside and spend the evening with us. And when Toby goes to bed tonight, I want you to go to bed with *me*."

He curved his hand around her cheek. "You've had a lot on your plate. You're sure? This isn't gratitude talking?"

"Are you crazy?"

"Crazy in love."

She kissed his palm. "Carrick, you know I love you, and now I can finally say it. You know I *do* and *have* and always *will*. Hopefully the custody issues are behind us, and now we can finally think about *us*. But no matter what else happens, it's time to start our life together."

"Toby needs a father. I hope you want to make this official."

"I think that can be arranged, don't you? Of course that means you won't get to live in that new house of yours — if it's ever finished. Unless you're planning to move us there."

"I always meant for that house to be your office and showroom. Don't you think it's time to give The Swallow's Nest its own digs? And time to just make this our home." He watched her expression, and then he laughed. "You had that figured out."

"Right from the beginning. Couldn't you tell from the floor plan?"

He leaned over and kissed her. She put her arms around him. Even with the center console between them, nothing had ever felt more right. As glad as she was to have her son home, she hoped Toby went to bed early.

Which meant they needed to wake him now.

She pulled away. "If you get him out of his seat, I'll unlock the door. After dinner we can hang Christmas stockings. I made one for you, too."

He got out, and while she went ahead to unlock the front door, he unstrapped Toby and lifted him out of the seat. When Lilia returned, the little boy was just waking up. He gazed around through half-opened eyes and saw the house. He smiled.

Lilia put her arms around both of them for a quick hug. "Toby's home."

"I'll take him in," Carrick said. "Want to get his stuff?"

She let them go and did a quick sweep of the backseat to get Toby's puppy backpack, slinging it over her shoulder.

She wasn't sure why she stopped and turned. Something had caught her eye, and it took a moment to make sense of it. Then, stiffening her spine, she walked down the sidewalk and stopped a few car lengths beyond her house.

She waited.

Ellen got out of the driver's side of her car and came around to stand beside her.

Lilia was the first to speak. "I'm trying to guess why you're here, Ellen."

653

The other woman looked haggard, as if days had passed without sleep. Her clothes were casual, and her hair was brushed but not styled. Her makeup was usually flawless, but today Lilia couldn't detect any.

"I had to be sure he got home safely," she said.

"He did, thank you."

"Thank God." Then Ellen began to cry.

Lilia didn't know what to say or do. She had never seen her mother-in-law in tears. In her kindest assessments, she had never given Ellen high scores for emotional depth.

She said the only thing she could think of. "I'm sorry you were worried."

"You were right about me, Lilia. I wanted a second chance, and I thought Toby would be my salvation. I wanted him to love me. I wanted to prove . . . I could be loved."

Lilia still didn't know what to say. She just started to talk, hoping for the best. "Look, Toby's fine. He really is. Marina's going to be fine eventually. It's over now. It's all over. Things are getting settled. You —"

"I've left Douglas."

Lilia stopped, stunned. This was one too many revelations to take in. "You *left* him?"

"I started moving out last night. He's away." Ellen sniffed and wiped her nose with a sleeve, something Lilia would never have expected to see. "That was thoughtful, wasn't it?"

Lilia had never expected to hear Douglas referred to as thoughtful, even as a joke. "Does he know?"

"He will. I'm moving into the first house we lived in when Graham was born. I'm starting over about thirty years too late. But I'm going to try."

"I'm glad for you, I guess. Am I supposed to be?"

"You don't have to be anything. I just wanted you to know." Ellen pulled herself a little straighter. "And I just wanted to tell you . . ."

Lilia waited.

"I am so sorry. For everything. I can make a list if you need one. But it would start with this. I *was* jealous of you. A son is supposed to love his mother, and only then the woman he chooses. But I was still waiting for the first when you came along, and I resented you so badly." She pushed her hair off her face. "I'm not making any sense, am I? I need to go. But please know I will never forgive myself, and I don't expect you to do what I can't."

She turned to get in her car, but Lilia put her hand on her arm. "You said the house where Graham was a baby?"

"We only lived there a little more than four years. He wouldn't have remembered it."

"Montclair . . ." Lilia tried to pull up the name. "Montclair Village?"

"That's the one. How do you know?"

"Because Graham took me to see it once. The man you were with at his funeral still lives there, doesn't he?"

"Hank."

"Right. He's in real estate."

"Yes, he was supposed to sell the house, but somehow he never got around to listing it."

"Graham was doing some work for Hank, and he had to drop off his estimate. I happened to be in the car. Graham stopped and showed me the house. He did remember it. He remembered playing in the backyard as a little boy. He remembered running through the grass in the front and laughing."

Ellen's eyes filled with tears.

Lilia reassured her. "Toby's going to be fine, Ellen."

"I can't tell you how glad I am."

Lilia nodded. She turned and started up the walk. Only then did she realize that Carrick and Toby were on the front porch. Carrick was squatting and Toby was trying to imitate him. As she watched he fell on his rump. She didn't know what they were doing, but she walked a little faster to see.

She'd been kinder than Ellen deserved, and she'd done what she needed to. Nobody could fault her. Nothing more could be expected.

Suddenly their Christmas lights came on. On the porch Carrick straightened, and Toby began to clap.

Lilia knew she needed to keep walking, but no matter what her brain told her, she couldn't take another step. She sighed and turned. Ellen was just opening the car door.

"Ellen?"

Surprised, the other woman looked up.

Lilia paused, just to be certain she was clear about what she was setting in motion. Family was messy, and nothing that had been decided today was going to be easy. She and Marina would probably disagree on how Toby should be parented. Sometimes she would have to give up time with her son when she didn't want to, have to live with Marina's choices, have to accept Marina's dysfunctional family into Toby's life. Surely that was enough. She didn't need more confusion, more decisions, more irritations.

But as she watched Ellen go still, saw her look of dejection turn to one of shy expectation, she knew she *could* do more.

"Damn it, Graham," she said, so softly nobody would hear it except the ghost of the man who had brought them to this place. "This is the very last thing I'm ever going to do for you."

She sighed, and to her surprise, she was able to smile.

She gestured toward the house. "We're going to hang Christmas stockings in a few

minutes. Would you like to come and help
Toby hang his?"

ACKNOWLEDGMENTS

At a certain point in a novelist's career we run out of things we know intimately and must rely on others. This book was no exception. Many thanks to the following sources.

My brainstorming buddies, Shelly Costa Bloomfield, Casey Daniels aka Kylie Logan, and Serena B. Miller. They helped me move past an idea to a plot, and I am so glad we spend that crucial week together every year.

The Burkitt's Lymphoma Society publishes moving online accounts of patients who have struggled with the disease, and I am grateful to those who shared their own. No two journeys are exactly the same, but the stories they told helped me fashion Graham's own.

I read and enjoyed many home and lifestyle blogs to help create Lilia's. Visit my website at emilierichards.com and the book pages for *The Swallow's Nest* to view recipes and craft ideas similar to those mentioned in this novel, and for recommendations of similar blogs you might enjoy.

From the time this idea formed I became enchanted by the lives of cliff swallows. Among other resources I'm grateful to the Cornell Lab of Ornithology, *ScienceDaily* and *New Scientist,* the sixth grade science class at Carmel Middle School, and Fernbank Science Center in Atlanta. The quotes from the fictitious *Ornithology Today* are my own, derived from information that these and other sources provided.

Even though I have attorneys in my immediate family, California family law is so specialized that despite pages of statutes and information, I knew I had to find a family law attorney, preferably from San Jose, to answer specific questions. I put out feelers, visited online writer's loops, and asked all my contacts for recommendations.

Fellow writers I hadn't met, Kristen Tate and Mary Kennedy, both with personal and professional experience, stepped forward to offer their insights and help. A neighbor, the Hon. Ed Smith, RPh, JD (ret.), spent an afternoon explaining how my plot might unfold in Illinois, where he was a judge and prosecutor. Ed's many insights led me in new directions.

In the end, my fondest wish was granted when Jennifer Isensee, a family law attorney in San Jose, spent two hours on the telephone, helping me think through the legal issues in the story. This would be a very different book if it weren't for her good-natured and generous assistance to a total stranger.

If any mistakes were made, even with the help I received, they were of my own creation.

Finally, thanks to Shane and Shelly Mc-Gee, who thoughtfully moved to the Silicon Valley just long enough to welcome me to that beautiful area so I could plot this story and research the setting. And to Michael Mc-Gee, who not only served as my first reader but also learned to cook (very well) as I finished this book so that we always had food on the table.

■ ■ ■ ■

The Swallow's Nest

EMILIE RICHARDS

■ ■ ■ ■

Reader's Guide

QUESTIONS FOR DISCUSSION

1. Graham loved, or was strongly attracted to two women. Lilia loved two different men, although she and Graham chose different ways of acting on their feelings. Do you believe in soul mates, or do you believe love is rarely cut and dried?

2. Three women in this book want custody and control over Toby's life. Could you understand each of their feelings? Could you understand their actions?

3. What makes a mother "real"? Is it a legal tie? An emotional one? A shared history? Is the swallow who lays her egg in another bird's nest the fledgling's real mother? Or is the real mother the one who feeds and raises the baby bird?

4. The temperament of a baby can influence the unfolding relationship between a parent and child. If you look at parent-child

relationships that you're familiar with, can you detect a difference between the way parents treat children who were hard to manage as infants and those who were not?

5. After Toby's birth Marina may have suffered from postpartum depression, but no one diagnosed it or helped her cope. Were you angry at her solution, or could you empathize with what she did, even if you couldn't empathize with the way she did it?

6. Lilia grew up in Hawaii where family (*ohana*) includes many people who others might not regard that way. Did this help her welcome Toby into her life and heart? Do you think it will help in the future with the challenges she accepts at the end of the book?

7. After so much time apart Marina doesn't expect to bond with her son, but she does. Do you remember a time when you bonded with a child? Was it gradual or sudden? Was it stronger for being one or the other?

8. Ellen wants to make up for the indifferent parenting of her son by focusing on her grandson, but she doesn't understand the mistakes she made and continues to make. Do you think she can eventually be an

important part of his life? How important are grandparents?

9. Do you read home and lifestyle blogs? Do you tune in regularly to see what your new "friends" are up to? Do you try new recipes or crafts because the blogs you like suggest them?

10. The similarity between a parasitic cliff swallow, who lays an egg in another bird's nest, and Marina's initial abandonment of Toby is obvious. Have you known situations like this one that have ended happily? Do you think that open or "cooperative" adoption can be a success?

ABOUT THE AUTHOR

Emilie Richards's many novels feature complex characterizations and in-depth explorations of social issues. Both are a result of her training and experience as a family counselor, which contribute to her fascination with relationships of all kinds. Emilie and her husband enjoy dividing their time between the Florida Gulf Coast and Chautauqua County, New York.